S0-BOU-875

Dan
Tabeshnick.

THE EMPEROR'S VIRGIN

THE
EMPEROR'S
VIRGIN

A NOVEL BY
SYLVIA FRASER

McClelland and Stewart

Copyright © 1980 by Sylvia Fraser

ALL RIGHTS RESERVED

The Canadian Publishers
McClelland and Stewart Limited
25 Hollinger Road, Toronto M4B 3G2

Printed and bound in Canada
by John Deyell Company

Canadian Cataloguing in Publication Data

Fraser, Sylvia.
  The emperor's virgin

ISBN 0-7710-3175-0

I. Title

PS8561.R37E56   C813'.54   C80-094119-5
PR9199.3.F723E56

ACKNOWLEDGEMENTS

My thanks to David Whitehouse of the British School in Rome; Roger Scudder and John H. D'Arms of the American Academy in Rome, for allowing me the use of research facilities. Also to D'Iberville Fortier, Canadian ambassador to Rome; Christopher Anstis, formerly of the Canadian embassy in Rome; Amleto Lorenzini; and Giovanna Capone, head of the Department of English, University of Bologna.

I especially wish to thank Sam Vaughan, publisher of Doubleday & Company Inc., and Lily Miller, senior editor of McClelland and Stewart Limited, for their extraordinary support and practical advice in the preparation of this manuscript.

Books by Sylvia Fraser

Pandora (1972)
The Candy Factory (1975)
A Casual Affair (1978)
The Emperor's Virgin (1980)

AUTHOR'S NOTE

The student of imperial Rome is likely to be either delighted or daunted by the amount of available research material. At its core are the histories of Tacitus, Suetonius and Dio; the letters of Pliny the Younger; the poetry of Juvenal and Martial. Attracted to such a rich source is an army of experts who plunder these biased, conflicting accounts to create plausible versions of their own, often as tenaciously supported as they are divergent.

Confronted by such confusing abundance, the writer of historical fiction at first finds his job easier than that of the historian. It is not only a prerogative but a duty to subordinate and mould the so-called facts to the telling of the story – not cavalierly or haphazardly but to enhance the storyteller's subjective vision. The main events in The Emperor's Virgin are historically based though imaginatively recreated; most major characters have real-life counterparts, some are composites, others have been freely interpreted. My greatest offence against the written record has been to telescope the final years of Emperor Domitian's reign, during which he grew progressively more irrational.

The Roman world will seem familiar to North Americans. The power of this ancient yet pragmatic people lay in the might of their armies and the efficiency of their road system; their genius, in the logic of their laws and the skill of their engineers who built monolithically in stone; their extravagance, in the creation of a leisure society with a rage for material comforts and mass entertainment; their dilemma, in the breakdown of traditional moral values – the rise of the divorce rate, the fall of the birth rate, the increase in promiscuity – leading both to an envy of Greek sophistication and a yearning for the purity of their Republican past.

By present standards, the Romans were a brutal people, not in the extent of their violence – one day of modern warfare renders puny all similar Roman efforts – but in their stolid acceptance, even lusty enjoyment, of battle, blood politics, slaughter in the arena. To engage the sympathy of today's reader, authors frequently filter the times through the sensibilities of a single character who is wiser, wittier, more humane or introspective than the rest. I have chosen instead to confront each character directly, to interpret him or her in a melding of past and present, with the balance depending on the closeness of the modern parallel and the availability of historical information.

In superimposing present and past, an author tries to create a human document capturing some of the richness and complexity of both, to be true rather than to be right. Those with no patience for such inventions, who prefer at least the illusion of receiving their facts neat, I refer to the original Latin texts.

CONTENTS

FLAVIAN DYNASTY

VESPASIAN, Emperor of Rome, A.D. 69 to 79

TITUS, eldest son of Vespasian. Emperor of Rome, A.D. 79 to 81

DOMITIAN, younger son of Vespasian. Emperor of Rome, A.D. 81 to 96

DOMITIA LONGINA, daughter of Domitius Corbulo, a general executed by Nero. Wife of Domitian. Empress of Rome.

JULIA SABINA, daughter of Titus. Niece and mistress of Domitian

FLAVIUS CLEMENS, cousin of Domitian. Consul of Rome

FLAVIA DOMITILLA, wife of Flavius Clemens

SENATORS

COCCEIUS NERVA, a former consul. Emperor of Rome, A.D. 96 to 98

CATULLUS MESSALINUS, blind prosecutor and informer

ANTONIUS SATURNINUS, a former governor of Upper Germany, and ex-lover of Titus

HELVIDIUS PRISCUS, a playwright and poet. Son of a Stoic philosopher executed by Vespasian

KNIGHTS

MAXIMUS MARCUS, a soldier and engineer, later promoted to senator

CRISPINUS CLODIANUS, a former fishhawker and wealthy freedman

RUFUS FELIX, an Alexandrian physician

MILITARY

PETRONIUS GETA, Captain of the Imperial Guard

CINNA CELER, a praetorian centurion

MAXIMUS NORBANUS, governor of Lower Germany

VESTALS

CORNELIA, head vestal, age 25
FAUSTA, former head vestal, age 55
AGRIPPINA, age 37
DIANA, age 18
HELEN, age 15
POPPAEA, age 10

SERVANTS

PARTHENIUS, African chamberlain to Domitian
HERMES, a dwarf and cup-bearer to Domitian
CASTOR, page of Domitian
PHYLLIS, former nurse and freedwoman of Julia Sabina and Domitian
VARUS, page to Domitian at his summer villa
STEPHANUS, freedman and steward of Flavius Clemens
BERENICE, Jewish maid and freedwoman of Flavia Domitilla, married to Stephanus
POLLUX, stablehand to Maximus Marcus

OTHERS

ZENO, Greek tutor to the vestalry and Domitian's imperial secretary
QUINTUS PISO, head priest of Mars, Jupiter and the Flavian Cult
PHOEBE, a prostitute. Mother of Castor
XERXES, a gladiator and strongman
PHILIP THE PROPHET, a Jewish leader
PETRAS, a Jewish prisoner
ASCELETARION, a soothsayer
LARGINUS PROCULUS, a soothsayer

CHAPTER ONE

A September morning in the Forum. Senators, recently returned from summer at their country villas, greeted each other on the steps of the Senate. Orators declaimed from the speakers' platform, slicing the air with gestures to make themselves understood over the noise. Idlers played on checkerboards scratched into the travertine pavement. Lawyers, already wearing the right and left eye patches, identifying them for prosecution or defence, gathered outside the Basilica Julia, where civil suits were heard.

The liveliest crowd swarmed around the *Daily Gazette* – the printed white tablets posted by the government, giving the news of Rome, which slaves copied each morning for their masters. Here was the price of grain; the day's birth, death, divorce and wedding notices; the content of wills; the dates set for law suits, Circus events, theatre productions, poetry readings; and the more savoury bits and pieces of the Roman mosaic – the wealthy widow who eloped with a gladiator, the senator's wife surprised in an act of adultery at the Temple of Isis.

Maximus Marcus, in red-plumed helmet and scarlet military cape, entered the Forum by the street known as Silversmiths' Rise. Around him towered the monolithic genius of Rome: triumphal arches, soaring vaults, arcades by the mile – splendid, startling, garnished with brilliant frescoes, marbles and mosaics.

In fifteen years' absence from Rome, Marcus had seen many wonders – the Great Pyramids, brooding and impenetrable, sentinels of the desert; the Acropolis, ascetic and inspiring as it glowed on its hilltop. Yet nothing stirred his blood like this life-soaked patch of earth encased in gilt and marble. Roman architecture was pragmatic and victorious. It recorded the progress of Roman might from mud hut to empire. No city had ever been so glorious, nor would be again.

As Marcus strode along Sacred Way, the oldest street in Rome, he felt energized by the mass and magnificence. To his right was a statue of Emperor Domitian on horseback, the tallest structure in the Forum. Twelve years ago Marcus had fought under the emperor as a tribune, against the Chatti along the Rhine. Three years later he had fought as a colonel against the Dacians along the Danube. Now at thirty-two, he had been recalled to Rome, having advanced as far up the power pyramid as the son of a wealthy knight from the provinces could, without imperial patronage.

He jostled his way through the crowds jamming Sacred Way, aided by his unusual height and the prestige of his uniform. As he entered Sacred Square, he was repulsed by beaters waving myrtle brooms and shouting: "Make way! Make way!" Marcus asked a hawker selling medallions: "What parade is this?"

"A virgin is being initiated into the cult of Vesta." The hawker held up a tin medal, depicting the Temple of the hearth goddess, adding: "That's one less kiss-and-cuddle for an honest man. The Temple of Venus is kinder."

A shout went up from the crowd.

The procession, startling in its whiteness, was making its silent way across the square. First came incense-bearers, swinging chalky pots that exuded curls of scented smoke. Then came the nineteen candidates, from which the initiate had been chosen, strewing white rose petals from alabaster bowls. Behind them, in a white cart drawn by a white goat, rode the initiate, also in white except for a bridal veil the colour of flame. She was escorted by two vestals holding silk banners that snapped in the wind.

Now came a splendid ivory chariot drawn by white asses. It bore the chief vestal, her red hair – almost the colour of the initiate's veil – just visible under her headdress. As the chariot passed Marcus, one of the asses caught a hoof and stumbled. Quick to read an ill-omen, the crowd gasped. The chief vestal smiled reassurances, and waited calmly for the beast to right itself. Gazing into her face, Marcus felt a shock of recognition. Where had he seen that face before, yet not exactly that face? As Marcus pushed forward, trying to get a clearer view of this person draped in white robes, the ass resumed its dignified pace, drawing the chariot past him, with the crowd swirling in its wake, eager to accompany the procession to the chief priest's house for the two-day initiation.

Marcus plunged once more into the Forum traffic, still perplexed but with more challenging matters occupying his mind. He was now at the foot of Victory Stairs, leading to the Palatine. The most strategic of Rome's seven hills, it had been established by Emperor Augustus as the imperial seat, and successive emperors had expanded his modest home into a glittering showplace that levelled both crests, and extended the hill with superstructures.

Marcus was to meet Flavius Clemens, consul of Rome, his late father's dearest friend and his own mentor, at the foot of the steps. Together they were to attend Emperor Domitian in his bedchamber – a rare privilege, as Clemens had been at pains to point out.

While Marcus was stationing himself for a better view, the consul's lictors broke through the crowd. Then Marcus saw the old man himself, borne in his sedan-chair, his silver beard resting on his chest. They greeted each other with affection. Marcus fell in behind the prestigious parade as it mounted the Palatine through a forest of fluted columns, golden roofs and purple awnings. At the imperial gate, Consul Clemens whispered the day's password. Eight praetorians escorted them through two more gates of decreasing size, then across magnificent gardens to the private wing of the Flavian palace – the largest and most luxurious ever built on the Palatine.

Marcus followed the tramp of praetorian boots down endless marble corridors ablaze in torchlight, to a cramped and smoky vestibule outside the emperor's bedchamber. Three others waited there – two wearing senators' togas with a broad purple stripe, the other in knight's toga with narrower stripe.

Dismounting from his sedan, Consul Clemens introduced Marcus to Antonius Saturninus, recently recalled governor of Upper Germany; Catullus Messalinus, the infamous blind prosecutor; Crispinus Clodianus, an Egyptian fishhawker who had risen to become a wealthy knight. Despite an elaborate exchange of courtesies, Marcus sensed none of these men liked or trusted each other. Here was a wary alliance in the forcing-house of imperial politics.

Almost immediately, the emperor's chamberlain indicated Domitian would receive them. A stately African, he ushered them through double doors into the emperor's bedchamber.

The room was dark, the shutters closed. Marcus peered through marble columns draped in purple to a golden apse containing an ivory bed raised on a dais. The bed's purple curtains were also closed. A hand reached through them. Even in the gloom he could see the imperial signet cut with the profile of Augustus. The emperor crooked his finger. One by one his visitors climbed the dais to greet him with compliments and kisses, taking their intimacy as far up the knuckles as rank and daring allowed.

Consul Clemens, tugging on his beard, inquired how well the emperor had slept. Prosecutor Messalinus remarked on the healthy timbre of the emperor's voice, which he, being blind, could best appreciate. Senator Saturninus, former governor of Upper Germany, bowed his vividly bleached head as he expressed joy at once more being in the emperor's divine presence. Wealthy freedman Clodianus, who overcompensated for his years as a fishhawker by importing perfume which he dumped by the galleyful on himself, complimented the emperor on his own spicy fragrance.

The emperor – still only a hand and a voice – received these blandishments with a perfect alloy of contempt and justice due. He signalled for Marcus to come forward. As the knight mounted the dais, he felt he was being inspected in the many mirrors angled about the bedchamber, but could glimpse nothing of his host through the curtains. There was an embarrassing pause during which Marcus, put off by the florid tributes this ritual seemed to evoke, managed no suitable greeting for this man he knew only as a commander. The emperor tapped his signet finger on the edge of the bed. As Marcus reached out to clasp the hand, the emperor scornfully retracted it. Descending awkwardly, Marcus rejoined the emperor's confidants in their semi-circle around the bed.

More silence. Then a long, breathy sigh from inside the curtains. In a bored, well-modulated voice the emperor said: "I have before me a legal case from the governor of Bithynia, who seeks my advice. Tell me what you think and what sentence you would give.... A prominent wine merchant discovered his wife and brother in adultery. He forgave them, only to have them run off together a week later with his jewel box. This time when he found them he slew them. Now, did the merchant commit a crime? If so, how shall my governor punish him?"

Freedman Clodianus, wiping sweat from his beefy neck, expounded a view which – when shorn of its metaphors and aphorisms – was the archaic Roman view: "The merchant had the right to kill his wife as his possession, do you see? He shouldn't have killed his brother. Him, he should have flogged. So he was guilty of murder – of his brother."

Consul Clemens held a more modern view. "It's forgivable for him to slay both his wife and his brother in an act of passion. It is not forgivable for him to slay either for theft. The man is guilty of double murder but with circumstances suggesting the mercy of a fine."

Ex-governor Saturninus gestured languidly from the centre of his bored and silky indolence. "Surely all acts of passion bring their own rewards and punishment. The only crime *is* the theft."

Only prosecutor Messalinus correctly assessed the emperor's streak of guilty puritanism, so at odds with how he lived his own life, for hadn't Domitian just restored to favour an adultress wife? "It was the duty of the merchant to kill his wife, having caught her in adultery, which the law defines as intercourse with a married woman. His crime was one of moral turpitude in failing to punish the guilty when catching them in the first place. Therefore, the merchant should be flogged."

In the emperor's second case, a slave had taken refuge in the Flavian temple after escaping from an owner who had nailed his hands to a tree. Here Consul Clemens, through enlightened pragmatism, and Messalinus, through clever second-guessing, anticipated the emperor, for in cases not touching himself he was usually fair. "While the power of master over slave is inviolate, it is in the interests of the system to outlaw extreme cruelty."

In neither case was Maximus Marcus' opinion solicited. He, of course, did not offer it.

The emperor ordered his African chamberlain, Parthenius, to open the shutters of the bedchamber, illuminating frescoes painted in the Fourth Style, with their pillars and draperies imitating those in the room. Another sigh from within the curtains. Now one of the emperor's feet poked through the drapery – pale, like his hand, with hammer-locked toes. It was joined by a second foot. Parthenius bathed them in rosewater, then fitted them into scarlet sandals.

Parthenius drew the emperor's bed-curtain.

Marcus found himself staring at the world's most powerful man – naked except for a loincloth. With his cornsilk hair tufted over his eggshell head, he yawned, stretched and blinked in the sunlight like a freshly hatched bird. It had been nine years since Marcus had seen the emperor, riding at the head of his troops,

PART I

IMPERIAL ROME

A.D. 95

and though Domitian was now only forty-four, he looked ten years older than that. His skin had an unhealthy pallor, his neck seemed emaciated, his tall and graceful body had slid down into a paunch.

Domitian's cup-bearer Hermes – a dwarf with the size, odour and hairiness of a large dog – handed him an amethyst goblet of hot Spanish wine poured over honey, while Parthenius treated him for baldness with a mixture of ground eagle's beak and sheep fat, then massaged the emperor's face: the high forehead and thrusting cheekbones; the gouged sockets with pale-blue eyes; the thinly pressed lips; the stubborn jaw.

As Domitian stepped down from the dais, half a dozen slaves converged. They wrapped him in fifteen yards of snowy Egyptian linen with a scarlet border, working under the exacting instructions of Parthenius, transmitted by gesture since his tongue had been cut out to render him a perfect servant. Now Parthenius swirled the emperor's hair evenly from the crown, in the style made famous by Julius Caesar, adding a laurel wreath dipped in gold – a ruse of both Caesars to disguise its thinness.

While Parthenius prepared the emperor, Hermes the dwarf imitated many of the chamberlain's gestures. As Parthenius arranged the imperial hair, so Hermes – with discouraged sighs and moans – arranged his own mingy tufts over his cone-shaped head, earning from Parthenius the occasional cuff. Domitian remained tolerant of this impudent parody – a thing of amazement to his intimates, who were always at pains to assuage his haughty dignity.

The emperor was now ready to leave his bedchamber. Petronius Geta, Captain of his Imperial Guard, met him at the door with twelve praetorians in scarlet kilts and four liveried sedan-bearers. They carried Domitian through marble halls so highly polished he could view his flank, followed by his entourage and trailed by the dwarf.

The emperor was to receive a delegation from the province of Judaea in the Throne Room – a gargantuan chamber with

21

vaulted ceiling supported by twenty-eight columns of yellow marble flushed with pink. Leaving the emperor's party with relief, Marcus joined the knights and senators assembled there. As the emperor made his gracious entrance, jealously flanked by prosecutor Messalinus and Captain Geta, a young senator beside Marcus remarked to his older companion: "I'd like to be a fly on the wall when those three meet in private."

"Not unless you have a liking for death by the stylus," replied his companion, referring to the emperor's well-known hobby of passing idle hours by stabbing flies with the sharp instrument used for writing on wax slates.

"At least the flies see the stylus coming, which is more than can be said for his human victims."

"Yes, those two informers always by his side slit throats with a whisper."

"And the one with no eyes sees the most. In Rome, injustice is blind."

As the senators' voices rose, a circle opened around them of men wishing to dissociate themselves from the dangerous conversation. Prudence told Marcus he too should edge away, but the sycophantism of the emperor's bedchamber had bred rebellion in him. He stood firm inside a widening sea of black marble.

The talkative young senator greeted Marcus with a broad grin. "I'm Helvidius Priscus, playwright and poet. Welcome to Rome – for I can see by the speed with which you did not leave my side that you must be very new here."

Imperator Domitianus Caesar Augustus climbed down from his sedan-chair. He mounted his ivory dais and seated himself on his throne, while the dwarf arranged his robes. As he leaned forward, chin cupped in his hand, a herald announced the twelve-member Jewish delegation.

The ambassador from Judaea – a pudgy man with the posture of an eternal supplicant – showered the emperor with wave upon wave of shameless flattery, far exceeding the 200-word limit put on such conventions. This was especially provocative to Domitian, who liked submissiveness in his friends but distrusted it in his enemies. He observed the ambassador with cruel detachment. It was, after all, the Jews who had provided the Flavian family with their bitterest battles, and his brother Titus with his most sensational triumph in the sacking of Jerusalem. Therefore, Domitian resented the Jews both as the enemy and as the instrument of his brother's success.

Domitian leaned forward in smiling intensity – a sign his intimates knew meant irritated boredom. Having completed his salutation, the ambassador was now inching toward the crux of his mission: His province wanted relief from the burden imposed by the permanent lodging of several thousand Roman legionnaires.

Domitian watched a fly buzz about the ambassador's pomaded hair as his voice droned on, praising Rome's might and her gift of peace, while complaining about the pillage of Roman soldiers: their rape of Jewish women; their disrespect for the Temple of Jerusalem. The fly settled in the ambassador's thick hair, bobbing and buzzing as he bobbed and buzzed. Domitian ran his hand impatiently through his own hair, which he had just heard variously described as "the gold of Caesar" and "honey poured on mead." He watched the fly land bull's-eye on the ambassador's nose. Still smiling encouragement, he beckoned to Hermes, whispered a few words in his ear, then settled back. Hermes leapt down the dais. He swatted the fly on the ambassador's nose. The ambassador tumbled backwards in a humiliated heap.

Domitian rose haughtily. "There would be no need for Roman soldiers in your province if you Jews could protect yourself from your own vermin. The hand of Rome strikes only where it sees the need." He swept from the Throne Room, to the applause of his senators, with the dwarf hopping behind.

Consul Clemens did not applaud. Neither did the young senator who had introduced himself to Marcus as Helvidius Priscus. Turning to Marcus, with his face pulled long, he said: "Come, my friend, let us get out of here. As a playwright, I find myself growing discouraged. When our emperor plays the buffoon so well, what is left for the theatre?"

The young men left the palace together. Though they parted at the foot of Victory Stairs, it was with the promise to meet again soon.

Marcus had one more visit to make on this his first day in Rome. Plunging once again into the Forum traffic, he worked his way southward to Upper Sacred Way with its double arcade of shops selling silks, meat, baskets, metalwork, fruit. He stopped at a perfume shop in search of a gift for a friend he had not seen for many years: Julia Sabina, niece of this emperor, daughter of the last, with whom he had shared childhood summers at his birthplace of Como. Urged by a turbaned Arab, Marcus uncorked and sniffed several porcelain flacons. He chose one containing the fragrance of violets, and left the Forum through the Arch of Titus.

Marcus easily found Julia Sabina's pink stucco villa on the Aventine – one of the seven hills on which Rome was founded, but certainly not the most fashionable. Consul Clemens had given him precise instructions, though he had at the same time warned Marcus against visiting Julia. Julia was the emperor's mistress as well as his niece. For two years she had lived with Emperor Domitian in the palace while his wife, Domitia Longina, was in exile for adultery. Two months ago the empress had been recalled, and Julia Sabina had been expelled. It was not the sort of situation in which a young man on the threshold of a senatorial career should risk involving himself.

Marcus had considered the advice of the consul, who had been his father's best friend, then had reluctantly disregarded it. The orderly, even spectacular progress of his career had made him trusting of his own good fortune.

Removing his helmet, Marcus presented himself to Julia's gatekeeper – a retired legionnaire easily impressed by the colonel's insignia. He led Marcus through a pink vestibule, with a statue of Juno, into a sunny courtyard.

Julia Sabina was sitting at an upright loom, her brown hair tied back with yarn. She looked up from her weaving, then beamed in recognition.

"Marcus! It *is* you." She jumped up from her loom. "When did you get to Rome?"

They embraced with affection. "I arrived from Egypt two days ago. I'm staying with Consul Clemens."

"Is Calpurnia with you? How is young Marcus and your brother Servius?"

"Calpurnia died of swamp fever six years ago. Marcus died at the same time."

She clasped his hand. "I'm sorry, Marcus. I hadn't heard."

Brushing aside her sympathy he said: "My brother Servius is well and sends his regards. He's still at Como, though he winters in Tuscany.... And you? How are you, Julia?"

She led him to her bench under the pear tree. "Surely you've heard my scandalous story?"

Marcus gave Julia the perfume he had bought for her.

She uncorked and sniffed it. "Violets!" She closed her eyes, remembering the wild flowers that had crowded the spring bogs where they had played as children. "What lovely memories just seeing you has brought back." She laughed. "Do you know what I'm thinking of now? You, racing the meadow in a goat cart, pretending it was the Circus Maximus. Tell me, Marcus, do you still race such a fine chariot?"

"Ten times finer but not with half so much fun. Do you still give your imperial colours to boys driving goat carts?"

"Even boys with goat carts find the Aventine too hard a climb for such a poor view, though when I lived in the palace I never lacked for admirers. Since you're staying with Consul Clemens, I'm surprised he didn't warn you not to see me."

"Clemens is your friend and supporter," protested Marcus.

"At court, yes. Though personally he doesn't approve of me.

25

He *did* tell you not to come, didn't he? I can tell by your face. If you're going to prosper in Rome, Marcus, you'll have to learn to hide the truth better than that."

Julia picked up her shuttle and slid it in and out among the purple threads gridding her loom. "How long will you be here?"

"A few months. Perhaps forever. I was recalled."

"By the emperor? Ahh, yes. For his birthday banquet." She held up the purple cloak she was weaving. "This is for the banquet, *if* I'm invited." She looked toward the palace, easily visible on the Palatine. "The first thing my father did whenever he took a new mistress was to banish me from the palace to Como. When the mistress was done with, he sent for me again. Why should I expect my uncle to be any different?" She added with bravado: "The emperor *will* send for me again. I'm used to waiting."

Maximus Marcus climbed down the Aventine, glad he had visited Julia despite Flavius Clemens' warning. As he re-entered the Forum, he saw a curl of smoke from the brazen roof of the Temple of Vesta, and remembered the procession he had seen that morning. He remembered the face of the chief vestal, and also where he had seen it before: not her, but her twin. His friend Nestor, who had died in the eruption of Vesuvius. Nestor had had a sister who became a vestal. It was she. It had to be.

CHAPTER TWO

As residence of the chief priest, the Regia was the site of the city's most sacred rites. White flowers, rotated with the season, grew in its red-walled garden. White banners fluttered from the myrtle trees, and an archway had been created of ostrich plumes.

The sixteen priests of the sacred colleges of Jupiter, Mars and the Flavian emperors had assembled in the garden to witness the initiation of a young virgin into the Order of Vesta, the hearth goddess. It was the duty of Vesta's six virgin priestesses to tend the sacred hearth of Rome, which had once been the source of fire for the original community of mud huts, and was now symbolic of the safety and prosperity of Imperial Rome.

The two-day ceremony, conducted by the elderly chief priest Quintus Piso, was drawing to a close. The white goat that had drawn the initiate's cart to the Regia had been sacrificed, and a favourable augury made from its liver. A torch, symbolic of a vestal's hearth duties, had been presented to the initiate. Now that initiate – a ten-year-old named Poppaea – knelt before the chief priest, repeating the awesome vows that severed all ties to her family and bound her to the Order of Vesta:

"I promise to conduct myself according to the will of Vesta, as interpreted by the emperor, the chief priest, the chief vestal, and my sisters senior to me.

"I promise to guard the flame of Vesta with my life. If I fail, may I be stripped and scourged.

"I promise to keep the secrets of Vesta. If I break this vow, may her wrath disembowel me and her fires consume me.

"I pledge myself to Vesta in chastity for thirty years. If I break this vow, may I be borne in shame to the Field of Ill-Luck and buried alive, with no prayers to attend me."

Chief vestal Cornelia listened to Poppaea with more than usual concern. Once initiation into the Order of Vesta had been an honour attracting girls of the best lineage. Now the vestalry had become unfashionable. Families who could not afford dowries were bribed with state subsidies of up to two million sesterces to sell their daughters to the Temple, while unruly girls of patrician standing were threatened with the vestalry as a spur to good behaviour.

The initiate Poppaea was the fourth daughter of a stonecutter who, if he'd been more practical than kind, would have exposed her to die at birth. When her name had been drawn that morning, she had flung herself screaming into her mother's robes, while her three sisters had sobbed as if at a wake.

The chief priest's reedy voice thinned to silence. Removing the initiate's veil, he held up her black hair in one hand and a dagger dripping with goat's blood in the other. "The pledge is given and received." Then he slashed off the hair. After hanging the child's severed locks on the sacred lotus tree already bearing the tresses of her five vestal sisters, the chief priest led her through the cheering throngs of Sacred Square to the House of the Vestals. To Cornelia he said: "I commit this virgin to your care in the service of Vesta."

Cornelia sent the attending priestesses to their tasks. Then she held out her hand to Poppaea. "Come. Let me show you your room." Together they climbed to the second storey of the luxurious vestalry, where Cornelia opened a shuttered door off the courtyard. "This is your bedchamber, Poppaea." Though it had no windows and was sparsely furnished, its walls were frescoed with cupids playing with hoops, and a vase was filled with chrysanthemums picked for her by the vestal Helen. Cornelia pointed to a statue of Juno, the mother goddess. "She will look after you if you are lonely."

Seeing the child set her chin against tears, Cornelia had a rare and sudden recollection of her own distant past...her first day at the vestalry, with the mysterious white figures in a ring around her, blotting out the world she had known, the shock of having her hair slashed off, the dark room in which she felt herself imprisoned, the homesickness that had overwhelmed her, wave upon wave like the ocean that washed the coast near her home of Pompeii. Taken off-guard by the vividness of her own recollections, she embraced the stiff-backed child, not caring that such an emotional display was against the traditions of the house, allowing Poppaea to give way to sobs.

Cornelia wiped Poppaea's face with perfumed water, and combed the ragged fringe of black hair that showed no tendency to curl. "Don't worry, it will grow back." Then it would be plaited into six braids, wound in a cone, and bound with six white ribbons – another symbol of chastity for priestesses of Vesta. Taking the child by her thin shoulders, Cornelia steered her back down to the courtyard with its three reflecting pools. Reclining on a couch outside the library was the vestals' Greek tutor, a scroll propped against his bent knee, his reed pen scratching so rapidly the papyrus seemed to flow like a foamy river under his fingers.

"Your court history must be going well today," Cornelia greeted him.

"Not so, not so!" replied Zeno, wiping sweat from his jowly face. "My recollections are being distorted by something quite unexpected growing like a tumor in my creative womb: a moral conscience! Whole paragraphs pour out, sounding more like the dour Cato than my own shallow self. I had hoped to make my fortune by pandering to the great, like that fawner Valerius Martial. There should be a god to protect rogues from their better selves!"

Cornelia laughed, used to her old tutor's irreverence. Propelling Poppaea toward him, she said: "Zeno will teach you, as he once taught me."

Poppaea did not accept Zeno's hand, jovially extended. She did not smile. "Perhaps in a few days," said Cornelia.

She showed the newest vestal the statues of the vestal chiefs surrounding the courtyard, emphasizing their humanity over their piety: "This is Junia, who loved animals. This is Fannia, who was the most beautiful woman in Rome. They are your sisters now, as they are mine. We are all women of the Imperial House, whose hearth we keep."

Still guiding Poppaea by the shoulders, Cornelia took her to the place she had saved till last: a grove of myrtles, concealing an aviary of parrots, goldfinches, nightingales, which she had created for the vestal Helen because of Helen's grief when the white doves she raised from nestlings were used in augury. Helen, who was here now, greeted them with the candid joy she took in tending her birds. "Look, isn't this parrot a beauty?"

A magpie swooped onto her shoulder, squawking what had become his own name. "Hello, hello!"

"He's jealous," explained Helen. "Would you like to hold a dove?" Coaxing one onto her finger, she offered it to Poppaea, who gingerly cupped it in her hands.

"I'm going to leave you here." Cornelia smiled. "Helen will bring you to dinner."

As Cornelia left the courtyard, she noticed Diana coming toward the vestalry gate with her buckets of sacred water slung as carelessly as milk pails over her shoulder. A buxom girl of eighteen, Diana was becoming increasingly difficult for Cornelia to handle. She knew she should reprimand her for her slovenliness, but shrank from the task. As chief vestal, it was Cornelia's desire to bind the vestals together in loyal sisterhood. In this, her first year in office, she had eased many of the traditions restricting vestal life and had revoked some of the privileges of seniority in favour of greater equality. Such changes had garnered stiff opposition from the vestal Agrippina, her senior by twelve years, and the logical choice as chief if the auspices had not ruled so harshly against her.

Cornelia walked across Sacred Square to the Temple of Vesta, a small circle of white Luna marble with a double portico of Corinthian columns and a cone-shaped bronze roof that vented smoke. As she entered the Temple, the smallest, oldest and most important in the Forum, she passed from sunlight into flame-streaked shadow, from the ordinary world into the world of spiritual mystery, from outer confusion to inner peace. Before her was an alabaster screen embossed with scenes from Roman festivals: Vestalia, the Festival of the October Horse, Saturnalia. Stepping behind it, Cornelia approached the sacred hearth where Fausta, who had been chief before her, was sprinkling wine. Once a woman of great dignity, Fausta had been overcome by madness – or the ecstasy of the godhead, as the chief priest pre-ferred to see it. Now, as she chanted around the hearth, her crabbed frame and unbound grey hair made her seem as one with the twigs and smoke of the fire.

Agrippina, the second-eldest vestal, was bent low over a dove whose guts she probed with a jewelled dagger – as skilled as any Alexandrian surgeon at preserving life while examining organs for irregularities. Since bad auguries had played a crucial role in ruling against her promotion to chief, she was diligent in check-ing up in this way on Cornelia's regime. The dove she held was plucked clean, its eyes were glazed, and yet its heart still beat. Remembering Poppaea's look of joy, Cornelia reached down thumb and forefinger and snuffed its life. Flinging the carcass into the flames, she said: "Please tend to your other Temple duties."

Agrippina stared up at Cornelia in hurt and humiliation. Set-ting down her dagger, she rose scornfully to her feet, and moved behind the alabaster screen. One day soon she hoped the College of Priests would discover their folly in promoting mere pretti-ness over piety.

Kneeling before the hearth of Vesta, Cornelia rebuked herself for bringing conflict here – right to the sacred flame. She had been too harsh with Agrippina just now, as earlier she had been too indulgent with Poppaea, encouraging a lack of restraint that would only hurt the child. Seeking guidance against her own impulsiveness, Cornelia gazed into the smoke, the crackling twigs, the flames. Of all the gods of Rome, Vesta was the only one who had no image, who existed only in the power of her symbol: her fire. According to its brightness, and the purity of those who attended it, so went the fortunes of Rome and the empire. Throughout history many plagues, floods and military disasters had been traced directly to carelessness or corruption in the Temple of Vesta. As Cornelia knelt in dedication before the hearth, she felt overwhelmed by her awesome responsibility. Yet more than duty, she felt love for Vesta. For Rome. From earliest memory, this was the only life she had wanted or known. To serve in so majestic a task – what a thrilling privilege.

Renewed in purpose and spirit, Cornelia sought out Agrippina behind the alabaster screen. To soothe the feelings of the sensitive vestal, she said: "Zeno showed me the will you transcribed for Senator Nerva. What a beautiful document. Nobody but you can get so much, so legibly, on a single page."

As Agrippina squinted in suspicion at the chief vestal she felt her hunger for approval war with her envy. She resolved the problem by greedily snatching up the compliment while rejecting its giver. Cornelia was jealous because she, Agrippina, could do everything more skilfully.

Cornelia left the Temple. As she crossed Sacred Square on her way to the vestalry, she saw a woman in imperial robes enter the gate. At first she feared it was the Empress Domitia, who had been wooing Agrippina with gifts. Then she recognized Julia Sabina. The two women embraced. They sat together on a bench among the roses. Holding her friend's face in her hands, Cornelia said: "Let me look at you. You seem happy for the first time in months. Can I guess the reason? You received an invitation to the emperor's birthday banquet."

Smiling radiantly, Julia pulled a scroll from her cloak, which she waved before the vestal. "Yes! This arrived an hour ago. Oh, Cornelia." She squeezed her friend's hand. "Do you know how long it's been since I was banished from the palace? Exactly two months, one week, three days and four hours." She moaned. "Oh, I hate her! I imagine them together, and I want to scratch out her eyes. When that rumour came last month that she was pregnant – thank god, untrue! – my whole body ached. I love him. I can't help it. Now they say he is tired of her again – after only two months!"

Cornelia looked into Julia's triumphant face, seeing only folly in this new hope of happiness. Choosing her words to support her friend without feeding her obsession, she said: "Yesterday I saw the emperor at the Temple of Jupiter, making a sacrifice for his birthday. Though the empress was with him, they didn't touch or speak, as if indeed there was some coolness between them. Even if that's true, she *is* his wife, as furious against exile as you are. She's cruel and clever in her passions, whereas you run hot and foolish. Guard yourself, Julia. Make peace with her. Didn't you used to be friends? Wasn't she kind to you when you first came to Rome? Be friends with her again. Control this 'love' of yours, which upsets me as much as the madness of Fausta."

Julia sighed. "I know you are right, Cornelia. But have you ever walked through mud and worried that you wouldn't leave footprints? Those are the kind of nightmares I have. When I look into a mirror, I see no reflection. That's why I weave and spin and paint. At least then I have some evidence that my hands exist, that I've been in that room because I've left a mark. When I feel love, or even pain, I know I exist. I know I've lived through that day."

"A ship leaves no mark, no matter how heavy the cargo," replied Cornelia, using reason against her friend's passion. "The fault isn't in the ship, but in the shifting substance of water – of life itself."

"But the ship at least has a captain and that captain has some course, even if he has to fight the winds for it," responded Julia before plunging into her own feverish justification: "Tell me – what am I? Where is my life without the palace and the emperor? Everything has always been out of my hands. When my mother died, my father sent me to live in Como, and that was an act of state. When I was sixteen, he recalled me to marry my cousin Flavius Sabinus, and that was an act of state. Then Domitian banished Domitia and took me into the palace – the place I had always longed to be, the place where I had a right to be. At last I had come home.... To have had all that and then to have it snatched away. What can I say? She doesn't love him. He doesn't love her. They just use each other. The only reason she was kind to me when I came to Rome was to manipulate me like the rest."

Cornelia took Julia's hand, intending to calm her, but feeling instead the other's hysteria bite into her own reserve. "What you fear is just the loneliness of life. You're unique only in this – you think an emperor or a palace can cure it. Can't you feel my touch? Can't you hear my words? You're real to me in my friendship for you though such feelings aren't as dramatic as the ones you are drowning yourself in."

Julia sighed. "I admire you, Cornelia, and I envy your life. For you, there are no compromises. No squalid jealousies. No uncertainties. No desperate choices. You know your duty, and you do it with a willing heart. I can find no such purpose to my life, but please don't give up on me. I do my best." She stood up, hugging her friend. "Now I must go."

Cornelia watched Julia dart through the vestalry garden, her purple cloak catching on the rose plantings, feeling – despite their closeness in age – like a mother helplessly watching a daughter take yet another step into folly. She touched the bulla of office she wore around her neck. Julia was right in this one thing: She was lucky in her life of service.

Cornelia walked toward her office by the library, intending to compile next month's schedule for all six vestals – her most boring chore. Her feet stopped well short of the door. Glancing wistfully back at the bench, she asked herself: What did she have to match the excitement of Julia's adventurous life? Squelching such a wayward thought, she hurried to her office.

Julia dashed through the gates of the vestalry toward her litter marked with the Flavian crest. She stopped in Sacred Square and glanced toward the Temple of Vesta, its smoke rising in a lazy plume. She looked back at the litter, again at the Temple, then rushed forward, almost tripping on her cloak as she climbed the Temple steps. She plunged into the smoky interior and pressed her palms against the marble wall, feeling its chill through their stickiness. She could hear Fausta on the other side of the alabaster screen, chanting as she tended the hearth. Julia edged toward the screen. Taking the bellpull in both hands, she yanked once then again. A strident jangle filled the Temple. Julia dropped the cord.

The chanting did not cease but instead grew louder, as if Fausta were shuffling toward her on the other side of the screen. Fausta's head appeared through the opening, her hair like a billow of smoke, her face stern. As the cousin of Julia's mother, who had died when she was three, Julia had known Fausta as an austere and dignified woman who could be kind. It was a shock to see how pitifully the vestal had changed in the year since her retirement as chief.

"Greetings, Lady Fausta. I have come to you in the name of my mother Marcia."

The mention of Fausta's dearly beloved cousin seemed to draw on memories deep inside her. She smiled. "How is Marcia these days? I haven't seen her for awhile. Why is she neglecting her prayers?"

Julia replied with gentleness: "My mother Marcia died many years ago, Lady Fausta. I have come to you for the blessing of Vesta and for Juno's gift of fertility."

Fausta scrutinized her face, then nodded. "I see." Taking Julia by the hand, she drew her further into the Temple, to a statue of Juno crowned with wild fig. Chanting in a single note, as if she had a swarm of hornets in her throat, she untied the sash binding Juno's waist. She dipped the rawhide into an amphora of goat's blood and, holding it at arm's length, dedicated it to Juno then to Vesta.

Julia stretched out her palms. Breathing deeply, Fausta slapped one then the other. Julia felt the leather sting her flesh...open her womb. The humming ceased. The beat of the leather ceased. The buzzing in Julia's head ceased. Fausta spread verbena lotion on Julia's palms, then gave her a moonstone to hold in each.

"Thank you, Lady Fausta." Embracing the old woman with gratitude, she said: "Tomorrow I'll send a goat for Juno and an amphora of oil for Vesta."

Clasping the moonstones, Julia left the Temple, feeling exultant. She had just made the first significant decision of her life. Now when the emperor called her to his bed, she would be ready.

Julia's bearers carried her through the Arch of Titus, commemorating her father Titus' sack of Jerusalem, then up the unfashionable Aventine. She heard the click of her own gate and felt the jar as her litter was deposited. Shaky but pleased with herself, she stepped out into her courtyard. To her surprise, Maximus Marcus was sitting on a bench under her pear tree. He stood up and hurried toward her.

"Two visits in as many days, Marcus? I'm flattered."

Smiling, he took her hand. "I've brought a friend who wants to meet you." Julia turned, expecting to see this friend. There was no one – just the wooden vat in which she was dying yarn with yellow madder. As she turned back to Marcus, something popped out of the vat of dye: the head and naked torso of poet and playwright Helvidius Priscus. Yellow yarn hung from his red beard like seaweed from the chin of Neptune. His chest – even his freckles – were dyed yellow.

Grinning with bravado, Priscus said: "I've admired you since you first came to Rome, but the Palatine was too high for me to climb. Any hill more regal than the Aventine and I get nosebleed."

Julia laughed. "Cleopatra had herself delivered to Caesar in a rug. Is this vat your version?"

Priscus stepped from the dye, shaking himself like a yellow mongrel. "The truth is, I came with my friend to ask you, artist to artist, if you would illustrate my love poems, which I have already boldly dedicated to you. Then I saw this dye – my favourite colour – and decided it would be more fun if you illustrated me, the poet, instead. When I'm fully illustrated with hearts and flowers, I'll recite my poems down in the Forum – same price for the rich as for the poor. My father was also a great man for the masses – it's a family trait."

Giggling, Julia tossed off her cloak, feeling light-hearted for the first time in months...her palms still tingling.

CHAPTER THREE

Emperor Domitian's Grand Hall was decorated for his birthday banquet. Nine ivory couches, divided by red bolsters so three guests could recline diagonally on each, were arranged around as many tables set with knives and spoons.

As a newcomer to Rome, Maximus Marcus was first to be announced by the heralds and borne to his couch-place under the hall's golden dome. Slaves perfumed his feet, replaced his sandals with embroidered slippers, arranged his emerald dining shawl. He settled back to enjoy the spirited competition in sedan-chairs and liveried servants as the rest of the guests were ushered in, according to rank. Each noisily greeted the others while keeping an eye out for more prestigious arrivals.

At last heralds proclaimed the imperial party. The guests arose, eyes strained toward the grand entranceway. As this was the first time Julia Sabina had appeared in public with the royal couple since the empress' recall from exile, everyone was breathless to observe this adulterous triangle that was the scandal of the empire.

As protocol demanded, Julia Sabina was borne in first. Unused to the strident luxury of court life, Marcus scarcely recognized his childhood friend, robed in orange silk, her almost-naked breasts roped in emeralds, her dainty features overwhelmed by a towering basketweave hairdo dusted with gold.

Again, the heralds trumpeted.

Emperor Domitian and the Empress Domitia appeared in a double sedan-chair, canopied with peacock feathers. Though the emperor was magnificent in gold-embroidered purple robes and jewelled crown, it was the empress who drew Marcus' eyes. Her haughty, handsome face was powdered white, with the veins of her forehead outlined in blue, her eyes in black and her lips in red. Her dark hair was tortured into a crown of curls wound with pearls.

As the empress was placed to the right of the emperor on the same couch as Julia, the women guests stared enviously from Domitia's corkscrew hairdo to Julia Sabina's basketweave. By tomorrow every fashionable woman in Rome would have a description of both, and by the following week they would be copied in all the better brothels. The competition among women for hairdressers was as keen as that among their husbands for chefs.

The elderly chief priest, Quintus Piso, shuffled to an altar cut as a sunburst in the mosaic floor, escorted by the chief vestal. After thanking Jupiter for the good health of the emperor, "one with you in godhead," Piso sacrificed a white ass, while the Lady Cornelia sprinkled wine on the altar.

Marcus had not encountered the vestal since seeing her in the Forum. Struck by her uncanny resemblance to her brother Nestor, he hoped he would have chance to acquaint her with the tragic circumstance that bound their lives, but was unprepared to see her lictors escorting her to the empty space on his own couch.

Slaves filled the diners' goblets with Falernian wine, chilled in snow and dipped from crystal bowls, while the poet Valerius Martial recited a poem celebrating the emperor's German victories achieved twelve years earlier:

"Thy sire and brother wear the Jewish crown,
The wealth the Chatti send is all thine own."

He ended with the toast: "Let us quaff our nectar to the god who lives among us."

As the guests drank the toast, the emperor's slaves distributed gifts to each: jars of beryl, amber, agate or crystal containing spices such as saffron, pepper and cinnamon, worth more than their weight in gold. Appetizers were then served while they reclined on their left sides and helped themselves with their right hands:

Jellyfish and eggs.

Sows' udders stuffed with salted sea urchin.

Portions of brains cooked with milk and eggs.

Boiled tree fungi with peppered fish sauce.

Olives, raw vegetables and apples.

Emperor Domitian watched in amusement as gluttons, like the wealthy freedman Clodianus, heaped their plates. His attention was caught by the couch containing the chief vestal Cornelia flanked by Maximus Marcus, recently recalled prefect of a legion in Egypt, and Antonius Saturninus, recently recalled governor of Upper Germany. Saturninus, a homosexual who had been the lover of Domitian's brother Titus, was lolling in a diaphanous toga, trying to catch the emperor's eye with the eloquent display of his profile – the flaring nostrils, the poetically brooding eyes, and with his top lip thrust provocatively over the bottom.

Smiling at Saturninus, Domitian lifted his gold goblet. "I propose a welcome-home toast to one of my most courageous officers." Preening himself, Saturninus started to rise. Domitian shifted his eyes to the other end of the couch. "Hail, Maximus Marcus! May your stay in Rome be a richly rewarded one."

Saturninus fell back in red-faced humiliation while Marcus stood to accept the compliment. "My return is rewarded, if only to hear the welcome of my Commander-in-Chief."

"How long has it been since you were here before?" asked Domitian, pleased to hear his military title.

"Fifteen years."

"Have we changed much in so long a time?"

"When I was here last, there were still many scars from the

Great Fire that blighted your brother Titus' reign. Emperor Augustus boasted that he inherited a city of mud, and left it a city of marble. You inherited a city of rubble, and turned it into a city of monuments."

"Just monuments, Marcus? As useless as that?"

Still talking confidently as an engineer, the knight replied: "The bricks under the marble and the principles that support them are as sound as any the world has known. Augustus built foursquare, which was right for the austerity of his time. You have moved on to the apse and the vault, which are right for the glory of ours."

This unexpectedly artful speech, delivered with a tourist's enthusiasm, touched the pride of the guests, so that they broke into applause. All but Saturninus. Picking at a sea urchin with the sharp end of his spoon, he asked: "Tell me, Marcus, since you have a provincial's keen eye for Rome's splendours, do you feel the same breathless appreciation for the statues planted so liberally about our forums? Or do you find a certain staleness of subject?"

It was a dangerous joke throughout Rome that the emperor's statues were becoming more numerous than the free population of the city. "The numbers don't matter to me," replied Marcus. "While the subject remains the same, each sculptor has carved it with his own eyes."

"Bravo!" exclaimed Zeno, who was the emperor's secretary as well as tutor to the vestalry. Picking up the compliment, he embellished it as his own. "I've been telling the emperor the same thing myself. His qualities are as the rays of the sun – too many to be caught by one flower or by one artist. If a man admires an orchid, is he to complain when he sees a field of them?"

Slaves cleared the debris from the first course, then refilled the goblets – this time with Chalybonium wine from Damascus. Each guest's slave bathed his greasy fingers and dried them with scented towels, while musicians passed among the tables playing the flute, cythra and lyre.

41

The second course was served:
Fallow deer roasted with onion sauce, Jericho dates, raisins, rue, oil and honey.
Boiled ostrich with sweet sauce.
Turtle dove boiled in its feathers.
Roasted parrot.
Dormice stuffed with pork and pine kernels.
Ham boiled with figs and bay leaves, then rubbed with honey and baked in a pastry shell.
Flamingos boiled with dates.

The conversation turned, naturally enough, to a discussion of food. Zeno recited a witty limerick in praise of Apicius, the Roman epicure, who committed suicide when he discovered he had only a small fortune left, after squandering millions to ransack the world for delicacies.

Clodianus, the former fishhawker from Alexandria, who had traded himself up to wealth and power, boasted about having spent more that morning for a single mullet than most men paid for their chefs.

"No doubt your guests will enjoy watching you eat it, as they gnaw their mouldy bread and drink their vinegar," joked prosecutor Messalinus, ignoring the fact that he too had a reputation as a pinchpenny gourmand who served guests different food at the same table, according to how he valued them.

"I am told by guests of yours, Messalinus, that some senators have as many grades of wine as they do friends – all bad," jibed Consul Clemens. "Tell me, do you invite people to dine with you or to envy you?"

Lovingly sniffing the wine which, being blind, he could not see, Messalinus replied: "Why pour fine drink down a gullet you don't like, or one that won't appreciate it? I discriminate among my friends as I do among my vintages."

More wine was served. The emperor's guests embarked upon their favourite topic: the vices of Rome, in which they took inordinate pride.

Clodianus, who seemed to be constructed of fleshy boxes set

one upon the other without neck or waist, leaned amiably toward Maximus Marcus. "If you want the true flavour of this city, try walking her streets by night. I swear by Mercury, god of knaves, there are ten thieves for every god of the crosswalk. Even the Temple of Mars the Avenger was robbed – not just the strongboxes but the god's own gold leaf peeled right off." He wiped his beringed fingers on the head of his slave. "It's dangerous to go out to dinner without making your will."

"It's not the thieves you have to watch out for," interjected Consul Clemens wryly, "it's the slops our good citizens throw from their balconies. That's the other side of Rome's extravagance: whether fish or fowl, it all ends up in the chamberpot. It's hard for a man to go ten yards at night and still keep his torch lighted."

"It's the foreigners who have ruined Rome," observed prosecutor Messalinus, delicately cleaning his teeth with a silver pick. "The only ones worse than the Syrians are the Greeks. Trust a Greek then get ten witnesses. We've become a city of mongrels."

Clodianus chuckled, anticipating his own joke. "Many a man's lock isn't to keep the thieves out. It's to keep his wife in. Since our women gained their freedom, many have never seen a sunrise. Their husbands get the greasy night creams at noon, while the midnight lover gets the skin freshened with asses' milk. Then there's this other part. If you get a guard to guard a wife, who guards the guard? Slaves and gladiators – they're our ladies' preferred meat these days, I'm told. No man knows, when his wife begets a kid, if he'll grow up to look like some thug from the arena."

"Speak for yourself!" exclaimed Saturninus, who had been sulking on his couch. "Admit it, Clodianus, the only reason you kiss your wife is to smell if she's been drinking."

Clodianus angrily gripped his spoon in his fist, for his wife's bawdy habits were the joke of Rome. "At least it's a woman's lips I kiss and not some man's asshole. You male brides grow bold. Next thing you'll be after is mention in the *Daily Gazette*.

I have five children. What do you muff-diggers pay for the future of Rome?"

"He's got you there, Saturninus!" applauded Emperor Domitian, pouncing with glee upon his pet complaint. "Rome needs soldiers. Every year the birth rate plunges. Our enemies boast they have no need to slay the Roman army. Our wives' repugnance for our seed does their job for them." He raised his goblet. "What Rome needs is less lust and larger families."

There was a chorus of "Bravo! Bravo!" which the vestal Cornelia cut short by addressing Domitian. "If Rome needs soldiers, my emperor, why do we kill so many babes at birth? Why do you allow the archaic custom whereby a woman must present her child to her husband at ninth day, and if he refuses to support it or acknowledge its paternity, that babe is exposed to die or sold into slavery?"

Resentful of this vestal who seemed too interested in politics, Domitian replied with hauteur: "Because, my priestess, there is too much hate in a bastard born of love. Venus gives a man happy nights, but the children of Venus shorten his days."

Saturninus, goaded by yet a second rebuke, interrupted with equal scorn. "What would you say then, my emperor, to the man with lawful wife whose womb he never fills? Would you suggest that she turn in frustration to the theatre?"

Now the emperor's table was gripped by silence, for what was this but a brazen reference to the emperor's own childlessness and his wife's adultery with the actor Paris? "I would say," replied Domitian, with the start of a tic about his thin lips, "that the wife who fails to breed should acknowledge her fault by presenting herself to her husband for divorce. But how much virtue can we expect from our matrons when our governors wear powder and plough the backsides of boys? Compare the length of your tongue with the width of your senatorial stripe, Saturninus, and see if you haven't gone too far with both of them. There's only one Caesar, and I am not looking at him."

Slaves cleared the table for the final course and set flower crowns on the heads of the guests. They served the emperor's favourite drink – calda, made of heavily spiced and heated wine from his own Alban estate – along with various desserts:

Fricassee of roses with pastry.

Stoned dates stuffed with nuts and pine kernels fried in honey.

Hot African sweet-wine cake with honey.

A cornucopia of fruits and mock fruits made of pastry.

The diners at the emperor's table welcomed this respite from conversation, and especially the women on his couch, who had spent a stressful evening. His mistress Julia had been chilled by the emperor's bitter comments about love children – a fear only partly allayed by the charm he now lavished upon her. The confidence of the Empress Domitia had also been shaken by the emperor's cruel remarks about barren wives. As she glared at her husband, now bending low over Julia Sabina, in laughing intimacy, a flush of pain seeped through her white makeup. Upsetting her wine, she stumbled toward Antonius Saturninus, a fellow outcast.

By now the light from the courtyard had faded to an uncertain grey. Slaves lit the oil lamps that hung in clusters from gold standards and were reflected in dozens of polished surfaces, as the diners retreated into private conversation: The gossip or "smoke" the slaves would sell tomorrow to be published in the *Daily Gazette*.

Cornelia searched the room for the other vestals, wondering how long they would have to stay in this unpleasant place, full of conflict and chaos. A hand touched her elbow. Turning, she found herself looking into the handsome face of Maximus Marcus. There was something reassuring in the presence of the young knight, and yet something disconcerting too...a powerful impact he seemed to have upon her, as if they had met some place before. How could that be? He said he hadn't been in Rome for fifteen years. She had scarcely left it. Feeling a queer sort of anticipation, she asked: "Do I know you?"

The knight smiled. "I *am* part of your past, though we've never met."

"That puzzles me. As a vestal, my life is Rome."

His smile broadened. "Your life before you became a vestal. You had a brother Nestor?"

Astonished, she asked: "Did you know him?"

"Very well. And your father Cornelius Quintus, and your mother Claudia. Nestor and I studied engineering together under the great Julius Frontinus. Later I visited him at your home in Pompeii."

She felt the first prickings of anxiety. "When was that?"

"Sixteen years ago. The time of the eruption."

Her fingers curled around the edge of the couch. "Were you with them...?"

He nodded recollecting: "Nestor and I were returning from a week on Capri when we felt showers of ash, which we took to be from a ship that had burned offshore. As we rounded the island, we saw a large and ominous cloud with a fiery underside. We heard rumblings. Then we knew – Vesuvius!" He stopped speaking.

The vestal was leaning toward him, her hands clutching the dining couch, mesmerized. Though Cornelia had heard many versions of the famous disaster, this was the first she had heard from someone who knew her family. She had been six when she became a vestal. Here was the life she had foresworn. She thought she had forgotten it. Now she knew, from the constriction in her throat, that she had not. "Please go on."

Marcus hesitated, as surprised as she by such a strong reaction to so old a tragedy. "Are you sure?"

"Please."

"We heard a crash as if the earth were exploding. Trees and boulders leapt into the air. Day turned into night.... Pompeii was buried under mounds of ash, like black snowdrifts."

She touched his arm. "My mother and my father?"

"Buried."

"And my brother?"

He felt the coldness of her fingers. "Dead, too. At sea."

"Drowned?"

"No." He frowned, remembering. "It's a strange story."

She leaned forward. "I want to know."

"Nestor begged the captain to take the ship in closer. He refused. Your brother stole a landing boat and set off on his own. Black waves pounded our ship so we had to jettison cargo. Yet we were in the first landing party." Marcus saw again the desolation of that shore, the wreckage of ships and uprooted trees, the piles of corpses, grotesquely coated in black. He said: "There were many bodies on the beach. One was Nestor, still in his boat as if the wind had thrown him on shore then sucked the water from under him. Whether he died from injury or from the poisonous fumes that killed the birds, I don't know. There was no mark on him."

Cornelia bowed her head. "This is painful, yet it seems to be the thing I yearned to know. I thought the past was closed to me when I became a vestal. Now I find it isn't."

"I'm sorry..."

"No." She repeated: "I wanted to know."

They sat in silence, caught up in that distant tragedy, suddenly more real to them than the party eddying around them. Cornelia felt grateful to the knight, yet frightened too, made vulnerable by this opening up of her past in a way she did not understand. She said, "Thank you," then turned her head, breaking contact.

By now banqueters were travelling drunkenly from couch to couch. A troupe of acrobats was building a pyramid. Jugglers tossed torches. Zeno called across the table: "Marcus, I've been trying to catch your eye."

The knight looked over at this jolly face entirely at odds with his mood.

"I'm host to a literary evening next week at my villa. The poet Martial, whom you heard tonight, will be there, and Messalinus here will give a legal dissertation. Will you add your talent to ours?"

Still mulling over his conversation with Cornelia, Marcus replied: "I'm sorry, Zeno, I'm not a man of words."

"I hope," bristled Zeno, "you're not one of those who thinks he's wasted an evening listening to poetry just because he hasn't wasted it somewhere else?"

"It wouldn't be *my* time I'd waste," said Marcus, "but yours."

Antonius Saturninus roused himself from the goblet he was sucking. "If you're not a man of words, Marcus, are you a man of action?"

The knight eyed him with suspicion. "Only as a soldier. As my duty requires it."

"Perhaps you'd like to race next month at our Festival of the October Horse?"

"I have neither the talent nor the training."

"Didn't you win laurels in Britain and in Germany?"

"Those were amateur laurels, as different as practise swords from steel ones, and very long ago. Taken as a dare."

"Then I *dare* you to compete in this year's October Horse."

Marcus repeated: "I have neither the talent nor the training."

The emperor interrupted his intimacies with Julia, amused at the rivalry he had aroused. "Nonsense, Marcus, nonsense! Look around you. What do you see? Rome's finest, stuffing themselves fat as sausages so they can purge and puke and begin again. All our Roman men exercise these days are their stomachs and their cocks – and our charioteers are our worst offenders. As for our women, they only leave their couches to douche. We need your fresh provincial blood – in fact, we should handicap you. You *will* ride in the October Horse. You will wear my colours. I will wager on you. Against Antonius Saturninus."

Clapping his hands, the emperor ordered more wine. He demanded the lamps be trimmed to cut down on the smoke, then dismissed the acrobats and jugglers, calling instead for female entertainment. He shouted to his cousin, Flavius Clemens, so loudly the consul's wife at the next table was forced to hear: "Clemens, I've a special treat for you. A Jewish girl who dances the Cordax like none Rome has ever seen."

48

Clemens was perplexed, for his shyness with women was well known. "Why is that a treat for me, my cousin?"

Domitian grinned. "I noticed you avoided the pork tonight."

"I also avoided the brains, the roast parrot, the dormice and all the rich sauces," replied Clemens. "A man my age is either a fool or his own physician."

Domitian turned sly. "Aren't you seeing a lot of the Jews these days – or am I misinformed?"

"My wife has a Jewish maid who is married to my steward, and they sometimes deal with Jewish merchants. All minorities flock as naturally as birds, don't they?"

Pretending more drunkenness than he felt, Domitian gave Clemens a coarse wink. "Beware of wenches who want to sleep with you, dear cousin. They may be in the pay of your enemies checking to see if you are circumcised."

Humiliated, Clemens arose from his couch. To prevent a quarrel, Cornelia interceded: "My emperor, why are you so harsh on this one cult with its pointless rituals when you turn a blind eye on the cult of Isis, which still practises the castration you forbid?"

Domitian discarded his mask of drunkenness. "The priests of Isis sheltered me as a young man during the civil war when my father's enemies burned Rome. Since the life of an emperor is a precarious one, I can't help feeling tolerance toward those who prolong it, and antipathy toward those who do not. My brother Titus destroyed Jerusalem, so now the Jews sneak one by one into Rome to destroy us. Every time I find an excuse to kill a Jew, I extend the work of my family."

Domitian returned with renewed vigour to pawing Julia on his couch – an insult both to the virgin priestess and to his wife. By now the whole party had taken a ruder turn. Many guests were gambling with dice or knucklebones. Three senators were making a game of urinating into a goblet.

Taking advantage of her prerogatives as chief vestal, Cornelia sought out the other priestesses. She bid a warm but hasty goodbye to Maximus Marcus: "Please, let's talk again." She bid a formal one to the emperor, who ignored her departure.

49

The evening grew steamier.

Xerxes, the famous strongman, tore off the head of a calf with his bare hands, and ate the brains. Two naked women, each five hundred pounds, wrestled in a vat of mud, calling upon the diners to join them. The freaks, for which Domitian had a taste, were paraded about by his cup-bearer, Hermes the dwarf, acting as ringmaster: A two-headed cow painted gold. A child, with flippers for arms, dragged on a leash. An armless, legless torso that juggled balls from tongue and nose.

Empress Domitia got up from the couch, where her husband and his mistress were now making love, and cast about her husband's guests, mortified and very drunk. Why had she been recalled from exile – to be mocked, then divorced? Why be so kind? Why not just have her guards strangle her the way he would anyone else?

Lurching toward the seat vacated by Cornelia, she sank down beside Maximus Marcus and leaned forward with a sultry smile. "You're very beautiful, the handsomest man in Rome." She lay her hand on his chest, then slid her fingers inside his toga. "I desire you."

Marcus felt her palm caress his flesh. "Lady, you are bold."

Leaning forward so her breasts grazed his arm, she asked: "Does that displease you?"

He gazed into her eyes, drawn by her power but paralyzed by her need, not knowing what was expected of him, or allowed. Falling back on traditional morality, he said: "You are the wife of my Commander-in-Chief."

She laughed, cracking her white makeup. "I see, Maximus Marcus. You are one of the noble ones. You never seduce a man's whore at a party." She dropped her hand to his crotch, and squeezed. "Another time."

Getting unsteadily to her feet, the empress flickered her tongue like the prostitutes of Tuscany Street, and stumbled from couch to couch, becoming drunker yet never quite taking her eyes off her husband and his mistress.

At last Domitian rose groggily. Summoning his sedan-bearers, he helped Julia into the other chair, and left the banquet hall, with Hermes the dwarf hopping behind.

Domitia turned in panic to Antonius Saturninus. He was fondling one of the pretty boys whose job it was to change Clodianus' shawl every half hour. She started toward Maximus Marcus. His head was lying on his dining table, his cup overturned. She looked back at the now-empty imperial couch. Parthenius, the emperor's African chamberlain, was standing with one leg locked into the other, the way he, as a hunter, had once stood motionless as a thorn tree in the grasses of the veldt. How she would love to wake up that ebony statue, that perfect slave! Staggering toward him, arms outstretched, she tripped on one of her ropes of pearls and passed out.

Maximus Marcus opened his eyes and peered around him. He saw the wealthy freedman Clodianus, with one of the 500-pound fat ladies and a couple of freaks, wrestling in the vat of mud. He saw Antonius Saturninus sodomizing a slave on the imperial couch. He saw Empress Domitia lying face-down on the floor.

Used to the plainer vices of military life, he felt both titillated and repelled: So, this was Rome.

CHAPTER FOUR

Maximus Marcus hiked down the Esquiline, feeling bleary-eyed from a month of hard drinking and soft living, but with a young man's resilience.

To the west he could see Capitoline Hill – tier upon tier of marble pavilions mounting to the Temple of Jupiter, the Greatest and Best. Below him, untouched by sunlight, was the Subura, vilest tenement in Rome.

Yet as Marcus stepped down into its slimy, clamorous streets, with their bouquet of grease and garlic, slops and urine, the buzzing of flies, the yelping of dogs, the jumble of stalls selling rope and fruit and jars and leather goods, he saw them still with the forgiving eye of the visitor. Now on either side of him loomed four-storey tenements of crumbling stucco, some dirty pink or yellow but most of them brown. Women on balconies washed pots and hung clothes as they shouted back and forth. There were sidewalk barbershops and blacksmiths working at their forges and hawkers ladling beans and sizzling sausages from sooty pots. Scrawled on the walls – the writing paper of the poor – were menus, an auctioneer's list, curses, jokes, political slogans and love laments:

"Dear Tertius, you are mean."

"The rich get sick from eating, the poor from not eating."

"Hey you, what are you loitering for reading this?"

"Helena – do have pity on me and take me back."

"Old goats lick instead of prick."

Jostling Marcus was the "mongrel" Rome prosecutor Messalinus had complained about: fair-haired Germans in wolf skins; red-haired Gauls in short tartan cloaks; white-robed Arabs; blacks in peacock livery. Here too were clients rushing to greet their patrons on the hill, and runners with dinner invitations, and children with slaves who carried their books. Six Syrians in red and gold bellowed: "Make way! Make way!" as an orange litter jangling with bells forced pedestrians against the wall. A member of the City Watch in half-armour and steel cap argued with a fishmonger whose stall protruded too far onto the sidewalk.

Muddy alleys and greasy stairs jutted in every direction, forcing Marcus to stop often to get his bearings at the corner fountains, where water spouted from the mouths of rams, of eagles, of nymphs, into stone basins to be collected by women with jars, or to overflow down gutters of slops.

At last he saw his destination: the fabled Circus Maximus, where in two days' time the Festival of the October Horse would honour Mars, the god of war. Despite the tense circumstances by which he had been drafted, he couldn't help but feel anticipation: He, Maximus Marcus, knight of Como, was to race against the finest charioteers in the world.

As he sauntered along the Circus arcade, Marcus recognized statues of famous charioteers, both living and dead: the slave Pegasus, who won 1,173 races and retired a multi-millionaire; Narcissus, a scoundrel of patrician family, who boasted he had killed more men on the race course than as a general of the battlefield. Before each festival, fans garlanded the statues of their heroes, kissed their lips, burned incense before them. Some matrons, it was rumoured, even stole them to sleep with – if they couldn't seduce the charioteer himself. Others immolated themselves on the pyres of their heroes killed that day, or slit their throats in front of their statues.

Garishly painted prostitutes, in short tunics and anklets,

beckoned to Marcus as they huddled around their night fires. Others enticed him from Circus windows, which they occupied like bees in a honeycomb.

Marcus entered through an iron gate guarded by four legionnaires. A clutch of urchins grabbed at his blue cloak, clamouring: "Give! Give! Give!" One lad of about thirteen stood disdainfully apart. After bestowing upon him a bronze as, Marcus tossed a handful of quadrans to the rest.

He was swept up instantly, passionately, in the lure of the stadium – the briny odour of horse sweat and manure, the tang of leather and brass polish; the clang of blacksmiths, the clatter of chariot wheels. But, most of all, by the majestic beauty of the horses – the world's finest, purchased at stud farms in Greece, Spain and North Africa, put into training at age three, then raced at five.

Marcus found the emperor's stable, draped in gold and purple. The head groom seemed unable to see his name on the list of competitors, though Marcus had no trouble reading it over his shoulder. He showed it to the man, who nodded curtly, then pointed to two chestnut stallions and a black chariot garnished in brass. "Those are yours." He kicked awake two stablehands asleep in the straw. "This is Maximus Marcus...the knight I told you about."

Grinning and bowing, the stablehands harnessed Marcus' horses. He followed them onto the oval track – 250 yards by 22 yards, the largest in the world, ringed with three tiers of seats for a capacity of 250,000. As he put on his helmet, one of the stablehands wrapped his calves and thighs with leather leggings, while the other held the reins. Marcus knelt in the chariot – little more than a set of wheels with a low platform and a backstrap. He trotted down the muddy track, holding the reins loose, for he liked to give his horses the kind of ride they wanted rather than to show off his skills. As he accelerated from a canter into a gallop, the team started to buck. He tugged on the reins. The leather broke in his hands. A wheel snapped off, flipping him into the mud. His horses bolted around the track, dragging the broken chariot.

Marcus tramped back to the starting gate, where a handful of charioteers were jeering at him. *So...the pros didn't like amateurs, eh!* With temper rising, he waited for his grooms to recapture his horses and to haul his broken chariot back to him. He inspected the wheel axle and found marks of a chisel. The reins too had been partially sliced through. He flung the wheel in the face of one groom and slashed the reins across the back of the other. "Don't come near me or my horses or my rig again, or I'll break your legs. I'd do it now, but you are such stupid louts I want you in good shape to work for my rivals."

Marcus returned to the stable, searching for the dribble-mouthed old manure-spreader he had seen on the way in. On finding the man he asked his name. The answer came back slowly: "Pol-lux." It was as Marcus had suspected. Here was one of the great charioteers commemorated outside, his body broken by one too many tumbles. After asking him enough questions to assure himself the old wisdom still lay under the jumbled words, Marcus presented him to the emperor's head groom. "Pollux will be my groom. I've ordered him to choose the finest horses and rig in the imperial stable. The emperor, who does not love to lose, has placed a large wager on me."

Returning to the entrance gate, Marcus singled out the boy he had noticed earlier. "Hello there – yes, you! Know anything about horses?"

The boy pressed his grimy face into the grating. "I used to work for the harness-maker Tullus."

"Would you like a job?"

"Yes, sir!"

"Come with me. Now."

As the legionnaires reluctantly opened the gate, the boy swaggered past them. He rounded the corner of the stable, then broke into a gleeful canter.

Marcus asked his name.

"Castor."

He laughed. "The fates must be with us. Meet Pollux. The two of you are to prepare my rig. See that as many pieces come back to the starting gate as leave it."

He returned to the track. Drivers in two-, four- and eight-horse chariots dashed confidently around it. As he glanced with impatience toward the stable, he spotted Pollux leading two balky, ill-matched horses: one white and the other jet; one a delicate mare, the other a powerful stallion. Castor was hauling a battered rig, much the worse for overuse. Marcus groaned. Was he doomed to be the clown of the games? The fool who drives goats for the amusement of children?

Grinning and drooling, Pollux showed Marcus a plaque on the chariot, bearing his own name. Marcus nodded grimly. Probably the bad-luck rig Pollux raced when he took his last tumble. Accepting the reins, he knelt inside the chariot. Though comfortably contoured for his knees, the platform was higher than he was used to. He started cautiously around the track. The horses felt off-balance, the chariot unwieldy. As he tuned in to the rhythm of each, its gait, its breathing, its draw on the chariot, he drove each separately with different hand movements, absorbing into himself the choppiness of the ride. At last he felt them begin to pick up each other's rhythms, to pull together as a team.

Stopping after three laps, he let Castor – who was more skilful with harnesses than he had a right to expect – make minute adjustments. Then he started round again, letting the horses run full out, feeling the wind slap his face as the mud fanned out in a red wake. The reins were as light as strands of hair, while the higher kneeling position allowed him to lean almost horizontally over his horses, making him part of their motion. They were pulling effortlessly as a team now, perfectly manoeuvring the turns, with the stallion swinging out on the right, and the mare pivotting inside. Marcus longed to ride them bareback, one foot on each, as he had when he was a youth, till the dignity of rising rank persuaded him to leave such stunts to the acrobats.

Muddy, sweaty, jubilant, Marcus returned to the stable. Castor rushed to him, his young face reflecting the wonder Marcus knew enough not to show around these cynical pros. Pollux took the reins, his lopsided mouth doing the best it could with a smile. "Picked right? Yas? Yas?"

Marcus clapped the old man on the shoulder. "No man could have done better."

He gave Pollux two goldpieces and Castor one, urging him to be early at the race course the next morning.

Castor hid behind a pile of straw and inspected his 100-sesterces goldpiece with the face of Apollo shining on one side and the emperor crowned in laurels on the other. Castor had unloaded fish and wine and grain at the docks in Ostia. He had baked bricks in the broiling sun at the House of Afer. He had slaughtered pigs, turned an oil press and sewed harnesses, but he had never before held a goldpiece in his hand. In a city of one and a half million, with half of them slaves and another one hundred and fifty thousand on the dole, it was impossible to keep a job. As soon as some general declared a victory, the markets were swollen with cheap slaves: Germans with strong backs, Greeks with learning, Egyptians with pretty bodies.

Castor closed his fist around the coin: enough to buy his mother fancy earrings; enough to buy himself a fine cloak! He dashed toward the gate, imagining how glorious it would be to display his new wealth to his former companions, then he stopped, street-wise. After sweated decision, he stuck the coin in his mouth and clamped his jaw. If anyone bothered him, he'd swallow it, and run like hell.

The young toughs were, as usual, playing dice for sulphur matches outside the gate. Castor strolled past, trying to look as if nothing extraordinary had happened, but he couldn't keep the self-important taste of gold from showing on his face. As the dicers nudged each other, one head then another poked up from the tight circle. "Hey, Castor! Where'd you get it? Ass end or mouth?"

It was common for the charioteers to solicit boys for a little lechery in the straw, though Castor had never gone with them.

"Fuck like mother, suck like son!" jeered another.

"Look! He got it in the mouth. He can't open it. How does a knight's cock taste, Castor? Same as the ones that plough for quadrans in your mother's cunt?"

Castor bit harder on the coin, feeling the imprint of Caesar in his triumphal robes, trying to imagine how he, Castor, would look on race day in his fine cloak, trying to blot out their taunts with the sweet security of wealth. A couple ran after him, taunting him. He ignored them. They returned to their game.

Castor's restraint lasted till he rounded the corner of the Circus. Then he ran home, like a small boy, to mother.

It was not yet three o'clock, the time when Rome's forty-five registered brothels opened for business. Sweaty, breathless, Castor hesitated outside his mother's house. He wasn't supposed to visit Phoebe when she was working. Squeezing the gold coin, he felt again the magic confidence of wealth, and lunged up the stairwell, taking the slivery steps two at a time.

Phoebe lived and worked in a cubicle on the fourth floor, where she squatted now on a straw mattress, patting powder onto a once-pretty mole that had sprouted three hairs. She saw Castor and, with a squeal, yanked her scarlet shawl across her breasts.

"Mother, look!" Castor held up the goldpiece.

A gnawing suspicion took hold of Phoebe. She drew back her hand to strike her son. "No! I have work. A knight hired me. For his horses. He's racing tomorrow at the Circus." Castor came to the best part, once more tasting gold. "He's paying me another goldpiece tomorrow."

Phoebe seized his arm, her black eyes glowing. "Tell no one, you hear me? No one." Castor's face fell. Phoebe's nails gouged his flesh. "Promise me, Castor. There are as many thieves as rats in a brothel."

Castor swallowed his disappointment. "I promise, Mother."

She dropped his arm. "Now get! There's guests expected."

Still staring at the goldpiece, Phoebe listened to her son scamper down the stairs. And another tomorrow! Enough to leave Rome. Enough to return to Tivoli, where her father worked in a posting inn. Picking up a tatty birdwing fan, she began to wave it, slowly, dreamily, with the coin still clasped in her hand. The fan had been the gift of an infatuated client when she had occupied one of the suites on the ground floor. As she had grown older, her price had fallen from eighteen asses to two, and her clients had had to climb higher. Now, on the fourth floor, she was far enough above the street that if fire swept the tenement, she was certain to be fried alive, but still not so low in fortune as the Old Contemptibles who lived above her. In the rain and heat of the eaves, the broken-down whores, with no teeth and little hair, turned the occasional trick for clients too senile or too drunk to notice, or those with especially filthy habits. There was as wide a gap between the fourth- and fifth-floor prostitutes as between courtesans and respectable matrons. It was the fate Phoebe and all whores feared most.

Phoebe peeked at her gold coin. She must hide it, but where? In the straw mattress? In the seams of her tunic? Those places were good enough for silver but not for gold. She saw the powder she had spilled on the floor. Of course! She shoved the coin to the bottom of her tin powderbox and leaned back against the sooty wall, too full of dreams to prepare for the day's realities, marvelling at the imprint of the goldpiece still in her palm. Once men had tossed coins at her as she danced. She had been the most exciting dancer in all of Rome. Knights had begged her to share their couches. Senators had showered her with gifts. Poets had composed poems to her on ivory tablets. She had slept with generals and even one consul...or had she? Part was true, part was not. She couldn't remember which. She had thrown away her past with her mirrors. Now the only reflection she allowed herself was the one etched in love in her son's eyes.

Hearing roistering in the street, Phoebe put down her fan. She should be sitting in her window right now, advertising her wares and undercutting the other bawds. Last night she had had only two clients: the first to pay the landlord, and the second to pay Caesar – the tax Caligula had instigated after setting up his own sisters in a brothel.

Phoebe thought of the gold coin in her powderbox. Not tonight. Tonight belonged to Castor. Barring her door – a thing forbidden by the management of the house – she sewed over a smoky oil lamp, making a cloak from patches of her old tunics, blurred to peach, rose, saffron, stitching her hopes, like seed-pearls, into the lining.

Castor spent the night rolled in a tight ball on her straw mattress instead of in the streets, hearing once again the sounds of purchased love reverberating through the brothel, striving to work the groans, hisses, thuds, and screams into a fantasy of his own, seeing himself racing in the Circus, his scarlet cloak streaming, his head crowned with laurels like the Caesar on his goldpiece.

He arose at still-time – when the cocks have stopped crowing but men are not yet awake. The cloak-of-many-colours was waiting for him. He put it on, feeling his shoulders broaden under its splendour, then dashed down the four flights scummy with piss, vomit and semen, to admire himself in the waters of the crosswalk fountain. As he studied his narrow face, with deep-set eyes pressed into an amber squint by high cheekbones, he felt for the first time the power of his own beauty.

Castor scrubbed his face and hands. He cleaned his teeth with a cedar twig. He gargled with his mother's rosewater, and combed his straight black hair with a bone comb.

The prostitutes, nodding over their fires, nudged each other. "What you got under your cloak, laddie? Hard flesh? Hard cash? We got use for both!"

Castor strutted past them on his way to the Circus.

His gang of indolents was still asleep in front of the gate, curled up row upon row, like fish scales. Castor nudged his way through them, disturbing one after another. They recognized their fellow-traveller under the patchwork cloak. "Hey! He's wearing his mom's coloured snatch!" Remembering himself reflected in the crosswalk fountain, Castor treated them with such condescension that they grudgingly made way before him.

The grand effect of his entrance was almost lost at the gate. The guards were not so easily impressed by a boy in a cape of whore's tunics. His face pressed to the grating, Castor pleaded with them to let him in, feeling prickles of panic creep like bedbugs up inside his splendiferous cloak. He saw Pollux inside and hollered. The groom shambled over to the gate. He tilted his head and slowly focussed his good eye: "Yas!"

The guards unbarred the gate.

The sacred spring of Egeria bubbled up in a hawthorn grove outside Porta Capena, the southernmost gateway of Rome. It was here each morning that one of the vestals drew water to purify the Temple of Vesta.

Concealed behind cypress bushes, Marcus saw the vestal Cornelia come through the yellow trees with silver buckets balanced like weighpans over her shoulders. He saw her climb the marble shrine built around the spring, and lift her arms to Apollo, just then rising over the Sabine Hills. She spoke the incantation:

"O most wonderful Apollo,
Source of all life, truth and beauty,
Let thine arms of fire
Spare this draft of water
That we might cleanse our Temple this day,
In love, joy and tranquillity."

Marcus felt intrusive. He should have announced himself immediately. Now it was too late. He turned to leave, but she called into the rustling shadows: "Hello, is anyone there?" Not wishing to frighten her, he emerged from the bushes. Cornelia retreated in confusion. "Maximus Marcus. I was just thinking of you. Don't you race today?"

He forced a laugh to cover his embarrassment. "Race? I play

61

the fool's part – the entertainment between the acts, with the midgets and one-armed jugglers."

"How is that?"

"My harnesses tear like uncarded wool. My wheels roll down the track like children's hoops. Perhaps it's a trick of the gods, but there are others, more human, I'd blame first."

She laughed, catching his humour. "I'd better pray for your safety."

"It's my dignity that's in more danger."

They stood smiling awkwardly at each other, with the vestal holding her buckets in her arms. Hanging them on a hook, she strolled down the steps toward him. "Since our conversation at the banquet, I've thought of little else."

He frowned. "I was afraid of that. I told you too much too harshly. If I were a more tactful man –"

"No." She shook her head. "It's true that for awhile I felt pain, but then other memories began to return – happy memories lost to me. My father carrying me on his shoulders through the streets of Pompeii. A terra-cotta doll that my mother gave to me and a tiny wooden carriage pulled by white mice. I remember playing with my brother Nestor on the slopes of Vesuvius, and stealing grapes, and my mother scolding me for getting stains on my tunic.... With your help I've been able to scrape away the ashes entombing my memories – to set them free."

He studied her strongly moulded face with broad cheekbones and widely spaced green eyes, as touched by her joy as he had been by her sorrow. "I have also been thinking about the past." He opened the pouch he wore around his waist. "This belonged to Nestor." He took out a turquoise ring. "Now it belongs to you."

"I recognize it. It was my father's!" Delighted, she put it on her finger, then folded her palm around it. "In losing a brother, I've found one." She remembered the Circus. "I must give you something to bring you luck in the race today." Impulsively she took an amulet from her neck. "This holds the blessing of

Apollo, from the priestess at Delphi. Take it, please. Wear it in good health."

Marcus held up the white stone so that it burst into colour when struck by the sunlight.

"For the love we share for Nestor. It's the thing I prize most."

"Then I'll prize it too."

Flushing, she turned from him. "Now I must fill my buckets." He moved to help her, but she warned him away. "No. That's forbidden. No one but a vestal can touch the vessels." She added with a rueful smile: "By the old rules, we shouldn't even be speaking."

He watched her climb the stairs, dip her buckets, then disappear through the hawthorns.

By the time Marcus reached the Circus, Castor and Pollux had already prepared the rig and were braiding Purple Faction colours into the horses' tails so they would stand up. He heard the urchins cheering outside the gate. Antonius Saturninus was just now being borne in on a white-fur litter by eight Germans with blonde hair – the first time he had come to the Circus this season, though his fellow Blue drivers had been much in evidence. Greeting each other perfunctorily over the altar of Mars, both drivers lit incense rods bound with their Faction colours, then Saturninus went to oversee the decoration of his chariot while Marcus returned to his horses.

Marcus had always loved horses, and as a cavalry officer his life had often depended on them. This team especially excited his admiration, for the intuition with which they worked together. Priam, his off-horse, was the aggressive, powerful one. Helen, the near-horse, was faster and knew how to think ahead more than any other he had ever driven. He had made up his mind to buy them after the race, no matter what they cost.

A crier shouted: "One waterclock to start-time!" Already Marcus could hear the clamour of fans in the stadium. It was perfect weather for racing – sunny and clear, with a chilly edge, like a grape that has felt the bite of frost. What his brother Servius, who owned a Tuscany vineyard, called wine weather. All around him were the giddy sounds and gaudy sights that would meld themselves into the most sensational sporting event the world had ever known. Anxious grooms rechecked the shodding of horses or polished already-gleaming brasses. Small boys forked straw and bumped into cach other with water pails. Hawkers advertised charms, for which they made ever-more-miraculous boasts. With pomp and pomposity, liveried servants delivered fans' gifts of amulets or silk scarves to the drivers, who knotted in small groups swapping bawdy jokes along with strategy. Touts begged snippets of gossip and got their ears boxed for their troubles.

Again the crier passed through the stables: "Parade! Parade! Ready for parade!" As grooms coaxed their teams into position outside the triumphal gate, horses reared, chariots locked their wheels, drivers cursed. The Purple Faction came first, sponsored by the emperor; then the Blue, favourite of the nobility; then the Green, favourite of the mob; then White and Scarlet.

A fanfare announced the parade, led by Consul Clemens, wearing the gold-embroidered purple toga of a triumphal general. In his hand he carried an ivory baton mounted by an eagle, while on his head he wore a gold wreath so heavy that a slave called Nemesis had to walk by his side to hold it up and to whisper at intervals: "Remember you are mortal."

Clemens passed through the triumphal arch, followed by the charioteers in their Faction plumage. Then came Pontifex Piso, followed by incense-burners and the sixteen members of the priesthood, carrying gold and silver images of Mars, Jupiter, Minerva and Domitian. As each charioteer passed the emperor's viewing stand, he saluted. "Hail, Caesar!" Saturninus, resplendent in white fox and well-remembered for his dazzling feats before his appointment as governor to Upper Germany, received an ovation.

As always, the stadium was filled to capacity: senators in the first two rows, knights in the next fourteen, with the plebs above that, many in togas, for only citizens could attend. Despite the blinding predominance of white, Marcus had no trouble picking out the vestals in their canopied stall beside the emperor's more commodious one, containing the empress and Julia Sabina.

The parade filed out of the stadium, with the cheers of the crowd ringing around the oval track. Pontifex Piso sacrificed a black pig to Mars and a white ass to Jupiter, as Consul Clemens climbed to the starter's gate at the end of the spina.

The October Horse race, in which Marcus was to compete, was the last of twenty-four – an event for connoisseurs who preferred the elegance of the two-horse contests to the flashier four-, six- and eight-horse clashes. As the morning wore on, Marcus stationed himself variously around the track so he could study it from every angle, for he liked to plan a race the way a general would a campaign, with due respect for both the terrain and his opponents.

By the twelfth race, which was the lunch break, the Greens, the Blues and the Purples were within four points of each other. Though Marcus had witnessed an endless variety of crashes, it seemed to his soldier's eye that the mishaps were more like pantomimes of disaster than all-out clashes. Many of the pros were in their late forties or fifties, with hundreds of races to their credit. Whether by collusion or by instinct, they seemed to have developed a strategy for survival, while appeasing their fans. It was easy to see why Saturninus was so popular with the spectators. He was a hell-raiser set on the mainchance. Whenever he raced, there were always messes of twisted harness and horse flesh from which one or more of the drivers did not escape. No wonder the pros hated the amateurs.

By the final race, just before sunset, the emperor's Purples were tied with Saturninus' Blues. There were twelve entries, representing the four top Factions: Purples, Blues, Greens, Whites. Dipping into Pontifex Piso's starting jar, Marcus drew No. 6 – a lucky middle position, since the twelve horses at the gate had to vie for six positions to the right of the spina.

As Pollux and Castor led his team toward the starting gate,

Marcus danced on the balls of his feet, swinging his arms to loosen his shoulder muscles, no longer aware of the crowd, his mind fully concentrated on the race. A page in imperial livery elbowed his way through the grooms and their drivers to shove a pouch into Marcus' hand. Thinking it might contain instructions from the emperor, he tore it open. He found a garnet amulet, carved on one side with a likeness of Saturn, and on the other with that of the Empress Domitia. Puzzled by such a gesture and irritated by its distraction, he looked around for the messenger. The fellow was gone. Frowning toward the imperial box, he recalled the empress' advances toward him at the emperor's banquet, which he had put down to drunkenness. This gift had an ill-omen feeling about it – or did it? What were the customs of Rome? Was the empress his patron, along with the emperor? Touching the white amulet he had received from the vestal, he shoved the garnet one into Castor's hand to rid himself of it till after the contest. "Keep this, lad. For luck."

Now the crier was calling for the horses to enter the starting gate. After putting on his helmet and adjusting his leggings, Marcus crouched in his chariot. Castor handed him his whip and his knife, to cut the traces in case of a crash. He took the reins from Pollux, and eased his chariot into the No. 6 position. Beside him was Saturninus, all glittering silver and nodding blue plumage, his twin black stallions pawing the ground, snorting to go.

A red rope restrained the horses. Consul Clemens stood on the spina, white scarf in his hand. As he dropped the scarf, eleven chariots broke from the gate in a thunderous clash and clatter, leaving one Purple entry rearing and bawking. Two other entries – a Green and White – were demolished in the press for position. Marcus was surprised to hold onto his inside spot. He had expected a vicious challenge from Saturninus, who seemed content for now to dominate the race from behind.

The drivers were to complete seven laps for a race of one mile. Seven bronze eggs marked the turning post at one end of the spina, seven dolphins at the other. By the second lap, Saturninus' strategy was obvious: He would squeeze up on less skilled opponents and, with a blood-chilling howl, run their chariots into the spina while staying in contention. By the fifth lap, only four entries remained: the lead Green, a Blue, Saturninus also for the Blues, then Marcus for the Purples. The Green, pushing his horse too hard, was forced to drop back, so that now the two Blues were in the lead.

Marcus could see that Saturninus' stallions – for all his flamboyant showmanship – were beginning to tire. Still, he was suspicious when Saturninus took the sixth turn too wide, forcing him to sail into the gap. Again, he steeled himself for a challenge that did not come.

Now in second place, Marcus could feel Priam and Helen gaining in unity and power. For the first time, he thought he might win this race. With a surge of the ambition that had brought him to Rome, Marcus drove hard on the inside, so that now it was as if his chariot was standing still and the stadium were rotating in a brilliant circle around him. He gained on the lead Blue more quickly than he calculated, hearing the thud of hooves as if it were the pump of his own blood, lusting now for the victory. Too late he saw the game. The lead Blue was sliding backwards and outwards, with Saturninus, his Blue partner, hemming Marcus from the rear. Now the lead Blue squeezed inwards in a sacrifice move designed to wipe out Marcus so Saturninus could swoop around them to victory.

The crowd – heavy bettors all – went berserk. Leaning horizontally over his horses, Marcus could see the finish line one hundred yards ahead. He heard the grinding of chariot wheels and, in a fury of impotence, saw that first day at the track when the other drivers had ganged up to humiliate him. With a single stroke, Marcus cut the traces, leapt forward onto the backs of his horses, one foot on each, as he had often done as a youth, jettisoning his chariot. It was a foolhardy trick, with horses untrained for it, but Priam and Helen accepted him with grace. The crowd cheered as the first Blue entry went down in the snap and pitch of chariot wheels, and Marcus, upright, dashed for the finish line. Unable to close the gap, Saturninus came in a poor second.

Pandemonium! Pontifex Piso disqualified Marcus, and awarded the victory to Saturninus, remembering the emperor had done that last time there was this sort of irregularity. The crowd would have none of it – the patricians because they hated the air of carnival Saturninus had brought to what was supposed to be the one contest of skill; the plebs because Saturninus had demolished too many of their own that day, on whom they had bet large purses. Hurling cushions, jugs and benches onto the stadium floor, thousands left their seats as they had ten years before in the Great Riot that killed thirty thousand.

The emperor's heralds trumpeted for silence.

The emperor himself appeared in the judge's stand. Holding the laurel wreath in his left hand and the bag of gold in his right, he awarded the laurels to Marcus and the gold to Saturninus. Amused to feed the rivalry between the two men, he declared the October Horse a tie.

The crowd was unappeased. They bellowed, hissed, booed and spat. With a dramatic snap of his blue cape, Saturninus strode across the judge's stand and magnanimously awarded the bag of gold to Maximus Marcus. Now there were cheers. The emperor declared Maximus Marcus winner of the October Horse.

With a whoop, Castor, Pollux and the other Purple grooms bore Marcus to the victor's chariot. They pulled him around the stadium to the shrieks of 250,000 fans. Marcus experienced the raw thrill of conquest, undercut by self-doubts he sometimes felt on the battlefield when the price of victory had been too high. It galled him to win through the generosity of Saturninus, whom he knew was the better charioteer. Why hadn't he thrown the gold back into his rival's face?

By the time Marcus had been cheered once around the stadium, his sense of fraudulence had been blotted up by the idolatry of the crowd. After all, he had outwitted Saturninus and been first across the finish line. Why shouldn't he let himself revel in his triumph?

Marcus watched as the sixteen priests of the sacred colleges of Jupiter, Mars and the Flavian cult converged upon his winning team. He saw Pontifex Piso garland Helen and Priam with myrtle, then lead Helen toward the altar of Mars. He saw Priam kick up his powerful heels, and the gentle Helen try frantically to slip her tether. He saw the sixteen priests of the sacred colleges assemble ropes, hooks and a large axe.

With a sick and slimy chill, Marcus realized what was about the happen – what he had allowed himself, in the conceit of his victory, to forget: The near horse of the winning team – his Helen – was about to be slaughtered to the god of war.

Marcus watched as the skittish Helen – who, with her rare and wonderful instinct, seemed to have sensed her danger – slashed at her priestly escort. It took all sixteen of them to bring her down with ropes, and to stretch her neck across the altar. Another twenty were needed to subdue the enraged Priam, who had broken his tether and was slicing the crowd with his forelegs.

In slow and gruesome ritual, Pontifex Piso severed Helen's tail. Then he hacked off her head, to such a renting of nays and whinnies from the two horses, that even the hardened were shocked into silence. The mangled white head was impaled on the standard of Mars and paraded around the Circus in front of Marcus' victor's chariot by a blood-soaked pontifex, while another priest, with tail attached, pranced behind.

Marcus watched in helpless grief. He had often had horses cut from under him in battle, and had routinely sacrificed animals to the gods. He had often had comrades slain by his side and given the order for the execution of an enemy. But he had never before watched something he loved slowly and wilfully dismembered – something which, moments before, he had felt as an extension of his own flesh. Of course, Saturninus had been magnanimous.

Marcus felt a hand on his shoulder. He turned. The poet Helvidius Priscus was beside him. Pointing in sympathy toward the twitching carcass, he said: "That's the hardest lesson you'll have to learn in Rome, my friend. He who wins, often loses. That was my father's last lesson. By opposing the Flavians, he won the admiration of every honest man in Rome. For that, he also lost his head."

Putting an arm around Marcus, he guided him through the crowd still cheering him as hero, still pelting him with flowers. They left the Circus, then went to Priscus' favourite tavern in the Subura.

That was the beginning of a long and reckless night, which brought them, drunk and disorderly, to the Forum just before sunrise. Having attempted, without success, to climb Domitian's mounted statue, Marcus lay on his back on the travertine paving stones singing bawdy songs, while Priscus staggered back and forth across the rostra, mimicking in word and gesture all of Rome's leading orators, and especially the mincing walk, hissing voice and verbal chicanery of prosecutor Messalinus.

Climbing to his knees, Marcus applauded, just as Priscus' manner changed. His voice grew deeper and firmer, his stance more authoritative. Now he was striding in full power across the platform, thundering down at the absent populace of Rome, quoting phrases then whole sentences from what Marcus guessed to be an oration of his father's. "Are you Roman citizens, or are you concubines of the emperor? Do you still have tongues to speak? Will you join your voices with mine?" At the point where Helvidius Priscus the Elder had shouted to his assassins: "Death to tyrants!" Priscus collapsed, his tongue stuck out, choking. As Marcus stumbled forward to help him, Priscus raised himself to his elbows and, grinning with the face of Mephistopheles, said: "Tell me, my friend, and let's be honest. Wasn't today's glory worth the neck of one horse? What is man's ambition against such a paltry price? If you had it to do again, wouldn't you?"

70

PART II

JULIA

CHAPTER FIVE

No one in Rome could remember a finer fall or a more bountiful harvest. As Emperor Domitian sat propped in purple cushions on his ivory bed, he unloosed upon his secretary Zeno that stream of edicts, warnings, penalties and patronage by which he ruled the world:

He granted Roman citizenship to a Greek ship owner sponsored by Captain Geta of the Imperial Guard, on whom the emperor's security depended. He denied it to a Greek scholar sponsored by ex-consul Cocceius Nerva, who was becoming too radical in what should be his declining years.

He rewarded his 1,000-member palace guard with another six goldpieces, for no reason more than that he was enjoying his life at the moment and wished it to continue.

He refunded, by one-third, the taxes of Aquitania because of hailstone damage to the fruit crop.

He ordered Maximus Norbanus, governor of Lower Germany, to increase his province's tribute by one-third to pay for border unrest.

He ordered grape production in Italy to be reduced by one-half to encourage corn production.

He accepted the offer of freedman Clodianus to erect a temple in his honour in Carthage.

He appointed prosecutor Messalinus to a prestigious priesthood in the Flavian cult, organized for the worship of his own family.

He accepted Zeno's request to add the epigrammatist Valerius Martial to those receiving priesthoods, but denied such patronage to Helvidius Priscus, even though his new play would open the emperor's Odeum.

He set aside the recommendation of Consul Clemens that Maximus Marcus be elevated to the Senate as a consul's assistant in charge of roads, preferring to dangle the young man a little longer.

He stiffened his legislation on moral reform: castration was to be more severely punished; he forbid prostitutes to use litters or to benefit from inheritance; he struck a knight from the jury roll because he had divorced his wife for adultery then taken her back; he ruled that if any juryman was proved to have taken a bribe, his colleagues must also be penalized; he expelled a magistrate for being too fond of dancing and acting.

Domitian considered publicly rebuking chief vestal Cornelia for travelling about Rome without litter or lictors. The lady's tongue was beginning to annoy him. He remembered how she had opposed him at his banquet, both for the exposure of babies and for his fondness for the cult of Isis. His mind turned lascivious: He could think of a better use for the lady's tongue.

Domitian yawned. It had been a productive morning, but now his concentration was broken. He dismissed his secretary in anticipation of an early bath and a long afternoon's bed-wrestle.... With whom? His wife? His mistress? One of his concubines? For the past six months Domitian had been feeling less lustful – more reliant on Hermes' freaks with special talents. That bothered him. It reminded him of the tragic decline in potency of his hero, Emperor Tiberius, so that he needed ever more disgusting stimulation. That fear was the reason Domitian had recalled his wife Domitia – that and his yearning for an heir. Now he was beginning to feel he'd made a mistake. Her demands, added to those of his mistress, were having the opposite effect.

74

Domitian thought once more of the vestal Cornelia. He imagined her standing before him in her white robes, her face proud yet fearful as he stripped off her garments piece by piece. He imagined forcing her to her knees, then pressing her face, her rebellious tongue, between his legs. He snorted, well pleased with that image. A vestal virgin. There weren't many fantasies left for an emperor.

With less enthusiasm, Domitian picked up a waxed slate embossed with the imperial crest. After dividing it vertically, he put the name DOMITIA over one column and JULIA over the other. He divided the slate again horizontally, then began listing the virtues and faults of each woman, above and below the line.

He put down his slate. First, his bath.

Julia Sabina was painting a bedroom mural of Cupid racing a chariot drawn by two dolphins. She was creating it with tiny squares of colour laid side by side, like inlay. Though such a technique was archaic, she preferred it to the illusionist style with its showy architectural perspectives. It suited her patient nature – or what her nature had been forced to become.

Julia had chosen Cupid because she thought it was what a young boy might like to see when he awoke each morning. That such a child lived in her womb seemed no longer in doubt, for Julia had shown no woman's blood since the emperor's banquet. That the child was a boy seemed just as certain, for Julia had taken an egg from a broody hen and warmed it with her own body, successfully hatching a cock-chick.

Such knowledge boosted her to the heights then dashed her to despair. The emperor had called for her only rarely since his banquet almost three months ago. Each day she waited for a summons that didn't come, while painting coloured squares to the drip of a waterclock and imagining where he might be: Now he would be awakening. Now he would be dictating to Zeno. Now he would be on his way to his bath. Now...now... Julia looked at the waterclock. Had the emperor reconciled with

Domitia? Was he with her now? That fear – too easily fanta-sized – filled her with blind jealousy. It was only when she was safe with Domitian that she could afford compassion. Then she felt as sorry for Domitia as for herself. Once they had been friends. What had caused their estrangement? Which of them had first attacked the other? Or had the emperor tired of the arrangement and played one against the other?

Julia put down her brush. The odour of the tempera with its gummy set of wax and egg yolks was making her nauseous. She wiped her hands on her tunic, feeling the slight swell of her belly, imagining the tiny hands and feet curled like a leaf in there...steadying herself.

Julia wandered through her small house plastered with murals of nymphs, birds, seashells, compulsively painted, one square at a time, since her exile here. She found Phyllis, her former nurse, on a three-legged stool in the courtyard, with the hindquarters of a goat imprisoned between her bulky thighs. Julia squatted beside her as she used to when she was a child, gaining comfort from the firm but gentle rhythm of the rough hands as they coaxed milk from the balky goat, the squish of the liquid as it slid down the earthenware jar, the salty smell of the flesh hang-ing in folds from Phyllis' armpits.

She said: "I am with child."

Phyllis pulled the teats ten more times before replying: "I know."

"What should I do?"

Phyllis did not look up. "Get rid of it."

"No!"

"Don't tell *him*."

Julia bound her arms tighter around her knees. "Why not?"

"She won't allow it."

"*She* doesn't rule Rome."

"She rules him. She gives him excuses to do what he wants to do. I love him as much as I love you, for I nursed him before I nursed you. I know his character. It was burnt too young. Say you are ill. Go to the country. I'll go with you. I'll raise the child as my own." She released the goat with a swat on the rump. "Don't go to him again. There are no secrets in a bed. She has the eyes of a potato and the ears of a bushel of corn. Go, while there is time."

Rocking on her haunches, Julia buried her face in her arms, trying to imagine herself galloping off to Como or Tuscany or Calabria...leaving Rome, the emperor, the palace. She thought of Helvidius Priscus. He too wanted to quit Rome – wanted her to go with him. Was that possible? For as long as she could remember, her feelings for the emperor had been a golden circle, strangling her. Was it possible to break free now that she had something else to live for...for the sake of her baby? Sometimes when she lay with her cheek against Priscus' chest, feeling cared for, safe, at peace, she thought yes, yes, she could do it. There *was* another world outside the selfish prison of her obsession, a world of mutual consideration, of affection.

Hearing a heavy footfall, Julia turned, seeing her gatekeeper behind her. Even before he spoke, she knew what he was going to say: "The dwarf is here. He's come to fetch you to the palace."

Stifling the rise of joyful panic, Julia again hid her face in her lap, binding her arms tighter around her knees, conjuring up the good feelings she had with Priscus, keeping herself earthbound. At last she raised her head. Avoiding Phyllis' eyes, she said: "Tell Hermes...I'm coming."

Stumbling to her feet, Julia followed her gatekeeper through her villa, holding her breath, her body erect yet with her hands fluttering like netted birds at her sides. Hermes was leaning against her statue of Juno – cocky, self-important, exuding his goatish smell. She stopped, feet rooted. Gesturing with his cap, he impelled her toward the litter. The silky curtains slid like cobwebs around her. Grinning, Hermes arranged her cushions, his manner full of innuendo. As the bearers lifted the litter, she felt a ground swell of panic and stood up, tried to claw her way through the curtains but was flung back by the motion.

By the time the emperor's bearers had hiked down the Aventine, Julia was losing her qualms in anticipation. By the time they mounted the Palatine, she had convinced herself she was right, even wise, to come. If she were planning to escape Rome, wouldn't it cause suspicion to refuse the emperor's invitation? Wouldn't it encourage retaliation? How could she gauge the royal mood if she were not there to experience it?

The emperor greeted Julia with charm and affection. He apologized for not having called for her sooner, and swore by the signet of Augustus that not a day had gone by in which he had not thought of her. As he prowled his bedchamber in swishing silk robe, exuding power and perfume, he spoke animatedly about the larger concerns of empire that had kept them apart, catching her up, catching him up, catching fire.

As a special mark of respect, he ordered Parthenius to see to Julia's needs, instead of the dwarf, who thereafter sulked in a corner. The African chamberlain changed Julia's sandals for slippers, he poured her a glass of Sicilian wine, and served them both sweets as they reclined on the emperor's day couch. Uncurling Julia's fists, the emperor kissed the palms, gently chiding her for the bitten nails and the mark of her weaving yarn. He shared his honeycake with her, licking the crumbs from her lips with his tongue, then sticking the tip deep into the dimple on her left cheek. He fluttered his tongue in her ear and called her his little hummingbird. He undressed her, instead of assigning her to his concubines, as he sometimes did, to be stripped, oiled and aroused to save his time. Holding her unbound chestnut hair to the light, he fanned it over her breasts, admiring its glossiness.

Once again Julia felt herself drawn into his ring of fire – his special world of vividness and light, where scents tugged sharply at the nostrils or broke like flowers in the mouth, where even thoughts had their special textures, and colours glowed so that everything outside seemed dull by comparison...muddy colours dabbed on cracked walls.

The emperor lifted Julia onto the imperial bed. Putting his hands on her breasts, he claimed each imperiously, as if for the

Roman Empire, seduced by his own spell, driven by his own needs; and yet – in the sureness of his touch and the headiness of her response – mapping out herself for herself, giving her the gift of her own flesh vibrating in awareness of him therefore of her. Hopeful, disarmed, eager to take her chances – incapable of doing otherwise – she opened her arms, her legs, her heart, offering herself to kindness or to cruelty, submissive to his whim, as he required her to be...a territory to be explored, a piece of clay to be fired and shaped, a vessel to be filled or destroyed...a foil, she knew, for the headstrong passions of his wife, for the three of them had often made love together.

These "triplings" had been playful as well as erotic, with Domitian and Domitia and Julia layered flesh upon flesh, interlocked in a shifting triangle of love, each inventing ways to amuse the others – a diligent hand here, a lickerish tongue there, coaxing small rosettes of feeling from some otherwise neglected erogenous zone.

Often the emperor – delaying his own participation – had ordered Domitia and Julia to make love together. Sitting on a curule chair, his chin propped on his hand, he would watch his women act out some small drama of seduction before pressing together lips and naked breasts, or losing their heads in one another's thighs, often ordering them to freeze in one position or another so he might admire the reediness of one against the ripeness of the other, the bulb of a breast cupped in a red-tipped palm, the graceful curve of a buttock ending in a tiny pink tongue – dispassionate at first, except for the fierceness of his eyes, feasting on erotic images tricked out in groans, giggles, the stroking of a finger until, unable to stand it a second longer, he would tear them apart and force or beg each to take him inside.

After Domitia's banishment, the sex between Domitian and Julia had become better, then worse – what had begun as long languid hours of privacy and tenderness being overtaken by experimentation best left to his bawds. Domitian would order Julia to masturbate for him in lewd poses on beds of muck or broken glass, demanding that she describe to him how aroused or debased she felt, and becoming sullen or abusive if he felt she left anything out. Instead of making love to her, he would masturbate upon her – between her breasts, in her hair – his mood contemptuous and sadistic, leaving bruises, like rotten spots across her flesh. Sometimes when drunk he would sodomize her with brutality and – by far the worst – once brought her to a fever pitch, then turned her over to the dwarf.

Today Domitian was once again the solicitous though forceful lover, progressing in hungry titillation from lips and tongue and ears and hair, to breasts and nipples and thighs, melting all of her into a funnel of hotly swirling flesh, sucking him inside. He fondled then opened her sex. Now she could feel him penetrate down into the ache and emptiness of her, right into her craziness, that unknown unloved part of herself that only he could reach, expanding now inside her, moulding her to him like fleshy lock to fleshy key, defining her insides as he had her outsides, commanding her blood to pound, her flesh to quiver, her juices to gush, to spurt, to overflow. He was losing control now, chest heaving, throat gasping like that of a beached fish, while the wiser, more primitive part of himself rammed up the silty birth canal he had once swum down.

She felt the bruising assault of him upon her vulnerability, felt her resistance stretch thin, give way. A scream grew out of the darkest, softest part of her, tearing itself free, its edges jagged with both relief and despair. She felt it explode up through her chest, lodge in her throat. She clamped her jaw, would not let it out, held it back, held herself back, hugged him tighter as his sweat-drenched body mounted to that convulsive moment when it would arch with head snapped back, *in pleasure! in pain!* while he lost himself, his mastery, his empire, for a few seconds in his need of her.

Taking her climax now, from the rush of him inside her, the bounty of him filling and feeding her, from the helplessness of him growing smaller, a boneless animal burrowed for comfort inside her, holding him, petting him, feeling such fusion, such joy, such relief. Feeling such hope, such stillness, such magic.

Feeling safe in the tranquil heart of time. Feeling tears of love, of gratitude, push up from quiet pools behind her eyes.

Later, when he had separated from her, turned from her, fallen asleep, she lay awake beside him, hearing his breath rumble through some grotto deep in his chest, his leg heavy on hers, pinioning her, feeling once again her aloneness, matching as best she could her breathing to his, not wishing to stir in case she awakened him, thus cutting short the brief time around which her life revolved, her hands between her legs, reliving the scene they had just played out, compensating already for what she was about to lose, recreating it detail by detail, like the murals she dabbed on her wall, storing up memories against the sterile times to come, marked out by the drip of the waterclock, fearing – yet happy too – that she could never break free. He would always weave just enough silk to bind her.

Julia lay her hand over her belly, where that other emperor rocked in liquid dreams.... His name would be Caesar Domitianus, and he would rule Rome as his father, as his uncle, as his grandfather had. He would be the link between them – a bond of flesh yet something of her own to love. Something real she had created cell by cell, as surely as she had created the winged Cupid on her wall with daubs of paint. She would be the mother of emperors. How could she feel lonely or insignificant again?

Julia looked over at Domitian, his head curled down on his chest like the head of a fern, his hair tousled, his thumb perilously close to his mouth, daring to see him as a larger version of the foetus she carried inside, feeling full of the confidence that marked these times of intimacy. Today would be a new beginning. How could it be otherwise? Wasn't she presenting him with the thing he wanted most: an heir to take the place of Flavius Caesar, who had died in his third year – whose image he still wore in gold around his neck? Hadn't that been the strength of his father Vespasian during the year of civil war ending Nero's reign? He had had not one but two sons to secure the empire and its succession – a dynasty. With a son, Domitian could put an end to rival claims. His position would be more secure. Surely he could see that? She thought of Domitia. Could they share the baby? Once it would have been possible. She closed her eyes, seeing the two of them, arms wound in a circle, with the child inside. Was it too late for that? Was there too much bitterness?

Julia felt Domitian stir beside her. She felt him fondle her breast, his finger plucking at a nipple, then cupping the flesh – fuller now – before sliding down to her belly...that fuller too. She closed her eyes, sucking in her breath. His palm found her navel, rubbing it around as if it were a talisman. Julia felt something sharp, unmistakable, alive. Her eyes flew open, still not sure if what she thought she had felt had actually happened. Domitian's stunned face, glaring down at her, told her the answer: a kick inside her womb still vibrating. She felt a thrill of pride, cut short by the sooty look in the emperor's eyes. He said, his voice sarcastic: "We are not alone in this bed."

She felt her mouth go dry. "The gods have been kind."

Domitian scowled. "That's a matter of opinion." He rolled over, his back toward her. Grabbing a pillow, she wrapped herself around it, rocking gently in the bed, hugging the miracle to her, ignoring as best she could the father thrashing in fury beside her. Throwing off the imperial coverlet, Domitian flounced out of the bed, down the dais, to the open window. He stared unblinking into his sun-drenched garden, re-aligning himself with the outside world. His fingers gripped the gold coin around his neck bearing the imprint of Flavius Caesar, dead at age three, sitting on top of the world...*Another son*. He felt tiny hands clutch in trust at his heart, and groaned: *a bastard*.

His face shattered into a dozen tics, his eyes stung with unshed tears. Pressing his hand to his chest, he felt such pain he thought he was having a heart attack. In helpless supplication, he turned to his patron, Minerva. Here was something outside his power as emperor to command. He felt mocked, betrayed. By whom? By fate? Or by the person now sharing his bed? He turned to his mistress to vent his spleen, saw her cradling the child as yet unborn, and felt a surge of tenderness far more

82

alarming. He stepped back from it, disowned it, despised it, dashed it by its feet against the wall. *How many emperors had had their lives cut short by a woman's ambition!*

Walking stiff-backed to the table where Zeno kept extra writing supplies, Domitian picked out a scroll of parchment bearing the imperial crest. With great ceremony he selected a reed pen, and in a flourish designed to hide the trembling of his fingers, wrote: "I sincerely regret that I was not able to attend you in your bedchamber this afternoon" – a simple message yet one he felt to be ripe with meaning. Rolling then sealing the parchment, he ordered Parthenius, erect as always by his door: "Take this to my wife, the Empress Domitia."

Parthenius loped down the hall with its polished walls reflecting his long legs as they slid in and out from under his equally long torso as if hinged with elastic. While carrying the emperor's scroll in his right hand, he played with amber dice in his left, bouncing them off an elbow, a knuckle, with his body now as mobile as it had once been still. Parthenius was never curious about the messages he carried – unlike the dwarf, who claimed to be able to re-seal scrolls using his own fake signet. The dice – along with a gourd of sour mead slung under Parthenius' livery – represented his worst vices, along with an occasional trip to a brothel.

A brass gong hung on the empress' door. Seeing his close-cropped head in the burnished surface, Parthenius drew back. It always startled him to be confronted with his own image, for while his body was in the service of the emperor, his spirit-self was usually thousands of miles away, in the savannahs of Africa where he had once hunted lions with a spear. To seem to be in one place while in another was a trick Parthenius had mastered, crouched for hours in the long grasses. In Africa the hunters of the tribe, the princes, had practised the discipline of silence, while the servants and women and children had been free to cackle like jackals. In Rome, he noticed, it was the servants who kept pride of silence, while the emperor brayed and ranted.

Parthenius struck the gong, shattering his image like a reflection in water. A pretty Syrian maid with a sulky look ushered him inside.

Reclining on a tortoiseshell bed was the empress, surrounded by objects exotic to the Romans but familiar to Parthenius: an erotic Nubian carving; an elephant foot containing ground-up rhinoceros horn prized as an aphrodisiac; a wall-sized mural of one of the wildbeast hunts in which he himself had been captured and sold into slavery. The empress was wearing a leopard-skin shawl slit to reveal breasts tipped in blood. Bowing low, perhaps emboldened by the familiar setting, Parthenius took this opportunity to ogle the empress' bosom.

He lifted his eyes. To his shock, the empress was smiling into his face, hungry enough for attention to relish even this show of desire from a tongueless servant. Still smiling, she reached for the scroll. He pushed it toward her, dropped his hands and his eyes, resentful that his privacy had been invaded.

The empress opened the scroll, her small flirtation over, her attention concentrated upon it. She read then reread the cryptic message: "I sincerely regret that I was not able to attend you in your bedchamber today." Scowling, she fixed upon one word: *not*. That Domitian had "sincerely" penned the note, using the familiar "I" and "you" instead of "the emperor" and "the empress" was too subtle for her mood of frustration. Heaving up from her bed, she crumpled the parchment and pitched it toward the granite bust of Saturn, her patron. Inclining her head toward the door, she dismissed the chamberlain. "No answer."

Domitia waited till the door had closed. Then clapping her hands she spun around to her maids. "Get out." She began to pace from her bed to Saturn, feeling panic build in her chest. She converted it into indignation – an emotion more suited to a general's daughter. *How could any woman with blood in her veins be expected to fill her day without a lover...even if it had to be her husband?* She put her hands between her legs and moaned. That was all she could think about. Soldiers with cocks as long as their lances! Gladiators with thighs that would tire a goat!

84

Athletes who could do pushups with their tongues! This new confinement, with maids paid to spy on her, was almost as bad as her exile on Pandataria. There she had nothing to compare her life with. Here she imagined everyone to be making love at all times – in the baths, under the beds, in bas reliefs on vases, birds in cages, snails on dinner plates – everyone but Domitia Longina, daughter of the great general Corbulo, Empress of Rome!

Seizing the bust of Saturn, Domitia forced herself to stop pacing, to control herself. No. She mustn't do that again. She mustn't give in to hysteria. It was too much of a confession of impotence. During her banishment on Pandataria, she had paced the island two miles from north to south before lunch, and half a mile from east to west afterwards, memorizing every rock, counting leaves on shrubs, staring out to sea till her eyes ached, willing each speck into a boat, whipping herself up into a frenzy. He had always known she slept with other men – had sometimes encouraged it. Paris had been different. Domitian had been jealous of Paris. *Domitian had wanted Paris, the toast of the Roman theatre, for himself.*

Domitia inspected herself in the brass mirror. Had she aged so very much in the past two years? Did she remind Domitian too poignantly of his own vanishing youth? She looked at her hips – spread but not fat. She looked at her buttocks – what the generous would call generous. If she could sneak away to the Temple of Isis or Cybele for an hour, she'd show the youngsters what she could do. Domitia thought of Antonius Saturninus – High Priest of Cybele – with whom she'd once prowled bars disguised as his page. Not yet. She was too closely guarded to risk sneaking out of the palace. Exile was too vivid a memory.

Domitia fondled her breasts, thinking of the last man who had admired them: the tongueless Parthenius. She conjured up his proud and alien beauty: the high unmarked forehead, the fluted bronze lips, the yellow eyes. Did she dare? Once she had come close...She thought of Parthenius standing stiff as a spear at the emperor's banquet, and then herself lying flat on the floor, with all of Rome jeering. The memory of that still rankled. Again she thought of Parthenius, now with gnawing appetite. What she needed as much as a lover were well-placed allies. The chamberlain scored on both counts, but how to lure him here? She thought of her doormaid Cynthia. Why was the girl always so sullen? Was there some grudge she could exploit?

Reaching for her bellpull, Domitia noticed her hand was trembling, and lashed herself with scorn. Had a few grey hairs and thickening waist cancelled her courage? She yanked the cord so viciously she cut her hand: two short tugs.

Cynthia appeared with such dispatch Domitia suspected she had been listening at the door. Good, that meant the girl had ambition. In an imperious voice from which all self-doubt had been scourged, she ordered: "Fetch me Parthenius. Then return to your quarters. Tonight when you prepare my bath you will find a surprise in my perfume pot."

The girl's eyes narrowed only slightly as she backed to the door.

Domitia did not hear Parthenius come in. She merely felt a hush in the air, and turned, knowing she would see him. He was standing in the shadows, his eyes burning like yellow lamps, correct but wary – once again the hunter, senses tuned for the telltale twitch in the grass.

Smiling into his eyes, Domitia said: "I was mistaken. There *is* an answer for my husband." She shifted her shoulders, letting her leopard robe slide from her breasts. "I didn't sleep very well last night." She dropped her robe to her waist. "I have a kink in my neck that the small hands of my maids can't ease." She rolled her robes down her hips, revealing dark hair softened by singeings with red-hot walnuts. "Would you give me one of the massages that my husband has recommended to me?"

Domitia stepped out of her robe, seeing a moustache of sweat bloom across Parthenius' full lips. Confident now, she yawned, then stretched, sinuously curling upward from some heated centre, like an animal reaching for the sun. Tossing her glossy hair, she turned her back upon him and walked with swivelling hips to the bed, where she flung herself face-down with her arms and legs spread wide. Again she sensed rather than heard Parthenius come up beside her, his whole body having taken on the stealth and silence of his missing tongue. His legs, as slender as bamboo shoots, were planted by her bed – gleaming, hairless, the sinews taut, bound to the calves in leather.

She waited, the craving delicious now, feeling a stir of wind as his hands swooped low over her back, prickling her to gooseflesh, till – *there*, his touch like forked lightning. *There*, too – the other hand, with square palms and tapering fingers, the thumbs touching, spanning her waist. Groaning, Domitia rubbed her breasts against the fur coverlet and plunged her fingers in the itch between her legs.

Reaching with one hand for his gourd of sour mead, Parthenius leaned forward on the other, pressing stale air from her lungs. Shimmying his knuckles down her spine, he buried them deep in her buttocks. Now she felt the steely fingers dig into the broad muscles, as if stripping them of their flabby casings, progressing downward to the thighs, twisting the flesh smartly, causing her whole body to shiver, and then – oh god, yes! – to shake.

Domitia clutched the fur bedspread with her fists, imagining his long brown body as one stiff phallus to stuff inside. Parthenius too was breathing hard, with the sweat oozing from his pores in scalding beads that spattered across Domitia's back and thighs. *Enough, enough.* She raised her buttocks, felt the weight of him on her backside and, with an astonishing nipping, gripping motion, seized his sex with hers, drawing him inch by inch inside. Domitia threw back her head to cry out as Parthenius clamped his hand over her mouth. Still more hunter than servant, he was used to killing silently, with a single thrust in the yellow grass.

Domitia stretched herself across her bed-couch, feeling much better. Wonderful, in fact, glorious. She looked in gratitude at her lover, his long brown legs sticking out from his trunk like the limbs of a fallen tree, and smiled rapturously – the act that always energized her put her lovers to sleep.

Heaving up from her bed-couch, she yanked open a leather trunk once belonging to her father. She put on butter-soft leggings, moulding them to her still-moist calves and thighs, then a breastband, a muslin tunic and suede lace-up boots. Next came shinguards and the helmet her father, the Great Corbulo, wore to defeat the Armenians.

Making a few practice thrusts with Spanish short sword and leather shield, she admired her wrist action in her brass mirror. Domitia had taken up the shocking sport of duelling when it was fashionable among patrician ladies with peculiar tastes. She continued it because she was very good at it and because it drained the energy which, when unused, turned into an acid that burned and festered. She had, after all, been raised on the smell of battle sweat, sweeter to her than perfume, then reluctantly weaned from leather to chiffon, from horses to litters. Her duelling partners were ex-legionnaires picked for their ugliness by Hermes acting on Domitian's orders. The one she had now was without teeth, had only one ear, and a face so scarred it was hard to find his nose. Domitia anticipated finishing him off.

Itching to get on with it, Domitia turned to her lover still sprawled over her bed as if he had taken root. She loved the male body – its leanness and efficiency, without annoying curves and flabby bulges. Putting her palms on his hairless torso, boned like the ribs of a boat, she leaned over and licked Parthenius' lips. He stirred. He opened his eyes.

Domitia cleaned him with a perfumed towel, then dressed him in his livery as attentively as if she were the chamberlain.

Correctly attired as a servant of the palace, he asked for, and received, permission to leave. Striding to the door, he turned, indicating with hand movements that he wished to speak.

Domitia nodded.

Being a man of no words, Parthenius came quickly to the point. He pressed a dimple into his left cheek. Frowning, Domitia interpreted: "Julia."

He smote his chest with his fist. She interpreted: "The emperor."

He clasped his hands. "They are together?"

He made a mound over his belly. Domitia's thick brows swooped downward. "Pregnant?"

Parthenius nodded.

Controlling her voice, she asked: "Does the emperor know?"

Parthenius nodded.

"What did he say?"

Parthenius thrust out his head, eyes bulged and piercing, so exactly like the emperor's bald-eagle look that Domitia laughed in spite of her anxiety. She sobered quickly. "How many months?"

Parthenius shrugged, then estimated with his fingers: *three*.

Domitia inclined her head. *You may go.*

Parthenius backed correctly to the door.

Feeling panic again build in her chest, Domitia took the muffle from her short sword. *So it was to be foils off? Good. She was tired of games.* She skewered a mounded cushion on her bedcouch. *A little bastard.* Snarling, she disembowelled it with a single thrust.

CHAPTER SIX

The baths were the preoccupation of idle Rome. For one quadrans – the price of oil and an attendant to guard one's clothes – any Roman could enjoy the same luxury as an emperor, in one of the city's dozen public baths. The greatest sculptures were there, the finest frescoes, the most valuable mosaics, along with libraries, barbershops, promenades, exercise rooms, poetry rooms, museums and restaurants. "For our baths!" was the universal cry of the beggar. The congenial greeting of one man to another was: "Have a good bath!"

Once a month Emperor Domitian attended the public baths built by his brother Titus – an act of diplomacy with which he kept in touch with the mood of the populace. An hour before, heralds would mark his route paying claquers to cheer. As soon as the imperial procession could be seen threading down the Palatine, a cry would go up: "He's coming!"

The friends of the emperor led the parade; then came the emperor, his lictors, his praetorians, his slaves and his servants, two of whom especially delighted the crowd: Hermes the dwarf, who pranced like Pan the goat god, making crude remarks in the emperor's voice; and a striking new page named Castor, who strutted in his livery as if he thought the parade was for him alone – the same self-possession that had attracted the emperor's eye as Castor had modelled his patchwork cloak at the Circus.

Domitian waved beneficently to the crowd from his litter, throwing coins and watching the scramble in amusement.

"Hail Caesar! Hail Caesar! *Bene lava!*"

The imperial party marched up Sacred Way, through the Arch of Titus, past a monstrous statue of Nero converted by a crown of sunrays into a statue of Apollo, then onward to the Baths of Titus, able to accommodate fifteen hundred bathers.

Now they streamed through a red marble arch into a colonnaded garden where prostitutes lounged among the fountains, wearing outrageously short tunics. The girls – mostly of Syrian and Egyptian ancestry – converged with whoops and squeals, making themselves conspicuous and alluring. Some bared their breasts, others stuck out their tongues or lifted their tunics to reveal bronze bodies plucked free of hair in the Egyptian fashion. One saucy wench, skirt held high, advertised herself with a tangle of orange body hair. Since Domitian took the same pleasure in depilating women as he did in skewering flies, he signalled Parthenius to include her in his selection.

The imperial party passed through a sienna portico to a lawn set with five round pools – of yellow, red, blue, green and purple marble. This was the Frigidarium, for cold baths. The emperor was borne to the imperial changing room, with its mosaic floors heated by air forced from charcoal furnaces, and its walls covered with prurient frescoes of the gods at play. Using secret ingredients prescribed by Hermogenes of Smyrna, Parthenius massaged the emperor till he stood in full erection. While his friends made ribald jests about the number of harlots he would crack like oysters that day, he plunged into the frigid waters.

"*Bravo! Bene lava! Bravo!*"

The others, wearing leather trunks – a custom begun with Nero due to his dangerous sensitivity about the shyness of his sexual organ lost in belly flesh – waded into the pool, making a fuss about its coldness to set the emperor's plunge in bold relief.

Hermes pranced naked about the edge, mimicking them in voice and style – an amusement for all except those mocked. After reclaiming their robes, the group trekked into the central and dominating hall: the Tepidarium, its grandiose dome set with multi-coloured glass supported by enormous yellow pillars. Sunlight streamed through the rainbow ceiling to spatter in breathtaking fragmentation over dancing fountains, mosaics and masterworks of sculpture, including the Laocöon.

Hundreds of bathers – laughing, singing, shouting, whistling – splashed naked in the four yellow-rimmed pools with emerald bowls, or sprawled on couches in the gentle heat.

Maximus Marcus floated in the tepid water, staring up into the vaulted, rainbow dome, watching acrobats, painted gold, dancing on a tightrope, seeing one spread his cape like the wings of the Roman eagle, then dive into the frothy water. All doubts he'd ever had about Rome sweated like impediments from his pores. He felt drunk on being Roman!

A large hand covered Marcus' face, shoving him under. Sputtering, he emerged to see Helvidius Priscus laughing down at him. Priscus jerked his thumb toward the entranceway. "Our Chief Peacock has arrived with his trail of peahens in leather trunks."

Looking where he pointed, Marcus saw the emperor with Consul Clemens, prosecutor Messalinus, freedman Clodianus and the dwarf. As the rebellious son of a senator, Priscus scoffed at all the honours for which Marcus, the son of a knight, had been taught to strive. Marcus was particularly nettled by Priscus' jibes against his sponsor Consul Clemens.

"Your cynicism makes everybody the same," he chided. "An eye that can't see the difference between prosecutor Messalinus and Consul Clemens is attached to a tongue that's not worth listening to."

Priscus laughed. "All men in leather trunks carrying a pea-cock's tail look like peahens to me."

"If your eyes are so bad, use your ears."

"I do, Marcus, I do. And the closer I get to the emperor's ear, the more the words sound the same. 'Shall we banish the philosophers?' *Yes, yes, yes.* 'Let's slit their throats instead.' *Oh, yessssssss.*"

"You wear your father's martyrdom as a badge. What good does that do? You never go to the Senate to protest, as Clemens does. You never oppose the emperor, except in private."

"What's politics to me? Why should I let myself be used in my father's causes? As for attending the Senate – I'd prefer a bawdy house, where at least everyone is honest about the business they're in. If you play the game, you *are* the game. I, my friend, am a poet."

"Yes, a *love* poet. With illustrations by the emperor's niece," jeered Marcus. "That's your choice, and I leave you to it. But when you talk politics you sound like a schoolboy drunk on Greek heroes. There are no heroes in real life, Priscus. It's the small differences in men that tip the balance between good and evil – the differences your scathing eye refuses to see."

"You're the one who's blind!" snapped Priscus, temper rising. "My father's death was no accident. Rome couldn't tolerate his stature. He was fated."

"Only because he chose to be. And his death doesn't make him a better man or a worse one. He was what he was, with the balance tipped toward good, as Clemens is today, though one is alive and the other dead. And *both* are miles ahead in goodness from that evil-monger Messalinus, though Clemens, in prudence, now seems to stand beside him."

"By prudence, do you mean leather trunks? Tell me, Marcus, is it because some day you see yourself dancing in the emperor's train that you look on these eunuchs with such tolerance?"

"I think you place too high a value on the sort of manhood that has to do with public display. Whether in leather trunks or toga, Clemens speaks his causes into the emperor's ear. He doesn't play with words in verse or tilt with shadows on a stage."

"Who says a stage holds only shadows? Why don't you see my farce at the Odeum tomorrow, then tell me who deals in shadows!"

"A *farce*, Priscus? Your father thundered about tyranny from the rostra!"

"He was a tragedian. I deal in life's absurdity. Have you ever seen the wound laughter makes in a pompous man? Come to the Odeum, my doubting friend, and see for yourself how words can be deeds, and how shadows can make an emperor bleed."

Marcus dove into the emerald pool, stung more than he cared to admit by Priscus' jibes about leather trunks, trying to recapture his sense of well-being. Once again he floated, watching the acrobats spread their wings, only this time thinking more sadly of Icarus.

The emperor's entourage reassembled in the Tepidarium to accompany him to the hot baths. When Domitian indicated he wished to continue alone, they repressed smiles of relief. The emperor's endurance for heat wore out the best of them. Besides, the best time for petitions was *after* those two great instruments of high-level diplomacy: bath and brothel.

The Caldaria were under red domes on either side of the Tepidarium, forming a cruciform, and no less splendid in their chaos of glass, marble and mosaics. In the centre of each was a bronze basin heated from below by a furnace which also circulated vapour between the double walls. Draping himself on a marble slab in a cloud of fumy mist, Domitian gave himself over to the thing he'd sought all morning: the luxury of violent shivering till the heat had soaked into the marrow of his bones and the goosebumps were sweated from his body.

It was in the hot baths that Domitian allowed his most acute expression of moods. Today he felt depressed. The unseasonably warm weather had reminded him more poignantly that winter was coming; and was it his imagination or had the crowds been more lacklustre than usual? He'd spent a lifetime striving to be emperor, and now after fourteen years the dictatorship meant nothing to him – except in the fear of its loss. If only he could stay here in the baths forever, with no court cases, no embassies, no favours to bestow. He laughed. If an assassin were forced to read the imperial correspondence for one day, he'd stab *himself* with Zeno's stylus.

Domitian called Parthenius to scrape the impurities from his skin with a bronze strigil and to pummel his slack thigh and stomach muscles which – being a physically lazy man – only got a workout when he bed-wrestled.

His mood rose with the steam. No wonder the Catos of history railed against the baths as yet another "Hellenistic contamination." Cleanliness as the handmaiden of decadence. Maybe as his last act as emperor he should ban the baths? He chuckled. It was usually while he was enjoying something that he framed the laws forbidding it to others. It was while he was tasting the fair and fleshy wife of Clodianus that he had thought of toughening his legislation against adultery. It was while he was sodomizing the eunuch Earinus, beloved of Titus, that he had decided to forbid castration. There was nothing like experience of evil to sharpen one's sense of duty toward wiping it out for others. There was nothing like the perverse use of power to prove one still had it.

Domitian took an exultant plunge into the hot pool, then stretched himself once more on the bench, face up, his hand gently laid over his crotch like a child protecting himself. What was the source of the black moods that had plagued him ever since childhood, sucking him down for days, even months, into a bog of pitchblend? Was it because he had had too much sorrow as a child? His mother had died after his birth, then his beloved sister had drowned when he was thirteen. He had worshipped both his brother and father, but they had kept him at bay, denying him the privileges and responsibilities that were his birth right. While his brother was tutored in the opulent court of Nero, he was shunted off to the family estate at Reate, in the Sabine hills. When he had tried to join his father and brother against the Jews, they had bid him write poetry. When he had attempted to lead an expedition against the Gauls and Germans, his father had publicly rebuked him. Of the six consulships awarded to him before becoming emperor, all but one was honorary. During the joint triumph of his father and brother over Judaea, he had been forced to follow their litter on horseback, collecting the crumbs of adulation. Worst of all, the half share in empire his father had promised him was rescinded in a later will – or was that will forged by his brother, who boasted he could imitate any hand? Domitian could never be sure, though he had considered assassinating Titus on the strength of his suspicions. Then, during Titus' two-year reign, Domitian had to watch his brother squander the treasury, purchasing the adoration which would later be denied him.

Domitian felt his body tighten like a fist. He had restored the treasury! He had rebuilt Rome! He had given the world fourteen years of stable government, and pushed back the boundaries of empire along the Rhine and the Danube. Yet what did his industry reap? Love? Admiration? Respect? Nothing but hate and calumny!

Domitian took another plunge into the bronze pool, then entered the steam room where he lay with his head thrust forward like a snapping turtle's, looking for a fly on which to fix his outrage. He seized upon a personal matter lurking at the edge of his consciousness. So...the gods, through the sweatings and heavings of the daughter of Titus, were about to present him with a Flavian bastard. What was he to make of such a "gift"? The longed-for son delivered by the back door of passion. Would the boy be a weapon against the intrigues he could feel coiling like snakes around him, or would he be a splinter of his brother's hate used to slit his throat? Imperial history was short on filial love, but rank with the blood of filial hate. What comfort had he ever received from his own flesh? What comfort could he expect from the flesh of Titus? And yet...*oh great goddess Minerva...* when he dared to remember the little boy who had warmed his lap, who had illuminated each day with the growth of his young intelligence...the last of the Flavians, now deified and immortalized on the coin around his neck... *What love, dear god, what love, what pain.*

Suffocating in steam, unable to catch his breath, Domitian

signalled for Parthenius to bring his litter. *The strumpets would earn their purses today*.

Marcus and Priscus strolled from the baths onto the colonnaded exercise court. Half of Rome seemed here, determined to take advantage of the weather. Men of all ages and a few women willing to defy convention romped in tights, loincloths or naked. Some lifted weights, some swung barbells. Four young men fought elegantly over a pig bladder puffed with air, which they tried to toss through a silver hoop. Others flung three red feather balls around a triangle, catching with one hand and pitching with the other. Two batted a blue feather ball with their hands. Another group, with feints and shoves, tried to carry a sand ball through opponents.

Still resentful of Priscus for his jibes, Marcus challenged him to a wrestling match. With a cockeyed grin, Priscus accepted. After stripping, the two men smeared themselves with oil and wax to make their skin supple, then rolled in the sand to give purchase. Marcus saw Castor, his former stableboy, eagerly watching these preparations. As he reached out to clap him on the back, he remembered the grime on his hand and, laughing, drew it back. "Castor, we seem to have changed places. Now I'm the urchin. You've progressed in the world."

Castor puffed himself up in his white-and-gold palace livery. "I am the emperor's personal page."

"If you used to be a plumber or a fuller or had any other honest employment, I'd say you've come down in the world," exclaimed Priscus. He winked at Marcus. "You and my friend here must be the only ones in Rome who think the best men rise, like cream, to the top." He ruffled Castor's hair against his vanity, dribbling sand down his tunic. "Be careful you don't shed your street wisdom with your street clothes. More murderers lurk in marble corridors than in the alleys of the Subura."

"My red-haired friend talks too much and sees too little," protested Marcus. "There is good and bad everywhere, depending on who does the looking."

With arms extended and weight evenly balanced on the balls of their feet, Marcus and Priscus circled each other in the sand pit. Though Priscus had powerful limbs and a well-muscled torso, Marcus was a foot taller with a longer reach. Relishing his position as underdog, Priscus taunted: "Hey, leather trunks! Come and get me." Furious at being derided in front of Castor, Marcus lunged at Priscus who darted away.

What began as a wrestling match quickly toughened into a slugging contest. Sensing the animosity between the two men, spectators chose up sides, urged them on, laying bets and offering odds. At first Priscus was the favourite simply because he was the hungriest. Keeping up a barrage of insult, he lost no opportunity to make Marcus look ridiculous, even stooping to an illicit knee in the groin. By controlling his temper and fighting with his head as well as his fists, Marcus soon uncovered his opponent's fatal weakness: apart from fancy footwork, Priscus refused to defend himself. It was attack, attack, attack. Timing his moves and punching steadily, Marcus closed Priscus' eye, loosened a tooth, split his lip.

Now the crowd was on Marcus' side, for Romans did not like to lose. As they cheered, Marcus' anger left him, for he took no satisfaction in humbling someone who so relentlessly played to his own destruction. Priscus could barely stand up, he could hardly see for the blood, yet he made it clear he would never give up. In exasperation, Marcus allowed himself to be pinned. Avoiding the disappointment in Castor's eyes, he returned to the shower room, disturbed by the dangerous flaw he had seen in his friend.

Emperor Domitian – powdered, pomaded and perfumed – lay naked on the bed-couch of his dressing room. Gesturing to Parthenius, he ordered: "The bitches."

Though it was usually Hermes who catered to Domitian's sexual desires, Parthenius was prepared for and had even competed for this particular commission. While Hermes climbed into a niche in the wall to fume and fuss, Parthenius ushered in the bawd with orange body hair, whom Domitian had chosen earlier. She posed voluptuously in the doorway, in matching orange wig and black mask of Hecate, goddess of sorcery. Producing a thinly braided black whip from behind her back, she asked in an accent Domitian could not place: "Would the emperor like a taste of Dionysian leather?"

Domitian admired the wench's audacity. The Dionysian cult had been banned, along with Cybele, for just such practices. He looked at the whip coiled like a snake around her arm and knew by the tightening of his groin that, yes, the emperor did desire it. "I'll test your skill," he said to her, "but remember: draw one drop of blood and I'll have you flogged by my praetorians."

As the bawd unwound tongs from her wrists, the emperor looked toward Parthenius on guard at the door, then at the dwarf hunched in a niche in the wall. Deciding it was safe enough, he spread-eagled himself. The bawd tied his wrists and ankles to the bed, then tested her whip with a whine ending in a brutal crack. Domitian's mouth went dry, and his buttocks gripped. He forced himself to relax.

The next time he heard the whip, it landed on his buttocks in a soft flicker, like a tongue. He anticipated the next stroke, then the next, as the leather teased and tingled. Beginning with his shoulders, the bawd scourged him downward to the soles of his feet. As she moved back up his body, she increased the pressure, adding more and more pepper to a hot stew, laying one length of the whip seamlessly against the next, so that his blood pulsed and his skin smarted in half-inch strips over his body.

The whip sharpened its bite – precise, measured, never missing a beat, like the drums that pound for the galley slaves. The relentlessness of the attack built up resistance inside Domitian and the first pricklings of panic. Perspiration oozed through the pores of his forehead and under his arms. A musky smell exuded from his stiffening sex.

The blows crossed the threshold from pleasure to pain. Domitian's hands constricted around the ivory headboard. His buttocks and stomach seized. Arching his body away from the whip, he pitted his endurance against her, his will to maintain control against her determination to break him.

At first he had wanted only to stimulate his sluggish body as an aid to waning sexuality, but as the blows struck, he began to sense some real and personal opposition in this bawd. There was a clog of something dirty and soft, like soot, in his throat. He protested with growls, screams and curses. He cursed this masked attacker. He cursed the gods. He cursed the woman who had given birth to him, only to leave him; and the sister who loved him, then dared to leave him. He cursed the father who had never loved him, and the brother who had displaced him. He cursed the wife who had deceived him, and every one of her cuckolding lovers. When he had no one else to curse, he cursed himself.

He tugged at the tongs, biting into his flesh. He thrashed about the bed. Still the blows found him, one after another, in perfect rhythm. He felt a shuddering through his limbs, then deep convulsions, exploding the clot in his throat. He broke into sobs, feeling himself at last in communion with the abject fear and self-disgust which he carried inside like a cesspool. He felt the relief of submission to a force stronger than himself – that thing most denied to an emperor. He felt inside himself the terrified child that was the perfect foil to his life of power. He begged, in the voice of that child, for the world to have pity. He babbled to his mother, his sister, his father, telling them he was a good boy and deserved their love. He pleaded for their indulgence, their blessing.

Now Domitian's breathing grew deeper and calmer, his body rising and falling with the blows instead of against them. Miraculously they ceased. He heard a thrilling silence, like the silence after battle. His body felt feather-light, purged, innocent. Nimble fingers unbound him. Palms cool with almond lotion annointed the gouges his resistance had cut into his wrists and ankles. He sat up on the bed as the bawd swaddled him in a silk sheet.

She posed before him, her left hand on her broad hip, her right hand once more holding the whip – chest heaving, sweat trickling from under her orange wig and black mask of Hecate. Tossing away the whip, she stripped off her orange tunic then her wig, and – last of all – the black mask. She stood before him, boldly revealed – his tormentor, his lover, his wife, his empress. When had he recognized her? When she had taunted him, tunic raised, in the garden? When she had brought the whip down on him for the first time? So soon? So late?

Stretching beside him on the couch, Domitia cradled his head between her breasts, crooning as she rocked him, so that he felt vulnerable yet safe. They made love slowly, with much tenderness, as they used to do many years ago, lying together in willow groves, by quiet pools, at his Alban villa, for days on end, with much that was known between themselves and yet much left to discover – before unslaked ambition, then too much power, had soured him, and she had taken her boredom, her grief, her frustration, her despair, into the beds of others.

At the point of sweetest sorrow, the empress leaned over her emperor, looked deep into his eyes, kissed his mouth, nuzzled his ear with her lips and whispered: "Julia is pregnant. She boasts of it all over Rome. It's known that she lay with many at the Temple of Cybele, and bets are being taken as to the father. One thing is certain: while your paternity is in doubt, your brother's claim is not. It *is* the grandchild of Titus."

Domitian hesitated only slightly: "The bastard dies."

They lay together a long time more, still holding each other, eyes closed, with Parthenius – lost in his own distant world – standing guard at the door, and Hermes glowering from his niche. At last, feeling the shredding of their bond and the intrusion of a difficult future, both burst into tears, to the mystification of the dwarf, who took only one truth from the afternoon: *Parthenius had received preferment over him again today. Oh, they would pay – all of them. They would pay.*

After bathing again, Marcus and Priscus went to the esplanade, where the mellow fruits of the splendid fall day could best be savoured. Professional athletes, their bodies stretched long, flung silver javelins into targets painted on the grass. Others, coiled like springs, sent discs zinging in arcs across the sky. Women in trailing gowns rolled hoops with hooked sticks. Others flirted from swings pulled on ropes by slaves or lovers. Prostitutes played tag among the masterworks. Hawkers bawled their wares, each in his own distinctive singsong. Fortune-tellers cast horoscopes or plumbed fates in cards and sand.

Their quarrel over and neither bearing a grudge, Marcus and Priscus strolled arm in arm to the barbershop, which was renowned as much for its gossip as for its styles, and which Priscus had dubbed The Talking Gazette. Several dozen clients waited on benches for ten barbers who wielded their razors over the heads of ten other clients. Each was aided by a master who lent himself to lengthy discussion on the cut and lie of each lock, and by two apprentices who sharpened iron tools on a whetstone, applied oil and staunched wounds with spiderweb soaked in oil and vinegar. Barbering, as practised in Rome, was an expensive, leisurely and dangerous craft, providing more than one lawyer with the bulk of his custom.

Seeing prosecutor Messalinus and freedman Clodianus on stools draped in muslin, Priscus couldn't resist shouting: "Wouldn't it be nice if Messalinus' barber would slit the throat that has slit so many others?"

Messalinus retorted in his sibilant voice: "If only my barber's razor could chop off the head and beard of Priscus, he would end the longest adolescence in Rome."

"I never prize my beard more than when I see the trembling chins of those who go clean-shaven," taunted Priscus. "I'll end my own adolescence by presenting my first shavings to the gods when our god-like emperor starts receiving better advice."

Freedman Clodianus, who was having his square jaw plucked, called over to the prosecutor. "Don't waste your breath on that one, Messalinus. That red-beard is a man no decent Roman would call a brother. He's more related to the he-goats who live on the shores of Cyniphs. I've trapped them, so I know by the smell."

"One more drop of scent on those dyed curls of yours, Clodianus, and no man will call you brother. He'll call you sister. Your enslavement to your barber is worse than the one you once had to Bibulus the fishhawker. By the time you get one cheek plucked, the other has grown in."

Priscus clapped Marcus on the shoulder, regretting his friend's disapproval at the same time as he courted it. "Don't be annoyed with me, Marcus. There are worse things than impudence toward liars, informers and cutthroats."

"You offend these powerful men to no purpose, Priscus. Your sting incites them against you, without deflecting them one inch from their course."

Priscus pulled a sober face. "You're right, Marcus, though it pains me to admit it."

By now they had passed the barbershop and were approaching Allectus Publishing House. Priscus steered Marcus toward the door. "I have to pick up some copies of my play for tomorrow."

Allectus consisted of three rooms: one for the preparation of materials, one for transcribing manuscripts, one for assemblage.

In the first room, slaves mixed ink out of pitch, soot and cuttlefish, or prepared papyrus by sorting it into grades, sponging it for re-use, worm-proofing it with cedar oil.

In the second room, out-of-work actors competed in volume as they strutted their narrow stages, dictating the works of contemporaries (Martial, Statius) or the Great Dead (Virgil, Homer, Horace), while scholars stroked their pens in unison, like the oars of a galley. Priscus greeted several of the scholars, then winked at Marcus. "I pay them, on behalf of schoolboys everywhere, to insert bawdy lines in the crankier texts of Cato and Seneca. It's my favourite charity."

In the third room, slaves pasted finished sheets into 100-page scrolls, which they glued to wooden rollers. Others gilded the ends or attached dangling labels giving title and subject.

Priscus picked up a copy of his new play entitled *Nemesis* – the name of the slave whose job it is to remind the emperor, when in triumphal robes, that he is mortal. Marcus frowned at the blood-red letters. "I hope you won't be goaded into rashness by anything I've said."

Priscus slipped the scroll into his tunic. "Don't worry. Only the Greeks are foolish enough to take their passion for truth to the stage. Our citizens want to be entertained, not challenged. Instead of wit, they want dancing bears. Instead of tragedy, they want volcanoes that erupt. Forget what I told you before. I was just joking. Even if I did want to incite the audience, I'd have to wake them up first – especially the senators in the front rows. Our actors have to fit their actions around their bellies and their words between the snores."

"If that's how you feel, why do the play at all?"

"For the money. Zeno got me a fat commission. And since the emperor confiscated most of my father's property along with his head, I thought it only fair to snatch at it. The truth is, there's only one Roman actor who was able to make himself heard over the shrieks of dying gladiators – the pantomimist Paris. If he were alive, I might be talked into risking."

"You mean the actor who was slain for adultery with the empress?"

"The same," replied Priscus bitterly. "The old fucker wanted Paris for himself. Never was there a more generous man – both to an audience and to his friends. Never a month goes by that I don't miss him."

"You knew him then?"

"Like a brother. I trained with him as a mime, though I've never appeared on the stage. Not, I can assure you, to avoid scandal among all our dear old senators who think the actor one below the whore. My pride was of a different sort, for with Paris to entrance, who would dare compete? He could reduce an audience to tears with a single finger, the lift of an eyebrow. He drew from our Roman clods a depth of compassion they never knew they possessed."

Marcus remembered Priscus' wicked imitation of Messalinus on the rostra – every flip of the cane perfect, every hitch of the eyebrow. "I saw your talent that boozy night after the October Horse."

Priscus grinned. "I try to keep in form."

As they left the esplanade, a small scarlet figure hurtled past them, nearly knocking Priscus over. Both recognized Hermes the dwarf.

"I wonder what he's up to?" mused Marcus.

"No good," Priscus replied.

Julia Sabina reclined on a couch in her library, reading poetry by Helvidius Priscus – not his love poetry but more recent verse, full of gloomy political allusions that confused and daunted her. She persevered because Priscus was someone she cared about and because she would be seeing him tomorrow night at the Odeum. She would also be seeing the emperor – the first time since she had confessed to him about their son, her baby. It would be her final chance to read his every gesture, to analyze his every word, the way women and slaves had always foretold their fates in the frowns and smiles of their masters.

Julia's attitude toward her life had changed since the last time she saw the emperor. From the moment she felt the baby quicken and stir inside of her, it had miraculously become a separate human being to her – not a bribe to secure the emperor's love, not an extension of herself to give herself importance, not a doll to play with so she wouldn't be lonely, nor an emperor to breed emperors, but a person with his own destiny. She wanted this child to have a fair chance at life more than she had wanted anything else – more than the approval of her father or the love of the emperor. For this she was almost ready to quit Rome. Her hesitation no longer rested on ambitions for herself, but on the child's right to be imperial if his father would accept him. Everything depended on tomorrow night.

Julia's gatekeeper appeared at the library door. "There's a man at the gate in an unmarked litter, m'lady. He wants in, but he won't say who he is."

Julia frowned. She had few visitors besides Priscus and Marcus. "I'll see to it, Brutus." Accompanying her servant to the gate, she found, as he had said, a black litter of the sort rented in the Forum. She addressed her intruder through the gate: "What is your business, sir?"

Cackling, high-pitched laughter. "My business is *my* business till I make it yours. D'ya think you're about to take in the Trojan Horse?"

Shivering in recognition, Julia ordered: "Bring him in."

Brutus opened the gate. "This way," urged Julia, leading the bearers through her vestibule toward her library.

The coarse black curtains parted. Hermes the dwarf debarked. With a sweep of his cap, he commanded: "Sit down," as if he were the host and she the underling.

Always before, the evil Julia felt in the dwarf's presence was countered by the joy the emperor's summons would bring. Now that balance no longer held. She perched on her reading couch, watching Hermes unfold his stool and arrange himself upon it, repressing nausea. "Do you have a message for me from the emperor?"

More cackling laughter. "From the emperor? Indeed, indeed, though not one he would have me deliver."

Straining forward, despite the musty odour that clung to him, Julia begged: "Please, Hermes, speak plain."

"Plain is it?" Jutting out his jaw, he scolded her as if she were responsible for some monstrous delay. "I've little time to lose, can't you see that? Do you think there are many times that our emperor lets me out of his sight?" He preened himself. "That's the price of being an emperor's favourite – whether his dwarf or his whore."

Shocked, she rebuked him: "Remember to whom you speak!"

Rolling his eyes from her face to her belly, he said: "I speak to both of you – to one emperor's daughter and to another emperor's bastard. D'ya think because I sit like a gargoyle on the emperor's bed that I neither see nor hear? In a palace even statues have ears and those without tongues speak." Cocking his head, face crafty, he lowered his voice in intimacy. "Here's the situation: The empress has convinced the emperor you've been dissolute at Cybele. After the Odeum tomorrow night, you'll be invited back to the palace. After that little treat, you'll fall ill.

106

The empress has a heavy hand in these matters. You'll be lucky to escape with your life. Certainly, the bastard will lose his."

His gloating words pummelled Julia like fists. She slumped over on the couch, overcome by his dank and dirty smell that acted like civet to her fears. "How can I believe you? Why have you come here?"

Hermes stared at her with surprise. "What choice do you have?" Hopping from his stool, he began to strut, arms folded, declaiming as he had often seen the emperor do, supposing his good deed entitled him to such indulgence, imagining he was being kind in allowing her chance to recover herself. "Motives are like a bag of cats, pulling in many directions. Perhaps I enjoy manipulating those who think they have power. Perhaps I like to pull some strings and loosen others just to see what will happen." Tossing his scarlet coxcomb, he ogled her with what was meant to be a tender smile. "Maybe it's less complicated than that. Maybe I'm here because you used to remember with a kind word that I am a man like others. Maybe I remember one night when – at the generous command of the emperor – *mine* were the hands that opened the white thighs, *mine* was the tongue, *mine* the cock, as good as any man's." Eyes limpid, lips moist, he put his hand on Julia's knee and squeezed. "Maybe I hope some day you will again come to see me as a man?"

Revolted, Julia flung the dwarf from her with such force he ended in a crumpled heap by the door. For a few seconds he gazed up at her with crushed and bleeding eyes, like a hawk that's broken his wing. Then, with the nimble responses of one who has learned to survive at the feet of power, he leapt up and brushed himself off. "Very well, you've had your chance." He puffed himself to full height and sneered: "D'ya think the empress will leave any trunk in Rome unopened? Any crypt unsearched? Where can you and the bastard find sanctuary except in those places known only to a dwarf?"

"You're mad!" shrieked Julia. "Get out!"

"Mad mad mad!" jeered the dwarf as he hopped down the hall. "Mad mad mad mad mad. The whole world's gone mad!"

107

CHAPTER SEVEN

Cornelia sat with Zeno the Greek by the vestalry reflecting pool where they often met toward sunset. It was a time Cornelia prized because she revered her worldly tutor. It was a time Zeno prized because Cornelia's respect made him feel more like the poet-philosopher he wished he had become than the ink-stained fawner of emperors he feared he was. As usual their talk began with Cornelia's inquiries about Zeno's students, then digressed to a discussion of the court history he was writing.

Zeno had served four emperors.

As a lyric poet forced to leave Rhodes because of scandalous adulteries, he had been taken up by Nero, who admired his musical skill, until that wretched day when he had been caught fornicating with one of the emperor's concubines, and unceremoniously transformed into a eunuch. Fortunately Zeno had befriended Commander Vespasian, whose life he had saved by preventing him from snoring during Nero's musicales. When Vespasian became emperor, he hired Zeno as tutor to the vestalry – a job of discretion for which he was now qualified by more than just classical learning.

Zeno's luck held: Vespasian's oldest son Titus, a charming degenerate with a taste for eunuchs, recalled him to a brief but flashy court life. For this the younger brother Domitian would surely have banished him, except that Zeno happened to have on hand an effusive, unpublished epic, written for Nero but now hastily revised for Domitian under the no-nonsense title: *Our Emperor, Our God.* It proved sufficiently shameless to regain for him his old job at the vestalry.

This was the spicy story Zeno wished to tell the world, though not necessarily the one he confided to Cornelia. "What is the title of your philosophic treatise?" she inquired with interest.

"*The Footless Chameleon,*" replied the tutor.

"You mean *Footloose*?"

The tutor smiled enigmatically.

While the vestal puzzled this, Zeno squinted toward the sundial, trying to see the slant of the red obelisk across its flower face. Since the Roman hour consisted of the day's allotment of light, divided equally by twelve, there were only two days a year when it told the right time. Though this was not one of them, he could see enough to know the day was drawing to that point when all visitors – including eunuchs – must leave the vestalry. Sensing there was something troubling the vestal, Zeno let the conversation lapse between them. At last Cornelia said: "Zeno, may I open my heart to you? I need your advice."

Zeno smiled. "As long as you don't mistake experience for wisdom. The two are not the same, as my biography will testify."

She laughed. "And as *I* discover day by day. My problem is one of childishness. I can't keep my mind on my duties. I start thinking one thing and it turns like a centaur into another. This morning I had to repeat the ritual of the salt cakes three times because of my stammerings. Poppaea and Helen started to giggle, and instead of reprimanding them I giggled too. Agrippina was scandalized."

"Agrippina is easily scandalized."

"True, but she was right. Precise ritual is important, though it's not something I enjoy. Besides, the reason I stammered through salutation was because I wanted to get it done with so I could moon over silly thoughts of my own, whereas I used to think of morning prayers as the best part of my day – a quiet time when I could clear my mind of detail and re-dedicate myself to Vesta."

"Perhaps you're tired of the gods for the time being? Perhaps you're caught up in more earthly feelings?" Zeno tilted his pouchy face in mock seriousness. "Yes, I can see it in your eyes. You're troubled by happiness. You must root it out. The more you have of it, the more you'll want."

She groaned. "Happiness? Is that what this is? This strange mixture? I want to laugh and cry. To run instead of walk. When Agrippina corrects me, instead of being grateful I want to box her ears."

Zeno grinned, delighted to feed irreverence in the vestal. "I've had that desire often, with less cause. Agrippina is a prig. All she knows of life is ritual which she performs with consummate smugness. The content of life entirely escapes her. I'm surprised it's taken you so long to become impatient."

"Sometimes I feel that way about myself," confessed Cornelia. "That I hold the shell of life from which the bird has hatched and flown. I keep remembering my time at Delphi. There, high in the mountains, I found not only the peace of the gods but also their ecstasy. I kept that mountain top inside me for a long time." Eyes cloudy, she beseeched him: "Perhaps if I returned to Delphi?"

Still leavening the vestal's seriousness, Zeno exclaimed: "Aha! It's as I've suspected. You're an imposter – a Greek in Roman disguise. For true Romans religion isn't supposed to be a matter of the spirit but the state of matter and a matter of state. You, as chief vestal, are supposed to bribe, beg and bargain with the gods as if they were a foreign power you'd like to stay on the good side of. It's not illumination you should crave, but results. Not thought, but action. Not motive, but deed. Your leaders regard morality as treason if it takes a man away from the authority of the state, which is why all emperors ban philosophers eventually. Your artists don't serve the ideal state but the Roman state.

You envy us Greeks our spiritual existence at the same time you condemn it as laxity. You see every chink in the armour of your pragmatism as decadence." He turned to Cornelia with affection. "At least, that's how all good Romans like Agrippina think. You, Cornelia, have fallen prey to the Greek disease. You want value beyond Caesar's gold coins and a peace that surpasses the Peace of Rome."

Cornelia stared down at the golden birch leaves floating in the pool. "Suppose what you say is true. What can I do to...correct it."

"Correct it?" Zeno slapped his knee in hearty laughter. "As your friend, I say *glory* in it, though as your adviser, I do urge you to hide it. At least it's the Greeks you've taken to, and not one of the more exotic cults on which Roman youths exhaust their pent-up frustrations: Isis, Cybele, the cult of the dead Jew."

"I've taken to nothing," reproved Cornelia. "I seek only one truth – the truth of Apollo. I have only one love – for Vesta. I have only one duty – to Rome. These joys fill my life to overflowing. This other thing is just a small annoyance that will pass. Even to mention it makes too much of it." She gave what she intended to be an airy wave of her hand. "You remember the knight Maximus Marcus? Well, he knew my family at Pompeii, which was a matter we gossiped about at the emperor's banquet. That started me reminiscing over my past. At first such idle thoughts were pleasant. Now they scatter my concentration. It's a silliness I must stop." She smiled too brightly, as if the problem were already resolved. "Though you're wrong, Zeno, in thinking me more Greek than Roman, you have, as always, given me much to think about."

Gazing at his beautiful companion, her hair a rich mahogany in the sunset, Zeno realized for the first time that she might indeed have a serious problem. At the mere mention of Maximus Marcus, her eyes had shone and her voice had grown soft. Did she understand so little of herself? Was love, as usual, deaf, dumb and blind? Laying his hand on his empty crotch, where

111

even now he sometimes felt a phantom twinge, he thought of all he had suffered for the same wretched cause, and prayed by everything he had once held sacred that this vestal would never become a tragic footnote to history.

"Thank you, Zeno," said Cornelia, rising from the bench. She saw a runner jogging across the courtyard toward her. The youth handed her cedar tablets which she knew, by their floral design, to be from Julia Sabina. Breaking their seal of crossed threads balled in wax, she read: "My life is in danger. I beg sanctuary with Vesta." Stunned, Cornelia stared at the message. The boy was still waiting. Snapping shut the tablets, she said: "Tell your mistress, yes. Yes, yes, yes. And may Mercury lend you wings."

She watched him sprint toward the gate. What had happened? Whom did Julia fear? Would it be necessary to hide her, or just to grant sanctuary? Who was tending hearth now? Poppaea and Agrippina. That would never do. She was going to have to think carefully about how to handle Agrippina. Still hugging the tablets, Cornelia called to Helen, just coming from the infirmary where Fausta taught herbal medicine. "Helen, dear, we have a small emergency. Please relieve Agrippina at the hearth. Ask her very respectfully to go to her room and to wait till I call her."

Hurrying to her own room, Cornelia collected a mattress and several blankets. Then she went to the Temple through the underground storeroom, emerging by the hearth where Helen and Poppaea were now tending fire. Behind the alabaster screen, she made a bed for Julia in an alcove by the statue of Juno, then stationed herself at the Temple door.

It was not yet nightfall. Cornelia watched the hawkers pack up their wares. She saw the Temple's shadow spill down the steps, then spread slowly across the empty square until it was an inky mat fretted with firelight. A drunk lurched past the vestalry gate, pausing to shout goodnight to the sisters within. A messenger with a torch trotted down the steps of the Palatine.

Now the square was silent and deserted. She saw a black litter enter its precincts. It halted by the vestalry wall, then sidled across to the Temple. A hand parted the curtains. Julia Sabina's chalky face peered out. Wound in a black shawl, she stepped from the litter and rushed up the stairs. Cornelia embraced her at the door.

"Cornelia, oh thank you. Thank Vesta."

"You'll be safe here. We'll look after you." She led Julia to the bed she had prepared in the back of the Temple.

Julia burst into tears. "I'm so terrified." She seemed feverish.

"Fausta will bring you a sedative. In the meantime...I'm afraid I must leave you for a while." Cornelia returned to the hearth. "Helen, please fetch Agrippina, Diana and Fausta, and come by way of the tunnel."

The vestals emerged one by one through the trapdoor: first Fausta, carrying twigs for the hearth; then Diana, rubbing sleep from her eyes; then Agrippina, looking aggrieved. Agrippina had not liked being ordered about by a younger vestal. She wanted that known.

"Join hands around the hearth," Cornelia ordered the vestals. "We have a guest seeking sanctuary, which is an ancient right we must not deny. Though you'll recognize this guest, you must never reveal her presence outside the Temple, or mention her name. Now in the name of Vesta, raise your hands."

All but Agrippina obeyed. Cornelia repeated: "I command you, by my authority as head of this Temple."

Agrippina obeyed.

"Repeat after me: O Vesta, Guardian of Rome, I do swear to protect with my life the secrets of the Temple..." With her eyes fixed piously on Cornelia, Agrippina intoned only as far as the word *Rome*. From then on, she merely mouthed the vow.

Cornelia smeared ashes on the lips of each vestal. Agrippina licked hers off. Cornelia sprinkled salt flour on their right shoulders and wine on their left. Agrippina managed to dislodge a bit of the salt flour.

Cornelia sealed the oath. "If I break this trust of silence, O

Vesta, let your fury disembowel me, and your fires consume me."

Tracing a blood circle around the five vestals, she warned: "No one is to leave the vestalry tomorrow but myself, and no messages are to be sent, except through me. Tomorrow night Fausta and Diana will tend fire. The rest of us will go to the Odeum, as scheduled. Now, please return to your tasks, all except Fausta. Will you help me?"

Diana, Helen and Poppaea left the Temple through the trapdoor. Cornelia and Fausta hurried around the alabaster screen. Agrippina took her place before the hearth, ear cocked for the slightest sound: *Who could it be? Someone important, obviously, but who?* Agrippina heard whispers but no words. At last Fausta came around the screen. Pouring an herbal liquid into a pottery cup, she heated it over the flame.

Leaning forward Agrippina whispered: "Who is in the Temple?"

Expressionless, Fausta replied: "Julia Sabina."

Agrippina felt her neck hairs prickle. *Julia Sabina.* The emperor's niece and mistress. Cornelia's best friend. *Her* own best friend's worst enemy!

Taking the cup of herbs from the fire, Fausta disappeared behind the screen.

Agrippina reached inside the bodice of her robes. She withdrew a scroll covered with notations in a precise, cramped hand – more words per page than anyone else, as Cornelia herself had had to admit. Recorded here were all the times in the past month when Cornelia had allowed a mistake in ritual to go uncorrected: the exact date the vestal Poppaea had sneezed in vespers and Cornelia had not repeated them; the time Diana had forgotten to put salt in the salt-flour cakes and some had been used. Once Agrippina had reported the misdemeanours of the younger vestals directly to Cornelia, and corrected errors in ritual as they arose. She had tried her best to help Cornelia, but that hadn't been appreciated. Cornelia was too jealous of her to accept helpful criticism, forcing Agrippina to keep a private record.

Agrippina tucked the scroll back into her bodice, right over the ugly birthmark like a bird's claw that her mother, unwilling to believe she had produced a disfigured daughter, had tried to scald off. The empress – her dearest friend – had given Agrippina the scroll along with a silk scarf and a silver cup. She had told Agrippina that she thought Cornelia's promotion to chief had been unfair, and that if there was ever any trouble in the Temple, to report it directly to her. Agrippina's hand over her scroll began to tremble. She had undermined the Oath of Silence merely to defy Cornelia. Now she wondered if she had actually taken it. She had been bound inside the circle of blood, but all the rest had been invalidated. As usual, Cornelia hadn't noticed any infraction. Cornelia never noticed anything. *Cornelia was unfit to be head vestal.*

CHAPTER EIGHT

Each morning Consul Clemens, like all men of influence, heard the requests and grievances of dozens of clients who sought his patronage in return for their loyalty. Though the political point of such a system was lost when the Republic was lost, this custom endured as a form of prestige and charity. Before firstlight, Clemens' clients began to collect in the vestibule of his villa to register with his steward and to be escorted, one by one, into Clemens' office.

On this late November morning, the consul and Maximus Marcus were sitting in easy chairs in the cosy, oak-beamed room hearing the complaint of a ropemaker who claimed to have been cheated of payment. Though it was past lunch time, Clemens listened intently, hand cupped over his ear, occasionally nodding his grey head or tugging his silky beard as he asked for clarification.

Because Clemens rarely spent money for public entertainments, he had a reputation for parsimony. However, no petitioner was ever sent away from his door unheard, and none ever went away hungry. In exchange he asked only that loyalty a man chose to give. He did not, as more vainglorious patrons, require his clients to call him "my lord," clamour after him at the baths, shout his name at gladiator shows, compose epics to him or advertise his virtues on public walls.

In the case of the ropemaker, Clemens promised to back his claim in court – either before the emperor, as was every citizen's prerogative, or before a magistrate at the Julian Courthouse.

Clemens asked his steward: "Any more, Stephanus?"

"None for a hearing, sir. All the rest wished their money, which I distributed."

With a grateful sigh, Clemens heaved up from his chair. His left leg felt stiff. Marcus took his arm, masking the older man's need for assistance. They walked into the courtyard with its colonnades of blue marble and its pool of tropical fish lovingly attended by Clemens. Shivering in the raw November air, Clemens dangled a hand in one of the heated pools. "A better day for fish than people."

Domitilla greeted them in the dining room. "You've had a long morning, Clemens. You must be tired. I'll speak to Stephanus about allowing in only the clients who have registered."

Clemens waved away her concern. "Their health is worse than mine, my dear, though most are half my age, for they don't have you to look after them."

Clemens and Marcus reclined on a cedar dining couch, surrounded by sideboards displaying fine Corinthian bronze plate collected by Clemens at auction, along with busts of such statesmen as Cicero, Cato, Seneca.

Berenice, the Jewish wife of Clemens' steward, dipped red wine from a bowl, while Domitilla sprinkled wine and bread over the altar of their household god. Then, with the consul's permission, she also asked a blessing of the god Jesus, whose cult she had come to respect from conversations with Berenice.

Clemens sipped his wine – a gift from Marcus' brother. "I'm happier than you know to have you as my guest, Marcus."

Saluting the consul with his goblet, he replied: "I'm happier than you know to see the world's first city from the side of her first citizen."

Clemens laughed. "You had better not let anyone else hear you say that, Marcus. There's only one first citizen in this town, and he sits on a throne, not on my cedar couch. But you must have guessed by now how selfish my pleasure is. As you know, my two sons are the emperor's nearest of kin and his presumed heirs. The terror of that has kept me in Rome longer than my duty and desire. At present they're studying in Greece with the great Epictetus. Given the evil vapours that too often blow through the Forum, I consider that safest and best. As I reach age sixty, when my attendance at the Senate is no longer compulsory, I begin to look for an heir to tend my city estates. That's why I'm hoping you'll take over my holdings as an adopted son."

Startled, Marcus put down his goblet. "Sir – I'm overwhelmed." He tried to find appropriate words. "What more can I say?"

The consul smiled: "*Yes*, I hope. In time. But I won't press you for now. Let's let the emperor make his move first." He winked conspiratorially. "I think you may find yourself named to the Senate in the next honours list."

"So soon?" Marcus felt an elation that good taste bade him conceal. He rose to thank the consul formally, but Clemens gruffly yanked him back to the dining couch. "Instead of gratitude, let me use up your goodwill with unwelcome advice." He studied the knight over his goblet. "I'm hoping, Marcus, you won't repeat your Egyptian mistake. I'm speaking of that matter of taking a mistress instead of a wife. The system of concubinage has ruined many a young man by undermining the basis of marriage. I hope, when you become a senator, you'll look toward producing a legitimate heir."

Marcus grinned. "When you mentioned my Egyptian mistake, too many possibilities came to mind. To marry – that's my intention. It has to be the intention of some good woman too. Am I mistaken, or are wives like your Domitilla in short supply?"

Clemens replied with sobriety: "It depends where you do your looking – which brings me to my second piece of advice. You have a brilliant career ahead of you, Marcus. There's just one fly in the ointment – and you know how our emperor feels about flies. Stay away from that hellion Priscus. Such men make amusing companions but they'll only bring you down."

Marcus started to protest, but Clemens hurried on: "No no no, I don't ask for agreement. Only that you consider what I have said. In the meantime –" he lounged back on his couch, indicating the switch to a more cordial topic "– do you have the million sesterces for Senate qualification, or may I have the honour of supplying them?"

Still brooding Marcus replied: "My brother Servius deposits regular earnings from the family enterprises in my name. My personal fortune is...well..." He calculated: "About twenty million sesterces."

"Ahh, then one day you'll be a wealthy man. Let's drink to your good fortune." Savouring the rough assault of the Tuscany wine on his taste buds, Clemens heaved an appreciative sigh. "Who knows?" He held his goblet to the light, admiring the garnet colour. "When I'm retired, I may grow my own grapes, write my memoirs, stock my trout stream..."

"Sir," protested Marcus, "you mustn't think of leaving. Rome needs you. When you rise in the Senate all eyes are upon you."

Clemens' smile was as dry as the wine. "All see, few listen. No, Marcus. There was a time when I believed that an active life in the service of the state was the most honourable that a man could strive for. Now I see that public service and personal virtue are sometimes two separate roads. I've spent long enough on the one. I'd like to explore the other." His voice grew husky, his choice of words more deliberate. "You have no idea how much I long for the brisk mountain air of Como where I can conjure up, at least in words, a government based on principles. Where vices are punished instead of individuals. Where laws are bent in the spirit of mercy rather than for greed or revenge. When the law is no more than what the emperor does, even senators catch the slaves' disease – the scramble for influence."

The Jewish maid Berenice arranged bread, olives, artichokes and trout before them on the cedar table. Domitilla herself served the consul and his guest. As Marcus speared an olive with the sharp end of his spoon, he asked: "What has caused this change in you, Clemens? Though I was just a small lad with large ears, I remember very well those long conversations between you and my father around our dining table in Como. Then you spoke out against philosophers who spent too much time in thought and too little in action. No man has influenced me more."

Clemens laughed. "Perhaps I now know the opposite sin: too much action and too little thought." Breaking a roll his arthritic fingers found difficult to grip, he continued: "To serve a Republic where justice has meaning and where power lies in the deliberations of good men is a purpose to which any man can aspire. But to serve the whim of one man under the sway of dwarfs, concubines, slaves and spies is quite another. These days, Marcus, your consul has less influence on your emperor than the last man to rub his back or the last woman to paddle her fingers through his chest hairs. No man – not even our emperor – can live in a vacuum. A man without peers is the first to become a slave to his slaves."

The older man's bitterness startled Marcus. "I confess I'm depressed by what I see at court. It seems no man tries harder than our emperor for a good public opinion, yet no man is more roundly hated by those closest."

Clemens nodded. "His brother was the best-loved of emperors. Domitian is both jealous of that and contemptuous. He pampers the people in competition with the memory of his brother, then draws away in arrogance and ill-humour."

"Isn't that just a fault of style?" prodded Marcus, trying to lure the consul from his usual discretion.

"True. But there's far more than style in the way he treats the Senate." Clemens picked up his fish knife and began the skilful filleting of his trout. "Though all three Flavians were dictators chosen by the praetorians and foisted on the Senate for legitimization, both Vespasian and Titus consulted us on important matters. Domitian showed the width of his purple stripe early by refusing to give the traditional assurances to the Senate that only they could judge and execute their own members. Then he had himself proclaimed perpetual Censor so all disciplinary action would flow through him. Then High Priest, so all honorary appointments were his as well. All that plus his personal vendettas. My own cousin Flavius Sabinus was put to death for treason because the emperor's herald mistakenly announced him as *emperor*-elect instead of *consul*-elect. Of course the man was also the husband of Julia Sabina, make of that what you will. Aelius Lamia, the husband of Empress Domitia, was executed for a harmless witticism about being cuckolded by the emperor – and that made ten years before. Only when the emperor's condemnations are the most obscenely self-serving does he get Senate ratification. Then he's likely to insert into the records a plea for mercy for the condemned man so the cruelty seems to be the Senate's. The last man he crucified, he had invited the night before to share his dining couch!"

"Of course I've heard the rumours," replied Marcus. "But in Egypt it was just as easy to believe that the emperor acted out of necessity against assassins. Throughout the provinces, he's known as a good administrator. Certainly, as his financial agent in Judaea I had no reason to complain about the promptness and sanity of his replies. As my commander, I found him fair and courageous. I wasn't prepared for the man I see now, indulging himself in petty slights and sucking up flattery that would make a whore blush."

Gesturing for Berenice to refill their goblets, Clemens continued his careful explanation: "The emperor, for obvious reasons, treats the military with a wet-nurse's care. As for his good reputation in the provinces – what is that but another symptom of rule by influence? The further one gets from the seat of power, the fairer the rule is likely to be." Waving his fishknife as vigorously as his rod of office, he asked rhetorically: "What does that snake Messalinus care about the government of Parthi? When our prosecutor connives, it's for the murder of his brother so he can steal his estate. What does the emperor's current couch favourite care about Egypt and the wheat problem? All she wants is an amethyst pin to flaunt before the other concubines. This emperor – like the others – rules best where he doesn't look." Clemens stabbed his knife into the eyes of his trout. "Bahh, in Rome even these fish eyes are likely to be in the emperor's employ."

The two men ate in silence, with Berenice frequently refilling their goblets and with the strong wine exaggerating the morose effects of the conversation on Marcus. He had been invited to Rome on the urgings of Clemens, to begin a senatorial career. To find that career perhaps not worth pursuing at the point when it was being handed to him, was unsettling. Though he'd grown used to Priscus' constant sniping, he felt betrayed when Clemens sounded the same note. Was this the habit of all Roman senators: to gripe continuously about the corruption of the court while living comfortably within its system of patronage? Was that what Clemens encouraged as his future? As he drained his glass, Marcus announced with more truculence than he intended: "This conversation bothers me, Clemens. Until now I thought this government worth serving if only because a man of your integrity serves it."

Neatly crossing his cutlery over the remains of his fish, Clemens pushed away his plate and confronted Marcus with dignity. "If it's me and not the system you wish to judge, then you'd better hear the worst." He held up his hand. "No, don't stop me now, Marcus. Let me tell you what it's *really* like to be consul of Rome.... Scarcely do I get to sleep at night before a messenger arrives to say Caesar is stirring. If I'm summoned, I feel like a dog at the bidding of his master. If I'm not summoned, I must fear for my life – has the emperor been more distant lately? Has Messalinus made up lies about me – worse, has he told the truth? After jogging by litter through foggy streets, I'm set down with the others to await the imperial bidding. Sometimes it's only a few minutes. Sometimes it's several hours. And do you know what we talk most about? Morality! The more it escapes us, the more we're obsessed by it."

The consul shook his head, as if scarcely able to believe himself. "Just last month a senator of one of our best families greeted our emperor outside the Senate. Domitian replied: 'Farewell!' and the poor man went home and slit his throat. Few thought a thing of it, because that's the way it is." He gripped his goblet, declaiming: "What is Rome but a pyramid of patronage with the emperor at the top? Zeno, the emperor's secretary, would, I'm sure, be the most decent of men in a decent world. Yet he thinks nothing the less of himself for hanging about the vestibule of the freedman Clodianus who would pick pennies out a dunghill with his teeth so he can run home and play broody hen for all his literary chicks. Our poets compose fawning epics to the emperor's face and then – out of self-disgust – rhyme dirty couplets on latrine walls. That's the true legacy of favour-grubbing: self-hate and jealousy. Prosecutor Messalinus boasts he can kill a man fastest by singing his praises. It's envy for a man's list of honours that drags that man down, and honours we all have by the chariotful. When there is no real power, false medals multiply. As you know, those of us who attend the emperor each morning have the privilege of writing the word *friend* after our names, as if it were a professional title, meaning 'I have favours to sell.' Any man who has travelled with the emperor can add *companion* to his name, meaning 'I have even greater favours to sell.' It's done every day."

Sticking his spoon into a pomegranate served to him by Domitilla, Clemens broke off his harangue and calmly began to eat. "Now that you know how bad things actually are, Marcus, how do you judge me: because I stayed here at all, or because I want to quit?"

Marcus stared at his plate, ashamed to have criticized his host, his sponsor, his father's friend, his own friend, especially in hearing of his wife. "I'm sorry, Clemens. I judge you...neither way. I judge you to be a friend of Rome." He concentrated on his artichoke, stripping the leaves clockwise to the heart, feeling his frustration build once more with unanswered questions, but channelling it into less personal channels, deferring to the wisdom he had earlier discounted. "Tell me, Consul Clemens – is it the system itself that's to blame for Rome's troubles, or is it the man who rules?"

Clemens shook his head, frowning. "That's a question I've asked myself many times. To be fair, it's not so much power that corrupts our emperor but the burden of that power – the excessive work, the excessive isolation, the constant fear of assassination. How can you judge yourself if when you get a boil on your nose, ten people praise your ruddy complexion?" He warmed to the dangerous criticism, too long suppressed. "Do you know what I consider the real cause of Rome's degeneracy? Success and the indolence that breeds. We live on the tribute that pours in from the provinces, and anything that doesn't amuse us to do, our slaves do for us. Clodianus the fishhawker turned perfume pedlar has two slaves just to run his waterclock: one turns it over and the other calls the hour. He has more liveried servants to staff his dining room than we have legionnaires on the Danube. The slave who puts on his right shoe isn't the same one who puts on the left. I'm considered to shamefully overwork my slaves because I run a household for two with only two hundred."

Marcus swirled the last of his wine around his goblet before drinking it to the dregs. "Where does that leave me, Clemens? What advice can you offer? Are there no good men? What of the Stoic opposition?"

Clemens sighed. "In the past ten years I've seen so many friends executed or expelled I can only think it's a judgement on me that I'm here. Still...good men? Yes.... When Pontifex Piso was younger he fought the emperor, though now he speaks out of both sides of his mouth and hears only with the ear that's convenient. Cocceius Nerva grows more radical with age – who knows how Rome might benefit there? As for the Stoic opposition – that ended with the death of Helvidius Priscus the Elder. He was the finest orator I've ever heard, and certainly no favour-grubber, but even with the Stoics one begins to suspect that those who miss liberty the most are the ones who want more power for themselves. Priscus came to believe that he owned virtue, which he would occasionally flash from under his cloak for the rest of us to admire. When he thundered like

124

Jupiter himself about the need to throw out inherited rule and to find a moral man to rule the empire, we all knew that he knew of only one: himself. How did that differ in principle from what the Flavians offered us?"

Smiling with affection, Clemens raised his goblet to Marcus. "I see only one hope: our emperor's new policy of inviting into the Senate the best men of the provinces to bolster Rome's ailing aristocracy. Only in that way –"

Clemens broke off.

Domitilla was standing in the doorway, her usually serene face puckered in distress. "What's wrong, my dear?"

She held out a cedar tablet with the seal broken. "This came from the vestal Cornelia."

Clemens reached for the tablet. "Is she ill?"

"No. It's Julia." Domitilla bit her lip. "It seems she's taken refuge in the Temple."

"What?" Opening the tablet, he scanned the brief message, then scowling to hide his emotions, turned to Domitilla. "Can you tell me more than is here?"

"Not for sure. Only with a woman's intuition. I believe our cousin Julia is pregnant with the emperor's child. If the father were unwilling, that would certainly be cause for hiding."

Clemens got up from his dining couch. "I see, I see." He began to pace, his hands behind his back, his brow furrowed, becoming the man of action Marcus knew and respected. "The Temple can serve only as temporary haven. Cornelia is a woman of strength as well as heart. She'll stand firm. I'm not so sure about our Pontifex Piso. Though his intentions are good, his resolution flutters like a white flag on a stick. We must get Julia out of Rome as soon as possible – by tomorrow if we can." He looked down at Domitilla's altar to the Christian god. "Do you think, Domitilla, that your Berenice and her people would be willing to help us?"

"I don't know, Clemens. I can only ask." Domitilla hurried from the room.

Clemens returned to his dining couch. "Are you familiar,

Marcus, with the Jewish cult that calls itself Christian after the dead Jew?"

"A little. From the two years I spent as financial agent in Judaea. I was surprised when I arrived in Rome to see how the sect has taken hold here."

Clemens nodded. "It's a sect to which my wife's maid belongs and with which Domitilla finds an affinity. Frankly, I'm too Roman to imagine myself worshipping a crucified criminal – I'd sooner stick to our own god-emperors if it comes to that. Still and all, I've nothing against them. They've learned ways of hiding themselves that only the fleas know. Every emperor can tell you it's easier to ban the wind than to ban the Jews."

Domitilla re-entered the dining room with Berenice and her husband Stephanus. Addressing both equally, Clemens said: "I have a favour to ask which is large and dangerous. Before I do, I give you my word that your choice is a free one." He turned to Stephanus. "Julia Sabina, my cousin and the emperor's niece, has fled to Vesta for sanctuary. Could you and your friends help us smuggle her from Rome?"

Stephanus looked at Berenice, for he was a recent convert to Christianity through her family. She smiled. "Yes. My people understand such problems."

"By firstlight tomorrow?"

She hesitated only slightly. "Yes."

"How could this be done?"

"By funeral cortege. It's done all the time with our people who are escaping."

Clemens stroked his beard, then smiled. "Well, Marcus, would you like to become a Jewish mule-driver for one day?"

CHAPTER NINE

Domitian's Odeum was a two-storey semi-circle with opulent marble façade. Tragedies played by day, comedies by night. Tickets were bone circles inscribed with the emperor's profile.

As the audience crowded into the 8,000-seat theatre for the debut of *Nemesis* by Helvidius Priscus, there was much speculation as to whether the playwright would use this showy opportunity to cause trouble for himself and the emperor. Maximus Marcus was one who approached the evening with misgivings. He had no confidence that either the disciplines of stagecraft or the diplomacy of statescraft could contain his hot-headed friend, or that he could be subtle enough to avoid censure.

Of more pressing concern was his need to help Julia Sabina escape Rome. *Her* danger at least was real. As knights and senators took their places in the lower stalls, Marcus manoeuvred a seat beside Cornelia, ousting Agrippina, who settled with bad grace in the stall ahead.

He greeted the chief vestal awkwardly, noticing she too seemed under heavy strain. "I'm glad we're side by side again, Lady Cornelia." As if making conversation, he pointed to the empty royal box. "I hope the emperor isn't ill this evening?"

Cornelia shook her head. "I haven't heard that he is. He won't arrive till the theatre is filled." She turned away to discourage the knight, beginning to sense, by the acuteness of her reactions when he was near, that he was a hazard to avoid, already disturbed that he had offended Agrippina by contriving to sit beside her.

Marcus persisted: "*I hope one of the emperor's party isn't ill or indisposed?*"

Something in Marcus' intensity alerted Cornelia. Frowning, she said: "A friend of mine fell ill yesterday."

"Oh?" His interest seemed exaggerated. "Seriously ill?"

"It could prove fatal. Unless she is helped."

He held her gaze and nodded slightly. "If she's ill, then she shouldn't stay in Rome. This drizzly winter climate will be harmful to her. South is better."

Cornelia nodded. "I agree." She shifted her eyes to Agrippina, who seemed to be straining back from the stall ahead. "Travelling too can be dangerous."

Marcus dropped his voice so she had to lean forward to hear. "Some times are better than others. I've always found still-time good for beginning a journey – after the thieves of night have gone to bed and before the thieves of day have arisen."

"Oh? What day of the week would you choose?"

"New moon is by far the best – for journeys, for battles, for plantings...for *burials*."

"That's tonight, isn't it?"

"The morning after this night."

She leaned back in her seat, confident she had caught his meaning, not wishing to arouse suspicion by whispering. "I'll remember what you've said, Marcus, if ever I have to leave Rome. Was it as a tribune responsible for the lives of many men that you learned to check auspices so carefully?"

"No, it was while I was the emperor's financial agent in Judaea. Do you know the so-called Christians?"

"Just as a group of Rome's unfortunates who compensate for the misery of their lives by their hopes for the next." Puzzled by this turn in the conversation, she asked: "Why do you mention those?"

He shrugged. "Coincidence. Consul Clemens' steward and his wife's maid both asked leave to attend a Jewish funeral tomorrow. It reminded me of the Jewish preference for starting journeys at new moon – especially those for the purpose of burial."

"I see." Cornelia nodded with eagerness. "The Jews must leave the city to bury their dead because they refuse cremation, isn't that so?"

"Yes. *They believe the body rises from the dead.*"

Cornelia touched his arm. "I understand, Marcus. I do understand." Their eyes met and held. Flushing, Cornelia became aware of her fingertips still resting on the knight's arm, and of the rise and fall of her amulet on his chest. Retracting her hand, she folded it with the other on her lap, and turned her attention to the empty stage.

The emperor had not yet arrived.

Zeno the Greek, who had been pacing the upper gallery, his hands tucked in his sleeves, regarded the emperor's lateness as a bad omen, but then Zeno – as Priscus' literary patron – regarded everything this evening as a bad omen. The owl he had seen – sure sign of disaster. His fig tree which had bloomed out of season.

Transporting his anxieties down to the stall where he was to sit with the younger vestals, Helen and Poppaea, he launched one of his "You Roman" lectures, beginning with: "You Romans use the theatre to confirm the social order, whereas we Greeks use it to challenge it."

To snag his pupils' attention, he told them the story of how he and Commander Vespasian had swallowed mild doses of poison to escape Nero's two-day one-man recital of the opera *Niobe*, only to discover neither death nor birth was sufficient reason to be allowed out of the theatre: a senator's wife having just been forced to bear twins in the aisle!

Deftly switching back to his original theme, he concluded in fine oratorical pitch: "When will your emperors learn that the leader who allows himself to be shafted on the stage seldom has to fear it in the Senate house?" There was a hush, followed by applause: the emperor and his entourage entered the theatre.

Imperator Domitianus Caesar Augustus and the Empress Domitia were borne in a double sedan-chair to the royal box. The emperor seated himself on a curule chair, with his empress at his right, and Captain Geta of the Imperial Guard behind him. Frowning, he drew the attention of the empress to the vacant seat to his left. Consul Clemens handed a note to Captain Geta, who passed it down to the emperor. Impatiently breaking Julia Sabina's seal, he read: "My lord, I regret I have been taken ill on the way to the theatre and must return home." He passed the note to the empress, who shredded it.

Clapping his hands, the emperor signalled for the play to begin.

Helvidius Priscus appeared at centrestage, with the torchlight drawing fire from his red hair and beard. Smiling up into the royal box, he thanked the emperor elegantly in verse for being "a cornucopia from which all patronage flows." As he exited, he was replaced by four singers, who carried the symbols of their class: a senator with his rod of office; a soldier with his dagger; a freedman with his moneybag; a slave with the shorn head of captivity. Each sang a verse testifying to the bliss of life under Emperor Domitian, and ending with the refrain: "In face and fame the fairest of the fair."

As the four danced off the stage, one tripped and the others tumbled over him. When they sorted themselves out, the soldier had the moneybag, the freedman had the senator's rod of office, the slave had the dagger, and the senator – having lost his wig – exhibited the shaved head of the slave. The audience tittered. An accident or risky political comment? Groaning, Zeno crossed his fingers.

The play itself took off on plot lines well-established by Plautus. Stock characters propelled by coincidence, mistaken identity, sex and violence, bungled their way toward a happy ending. In this case, a prostitute and her pimp had both fallen in love with a masked dancer. Each set out to discover his identity for the purpose of seducing him.

The action was brisk and the stage effects as flashy as anything seen before in Rome. Fauns with pink horns leapt through dancing waterfalls. Bears and leopards popped up through trapdoors. Naked prostitutes engaged in bizarre sexual acts as they hung from trapezes. A fire, intended to burn down a forest, almost took the theatre with it. Here was everything Priscus claimed to despise, done with panache. Was that his joke? Was he feeding pigs pig-fodder? Was he taunting the radicals who sought to use him in his father's cause? Or was it as he himself claimed: that he had decided to take the money and run?

INTERMISSION

The plebeians in the upper seats crowded out onto the galleries while the patricians from the lower stalls streamed down onto the stage to become the stars.

Zeno rushed backstage to congratulate Priscus on a play he judged, in mass appeal, to be nectar sweetened with honey – hard on the literary digestion, but given the political climate, exactly right.

So as not to arouse suspicion, Marcus, Cornelia, Consul Clemens and his wife Domitilla took pains to keep apart, with the result that Cornelia found herself talking to the man she dreaded most: pock-faced Captain Geta of the Imperial Guard, whose legendary ruthlessness made her skin crawl. Though boorish with almost everyone else, he was worshipful of Cornelia – clearly seeing her as the epitome of womanhood, saintly and sublime. Servility from such an unlikely source unnerved Cornelia. And it didn't reassure her to discover Geta wished to donate money to erect a statue of her at Egeria spring. Shuddering, she touched her bulla, as if to ward off evil. She would pity herself if ever the captain should doubt her integrity.

The emperor and the empress cast about the stage, their minds elsewhere – a circumstance noted by Geta despite his attentions to Cornelia. As captain of the Imperial Guard, he kept himself as attached to the emperor as a dagger in his master's hand.

The vestal Agrippina was as keenly focused on the empress – her patron, her friend. That she now believed she was *not* bound by the Oath of Silence terrified her. What was she to do with choice once she had it? What did Vesta want of her? Where did her sternest duty lie: to obey her vestal chief whose fitness she doubted, or to alert the empress, her friend?

Enviously, Agrippina watched Cornelia thread her way through the fashionable crowd, smiling at this person, chatting with that one. She saw the empress turn from prosecutor Messalinus as if looking for someone else. *Now* was the time. Straining forward, eyes glittery, body taut, Agrippina reminded herself of the grievous shortcomings by which Cornelia imperilled the Temple, the city and the empire. *Unfit, unfit, unfit to be head vestal.*

Working her elbows like a chicken's wings, Agrippina propelled herself down the crowded aisle. She saw the empress approach Antonius Saturninus and with stupefying boldness inserted herself like a knife blade between. Annoyed, the empress side-stepped. Agrippina moved with her. "I'm sorry about Julia Sabina," she blurted. "About her illness."

The empress stopped in mid-turn. She swung back. "Oh?" Her eyebrows lifted over wary black eyes. "How did you know my niece was ill? Were you with her?"

"Only afterwards," replied Agrippina, intoxicated at being the focus of the empress' attention. "At the Temple. Fausta had her under sedation. She and Diana are tending fire. I hope she spends a peaceful night."

Domitia's lips twisted into a chilly smile. "I'll look in on her...as soon as I can."

"As soon as possible," urged Agrippina, trying to prolong her heady turn in the limelight. She snatched at something she might have heard: "I think she may be going on a journey."

"Oh, when?"

Squinting, Agrippina tried to remember. "Tomorrow. At firstlight."

The empress brushed Agrippina's hand with red-tipped fingers. "My thanks for your concern." She added with what Agrippina took to be great significance: "We'll talk again."

Stepping back from the empress, Agrippina allowed the crowd to flow between them, feeling jubilant for as long as she could see her, then nauseous as if a chasm had suddenly opened under her. Clutching her scroll, she stumbled back up the aisle, afraid she would faint, knowing from the stench and stickiness of her robes that she had soiled them. *If I break this trust of silence, O Vesta, let your anger disembowel me and your fires consume me.*

Emperor Domitian signalled to the empress that he wished to return to the royal box. As he sank morosely into his chair, he began to wish he were anywhere but here. Why had he built this damnable theatre in the first place? Too bad it didn't burn down in the opening act! He'd walk out now, except he couldn't think of anywhere else he wanted to be. He glared at the empty chair beside him – a thing he'd been avoiding. He had felt relief when he read Julia's message, then anger, then relief, then anger again. The conflict had paralyzed him, sapped his energy. Forcing his attention back to the stage, he almost wished Priscus would try to prick him so as to snag his interest.

The play resumed. The prostitute had tracked down the masked dancer with whom she and her pimp had fallen in love. By posing as a wealthy patron, she lured him to an assignation in her bedchamber. On discovering this plan, the pimp hid behind the prostitute's statue of Minerva. Spotting him there the masked dancer began to undress both for the pimp and for the prostitute on the bed, in a mime that started out playful, grew seductive, then richly melancholic.

Domitian became absorbed by the play – in vague unease, then in acute distress. Its characters – at first clichéd and silly – now seemed all too real. Could the fat brothel-owner be Clodianus?

Was Consul Clemens the silly uncle who kept worrying his beard? Certainly the blind parasite was Messalinus. As for the prostitute and her pimp...Domitian felt his mouth twitch as the dancer, naked but for his mask, swayed to a single lute, poignantly torn between the prostitute on the bed and the pimp behind the statue.

By now the senators in the lower stalls had recognized the actor playing the masked dancer. The broad torso and bandy legs were unmistakable to those who knew him, yet so graceful in their movement that he seemed, by illusion, to be perfectly formed. One senator whispered to another: *Priscus, Priscus, Priscus, Priscus*, till the whole theatre seemed to buzz with that name. Domitian strained forward in his seat, his livid face jumping with tics, mesmerized by that single figure soaring and spinning across the stage.

The flute ceased. The dancer ceased. Poised at centrestage, he put his hand to his mask – a black helmet covering all but his eyes. The hushed audience awaited the signature flash of red hair. Teasing them, Priscus dropped his hand. Again he danced, filling the theatre with sadness, grace and beauty. He froze once more, his back to the audience. Flinging off his mask, he spun around. A startled gasp. Not Priscus but *Paris* seemed to confront them. The same bent nose and high brow! The same faun-coloured hair! He was dancing now in silence, controlling the audience with the crook of a finger, the widening of the eyes...a single tear. Domitian heard the empress beside him groan.

Paris-Priscus climbed into bed with the prostitute-empress – *for it was she!* – while the pimp-emperor – *for it was he!* – began to writhe on stage with the pain Domitian now felt. At last, unable to endure his jealousy a moment longer, the pimp-emperor on stage drew his dagger.

The emperor in his box nudged Captain Geta of the Imperial Guard. Geta put his hand to his dagger.

The pimp-emperor flashed his weapon toward the audience. Geta unsheathed his.

The pimp-emperor sprung upon the bed containing Paris-

Priscus and the prostitute-empress. He yanked the lovers apart. As his fake dagger found its mark, so did the genuine dagger of Captain Geta, pitched from the royal box. Paris-Priscus toppled onto the bed, oozing blood. At first the audience did not grasp that his suffering was real. It was only when Priscus stumbled to the front of the stage and, shaking his fist, screamed, "Death to tyrants!" that they realized the play had burst its bonds.

A wail of mourning rose from the audience, many of whom remembered Paris with fiercely loyal hearts. It was as if they were seeing their hero murdered all over again, for so precisely had Priscus captured Paris' every nuance that he seemed mystically inspired. The plebeians began to holler: "Bravo, Paris!" while Marcus and a few senators rushed to the stage in aid of the fallen playwright. Marcus got close enough to receive a wink and a grin, before Captain Geta and his praetorians yanked him away.

After peeling off Priscus' faun-coloured wig and wax nose, Geta forced him to his knees by the simple expedient of breaking both legs. Then, prying Priscus' jaws open, he hacked out his tongue. He flung it up to the imperial box, where it flopped into the chair belonging to Julia Sabina.

Leaping to their feet, shaking their fists, many continued to shout: "Bravo, Paris! Bravo, Priscus! Death to tyrants!"

Geta gashed Priscus' throat, all but severing his head. Now the howl that went up proved Domitian's boast that the acoustics in his Odeum were the finest in the world.

At Domitian's orders, the lead actors were instantly hauled onto the stage and flogged. Some had their hands chopped off. It wasn't until this orgy of revenge had swept to its conclusion that he or anyone else noticed that the Empress Domitia was missing from the imperial box.

The Empress Domitia had had no clear idea where she was going when she bolted from the theatre – only that she had to escape that hideous place where her beautiful Paris had been slaughtered once again, and that obscene thing – his tongue – pitched almost onto her lap. Beating her way with her fists to the nearest exit, she had bribed the guard with her garnet ring to let her out. Then, with her garnet necklace, she had bribed another guard for his cloak and his black mare.

Striking out across the Field of Mars through the pitchy night, Domitia galloped as she had once done with her father, across the battlefields of Armenia, slapping the withers with her hand, the hooves flinging out divots of mud, then echoing over the travertine of the Forum, without destination, until she saw the smouldering cone of the Temple of Vesta. Here Domitia reined her horse so harshly she gashed its mouth. Dismounting, she bounded up the steps of the Temple, propelled toward some significant act that would blot up the blood on her imperial robes, which she now imagined – in her hysteria – to be the blood of Paris. The Temple felt hot, oppressive, after the head-long freedom of her ride. She could hear the mad hag Fausta chanting on the other side of the alabaster screen, and another sound – distressed breathing, like the labours of someone with fever. Impelled toward that sound, she stole deeper into the Temple, toward a statue of Juno where she spied someone curled at the feet. She retreated into the shadows behind the statue, her hand resting on the rawhide around the goddesses' waist.

Julia Sabina could hear Fausta chanting behind the alabaster screen – sometimes softly, sometimes stridently, as she passed in and out of consciousness, the same sound she had heard for several hours, or was it days? Fausta's sedatives had robbed her of all sense of time and even place, so that sometimes she seemed like a child trapped in a slimy tunnel which she tried to transform into a thing of beauty with daubs of paint; and some-times she was herself, with enormous belly, pursued by the dwarf through forests of snakes. Though she was still feverish, the nightmares had subsided, so that she was beginning to remember the good times of her life: how her father had once

136

taken her on his lap and wept that he didn't see more of her; how he had placed a statue of her in the Forum for her fourteenth birthday; how Domitian, as her uncle, tucked presents under her pillow. Julia tried to remember her mother – the warm, shadowy figure who had died when she was only three, and whom she imagined to be strong and loving like the goddess Juno. Laying one palm on Juno's toe, and the other on her swollen womb which was Juno's gift, Julia imagined she could detect a tiny heartbeat and felt a surge of love, of kinship, with all women: Cornelia, Phyllis, Fausta... Even Domitia, for wasn't Domitia a person of compassion where children were concerned? Hadn't she grieved more than a year for her own son? Many people said that was the true cause of Domitia's enchantment with Paris: grief, despair, a sickness of spirit.

She remembered Domitia's kindness to her when she had first come to Rome. How Domitia, as the sophisticated aunt, had helped her to choose gowns as stylish as her own. Later, of course, there had been the more intimate times. She missed Domitia, oh she missed her! She could admit that now that she was no longer afraid, now that she was beginning to see things from a more adult perspective, as if the child in her womb had displaced her own childish self, forcing her to grow up. She thought in admiration of Domitia's strength. Her boldness. Her courage – so unlike her own timid ways. They still had much more in common than at odds. Both were pawns of politics neither understood nor even cared about. Each had retreated into selfishness, seeing the emperor – the whole Roman Empire – in terms of her own emotional needs.

Julia was beginning to believe that she had been foolish to run away. The time for that had passed, when the emperor had learned of her pregnancy. Now she had no choice but to trust people. What evidence did she have that her life was in danger? Only the accusations of the dwarf. Tonight, when Cornelia returned from the theatre, she would ask her to write to the emperor, begging his pardon, and bargaining in good faith for the well-being of her child. If he wanted her to take the child to the country, to renounce all rights of succession and never to return to Rome, she would do it. She was even prepared to give him up to the emperor and Domitia as their adopted heir, and to accept banishment for herself. Surely, if the emperor had a son, uncomplicated by his relationship to her, he could accept it as his own? Surely, if Domitia had a son of the emperor's she could love it as her own? If only she could see Domitia now, to pour out her heart to her, she knew she could dissolve the bitterness between them.

Julia had the sudden instinct she was not alone in the Temple – not even in the nebulous ring surrounding the hearth. A shadow close to Julia was taking on substance and shape: a woman, muffled in a long black cloak. As that person knelt beside her, Julia smelt a familiar fragrance – musky and exotic. Reaching out her arms, she spoke the affectionate name that went with that scent: "Mitia..." Julia felt answering hands upon her, cool from the night air, and the frosty breath of a coarse cloak. But there was something disturbing about those hands. They were not loving hands. They were locking themselves around her throat. As the pressure of thumbs against her windpipe increased, Julia started to choke. She tried to whisper the magic name again – "Mitia!" – but, held down by too powerful a force, she could only gag.

Julia tried to tear the hands away. Feeling the child kick in her womb, she too began to kick and claw and punch. But the hands had taken too strong a hold. For a moment she thought she could break free, but the hands were joined by something else – a length of rawhide. Julia saw the face belonging to the hands floating over her – veined in blue, rouged with red, ringed in black...and very very frightened.

CHAPTER TEN

A curious crowd swarmed around the *Daily Gazette*: merchants of Upper Sacred Way, prostitutes of Tuscany Street, runners from the Julian Courthouse. Senators and their slaves competed for elbow room in front of the printed boards. What they saw made no sense at all.

There was no mention of the play *Nemesis*, or of Helvidius Priscus, or of the bloodletting at the Odeum. That was not too surprising. The official line had not yet been worked out. What stunned everyone – caused such disbelief – was a discreet black tablet, lettered in gold, slipped in among the white ones detailing the economic and social life of the city. This black tablet reported the death of the emperor's niece, Julia Sabina: how she had fallen ill on her way to the theatre; how she had sought refuge at the Temple of Vesta, where her fever had worsened, causing her to choke on her own bile. The tragedy, it was stated, had been discovered by the August Lady Cornelia on her return from the Odeum. Since the vestals Fausta and Diana, who were tending hearth, had heard no sound, it was assumed she had died peacefully in her sleep.

No one – patrician or plebeian – could believe such a story. It was clearly a distortion. Was this death connected with the murder of Helvidius Priscus at the Odeum? It was known he had dedicated love poetry to Julia. Had the emperor sought jealous revenge in the same way he had slain Paris and banished Domitia?

For years the imperial triangle had fed the prurient fantasies of Rome, so that there were few in the city who hadn't taken sides, laid bets and generally felt themselves as informed as the principals. Significantly, in this cruel and final twist, Julia Sabina was not viewed as the niece or the mistress of Domitian, but as the daughter of their beloved emperor Titus. On this cornerstone, monuments to her sainthood were hastily erected: the gentle Julia Sabina – so like her father Titus – had always sided with that which was most honest in Domitian, whereas the empress had played shamelessly upon his excesses.

The body of Julia Sabina was prepared for burial by the vestals Cornelia and Fausta, and by Julia's nurse Phyllis. The emperor, as nearest relative, closed her eyes and put a coin in her mouth for Charon – though not without difficulty. The eyes that had been blind to all of his faults now refused to give up their accusing stare till the lids had been stretched and stitched. The jaw – once so yielding – refused to open till it was broken and rewired.

Julia's body was transported to the palace, where it lay in state in the Throne Room, with its columns of yellow marble draped in black. On the eighth day, the emperor's herald invited all citizens to attend the funeral. Because resentment still ran deep over the debacle in the theatre, this announcement sparked many riots, so that Julia's death – as most events in her life – was but another manoeuvre in the game of imperial politics.

It was a cold and murky day, the sort on which nothing casts a shadow. The cortege flanked by praetorian guards wound its way down the Palatine, then along Sacred Way to the Temple of Vespasian and Titus, at the foot of the Capitoline.

First came the torch-bearers, then the flute players, then the chief priest and the vestals Cornelia, Fausta, Agrippina and Helen, bearing cypress branches sacred to Pluto. Then came the bier, borne by eight priests of the sacred colleges followed by the emperor, barefoot, face smeared with ashes, black robes rent;

the Empress Domitia, heavily veiled; Consul Clemens and his wife Domitilla; Maximus Marcus and other prominent citizens; Julia's freedwoman Phyllis and her slaves, wearing new red caps of freedom. Last came a phalanx of professional mourners – actors wearing death masks of the ancestors of the deceased, beating their breasts, uttering heart-rending wails, and appearing to tear their hair.

A pyre had been built in front of the Temple of Vespasian and Titus. There the bearers lay the body on its bed of cypress faggots. The flute-players stopped piping, while the torch-bearers formed a semi-circle around the bier.

Domitian climbed the steps of the Temple. Raising his arms, he addressed himself to Juno, to Jupiter, and to the deified emperors Vespasian and Titus, delivering his oration in a voice from which all emotion had been squeezed. "Here lies Julia Sabina, my beloved niece, the daughter of a god, the grand-daughter of a god, and now one with them in godhead. Her beauty, her joy, her innocence have passed from the light into the shadow, out of our power to see, but not out of our power to worship and to entreat." Receiving a torch from the chief priest, he turned aside his face, as was the custom, and touched it to the pyre, adding in a wispy voice few could hear: "God speed, my little hummingbird, and a safe journey."

During the oration, Cornelia found herself standing beside Maximus Marcus. Though they did not touch or speak, she could feel the depth of his sorrow in the slump of his shoulders and the weary tilt of his head. Here was a different man from the confident young knight she had met at the emperor's banquet. His eyes were pouched and bloodshot, his features smudged, as if some certainty inside him had broken. Together they watched the flames lick up the side of Julia's bier, then embroider the simple robes and dark coils of her hair. For a few moments the face glowed, incandescent, inside its curls of flame, then it slid behind a veil of smoke and was gone.

Remembering the many intimacies she had shared with Julia,

the generosity of her friend, her consuming loves and reckless hates, Cornelia felt grief push in a fist up through her throat. Julia's death left a vacancy in her life she could never fill. Already she felt lonely. Yet, as she shivered in the heat of the fire, she knew there was something more...some fear beyond loneliness, some terror she could feel creeping in an icy wave over her. Julia, she was beginning to suspect, had been more than a friend. She had been the only person who spoke frankly to Cornelia of the forbidden emotion called love which caused more misery and bliss than any other, and which she as a vestal must wrench out with prayers and sacrifice if ever she felt it take root. In sharing with Cornelia the turbulence of her life, Julia had been a vicarious outlet for longings that had no place in a vestal's life. She had provided a bulwark against a dynamic, irrational part of Cornelia whose existence she suspected but dared not face. Now, as Cornelia stood beside Marcus, she felt naked, ripped raw, exposed, like a sea creature without its shell. His very existence posed a threat – the sombre shadow he cast over her, the roughness of his cloak as it brushed her hand, the heaviness of his breathing, the smell of his freshly waxed leather boots, the salty tang of his flesh. In panic, she stepped away from him, closer to the bier, reaching out her cold hands to the flames, imagining she was kneeling by the hearth of Vesta, sealing herself off from such unthinkable thoughts, turning her mind to another problem – one that disturbed her as much but did not erode her: how Julia Sabina had died. Not peacefully, as reported in the *Daily Gazette*. How then to account for the purple bruises on her throat, the twisted face and bulged eyes that would haunt her for the rest of her life? Who was responsible for such a shameful and desperate act?

Cornelia looked at the Empress Domitia, muffled in her impenetrable veils, and at the emperor, his face as masked as those of the actors disguised as his father and brother. How had they known Julia was in the Temple? Her eyes shifted to Agrippina's saw-toothed profile just visible over the empress' shoulder. To break an oath of Vesta? Never. Only the sourness of her own feelings for Agrippina could make her imagine such a thing.

Dousing the embers with wine, the chief priest collected the smouldering bones from the altar, then wrapped them in linen and gave them to Phyllis to wash with milk and place in an urn along with roses and aromatic plants. The wax masks of the actors blurred in the heat from the embers. Cornelia looked at Emperor Domitian. Did he grieve? Was it a trick of the smoke and the flames, or had his face too begun to melt?

Domitian lay in his shuttered bedchamber, swaddled in furs, as close to the brazier as he could draw his couch. Though he was sweating, he couldn't stop shivering. He had always had trouble keeping warm, but tonight it seemed much worse. He stared into the brazier, seeing again Julia's pyre, with the flames riffling like fingers through her robes, picking the flesh from her bones.

Would he at last feel warm on his own pyre, or would his shade already be off with Charon, cheeks hanging with icicles as they plied the frigid Styx? Could spirits feel heat or cold? Did they know joy or sorrow? The testimony of the poets and prophets was confused and depressing – a world like this, without colour or sound or taste or beauty or desire...a pallid reflection, in swirls of smoke and vapour...timeless...without end. He laughed cynically. Would he notice any difference?

Domitian gripped his cup of spiced calda, prepared for him by Phyllis, Julia's freedwoman, once his nurse and now again his nurse, remembering his sister who invited him into her warm bed when he was frightened, and initiated him into the mysteries of the flesh. She had drowned when he was thirteen, failing, on his dare, to swim a flooded river. They never found the body, though he had spent a year in a dinghy rowing back and forth, staring into the currents, seeing seaweed as hair, the pale faces of fish as her face. Was that when he had become so cold?

143

Had the fog seeped into his bones? Was it the clammy breath of her spirit forced to wander in wretchedness for a thousand years along the banks of the Styx because she had not received burial?

Domitian turned his eyes from the fire to its reflection in an urn on an ivory stand: the ashes of Julia Sabina, her earthly remains. They should be in the Flavian Temple, but he had wanted them for a while longer to give focus to his memories. He had thought more about Julia since her death than he had in her lifetime. He had talked more to her ashes than he had to her. He had first seduced her out of malice. To spite Titus, after a quarrel. To spite Domitia. Had he ever loved Julia for herself, or had she merely been a convenience? When he looked in her eyes, had he seen only a flattering reflection of himself, the way the urn now reflected his face ringed in fire?

Domitian downed his calda. *Ghosts, so many ghosts.* He could feel their oozy presence in the room. Was this the curse of the Flavians? No sooner did he reduce one of them to ashes than its shade slid back to haunt him, eyes frosty with reproach. Julia had been his plaything. Now she was one of them – strong as they were strong. Becoming drunk, Domitian gulped more and more calda, seeing another image more vivid than the rest: Domitia, his empress-wife, standing in moonlight, her toga putrid with blood, not yet having had chance to wash off the evidence of her night's work. Taking the urn into his arms, he rocked it, hugging it. He had agreed to the abortion, yes, but *not the rest, not the rest, oh, dear little bird, not the rest.*

The Empress Domitia paced her bedchamber, thinking of her husband swaddled in darkness and furs, with the heat as high as it would go, tended by his ancient nurse Phyllis, drooling into his calda...a baby crawled back into the womb.

That had always been her trouble: men who were too weak. She had first experienced life from the shoulders of her father, the great Corbulo. That had given her a false sense of her possibilities as a woman – or, at least, of the strength of the shoulders she could ride on.

If only Domitian hadn't seen her with the blood spewed all over her robes. That bastard! It wasn't fair. He had agreed, no matter what lies he told himself now. What had he expected her to do? He had debauched the girl. He had been willing to believe she was unfaithful to him at Cybele. What he wallowed in was not grief but a parade of grief to cover his guilt. He had used her, Domitia Longina, as the instrument of his will to kill his brother's bastard, the way he had used assassins to kill Paris.

As for Julia Sabina, her little niece – she had got what she deserved. She had been kind to Julia. She had befriended her. She had generously allowed her liaison with the emperor, but the little bitch had tried to wean him from her, to squeeze her out. Domitia conjured up that mortifying image of herself lying in her own vomit at the emperor's banquet. Yes! In killing Julia she had done only what was necessary.

With a moan, Domitia slid to the floor, clasping her statue of Saturn. Again she was hearing the chant of the hag Fausta as if she were here in the room, and then that other sound – of laboured breathing. She was following that sound to the throat that made it, fitting her fingers in a collar around that throat – lightly, still experimenting with her strength and will. The flesh had been pulpy like the cheek of a very old grandmother that used to swallow her lips whenever she was forced to kiss her. Even then she might never have begun to press. Even then she might have released the throat...fled the Temple. It was only when Julia had opened her eyes and, reaching up her arms had spoken the affectionate name, that Domitia had panicked, unwilling to answer that plea to love, to be sucked in again, seduced, ensnared...then cast out.

Well! Domitia yanked herself back to present time. The thing was done, whatever its consequences. *He* had always acted quickly, decisively, to rid her of the men who were important to her. Now she had done the same with the niece and mistress. He was the worst tyrant since his hero Tiberius – all of Rome said it. He murdered by decree as easily as other men wished it, yet bore no mark. What right had he to condemn her?

145

She hated him. No, hate was far too clean a word. She despised him. How easy it had been to shape him to her will at the baths – like putting her thumb into hot wax.

Domitia smiled into the glowering face of Saturn. During her exile, she had vowed that when she got back to Rome she would seduce every man in the city. It was time to make good her boast. Right now! While the emperor was moaning over his urn, while he was weak and vulnerable. She would consult her old friend Antonius Saturninus, High Priest of Low Tastes. The Saturnalia – great Festival of Misrule – would soon be upon them. It was time she made plans.

PART III

DOMITILLA

CHAPTER ELEVEN

Roads were the triumph of Rome. They radiated outward through fifteen gates to the mountains of Spain and the pine forests of the Rhine, to the deserts of Africa and the plains of Parthi – fifty thousand miles of them, binding the empire in a web of stone. They carried wagons of wine, oil, meat and booty into Rome. They carried troops and imperial edicts out.

Maximus Marcus, newly appointed senator and assistant to the consul in charge of roads, galloped around the Servian wall, with the December air riming the jet flanks of his horse Priam. Here, happily, was crisp weather more like that of his native Como than the stingy days and glutinous nights that had sapped his energies and curdled his moods in the past month in Rome. He was not used to feeling despondent. He was not used to restless nights. He had always been able to sleep before battle with his head pillowed on his shield, or leaning on his spear. He could sleep on horseback and in gutters of mud. He could not sleep in the beds of Rome.

Perhaps it was grief. He had lost a dear friend and someone who had been like a sister...yet why should that disturb him beyond the period of mourning? He had known much of sudden death. It was the condition of his life: comrades slain in battle; his wife and son, stricken with swamp fever; his adopted family obliterated by Vesuvius; his own parents, suicides when he was nine – his father because of the onslaught of incurable illness, his mother because she felt it her duty to accompany him. What was one life more or less to the gods? To mourn too indulgently was to make too much of one's own life, one's own importance to the universe.

Marcus was aware of another emotion lurking like quagmire under his sorrow. He prodded it, a layer at a time, the way an engineer sinks piles into bog to see if there is enough firm ground to hold. He found resentment and then, under that, an obdurate fury. He was enraged at Priscus for the stupidity of what he had done. Julia had had no choice, but why had Priscus thrown his life away? What had he accomplished? At least his father had died for radical political beliefs. What had the son died for? A lampoon of the emperor's love life!

As a soldier, Marcus had been trained, under the bleakest of circumstances, to preserve his own life. Priscus had once again struck a wrecker's blow at the cornerstone of his values. But it was more than that: Marcus had opened his heart to Priscus as he had to few others. Why had Priscus thrown that love away?

Marcus urged his horse to a hard gallop, taking relief from the pound of hooves over the tough Roman road stretching before him as dauntless as the Roman will, letting the clatter fill the cavern of his head, tasting the bite of the wind. He felt a burden fall from his shoulders. As he left Rome behind, it was as if he were sluffing off the equivocations of that whole deceitful city which he had foolishly adopted as his own. Perhaps this was all he needed. Respite. To exchange Rome's clamorous rat-infested alleys for the sweep of open country; the stink of vomit and putrefying garbage for the tang of brisk air and frosty loam.

Marcus felt the blind impulse to strike north and to keep going till he reached his family estate in Como, while he still held onto his own values, his own illusions about life. After all, if all roads lead to Rome, it was equally true that all roads lead from it. Dismayed by such an irrational impulse, he concentrated on the job at hand: inspecting to see which roadside walls had crumbled; where drainage ditches were clogged; what secondary roads demonstrated, by heavy rutting, that they too should be paved; and, in each case, using the markers set every five thousand feet out from the Forum's Golden Milestone to fix location.

It was a job for which Marcus was well suited. As a student under the famous engineer Julius Frontinus, he had helped maintain the eight aqueducts that poured over 200,000,000 gallons of water into Rome each day, through 150 miles of subterranean channels, and on arches of triumph so carefully graded there was no need for pumping. As a tribune, he had often functioned as an engineer, for an axe and pick were as much a part of a legionnaire's equipment as javelin and short sword. He had constructed roads and bridges along the rough, pine-clad Rhine frontier, and he had built the machines with which Romans developed the science of war: 70-foot assault towers that could be rolled up to the walls of forts; fire-throwers that could fling flaming darts 2,000 feet; mobile catapults that hurled bagfuls of stones; giant onagers that lobbed 60-pound missiles a half-mile.

Marcus looked forward to honing his skills for civil use, for the construction of permanent roads was as exacting a craft as the setting of fine jewels. First the site had to be levelled and firmed with rammers; then the bed had to be prepared with a nine-inch layer of rubble and a six-inch layer of fine lime; then polygon blocks of lava or tufa or basalt, with their undersides carved into a cone, had to be set so their seams were invisible.

Marcus spent the whole day outside Rome, stopping every three miles to inspect the posting stations with their stables of fresh horses enabling letters to travel two hundred miles a day by horseback, twenty-five miles a day by foot. At last, he felt satisfaction in his new appointment – the dream of a lifetime fulfilled. Rome had created a mobile civilization, of which he was master. Rome had paved the world.

On re-entering the city by Porta Capena he passed the spring where the vestals drew their water. He touched the opal given to him by Cornelia, realizing, as he did so, that disturbing thoughts

151

of her were never far from his mind. Again, Marcus felt as if ground were shifting under his feet. The whole damned city of Rome was built on sewage and the Pontine marsh! Every step he took, he found another bog-hole. Flavius Clemens was right. It was time for him to remarry, to put down roots, to produce an heir...to bring some stability to his life.

After leaving Priam in the care of old Pollux at the Circus Maximus, Marcus struck out by foot for the Esquiline. He had hiked only a short distance when a runner thrust a leather tube into his hand, then sprinted away. Marcus opened it. It contained a parchment, heavy with the scent of musk, which read: "Once I gave you an amulet that brought you luck in the Circus. Now do this thing for me. Go next Friday, the last day of Saturnalia, to the Marble House of Lucius on the banks of the Tiber. Wait for my messenger by the statue of Saturn."

Marcus reread the note. What was he to make of this? Was Cornelia in trouble, or did she wish to see him as a friend? He stuffed the message back into its container, with that now-familiar feeling of impotence: Rome was a fool's game in which everyone but he knew the rules.

Castor the page crouched in cypress bushes near the spring of Egeria, wrapped in a brown cloak against the morning's chill. He was waiting for the vestal Helen to visit the well. At least, he prayed to Venus it would be Helen. Once he had spent an hour in the bushes, only to be treated to the sight of the mad hag Fausta.

Hearing the rustle of shrubbery, Castor caught his breath and exhaled slowly: Helen. She passed mere feet from him, her midnight cloak brushing the bushes where he lay. He watched her lift her arms, with their faint gilding of hairs, to the rising sun. He watched her lips press then part, releasing shivery little puffs of mist, as the vestal recited the incantation. He put his hand over the bulge in his tunic – not to arouse himself, but like a lover gallantly touching his heart. His adoration of Helen was pure, fed by Ovid's *Art of Love*, the book with which his mother had taught him to read. He did not associate such lofty sentiments with the humpings and groanings of the hairy army that thrust itself, spearman by spearman, between his mother's thighs, or with the ruttish dreams that tortured his sleep and soiled his linen.

Though Castor had never spoken to Helen, he had composed letters to her in the style of Ovid, and once he had copied out a love lyric by Catullus, which blew away before she found it. She was a luminous vision in white, of which he caught tantalizing glimpses at public events as she intoned ritual, untouchable by the prurient confusion of his thoughts.

Castor watched as Helen filled her silver buckets from the spring, almost groaning as her breasts broke against the opening of her cloak. She shouldered the silver harness and glided gracefully toward him, seeming to look right at him before floating by. He waited till her footsteps receded, then Castor uncoiled himself from the bushes, studying the path to see if it bore an imprint of her shoe, before putting his own clumsy foot there. Hurrying to the spring, he looked hungrily into the water as if he hoped to find her reflection still shimmering there. He saw only his own brooding face, with the amulet of Saturn dangling from his neck. He kissed the amulet, having concocted a romantic fantasy of its origin and dismissing completely the accidental circumstances by which he acquired it from Marcus and the empress.

By now the sun had risen. Castor had another important errand before returning to the palace: to escort his mother from the brothel in which she had worked thirteen years to a flat he had rented for her at the foot of the Aventine.

Phoebe was dressed and waiting when Castor arrived. Together they climbed from the fourth floor of the Circus brothel, with Pollux limping behind, carrying Phoebe's miserable possessions: her tinbox of white powder, her trinket box and a worn leather canister containing Ovid's *Art of Love.*

153

Though she was prevented by law from wearing the long gown of the respectable matron, Phoebe had sewn up the slit of her most conservative tunic and added a white border which she was careful to display in the opening of her new blue cloak. Her dyed black hair had been corkscrewed into an imitation of the style worn by Empress Domitia to the emperor's banquet; her pocked face was chalky with powder; the mole on her chin had been converted into a beauty mark, and she wore false eyebrows. Phoebe waved her birdwing fan, teetering on the edge of hysteria as she left the life already she pretended she had never known.

As yet there were no clients in the house. Slouched in their doorways, the bawds watched Phoebe's departure with envy, anger, curiosity, hope, under a common mask of sullen indifference. She was not a favourite. The higher she had been forced to climb in the brothel, the more airs she had assumed to cover her mortification.

The ragtag party stepped into the street opposite the Circus. By now it was drizzling. Since prostitutes were forbidden litters, Pollux grandly raised a parasol and, heads bent, they picked their way through the guttery street, clinging to their buoyant mood.

They trudged south to the labourers' quarters at the foot of the Aventine, where Castor had rented a flat in a four-storey stucco tenement identical to hundreds of others that housed ninety per cent of Rome's population in stink and squalor. On the arcade level was a flour shop and a blacksmith shop. On the next floor was a bricklayer and his family; then came Phoebe and, above her, in the bluster and stuffiness of the eaves, three bath attendants.

In renewed good cheer, Castor lifted his mother over the threshold of her new home. Through smudged selenite windows she could see a cramped courtyard with a Pan fountain. She now had a charcoal brazier for heating and cooking and a pipe for slops.

Shining with pride, Castor showed her the adjoining room where an artist, possessing more gall than talent, had attempted a pastoral scene, framed in drapings and pillars, of the illusionist style. Castor had already brought her a tin bed-couch. Next month he would buy her a new robe and a trunk to keep it in. But now it was time for him to return to the palace.

With the first tremors of fear, Phoebe listened to Castor's footsteps fade down two flights of stairs. Then, to reassure herself, she wandered around her two rooms, fluttering her birdwing fan as if showing guests the fine appointments. She admired, aloud, her new couch – the first real one she'd owned in thirteen years. She lay upon it, at first stretching luxuriously, then drawing her cloak more tightly about her thin body to counter the chill.

The pastoral scene over her head, with its cascading waters and grazing sheep, reminded her of her native village of Tivoli, just outside of Rome. She put her hand against one of the sheep, imagining she could feel the matted wool, wishing she could go home to Tivoli, but knowing she had Castor's career to think of now. The painted pillars and drapes looked as if they might topple down on her. She shoved her bed to the opposite wall and lay down again. This wall was scratched with the pronouncements of a previous tenant, who seemed to fancy himself a philosopher. She read:

"If a man spent half the time on philosophy that he did trying to get better bread from his baker, he might become a moral man."

"A god-fearing man is as hard to find as a pregnant mule."

"Never trust a mad dog, or a Jew, but if you must, choose the dog."

"Let us hope chastity has not retired from the earth."

"A prick like a stick is fit for screwing.

A prick like boiled asparagus for naught but stewing."

"A whore past her prime is like this peeling wall."

Phoebe buried her head in her cloak. Seldom had she spent a

night by herself. She could hear music from the tavern on the corner. She could not stop shivering.

Of the 159 days marked as holidays in the Roman calendar, Saturnalia was the rowdiest and randiest. From December 17 to 23, schools and businesses closed and Rome turned into one hard-drinking, high-flying brothel. On the final night, slaves, donning the tall cap of liberty, took over their masters' households. Priests of the secret cults of Cybele, Isis, and Mithra, pranced through the streets bashing cymbals and gongs, striking drums and bells, chasing Saturn's spirits of darkness from the city. Rampant youths overturned urinals, torched sheds and looted stores. Modest women turned bold in love.

Maximus Marcus threaded his way through the swarming downtown crowds to the industrial area along the wharves of the Tiber. On either side of the widening streets were warehouses for oil, flax, wool, lumber, spices, along with the gaunt storehouses – three hundred of them – containing the grain each male citizen was entitled to draw every month, ten gallons dry measure. Even here, gangs were pirating the flat-bottomed boats used to haul produce from the port of Ostia, and sailors who had broken open a keg of wine were holding a pissing contest from the riggings.

At last Marcus found the Marble House of Lucius beside a quarry in a limestone cliff. The ornamental iron gate was ajar. He went inside. Freshly cut limestone glowed eerily under a full moon, along with blocks of marble out of which figures were beginning to emerge: a scowling orator, with hand raised as if to instruct his sculptor on how to finish the job; a beetle-browed Thracian gladiator, sword unsheathed, wanting only legs to rush his opponent; generals and senators, bearing blank blobs for heads, intended with a day's chisel work to receive the features of their purchasers – or those their vanity dictated; a row of imposing statues, mass produced, to dominate a public square or forum as Emperor Domitian.

Far more compelling was a platoon of torsos with heads lopped off and names scratched from their pedestals – symbolic of the fate which had overtaken these men in life: philosophers, magistrates, actors, row upon row, to be fitted with the heads of their successors, and with the originals in a grisly pyramid nearby. Marcus turned over one severed head, then another, with the toe of his boot. Some faces were haughty, others kind, some were idealized in the Greek tradition, others showed the disfigurements of age. He recognized several with the pudgy, pretty features of Nero, and another with a freshly cut stem of...

Marcus strode off to a different part of the compound. He felt no more anger at Priscus. That had burned away. What was left was sorrow for his friend, and a deep and bruising child's hurt.

Marcus spotted the statue of Saturn just ahead – twenty feet high, in black granite, with face twisted in a leer. A seat was carved in the base. He sat on it – suspicious, alert. As seconds dripped by like drops in a waterclock, he felt he was being watched – or was that the suggestiveness of the setting? Was he the victim of a Saturnalian hoax? The more he thought about it, the less likely it seemed that the vestal Cornelia would summon him here.

Hearing a foot crunch on gravel, Marcus turned, hand on his dagger. A woman as tall as himself was undulating toward him, carrying a torch and trailing diaphanous peach robes. Though there was something familiar about her bearing, he did not recognize the powdered face under its gold eye mask, nor the waist-length blonde hair dusted in gold.

She handed Marcus a scroll on which was written: "Welcome to the Marble House of Lucius." Flourishing a red scarf, she indicated she wished to blindfold him. Marcus submitted: *When in Rome...*

Putting Marcus' hand on her waist, the guide tugged him forward with a gentle roll of her hips, upward on gravel, then through cedar and pine trees over rutted turf. They struck limestone again, and started downward.

Marcus' guide was shivering in the gusty air. Though he

offered her his scarlet mantle, she spurned it by her silence. Once she seemed lost, and when she missed her footing she choked on a very unlady-like curse. Marcus was sure they were circling back to the Marble House of Lucius. Feeling gravel under foot once more, he grinned. Suspicions confirmed.

Now Marcus' guide ordered him down on his hands and knees and pushed him into a tunnel. The limestone under his hands was mossy and cold. He could hear dripping water.

At last she removed his blindfold. Marcus discovered himself to be in a magnificent limestone cave lit with torches. Firelight shimmered over pink- and green-tinged columns that hung in clusters or thrust up from the floor. A cacophony of sound – bells, cymbals, laughter, chanting – reverberated through the tunnel.

Now hurrying toward the music, they veered around a corner and emerged into a soaring black dome hewn from the rock, spangled with reflectors imitating the constellations, and double-ringed with Corinthian columns like the natural formations.

In the midst of this ethereal beauty was a scene of shocking carnality. Naked men and women, painted ochre, white and blue, many with snakes wound around their bodies, tossed their scarlet-plumed headdresses, stamped their feet, rolled their hips and shouted obscenities to the beat of drums and cymbals as they danced around a ten-foot red-veined phallus, embedded in a black stone and encircled by two trenches – one of fire, one of blood.

As Marcus' guide joined the women banging cymbals, a slave with shaved head and oiled body led Marcus to a ring of couches and presented him with a steaming phallic cup. He sniffed, then tasted it: fortified wine, very bitter, very heady. With the aphrodisiac satyrion added?

The dancers spun, shimmied and vaulted to a faster and faster beat. Occasionally one, eyes rolled back so the whites glowed, would plunge into the trough of blood or dare the hot coals to kiss the phallus. As Marcus now knew, he was in the forbidden

Temple of Cybele – the earth goddess represented by a black stone whose eunuch priests were called Galli. Imported from the Near East, the cults of Cybele, of Mithra, of Isis, of Dionysius and of the crucified Jew were spread throughout the empire by Rome's superstitious legionnaires who became infected while fighting for the Roman way. When Marcus was an imperial agent in Judaea, and later as prefect of a legion in Egypt, he had avoided contact with the orgiastic cults, proud of being Roman and wishing to avoid contamination. It was strange that it would be here, in Rome, that he would have this experience. Stranger still that this alien mood, here in this cave, seemed to catch and counter exactly the restlessness he found just under the gilt-and-marble skin of the imperial city.

Sinewy fingers gripped his arm. His guide was beckoning him to follow her further into the limestone cliff. This time the tunnel ended at a door, like a shield, which she urged him through then closed behind him.

Now Marcus was in a cosy chamber decorated with the pelts of exotic animals and the trappings of war: shields, banners, helmets, spears. Under a canopy of peacock feathers was a leopard-skin bed lit by two torches, and lounging on the bed was a woman naked except for a gold chain tilting her breasts and an apron of pearls. Her jet hair was clasped with rubies, like drops of blood, while her nails, her lips, her eyebrows, her nipples, were gilded. The torchlight licked her olive skin, shooting tongues of flame through her hair, so it seemed she too was on fire. She laughed at his bewilderment. "Welcome, Marcus. You look astonished. Have you never seen a naked woman before?"

Recovering aplomb, Marcus replied: "Naked women I have seen by the hundreds. Never before have I seen a naked empress."

"Saturnalia is full of surprises, which is why Saturn is my patron. His boldly changing moods please me." She arched a golden brow. "But surely you expected this liaison after receiving both my amulet and my invitation?"

Marcus suddenly remembered the garnet charm which the

empress had sent to him before October Horse, and which he had passed to Castor, then deliberately blocked out of consciousness.

Sipping her phallic goblet, the empress smiled in intimacy. "From the moment we met at the emperor's banquet, I made up my mind I would have you." Fondling her breasts she taunted him. "Last time we met you seemed to worry about cuckolding your Commander-in-Chief. Do such thoughts trouble you now, Maximus Marcus?"

Watching her tease her breasts, he replied: "I have learned many things since coming to Rome, not many of them honest."

"Good! Then I hardly need remind you that tonight, in celebration of the Festival of Perversity, Hermes the dwarf sits as emperor on the throne, while my husband grovels at his feet. Many will say Rome has not been so well ruled in fourteen years." Holding up her goblet she said: "I hope this time your neck won't be the stiffest part of you."

Depositing her drink on a drum stretched with zebra skin, the empress rose from her bed and began to pulse and sway, at first slowly and sensuously to the music that throbbed through the chamber, then becoming more abandoned as she advanced toward Marcus and retreated, rotating her hips, sending shudders around her belly and shivers up her thighs. Marcus could feel the beat of the drums in his veins, the froth of wine through his head, the pump of blood to his groin, deeply aroused but holding back, mesmerized by the strangeness of the situation and the empress' aggressive sensuality. At last she flung herself onto the bed. Flickering her tongue, fixing Marcus with mocking eyes, she parted the pearl apron and slowly spread her legs wide. Stroking her thighs, entirely caught up with herself, jerking her head and moaning, she opened herself, layer by layer, as if peeling a ripe fig. With one gold finger she touched then caressed then pierced her sex. With the other hand she reached for the phallic goblet...

Ripping off his tunic, Marcus strode to the bed. He twined his tongue with hers and with a groan lowered himself between her thighs. As he began the ardent rhythm of love, the empress countered with an astonishing gripping, shimmying motion that sent shivers shooting up his spine. Never in the brothels of the world had he enjoyed a woman so wanton, so greedy, so alive. As she raked his back with her nails, snarling, spitting, drawing blood, she fought him with her arms while embracing him with her thighs. At first Marcus tried only to subdue her, then he fought back with all the frustration he had felt since encountering the duplicity of Rome, pinning her and driving deeply in a way that would have been brutal if she had not desired it, needed it, revelled in it, must have it, feeling all of his tensions collect in some high place like an eagle spreading its wings. As he moved to climax, the empress took his lower lip between her teeth and bit through it.

Marcus exploded in a shattering spasm like a volcano erupting in a closed space, an implosion sending out shockwave after shockwave, reverberating through her flesh, meeting resistance, then rippling back and back. After an unknown passage of time, he came to in a sprawl of sweat and semen, still tasting blood, with the empress smiling sweetly down upon him. In her hand she held Cornelia's amulet. "What is this? Do you come into one woman's bed wearing the charms of another? Don't deny it. I recognize this. I know where you got it."

Before he could reply, she tossed the amulet aside, as if she had already forgotten it. Becoming playful, good-humoured, childlike, she cleaned him as a mother cat, relishing the taste of him. Indeed, there was no part of the male body she didn't adore. She cherished the back of him as much as the front, his nether lips as much as those of his face, working gently, insistently, expertly, to open them, sending out swirl after giddy swirl of sensation, and then with an astonishing flutter, sodomizing him with her tongue. Marcus had never before felt every part of himself to be so ardently acceptable, so acceptably male.

The empress' special taste, it seemed, was for imitating the copulations of African beasts. Using their pelts as costumes,

161

she demonstrated their mating habits, about which she seemed remarkably informed. Afterwards, laughing at his exhaustion, she said: "Even in your fatigue you smell of leather and sweat, not of silk and perfume and dust and cobwebs like some of the aging eunuchs who still try to pump the beds of the palace." Then she tore the amulet from around his neck and would not give it back. "Can you deny me this trinket? Would you treat a bawd so stingily?"

Several hours later Marcus and the empress returned to the main chamber of the Temple of Cybele, with Marcus feeling as if he had just restocked the herds of Africa and conquered the throne of Rome. As the empress joined the celebrants, Marcus retired to one of the couches, savouring a steaming cup. The dancers were still swirling around the giant phallus embedded in its black stone, to the clash of cymbals and the beat of drums, but more of them had leapt into the trough of blood. More were tempting the inner ring of fire to kiss the phallus. Some were using their teeth to rip off the heads of the snakes wrapped around their bodies, drinking the blood and lashing themselves with the twitching bodies.

Marcus knew the legend of Cybele only too well: The earth goddess finds a mortal child in the reeds. Calling him Attis, she nurtures him to manhood, then takes him as her consort. After breaking his vow of fidelity to Cybele with a wood nymph, Attis chops off his genitals in remorse. Though he dies of his wounds, Cybele restores him to life after three days of mourning, during which worshippers drink his blood.

Devotees of Cybele liked to celebrate their festival over seven days. It became clear to Marcus what stage they were now reaching. Draining the bitter liquid in his goblet, he fortified himself.

Some of the male dancers had already drawn knives from their plumed helmets. Others had acquired axes. Tossing their bodies to even more demented rhythms – now hanging on the precipice of madness – two hacked off their genitals in imitation of the sacrifice of Attis. Others followed. Kissing their severed parts, they hurled them onto the black stone to impregnate the womb of the earth goddess Cybele. In final burst of ecstasy, these newly created Galli dove into the trough of blood, then flung themselves on the red-veined phallus, some falling face-down on the carpet of fire, others bleeding to death at its base. Marcus felt the room glisten and throb about him like a freshly plucked heart.

The drums ceased.

Marcus lay back on his scarlet couch. His guide was standing over him in the tattered remains of her gown, still masked. As he stared groggily up at her, she stretched herself flat upon him, long blonde hair falling over his shoulders. During their long kiss, Marcus felt the rise of a sex that was not his own. He peeled off the blonde wig, yanked off the gold mask: Antonius Saturninus!

CHAPTER TWELVE

The Senate House was con-
structed by Julius Caesar at a time when Rome was evolving
from republic to empire and the Senate was being shorn of its
power. It was grandly restored by Domitian, who reduced the
Senate to a new low in prestige by his vain-glorious behaviour.
Consisting of 600 members – some by birth, others by appointment, all with property qualifications of one million sesterces –
the Senate convened twice monthly and by request of the
emperor.

This special session, which Domitian called for January 15,
was to be his first public appearance since the death of his niece
Julia Sabina. All manner of rumours circulated as to his mental
and physical capacity. He had not presented gifts to his chief
officials at New Year's, as was customary, and the only intimates he allowed in his bedchamber were Captain Geta of the
Imperial Guard, and prosecutor Messalinus, who daily fed him
poisoned gossip.

Wearing broad-striped toga and red senatorial shoes, Maximus
Marcus approached the bronze doors of the Senate for his first
session as assistant to the consul. Since the emperor's reclusive
behaviour had brought out the curious, Marcus had to jostle for
space on the small, noisy portico.

The hall itself was 150 feet long and 60 feet wide, with a

magnificent polychromatic marble floor, and a lofty timbered ceiling designed to dwarf the individual to the glory of the whole. Its focal point was a statue of Victory captured during the Punic wars. Before her outstretched arms bearing a crown was the throne for the emperor, and a line of curule chairs for the consul and other senior officials. Running the length of the hall were three marble tiers – the first with chairs was for former consuls, criminal investigators, ministers in charge of roads, water supplies, archives and so forth; the second two tiers with carved benches were for the rank and file.

The side door opened. Consul Clemens entered, preceded by twelve lictors. As the Senate rose, Clemens lit incense rods and sprinkled wine on the altar of Victory. Now the emperor marched in, preceded by his twelve lictors and wearing – to everyone's astonishment – triumphal robes.

Consul Clemens demanded: "Bring in the chickens."

Two augurs, carrying ivory staffs, set before the assembly a cage containing three barnyard fowl that had been starved for a day. Clemens scattered grain in easy reach. The chickens were slow to eat it – a poor augury. Clemens turned to the emperor who, with a curt nod, accepted the auspices.

Clemens intoned: "Since there is no evil sight or sound, let our affairs begin."

Though Domitian usually insisted on speaking first, this time he waived the privilege. Clemens asked: "Who among you wishes to begin?"

There was a prickly silence as the senators peeked and peered from one to another. Though many resented the emperor's usurping the right to speak first, they liked it even less when he teased them by refusing, for then they were likely to stumble into ill-advised opposition. Also, since the emperor had called this session, the business was his own.

Maximus Marcus had intended to thank the emperor for his new appointment, as courtesy demanded. However, the sight of Domitian – his cuckold! – in triumphal robes paralyzed his tongue. He endured an uncomfortable three minutes by the

165

waterclock till the emperor indicated that he himself would speak. Leaning forward with a benign smile – in itself a worse augury than the sluggish chickens – he addressed the assembly.

"Consuls and senators, since you are so shy, I will fill the empty air. My legislation is in two parts. The first has to do with" – he pulled a sober face under which lurked a quirky smile "– myself. I come before you as a man condemned. By whom? By myself. For what? For the crime of laxity. Laxity in allowing such things as friendship and a soft heart to interfere with my judgement. Those qualities – while attractive in a private citizen – are flaws in an emperor when they get in the way of the *execution* of his duties." The emperor's emphasis on the word *execution* drew a groan from the Senate, who had seen too many of its members executed for treason.

Allowing a touch of irony, he continued: "I hear by your response you can do nothing but agree with me, so now I stand condemned by you as by myself. Yes, I confess it. I've been lax." A sinister smile began to break loose. "How can I correct this flaw? First I must remove myself from temptation by allowing you to elevate me beyond the reach of too human a compassion. I propose, therefore, that I be addressed by the title *Lord and God*, so that every time I hear myself named I am reminded of my imperial responsibility.

"Since you have already voted to me the honorary title of Germanicus, after that beloved general whom I am said to resemble, I allow you to mark this honour by changing the month of November to that of Germanicus, and the month of October to that of Domitianus.

"I also propose that you vote to me an increase of lictors from twelve to twenty-four, and that in recognition of my military triumphs, my imperial fasces be permanently wreathed in laurels.

"I further propose that henceforth all statues of me be only of silver or gold, and that those already standing be gilded in private subscription raised by yourselves."

Maximus Marcus stole covert glances at his fellows. Consul

Clemens pushed back in his chair, nervously tugging his silver beard. Ex-consul Cocceius Nerva – leader of the opposition to the extent there was any – leaned forward, his dark brows knit under a billow of white hair. Pontifex Piso clicked his false teeth and worried his ear lobe. Antonius Saturninus reddened to the colour of early sunrise. Prosecutor Messalinus tapped his ivory cane. Captain Geta patted his dagger. Others mopped sweat, shook their heads or twisted in their chairs – most seething with indignation.

Thoroughly pleased with himself, the emperor continued: "Considering the love you all bear me, my next suggestions will be more to your liking, since they concern the protection of my person. I propose you vote a supplement of four goldpieces to every member of my praetorian guard, and a pay increase of one-third for our noble legionnaires. I also propose that all persons entering my divine presence be required to strip before my praetorians for search."

Almost choking with laughter, the emperor continued. "Having dealt with my own shortcomings, I can proceed with easy conscience to the shortcomings of others and –" here, his voice hardened "– especially those who hide improprieties behind the broad stripe, for the higher the rank, the ranker the offence.

"As the divine Augustus knew, the cornerstone of Roman morality is the family. How can we guarantee world peace when our enemies breed like flies while we commit genocide through our plummeting birthrate? Do you suppose, senators, that the cause of our fruitlessness may be that Rome's noblest feed their seed into their strumpets! The backsides of pretty boys! Other men's wives! Instead of into the wombs of their wives? Do you suppose it's because the good matrons so flagrantly mix seed in their wombs that the fruit must be destroyed because its ancestry is so wretchedly in doubt?

"I will say it again: It is the duty of Romans to breed soldiers! Therefore, fines for citizens with less than three children will be doubled, and anyone over sixteen who remains unmarried for over a year will also be fined. The estates of those who die without direct heirs will be confiscated along with the property of those judged guilty of adultery, with informers receiving one-third as a reward.

"The practice of abortion must now be considered a capital crime. Those found guilty of having or performing an abortion will be sewn into a sack with a dog, a cock and a snake, and thrown into the Tiber. All poets or playwrights who write about adultery or abortion will have their hands cut off, and those who perform such works shall have their tongues cut out."

Having whipped himself up into a fine rage, Domitian thrashed about as he continued. "I must now address you as your High Priest, for I find myself appalled by the irreligious life of this city. Though it has been Rome's policy to welcome the gods of other nations, we must not tolerate those cults which undermine Roman virtue. I'm informed that the filthy practice of Cybele –" and here, unmistakably, a glare at Antonius Saturninus – "has sunk so low that even to attend such a cere-mony must be judged an act of crapulence punishable by death, for those who lust after an unworthy object become the thing depraved.

"As regards that other bothersome cult – that of the Jews – I offer this warning: Those born Jews, bearing on their organ the mark of their sect, who pay the tax levied on them by my divine brother, will remain under Roman protection. Those born Jews who try to avoid payment, I condemn to property confiscation. Those born Jews and calling themselves Christians, who wor-ship one god above all others, those I condemn to death."

The emperor turned to Consul Clemens. "Those Roman citi-zens, and especially those with lictors, who harbour such persons, I charge with conspiracy, for which the penalty is death." His voice softened to a hiss, so it seemed that prosecutor Messalinus might be speaking through the emperor's mouth as, in fact, he was. "Those born Romans who cross the line into membership in such a cult, I charge with treason, for which the penalty is execution in the old way which, if your memory fails, means thrusting your head in a wood fork, being flogged to death with

168

sticks, and having your body thrown down the Stairs of Mourning to be a plaything of contempt for the mob."

Lounging back in his chair, he continued. "Those are my few proposals." He looked the length of the Senate. "I trust you will accept them in full, without the need for picayune debate?"

Consul Clemens rose and spoke courageously. "I open the floor for debate." There was an embarrassed hush, during which the senators studied their feet, the floor, the ceiling, everything but the consul or each other. Clemens tolerated the silence as long as he dared. "Since there be no debate, please divide yourselves on the floor according to ayes and nays."

Prosecutor Messalinus and Captain Geta strode to the right of the Senate. Others took their time doing so. After much coy foot-shuffling, over nine-tenths of the Senate approved the emperor's legislation in full, while a handful – including Marcus, Saturninus and Nerva – voted against it or abstained.

The emperor fixed the dissenters with a sour eye, and – without bothering to thank the rest – swept from the Senate.

Domitian felt buoyant most of the trip back to the palace. It had amused him, after weeks of solitude, to taunt and debase the Senate. To play emperor. He imagined the turbulent scene he had left behind – how the fools would mill about, blustering with outrage, trying to save face by pretending the crow he'd just fed them was pheasant. He remembered how Saturninus' powdered cheeks had flushed a pretty pink, with his dainty nostrils flaring. How Pontifex Piso had worried his ear lobe and clicked his false teeth. How Cocceius Nerva's black brows had flapped like bat wings. How his grave cousin Clemens had tugged at his beard as if it were a tit that might save him, looking even graver...grave, indeed. Why not grave? It was time the old ditherer visited the Shades; and if he kept fooling around with the Jew-God's chosen people, he, Imperator Domitianus Caesar Augustus, would be happy to advance Charon his passage money. Of a sudden, Domitian's thoughts seized on Maximus Marcus, his consul's new assistant in charge of roads. Was he

169

too gauche to understand he should thank his emperor for his patronage, or was he still sulking over Priscus' death? He would have to watch the young man. When innocents started to think, they were more trouble than philosophers.

As Domitian's litter jogged up the steps of the Palatine, he felt his bravado fray. It was colder than winter in Gaul. Shivering despite the chest protector, woollen gaiters and four winter tunics he wore under his triumphal robes, he was forced to note a galling crack in his omnipotence: No matter how he changed the names of the months, he could not force spring to come one day sooner.

It felt no better in the palace, with its frosty marble walls too much like a mausoleum. After demanding to be taken to his bedchamber, Domitian huddled beside his brazier, nursing hot brine, dreading the melancholia he knew would soon devour his high mood. The pocked face of Captain Geta, whom he now kept in constant attendance, did nothing to liven the chamber, while his page Castor, though decorative, stared dreamily into space, almost as blank-eyed as Parthenius. Was the young man smitten? Domitian studied his moony face. Well, he knew the outward signs, though it had been a long and sterile time since he had felt those inner stirrings. Suddenly morose, he kicked the dwarf from his bed. "Get up, you hairy whore's cunt! Bring me bawds, music, dancing girls!"

Startled into action, the dwarf loped from the room, to return minutes later with a motley retinue that soon turned the bedchamber into a circus of bizarre talents: an armless juggler, a parrot that recited Catullus, a musician who plucked the lyre with his toes, a baboon wearing a toga.

Nudging the dwarf, Domitian asked in a loud derisive voice: "Who does Grumpy the baboon remind you of?" He answered himself: "My cousin Clemens, of the dour complexion."

The baboon lifted his toga and began playing with his genitals. "The perfect image!" howled Domitian. "We could switch him with my cousin and even Domitilla wouldn't know the difference."

170

"Put him in her bed, my Lord and God, and she might think herself far better served."

"We could replace every senator in Rome. They're prettier, they're franker about their vices, and they're not so talkative, though I'll grant you there were quite a few who had trouble finding their tongues between their legs this morning." Domitian roared at his own joke, then smirked at Geta and Castor, attempting to snare them with his laughter. Needing sharper stimulation to keep his depression at bay, he again kicked the dwarf. "What has your lecher's eye picked for me in the brothels and slave markets of Rome?"

"Many delights, Caesar!" exclaimed Hermes, flashing his yellow smile. "They wait outside your door."

"Fetch them, whoremaster!" He clapped his hands. "Parthenius, show these jugglers the exit."

Hermes ushered in twelve scantily clad young girls of assorted colours and shapes, which he displayed one by one to Domitian. "This is Deliah of Medi, whose tongue would cause a marble cock to rise. This is Cynthia of Athens – see, my Lord, *three* breasts, each as exquisite as a breadfruit." Prancing before the emperor, the girls simulated the perversities for which they were trained.

Domitian turned to Castor, whom he had been observing out of the corner of his eye. "Page! Which piece of flesh would you choose?"

Surprised to hear himself addressed, Castor glanced toward the bawds, too much like the ones he had known in the streets of Rome. He thought with adoration of the vestal Helen and grimaced. "None, my emperor."

"What? Don't you like bitches? Are you happier then with the company of pretty boys like yourself?"

"No, my emperor." With the superiority of his one pure love, he added: "I am a virgin."

"A virgin!" Domitian snorted. "No wonder the birthrate tumbles. How old are you?"

"Fourteen, my Lord."

"You aren't mutilated, are you?"

"No, my emperor." Again that fateful touch of pride. "I am saving myself."

Now Domitian was thoroughly intrigued. "For what?"

"For love," replied Castor. The prettiness of the lad's speech, inspired by the lyrics of Ovid, lit him with the shy glow of innocence.

Looking from his fresh angular face to the bawds so shamelessly over-advertising their wares filled Domitian with a nausea for the flab and stink of women's flesh. "Take this mess away," he ordered Hermes. "Next time you shop for an emperor, don't used your own gross tastes as a guide."

As Hermes hustled the girls from the room, Domitian smiled upon his page. "Come here." He pointed to a spot in front of his couch. The boy stepped gracefully forward.

Domitian's eyes roved from the full lips to the slim hips and sturdy thighs. The boy was even comelier than he had noticed. "Come closer." Castor did so. Taking hold of his chin, Domitian gently forced open Castor's jaws. He examined the cavern of the throat, the pulpy tongue, the white teeth. "You have a strong fresh mouth."

Castor clamped his jaw. Domitian slid his hand down the boy's tunic. Reeling from the emperor's grasp, Castor darted behind the statue of Minerva. His resistance aroused desire. Pointing to the boy, Domitian ordered Captain Geta: "Bring him here to me."

For the first time, Geta hesitated before executing a command. Though few knew it, Geta was a prudish man. He was also a pious man. At age seven he had seen the Gauls rape his mother, then disembowel his father before sexually abusing him. He had taken a shine to the naive page, and felt a powerful resistance to wrenching him from the skirts of Minerva.

Thinking his captain had not understood, Domitian repeated the command. Obedience won out over scruples. Geta dragged Castor to the place designated by the emperor's finger.

"Now," ordered Domitian, "hold him there."

172

Clamping his burly arms around the boy, Geta did as instructed, while Domitian fondled Castor's sex through his tunic, taking his time about it, enjoying the boy's fear, as stimulating as an aphrodisiac, with the look of distaste on Geta's face as an unexpected bonus. Casually he reached under Castor's livery and drew out his genitals. He caressed them in his palm, the balls heavy in their slippery bags, the shaft collapsed. Terrorized, Castor made token resistance.

Domitian fumbled under his pillow. Still holding the boy by the testicles with one hand, he withdrew a knife with the other. Flashing the blade for the boy to see, he teased him with his power. Now it took all of Geta's strength to hold Castor. Amused, the emperor lay the cold blade against the boy's warm shaft, seeing the flesh jerk convulsively. He rubbed the blunt edge of the blade back and forth, and then, flicking the blade, nicked the boy's sex. Blood spurted. Dipping his finger, the emperor smeared it on the boy's lips. "A virgin's blood...so, now you have lost your maidenhead. Be shy no longer. Take me in your mouth and treat me reverently or –" he tapped the knife – "you will never treat a woman in your life."

Digging into his own loincloth, Domitian withdrew his genitals, in full erection, and displayed them for the boy to admire. "You see? I've already done half your work. You have a chance to show your love for your emperor to which few dare aspire."

He ordered Geta to bring the boy down between his legs. By snapping his knee in Castor's back, Geta propelled him forward. On command, Geta also pried open the boy's jaws and, grabbing him by the scalp, initiated a rhythm that Castor was forced to take up. Swaying on the edge of his bed, Domitian felt heat rise from his crotch in rich pulsations. Eyes closed, he swooned, drawing the boy's head with him, kneading his face into his groin, feeling the fleshy lips complete their work, groaning as the colours of red and yellow and purple and blue intensified in his head, feeling himself engorged in flesh, finally pitching backward in a spasm of warmth and wet.

The emperor lay upon his couch, feeling the fusion of flesh to flesh begin to dissolve, groping his way back to his own separate reality, aware now of the stickiness of fur against his back, a kink in his toe, an ache in his neck. Pushing the boy from his crotch, he sat up on the bed, rearranged the silky hair about his head, and crossed his legs. The boy still crouched before him, head bowed, with Geta hovering behind him. Castor's misery and full cheeks did not please the emperor, now detached from the former object of his lust. He ordered the cringing boy: "Swallow! The seed of Augustus must not go unattended."

Castor gagged, then heaved, as Hermes nimbly caught the regurgitation in a chamberpot.

The emperor watched in anger, feeling drained rather than satisfied, flushed empty instead of clean, for which he could find only one scapegoat: this boy and his lack of love. "All the world knows the importance of Caesar's seed. Who are you to place so low a value on it?"

Eager to recoup lost prestige, Hermes forced the boy's face into the chamberpot.

"That's right. Let him lap like a dog, if he knows no better way. The boy is stubborn in his simple-mindedness." The emperor's eyebrows rose with his voice. "Or perhaps I have been using him against his talents? A man has two ends, the way a horse does." Hoisting the boy's tunic, he probed with his index finger. "This one's as tight as a vestal in a court of eunuchs."

The dwarf produced a pot of Egyptian lotus ointment. The emperor dipped his finger. "Release your muscles." The boy tried but was still in shock.

The emperor anointed the hilt of his ivory knife, then thrust it into the boy's buttocks. Screaming, the boy jerked forward. Withdrawing the knife smeared with blood and excrement, the emperor tossed it to the dwarf, while the boy flung himself at the emperor's feet, pleading for mercy.

"Mercy?" snapped the emperor. "What do you think you have just felt but my mercy? I used the blunt end of my knife instead of the point, which I use on the flies."

He yanked his feet from Castor's moist clutch. The thing

174

which had attracted him – the boy's innocence – was destroyed, unlike that rare innocence of his niece Julia, which resisted every debauch like a pearl shedding dung.

He said to Hermes: "This one has broken too far. He's dogs' meat. I give him to you for your pleasure."

Hermes covered the emperor's feet with slobbery kisses, a thing not displeasing to Domitian, for what was that but a dog behaving like a dog? He leaned back with the first twitchings of a smile. The morning had had its diversions, but he needed one more act of outrage to sustain him against the depression he knew was waiting to smother him.

"Hermes, the chamberpot."

The dwarf retrieved it.

Setting his buttocks upon it, Domitian defecated long and lovingly into it, while musing aloud: "Why should one effusion of the emperor receive special consideration and not the rest?" He pondered that, along with its codicil. Whom should he favour?

That decision was not difficult.

The next one was trickier. Who should his messenger be? He would like to have sent Geta, but dared not take that risk. Beckoning to the dwarf, he commanded: "Deliver this, by ass, to the residence of Antonius Saturninus, with the compliments of the emperor." Domitian fell back laughing. A good day to be an emperor.

The family of Antonius Saturninus was not only one of the wealthiest but among the most aristocratic in Rome. His villa on the Viminal was one of the grandest and the most eccentric. It was a palace of pleasure and illusion for which Saturninus and his ancestors had plundered the world over the centuries. There were no straight lines in Saturninus' villa, only curved space, and nothing was as it seemed: secret panels, mirrored walls, doors that opened into blank walls. His frescoes were painted to look like mosaics; his mosaics – at 150 squares to the inch – to look like frescoes.

Most of Saturninus' life and all of his entertainments were devoted to celebration of the senses. In his banquet room – the largest in Rome – the world's finest chefs gorged his guests on dishes gleaned from generations of gourmandizing. While musicians hidden in the floors and walls turned the whole into a vibrating music box, sliding panels showered them with perfume and the riper smells of his orgiastic pleasures. The addition of swirling colours and flashing lights had driven more than one guest from ecstasy into insanity.

Saturninus was a true decadent: a man who caroused by night and slept while decent men worked. He had a physician for every orifice of the body, and another who spent his time inventing formulas to preserve his virility, youth and beauty. There was no fashion Saturninus failed to pursue, and even his statues had marble toupees so he could change their hairstyles. It was said in Rome that no one had such exquisite bad taste.

Having learned libertinism at his mother's knee, Saturninus had preached it in the court of Nero, where Titus was his chief lover. A brilliant singer, he teased Nero unmercifully by devising ridiculous exercises to improve the emperor's weak voice: gargling with urine; the constant use of emetics to lower his weight; sleeping with his legs tied to the ceiling to rush blood to his voice box.

It was also Saturninus who added a pragmatic edge to the emperor's pleasures. He suggested that Christians be dipped in pitch and resin and tied to stakes as slow-burning torches for the emperor's night games. It was his idea that slaves too old to work be taught swimming in the emperor's tank of piranhas.

Saturninus' tastes had led to his joking appointment as consul's assistant in charge of sewers, which, in turn, led to one of the more useful features of his villa: It was connected by sewage tunnels to three buildings below the Viminal, all of which he owned – a brothel, a paupers' crematorium and a shop with whips and manacles for slave control (or miscellaneous amusements). The tunnels ended in a chamber under Saturninus' villa, which could also be entered by his bedroom. It was typical of his arch humour that the concealed tunnel entrance was painted to look like a tunnel entrance, and the concealed entrance to his bedroom had been painted to look like a bedroom door.

When the emperor's "gift" arrived, Saturninus had been pleasuring himself with a eunuch, to whom he was engaged. Thinking that the emperor wished to make amends, he tore open the elegant wrappings, saw the contents and flew into a rage, smashing everything he could find bearing the emperor's image. After an hour, he collapsed in hysterical laughter: The perversity of Domitian's gesture appealed to his warped humour. Even Nero had never hit upon so direct and simple an insult. He was glad to have the tension unequivocally settled between them.

Taking up his gold stylus, Saturninus wrote on wafer-thin ivory tablets: "To the Imperator Domitianus Caesar Augustus, Lord and God: Your thought-provoking gift arrived while I was taking my bath. What did I do to deserve such a personal mark of favour? I urge you to share your imperial bounty with others, so that I may not be destroyed by the jealousies brought on by such groaning patronage."

On posting the letter, Saturninus called a secret meeting in his subterranean chamber. Unable to resist the seduction of his own perversity, he arranged for the abstemious Clemens to arrive through his brothel; the moralist Nerva, through his slave-torture shop; the glutton Clodianus, through his paupers' crematorium. Domitian's newly appointed senator in charge of roads, he routed through Rome's cruddiest sewers, beginning with the latrine at the southeast corner of the Forum which, despite its pretty marble seats with dolphin trim, stank like what it was – the entrance to Rome's most malodorous cesstrench.

Though Saturninus had put away his sexual toys for the occasion – the whips and wigs of flaxen German hair, the jewelled spurs and bridles – there was little he could do about the erotic murals painted by one of his lovers using them both as models. Against this backdrop, he waited in languorous elegance for his guests to arrive. Last – as he expected – was Maximus Marcus, stinking of dead rats and sewer slime. He wrinkled his nose as he handed Marcus a perfumed towel, also making a suggestive moue with his lips.

Even then, the sober faces of his guests brought out the prankster in Saturninus. Setting the gold chamberpot iced and covered before them as if it were a rare wine he would serve later, he balefully intoned: "Gentlemen, forgive me if I dispense with the civilities and plunge to the gut of the matter. Though I count you more my peers than my friends, we have this thing in common: all of us sat in the Senate – within the walls that have echoed with the eloquence of Julius Caesar, the earthy wisdom of Vespasian, the lyricism of our beloved Titus – and we have been forced to listen to the ravings of one who proclaims himself our Lord and God. We have heard this person, who calls himself a god and who publishes victories on battlefields he has never seen, demand his fasces be permanently bound in laurels. When have you ever seen our triumphant general on a horse, except on the colossal statue which we are supposed to gild at our own expense?"

Saturninus struck a provocative pose. "We have heard this god-general raise the pay of both his praetorians and the legionnaires, with all the dangerous implications of that. Where do you suppose he plans to get the money? He has already told us: through the execution of anyone whose wealth he desires on trumped-up charges of adultery, abstinence, debauchery or religious treason. I tell you, friends – for I believe in our common distress we will soon become that – Rome has another Caligula at its throat."

Saturninus heaved back into his silken cushions, anticipating the centrepiece of his speech. "Do I see skepticism on the faces around me? The emperor is just out of sorts, you say? He is still grieving over his niece, you say? Well, gentlemen, let me show you what the emperor sent to me, Senator Antonius Saturninus, ex-consul with his brother Titus, and former governor of Upper Germany." Saturninus swept the cover from the chamberpot. His guests gasped. "Fasces for him, feces for me! Smile, laugh, turn away, but what Domitian makes bold to send me today, he will send to you tomorrow. The emperor – though a god – has more bowel movements than senators, and even now one that began as a fine dish of sow's udders may have your name on it."

Observing faces stamped with disgust, Saturninus pushed the chamberpot from him, and signalled a slave to remove it. "That is but a joke of madness. The real peril comes next, with his attacks on our property and our persons. Did you enjoy being denounced for moral laxity by a man who seduced the daughter of our beloved Titus, then tried to brand us with the guilt of her death by his laws against adultery and abortion? Who turns one blind eye – his own – on himself, and two – belonging to prosecutor Messalinus – on the rest of us?"

He pointed to Clemens. "Domitian proclaimed your death this morning as clearly as if he spoke your sentence." He inclined his head toward Nerva. "You too dangle on the thin thread of sufferance, which would be severed today if you had enough property to make it worthwhile." He nodded at Clodianus. "Your wealth proclaims your death. It's said the emperor only accepts your dinner invitations to check the growing value of your silverplate." He grinned at Marcus. "Think of Paris, his crime and fate."

Saturninus again addressed the group. "I for one know when the period of tolerance has passed. The next time I see our god's excrement, I hope he lies steeped in it. Tonight I leave for Upper Germany, where four legions await, faithful to me. We shall be joined by an equal number of Chatti. Together we shall conquer Germany. Then, gathering dissident legions, we shall march against an emperor too mad, too cowardly, to leave Rome. We shall swoop down upon the imperial city. In the name of Titus, whom we all love, we shall assassinate this upstart, who so often plotted against him.

"All that I will do. I ask only that you don't oppose me. Well? Will you put your seal on this?"

Clemens, Nerva, Clodianus and Marcus stared at their host. Gone was the fop who pranced in diaphanous robes, blowing perfumed kisses. Before them, hard as steel, sat a victorious general. All had agreed with his assessment of Domitian; but what better could they expect from a man who revelled in his reputation for harlotry, who sought to seduce them to battle in this shameless playground? What guarantee did they have that as soon as he was enthroned he would not turn his sword against them or drown all Rome in his lechery?

Each set about to pick his way through Saturninus' swampy challenge to high ground, and none more skeptically than Marcus, with the stink of Rome's sewers still clinging to his flesh.

Castor was ill for a week after his abuse by the emperor, while Hermes solicitously waited on him, tempting him with delicacies smuggled from the emperor's own table. Castor's illness took the form of delirium, in which he relived every encounter he had witnessed or imagined between his mother and the men who paid or forced their way into her cubicle: a sailor with hair all over his back; a masked man in a cloak, who watched her do things with his female companion; men who robbed her; men who beat her; the brothel owner who made the bawds perform repellent acts for him with goats and snakes.

On the eighth day, Castor's fever broke. He faked illness till nightfall, then tiptoed past the sleeping dwarf and, wrapping himself in his cloak-of-many-patches, stole from the palace through the tunnel Nero had built to the Forum.

At the foot of the Palatine, he began to run and did not stop till he reached his mother's flat. This very night they would strike out along the Appian way for the posting inn near Tivoli, where his grandfather was a stablehand.

Climbing the two flights to his mother's flat, Castor let himself in her door, feeling pride that he had at least done this much for her. As he was lighting a lamp from her brazier, he heard laughter. Was he mistaken? No, there it was again. He had already noticed smudges of white powder on the floor. Now he saw that they led to his mother's bedchamber. Following the trail, he listened in mounting panic outside her door. He heard the laughter once again. Kicking open the door, Castor thrust the lamp inside, holding it high. A large pair of sweaty hams pumped over his mother lying spread-eagled beneath. Seeing Castor, she screamed and snatched for her robe. The owner of the hams, whom Castor recognized as the baker from the shop below, scrambled to his feet, then charged past like a bee-stung bull.

Castor's hand closed over something on his mother's trunk: her powder tin. As she cringed before him, her face smeared with kohl, her eyes full of the same terror with which he had cowered before the emperor, he hurled the tin into her face. She ducked. It smashed into the meadows of the fresco, spattering her with gold coins and powder. Picking up the baker's belt, he slashed it across her breasts, leaving red welts. Then, flinging the belt from him as if it had suddenly turned into a snake, he fled down the steps from his mother's flat, feeling rage, then despair, then rage again.

A bitter wind blew through the narrow street, rattling shutters, flapping signs and flinging fistfuls of sand into Castor's face. He spotted the baker's sign and, leaping high, seized it with both hands, yanked it from its leather hinges, broke it over his knee hurling the pieces into the doorway. He tore off his patched cloak that now looked like what it had always been – a rag made of whore's tunics. Ripping it into a dozen pieces, he pitched them after the broken sign. His eyes burned. Moaning with the pain, he rubbed them with his fists, unable to scrape away the filthy picture scorched into them.

Castor was even with the corner fountain. Plunging his head into the frigid water, he felt relief for an instant, then the burning once more. Again he plunged his head, sobbing now, not daring to take his fists from his eyes, knowing – if he did – what he would see: *their* eyes – the eyes of all the other men who had abused her – staring back at him.

181

CHAPTER THIRTEEN

The number of troops immediately available for the defence of the imperial city was 20,000. This included police and firemen, the riot control squad and the emperor's praetorians. Rome also had an army of thirty legions, for a force of 150,000, plus an equal number of auxiliaries. Most of these troops were deployed along the northern and eastern frontiers.

The rebel Saturninus' challenge came to Domitian from Mainz, in Upper Germany, where he had fled: "Imperator Lucius Antonius Saturninus Caesar Augustus to Our Lord and God of the Chamberpot:

"I address greetings from my winter capital in Mainz. I shall arrive in Rome next month at the head of the Roman Army. I trust you will vacate the city in good order."

In hysteria, Domitian commanded Maximus Norbanus, governor of Lower Germany, to march against Saturninus with Rome's four German legions and whatever auxiliaries he could muster. He also commanded Trajan, his legate in Spain, to cross the Pyrenees with his Spanish legion. He himself prepared to march from Rome at the head of his praetorians, with Maximus Marcus as second-in-command.

Marcus received his battle orders with relief. His growing disillusionment had caused him to want to quit the city as soon as possible. He was also under pressure from the emperor's wife, who showered him with love tokens, messages and invitations, which he refused – at first with courtesy, then in exasperation which matched hers. Now that the spell of Saturnalia was no longer upon him, he knew the political realities of a liaison with the empress.

Marcus looked forward to the campaign against Saturninus as a way of renewing faith in old Roman virtues: Days spent in the saddle at the head of his troops. Route marches covering twenty-four miles in five hours, with each man carrying a javelin, a short sword, helmet, cuirass and five days' food. Let the Trojans build their horses; the formula by which Rome had brought peace to the world remained the same: to have more troops, better trained, equipped and paid than the enemy; to have the best roads and supply lines; to value courage over genius, opportunity over courage, and siege over surprise; to see war as a natural part of life and the first condition of peace; to fight where possible in a three-line phalanx behind a solid line of spearmen; to drive the main body of one's own forces against the enemy's weakest spot, and never to make peace until after victory.

It was said that Rome's legionnaires fought as if their weapons were permanently attached to their hands. The praetorians were paid twice as much. Marcus hoped they would prove half so good.

Marcus arranged to meet Cornelia at the spring of Egeria before firstlight. As he entered the pavilion guarding the spring, she greeted him formally in case of spies but also to establish for both of them the basis of this rendezvous: as chief of Vesta and a senator concerned for Rome. "Hello, Maximus Marcus. You're at your prayers early this morning."

Matching her caution, he replied: "Yes. I'm leaving Rome. I've come to ask you to make sacrifices for me."

Hanging her buckets on their hook, Cornelia wrapped her white wool mantle more tightly around her, already aware through the treachery of her body of his power upon her. She preceded him down the back stairs to a bench buried in birch and hawthorn trees and, perching on one end, gestured toward the other.

He leaned toward her. "May I trust to your discretion and goodwill?"

Threatened by his closeness and the stir of moist air from his lips, she inclined her head away. "You have both...as always."

"The emperor has commanded me to march with him against Saturninus."

"Oh." She tensed. The rumours were true then. Rome was in rebellion. "When do you leave?"

"Tomorrow morning at cockcrow."

"So soon?" Her glance caught his, then skittered away. "Does that plan suit you?"

"It's the best of bad choices." He grimaced. "These days to love Rome isn't necessarily to love her Caesar. To choose between Saturninus and our emperor is like choosing between a donkey and a jackass!"

She might have been offended by his disrespect for the emperor; instead, she felt stirred by his passion for Rome. "Can Saturninus persuade his legions to support him?"

"Not from loyalty. He's seized the retirement savings of two of them at the bank in Mainz, and won't release the money until the battle has been won."

"What about our other two German legions?"

"They stand with the emperor – and why not? As troops they're better housed and fed than half of Rome. The emperor's always been shrewd there. Saturninus is counting on the Chatti to join him." He snorted in disgust. "This is to be a war of the purse, not of honour: goldpiece against goldpiece, with foreigners holding the balance."

"And this city? Who is in charge here?"

"Clemens for administration. Geta for defence."

She felt a ray of hope. "Consul Clemens is still in favour then?"

Marcus' response was grudging. "For now. While convenient. The emperor knows a loyal heart. Because Clemens was publicly denounced, he feels doubly bound to stand by the emperor so as not to seem to act from self-interest."

"As you stand firm by him?"

"As firm as I can on shifting sand." Frowning, he reconfirmed his years of military training. "He *is* my Commander-in-Chief."

They sat side by side, the exchange of vital information over, neither looking at each other nor speaking nor touching, yet beginning to relax, to enjoy each other's companionship despite the morning's chill. A freak sleet storm had frozen golden birch leaves and red hawthorn berries to their branches in icy casings that made them tinkle like chimes in the wind. Aroused by the beauty and the imminence of danger, Cornelia turned to Marcus and, breeching the barrier she had so carefully erected, smiled. "Of course you have my prayers. Is there anything else I can do for you?"

Hearing the intimacy in her voice, catching the vulnerability of her eyes, Marcus launched a speech he had rehearsed without daring to believe he would deliver it. "I see peril ahead for Rome. And great confusion. I know better than to ask a vestal to abandon her post any more than I would ask a general to abandon his. But for my peace of mind, I must speak out." Hesitating now, he let the silence pile up between them, waiting till at last she raised her eyes from her hands knotted in her lap. "Do you see a time and a place ahead for us, no matter how difficult or how far?"

Cornelia felt her throat constrict. She opened her mouth to protest, to chide him and herself with a recitation of her duty. Instead, she said: "The term of a vestal is thirty years."

"When did you become a vestal?"

"When I was six." She added in a rush: "I am bound for eleven years more."

He calculated: "When you're thirty-six, I'll be forty-four." A jubilant smile lit his face. "As I grow older I've noticed time goes faster. That's a trick I resented till now. Now I see that as a gift."

She shook her head. "You don't understand. I love Vesta. I love Rome. It's my *privilege* to serve." Belatedly, she rebuked him. "It's on the quality of this service, as much as on her armies, that the fate of Rome rests."

"But in eleven years –"

"No!" Again she shook her head, this time so vigorously she almost dislodged her headscarf. "I won't leave the Temple. Not even then. Few do." Flustered, she turned away, repeating in a whisper: "You don't understand. It's hard after this kind of life to live another kind. Let Fausta be a witness to that. Six months after her retirement she was back at the Temple in the state you see her now."

"Fausta is a witness only to Fausta."

He tried to impel her to look at him, but she would not be caught in that trap again. He reached for her hand, but she snatched it away. Her voice flat, she said: "Such unions...of the sort you suggest...are always ill-fated."

"Always?"

"Almost always."

"*Almost.* Then there is a chance?"

Gathering her mantle around her, she huddled on the edge of the bench, so that only the edge of her profile showed. Part of him wished to take her in his arms, to warm her, to comfort her. Another part – perhaps the kinder – knew he should turn away. Choosing each word carefully, he said: "If there were another life...and a person who loved you to share it...would that life ever seem desirable to you?"

His question hung between them, each syllable in its own puff of mist, a permanent part of the landscape like the birch leaves and hawthorn berries. Her hands ceased to tremble; her shoulders straightened; her mantle – no longer clutched at the neck – fell in graceful folds. As she turned to confront him, Marcus prepared for the cool affirmation of her devotion to Vesta, her duty.

Cornelia was smiling. Tears filled her eyes. She said in a voice that sounded like the chiming of the leaves: "Such a thing would seem...the miracle for which the first of my life was lived."

Feeling the rise of exultation, Marcus moved to embrace her, but she shrank back, her hands between them, warding him off. "No, Marcus. Please. No more." Sliding off the end of the bench, she darted toward the fountain. He strode past her, caught her by the wrist, swung her around. They gazed at each other, scarcely breathing, only an arm's length away, but neither daring to move closer, knowing the consequences, the danger. He dropped her wrist. They continued to stare, unable to close the gap yet unwilling to pull away. Cornelia gasped, a stricken look on her face. Spinning around, she called toward the pavilion: "Is anyone there?" She wheeled back to Marcus. "Did you hear a noise?"

He shook his head. "Just the wind chiming the trees. A pretty sound."

Trembling, she backed away from him. Understanding her fear, not wishing to damage their fragile bond, Marcus placed his hand upon his heart in farewell.

"May the gods go with you, Marcus." She added, with a fierceness that surprised them both, "I wish I could!"

Fixing her image in his mind, white and flame against the backdrop of gold leaves and red berries, he strode down the path and disappeared through the cypress bushes.

Cornelia climbed the steps of the pavilion, legs shaky, on the verge of tears but too frightened to cry, not daring to look at the statue of Apollo, still rubbing her wrist where he had clasped it, holding off recriminations. Anxious to get away from this dangerous place, she hastened to fill her buckets. She stared. They weren't on their hook. She cast about, looking for them – by the fountain, among the pillars. Catching a glint of silver by the toe of Apollo she scooped them up in relief. They seemed undamaged. Could they have been blown there? Was that the sound she had heard? A more ominous thought struck her: was this a sign sent to warn her?

187

Quivering so she could hardly stand up, Cornelia supported herself against one of the pillars of the Temple, feeling the first strong rebukes of conscience. Why had she agreed to meet Maximus Marcus here alone when she knew her vulnerability? Their mutual concern for Rome was hardly reason enough. In fact, it was because of the rebels' threat to the empire that she must especially guard her purity so no fault in the Temple would anger the gods against Rome. Clasping her bulla, she thought of the risk she had taken against her duty. Closing her eyes, she vowed to cast his image from her, to exorcise his words. She must never see Maximus Marcus alone again.

Shored up by the strength of her resolve, Cornelia dipped her buckets in the spring, shouldered them, hurried down the path, away from the pavilion, already warming herself with a vision of the fire of Vesta.

Someone stole from behind the statue of Apollo: a vestal dragging a duplicate set of buckets. She stood with hands on broad hips, peering up the path where Cornelia had just disappeared.

Diana had forgotten the chief vestal had said she would fetch the water this morning. She had arrived at the spring – late as usual – and found the other buckets. As she was examining them, she had glimpsed Cornelia and hidden behind the statue.

Diana grinned. She knew now why the chief vestal had offered to replace her this morning.

Maximus Marcus hiked from the spring of Egeria to the Esquiline where he was to have a farewell lunch with Consul Clemens and Domitilla. There were still a few clients in the vestibule to whom Clemens' steward was doling out money. Clemens himself stood at his courtyard fountain, his back to Marcus, feeding his fish. It shocked Marcus to see how stoop-shouldered and frail-looking the older man had become.

Hearing Marcus' feet on the paving, Clemens greeted him without turning. "You're leaving Rome tomorrow, my son?"

"Yes. We begin our march at firstlight." Marcus stood behind the consul. "My horse and gear are already at the Praetorian Camp. I'll be staying there tonight."

Nodding, Clemens drew Marcus closer to his fish tank. "Come share with me one of my keenest pleasures." He chuckled. "Do you know what I think of when I tend my fish tank? I think how much watching my fish is like watching the shenanigans of my fellows in the Senate. There are clown fish. Fish who skulk in the reeds. Fish who puff themselves up when others are near. Fish who nip off the fins of prettier fish. Fish who hunt in packs. Fish who swallow whole. Fish who dart away. Fish who spend their lives hiding in seashells." Crumbling the last of the bread into the water, he added: "I'll miss you, Marcus. I enjoy your company. I also envy your chance to fight an enemy who calls himself an enemy with weapons you can see."

Marcus nodded. "I admit I'm glad to be going. I'm also relieved that the emperor leaves his fish tank in good hands."

The two men strolled arm in arm into the dining room where Domitilla had set the table with her husband's prize bronze plate.

"You've been tending your tank without your cloak again, Clemens," she said in gentle rebuke.

"True, Domitilla, true. My pleasure warms me against the chill you notice on my behalf."

She smiled. "You forget the fishes' water is artificially heated. Your blood is not."

As Marcus and Clemens reclined on the cedar dining couch, Domitilla drew the brazier closer, then wrapped her husband's legs in a brown cloak. After twenty-five years of marriage, the interplay between them remained polite, even formal, in the old Republican tradition, with affection expressed in consideration for each other's health, a fond compliment, a tolerant glance that held after the words had been spoken. Clemens knew it was not a style that had come easily to Domitilla – a pretty young girl of twenty, married off for political reasons to a cousin fifteen years older and one head shorter. At first she had chafed under what she took to be his austere and uncaring ways, but

189

time and maturity had forged a link between them so unalloyed with selfishness that now she often experienced his moods before he was aware of them, and even had prophetic dreams.

In honour of the occasion, Domitilla joined Marcus and her husband on their dining couch while her maid Berenice, who was pregnant with Stephanus' child, brought them cheese, black bread, mullet with pinenut sauce and calda. As Domitilla served her husband, she said: "I hope, my dear, that when you're at the palace you'll dine with consideration for your stomach."

Laughing, he teased her. "Yes, and don't forget my liver and my bowels for they never forget me. I imagine the emperor's staff will be able to gear down to my modest needs though with nothing like the pleasure your cooking gives me."

"Will you be back for dinner this evening?"

"Yes, if the gods are willing." His face clouded. "And every evening for a few months more if the emperor is willing." He put down his fish knife and took Domitilla's hand. "I want you to know, my beloved wife – and you, Marcus, as my witness – that I have had the best life with the best woman a man could ever have." He laced his fingers through Domitilla's. "I was born old...a fussy old man with fussy ways. My uncle Vespasian was said to look as if he were striving to pass a peach pit whenever he tried to express his emotions. I seem to have inherited the Flavian beauty. I sometimes wonder how much happier you might have been if you had married someone... more adventurous?"

Domitilla squeezed his hand. "I've had the best of lives too, with the best of men. I wouldn't change one minute of it." She studied his face. "You seem troubled this morning. Is there something wrong?"

Patting his stomach, Clemens smiled wryly. "Just indigestion, I hope. But I think that in the times I smell approaching we should be prepared for the mildest attack of biliousness becoming fatal."

Domitilla put down her bread roll and looked from Clemens to Marcus. "Are either of you hiding something from me?"

"No more than the gods hide from me. I'm not much in their confidence, though I warm the throne from which my cousin stepped onto Olympus." He turned to Marcus. "It's not the most comfortable seat, though it does have this advantage: I don't have to get up at cockcrow each morning and rush up to the Palatine to kiss myself." Picking up his knife, he shook it by the bone handle. "If Saturninus returns victorious, he'll have a vengeful eye for the support we didn't give him. If the emperor triumphs, as is my guess, well...he'll be no happier for the insult he's had from one of senatorial rank. The rest of us will be guilty by association – especially if our rebel was unkind enough to keep a record of those who met with him in secret."

"That's a problem worth thinking about," agreed Marcus, pausing as he cut himself some cheese. "Be sure of one thing – if I can, I'll destroy Saturninus' correspondence."

They finished their lunch in silence. Berenice cleared the table, then set out fresh fruit in alabaster bowls. Picking up her knife, Domitilla began slicing an apple for her husband. "There *is* something important I want to discuss, Clemens, though I dread it. No, don't go, Marcus. We may need your opinion. There's more at stake here than one man, for Clemens is more than just my husband: he's the mainstay of Rome."

Clemens laughed, pleased though embarrassed. "If you want Marcus and I to see clearly with our heads you had better set a good example. You see me now with a wife's loving eye."

Placing the apple in front of her husband, Domitilla began: "In the past year I've listened to Berenice talk about her Christianity – at first as an indulgent mistress, then with an interest I can no longer deny is my own. Berenice's faith has become my faith. The doctrine of love, of repentance, of eternal life, has become dearer to me than the gods of Rome or the philosophies of Greece. At first this didn't matter – one faith among the many tolerated by Rome. Now I find this belief dangerously out of favour. I don't care for myself, but I'm sick with guilt when I see my joy become the dagger at your throat. Clemens, the time may come when – for your own safety and your duty to Rome –

you must renounce me as your wife. I couldn't live with myself if –"

"No, Domitilla, no." He pushed his plate away with one hand and touched the other to her lips. "Say no more. You are my life. Our fates are bound like the fate of a two-headed calf. I can't accept your dead Jew. He seems too much like Cybele's Attis tricked out in Jewish dress. But what a small thing to all we do share! Do you think the danger you bring to me is worse than the danger I bring to myself and you? We are one, my love, and if our last dream of growing old together at Como is not to be, let it be known that we have had a life that others only dream of. All that the gods had to give, and more."

Too overcome to go on, Clemens rose from his dining couch. Domitilla stood as if to join him, but he waved her back. "No, my dear, please. I must collect myself. Stay with Marcus. He's going further for much longer. I'm just going to the palace."

Still with eyes averted, he embraced the younger man. "Take care, my son." He trudged to the door of the courtyard, stood for a few moments with his back toward them, then turned. "Now that we are discussing...this sort of thing, there *is* one question more. Do you think, Domitilla, it's time we wrote to Epictetus in Greece and asked him to prepare for the abduction of our sons?"

She considered this doleful matter, her face unchanging. At last she nodded. "Yes, Clemens, I do."

He bowed his head. "It may be in the weeks to come that our sons must cease to be Roman." The consul walked stiffly across the courtyard, trailing the brown cloak, as Marcus and Domitilla gazed after him. To steady her hands, Domitilla picked up a robe she was mending for Berenice to take to her Jewish family. Matching its dark-green colour with a length of yarn, she hunted for a needle in her sewing kit.

"Consul Clemens has been like a father to me," observed Marcus, still affected by the scene he had just witnessed. "And you, Domitilla – you have all the virtues I've ever admired in a woman: beauty, serenity, loyalty, warmth."

192

Domitilla glanced up from the bronze needle she was threading, and smiled. "I think, Marcus, you credit me with the qualities I wish I had rather than the ones I possess. I *am* content. I'm married to the best man in the world but I didn't always have the sense to know that." An impish expression, quite out of keeping with their conversation, crossed her face. "When my father betrothed me to Clemens, there was no unhappier bride in all of Rome. You see, I was madly in love with a charioteer. I used to hang around the Circus, dressing his statues with flowers, hoping to catch a glimpse of him, always in terror he would be killed, yet planning how extravagantly I would mourn him."

"*You*, Domitilla?" queried Marcus, puzzled both by her confession and her abrupt change of mood. "You and a charioteer? I can't imagine such a thing."

Domitilla chuckled, pleased to have shocked a young man who seemed to feel, through the privileges of age and sex, that he had sole possession of all the vices. "It's true. Poor Clemens had no idea what a ninny he was marrying. And things didn't easily improve between us," she confided, weaving her yarn through the frayed wool. "Since all I understood of love was this obsession I had for my charioteer, I believed my shy husband must have a mistress on whom he lavished the passions I never saw. One evening when he hadn't come home by midnight, I ran to my father in a fit of jealousy and demanded a divorce. My father packed me off to the Temple of Juno Viriplaca, where husbands and wives can speak their hearts and vent their tempers without penalty. Then he sent Clemens to get me, telling him not to come back till we were reconciled.

"Well, it seems by then I had become fonder of my husband than I knew," exclaimed Domitilla, warming to her story. "I berated him so tearfully, there under the protection of the Goddess of Difficult Lovers, that he broke through his reserve and swore he loved me with all his heart and that he always would. After that, whenever I've felt less than satisfied with my lot in life, I've returned to Juno Viriplaca, and sometimes Clemens and I return together."

Domitilla tied then broke her yarn. "That's a story I've never told anyone before, but I have a special reason for dredging it up for you today." Though her voice remained casual, an odd light gleamed in her eye as she explained: "The man I once loved with such abandon – can you guess who he might be?"

Frowning, Marcus shook his head. "I can't even imagine. I haven't been in Rome long enough to know all your old friends."

Folding her hands tidily over her mending, Domitilla announced: "The man I loved is the man you are going to fight tomorrow."

"What? Antonius Saturninus?"

She nodded, wearing the smile of fond indulgence Marcus thought reserved for Clemens. "Saturninus wasn't always the way you see him today. Spoiled, yes. Too rash. Too rich. Too handsome but –" Seeing Marcus' discomfort, she broke off. "Don't judge me, Marcus. There's not much logic in the human heart, as I think some day you'll discover."

Remembering the last woman to whom he spoke of love, Marcus nodded with gruffness. "Though Saturninus is my enemy, I'll respect him for your sake and treat him with dignity. For whatever good you once saw in the man." He stood up. "Now I must be on my way."

They strolled together to the vestibule, with his arm around her waist, feeling close in both age and folly. Domitilla was glad she had spoken out after twenty-five years of silent loyalty... that she had paid her respects to her own past even if it meant trading in some of Marcus' admiration for his understanding.

As Marcus started down the Esquiline, she wandered back to her room and, kneeling at her Christian altar, said a prayer both for Clemens and Marcus, with a furtive postscript for Saturninus. Then, feeling light of heart and head, she picked two bouquets of daffodils from the indoor garden she nurtured as solicitously as Clemens his fish. One was for the altar of Juno Viriplaca. The other – though she did not know it yet – would be laid by a broken statue outside the Circus Maximus.

194

CHAPTER FOURTEEN

Emperor Domitian galloped off, with Maximus Marcus by his side, in the vanguard of his splendid 9,000-man praetorian corps, heading northeast to the Adriatic Sea. It had been twelve years since he had last left Rome to make war in response to sneak attacks by the Chatti, who surged across the Rhine to burn and massacre Roman forts. Pretending to be taking a census in Gaul, Domitian had collected four legions at Mainz, plus a detachment of British legionnaires. During two years' fierce campaigning, he had laid bare the hiding places of the Chatti, and pushed back the frontier with 120 miles of forts and watchtowers.

Now, as Domitian listened to the thud of praetorian boots on the paving stones of the Flaminian Way, he believed what he longed for was to recapture the thrill of conquest. After a day on horseback, he began to suspect that what he would first have to recapture was his youth. He had never liked exercise except under the goad of proving himself to his father, so that at forty-four he was badly out of condition. By the time he reached Rimini on the coast, the clamour of his tramping, brawling, galloping troops, undulating behind him like a scarlet-and-gold dragon's tail, had given him a migraine. He switched from horseback to carriage and – to the dismay of Maximus Marcus, who thrived on the rigours of the journey – took some of the trip by litter.

At Rimini the troops veered northwest along the Aemilian Way, straight as a spear into the heart of the enemy. Now the muted, wind-blasted sweeps and scallops of the Apennine foothills gave way to the icy peaks and tumbling valleys of the Alps which were in turn overtaken by the gloomy pine forests of the Rhine.

In the first romantic flush of the campaign, Domitian had intended to eat the coarse bread, wheat porridge, salt pork and sour wine cut with vinegar, which was the fare of the ordinary soldier: to be a general in the warrior tradition of his father Vespasian. However, the further he got from Rome, the louder the wind howled, the fiercer the blizzards blew, and the more despondent he became.

The stone roads of Rome turned into the plank roads with which Augustus had netted these hinterlands for the Roman Empire. Rome's civilizing influence also seemed to end at the same time. Now Domitian's litter-bearers waded through waist-high snowdrifts to an abandoned earth fort Domitian's troops had built twelve years earlier. They pitched camp for one night and then – when Domitian refused to budge – for another and another.

Regaining his optimism, the emperor would strut along the stave walls of the fort, swirling his fur cape as elegantly as if he were pacing the galleries of his palace, deploying troops into the forest to catch game birds for his dinner. Soon, however, the sight of all that dense, dead, drifting snow seemed too much like the desolate landscape he carried inside himself. He retreated to his pine-log quarters in the centre of the complex, where he slouched, heaped in furs with a brazier burning between his legs, so that it quickly became a rude jest to reply to any inquiry about the emperor: "He's in his bed fucking Vulcan."

During the interminable nights, the emperor's isolation, which had begun with his estrangement from Domitia and escalated with the death of Julia, took more desperate hold. Now he was heard to address the shadows, calling them by his father's name, alternately demanding praise for his virtues and forgive-

196

ness for his sins, which he deemed to be only those of a head-strong youth with too large a heart.

He also persuaded himself that the howling of the wind was the chant the Chatti used to prepare themselves for battle – a harsh, intermittent roaring, created by using their shields as amplifiers. His officers came to understand that when he asked for news of the battle, he meant the one he had fought here twelve years before. Always they reported outstanding success, and he was generous in his promise of decoration and booty.

The one thing which nailed Domitian to present time was his hatred of the rebel Antonius Saturninus. As Titus' lover, Saturninus became heir to all the vicious jealousy Domitian had not dared show against his brother. Now the emperor invested as many hours as he used to spend skewering flies inventing tortures he would inflict upon Saturninus: castration with heated wires, eyeballs plucked out by his own hands, spikes driven through his body at one-inch intervals, burial in a tub of excrement. Added to every dispatch which he sent to Maximus Norbanus, governor of Lower Germany, was the postscript: "Deliver to me Antonius Saturninus ALIVE."

After a week's delay, a delegation of tribunes approached Marcus on behalf of their disgruntled troops. They wanted him to present to Domitian a note, allegedly from Maximus Norbanus, stating that Saturninus had mustered the Chatti and was overwhelming his army. By now Marcus had given up all hope that he would ever again see the emperor in sane and courageous command of his troops. Still, such an act was treasonous. After much brooding he agreed to take part in the scheme. Right and wrong did not stand out in such stark relief after six months in Rome.

Marcus presented the note to Domitian as he reclined on a fur couch by his brazier, eating pheasant stuffed with pinenuts. The emperor read it, crumpled it, tossed it into the flames, then looked at Marcus as if to inquire why he was still standing there.

"Will we be breaking camp tomorrow?" ventured Marcus.

Domitian wiped his hands on a perfumed square. "Not till

spring. Not till spring." He added sardonically: "The auspices from my dinner pheasant advise against it."

Marcus scanned the emperor's face. Was he baiting him or could he actually be so callous? "What about Norbanus?"

Domitian's only answer was a shrug.

"Is he to be sacrificed then?"

"That's your term for it," replied Domitian, picking his teeth with a sliver of bone. "If he had been doing a proper job as governor, the Chatti wouldn't have rebelled."

Becoming devious in the manner he despised, Marcus asked: "What about all your plans for Saturninus? Is he to be spared to grow in strength?"

The emperor thought about that.

"Perhaps if I could sprint ahead with half the troops, I could capture him for your triumph," urged Marcus.

Domitian cocked his head. "Permission granted. But take only two thousand men, and none of the heavy equipment." He grinned. "What if this note is a forgery? What if Saturninus is waiting in the bushes to attack me?"

Commander Maximus Marcus set off next morning at the head of a cavalry of 2,000 picked men – northward, down the frozen Rhine. Though he was chagrined at leading so few against Saturninus' superior forces, the emperor's irrationality made that the best and only choice. As for the lack of heavy equipment, that proved a boon. The German winter had been a severe one, striated with freak mild spells so that the ice was fretted with air pockets. The praetorians, unencumbered, flew swift as Valkyries down the river.

Far from finding the landscape bleak, Marcus – bred on the alpine slopes of Como – rejoiced in the crunch of hooves on the wind-dried snow, the icy cascades that hung from the lip of precipices, the snow's subtle mottlings of pink and purple and blue. Occasionally they passed a farm or an enclosure of log cabins where blonde savages in furs and leather breeches peeked out at them. Some of these seemed deserted – a bad sign since it probably meant the Chatti were massing further downriver.

Toward evening on the second day, Marcus' force was attacked by a cavalry that swooped down from an anonymous pine knoll on the left bank of the river. Behind him, on the opposite shore, jutted a promontory that would provide cover. About to order retreat, Marcus had a sudden vivid recollection: the October Horse race, with Saturninus, all blue and glittering silver, whipping his black horse up from outside and behind, while his Blue Faction partner crushed Marcus from the inside.

On impulse, Marcus signalled a charge. His instincts proved sound. Only 1,000 men blocked him in front, whereas a force three times that size – led by Saturninus himself – waited behind to ambush. Though Marcus' praetorians were outnumbered two to one, they easily held their own against Saturninus' rebels, coerced into fighting by the theft of their pension fund, and now denied the showy victory Saturninus had promised. Despite their commander's own fierce and spectacular courage, they fled into the forests – no doubt to regroup for attack further downriver.

Marcus pitched camp in the traditional manner of the marching legion: inside a square palisade, with every tent in the same spot as the night before. He inspected the icy battlefield, gory with blood – all of it, he reminded himself, Roman blood. The severed hands still clasping their swords were Roman hands. The gashed heads were Roman heads. Marcus had never before fought his own countrymen. Instead of absorbing Rome's shame, as the kinder earth would do, this foreign river displayed it in rank and steamy piles. Unwilling to add to its measure, Marcus ordered no distinction be made in treating the wounded. All the rebels who would renew their oath of loyalty were welcomed and, indeed, it was discovered that some of Saturninus' soldiers had faked injuries to change sides. On questioning these, Marcus learned that Saturninus was encamped in a permanent fort a half day's journey down the river. A force of

Chatti was assembling on the right bank preparatory to joining him, while Maximus Norbanus and his troops were at least two days' journey north.

Marcus and his troops set off at dawn, this time picking their way along the forested shore – partly to maintain cover, partly because a rise in temperature made him cautious of the ice. They pitched camp during late afternoon, in pine forests near Saturninus' fort – ironically, one Marcus had constructed twelve years before, that crowned a hill overlooking a plain spotted with stumps, and a broad sweep of the Rhine. The twenty-foot stave walls were topped with siege terraces, providing protection for spearmen. From its corner tower, Saturninus impudently flew the imperial banner.

All day Marcus' troops had seen evidence of the massing of the Chatti on the right bank of the river – unbridgeable here because of the width, thus a natural frontier except in winter. His scouts warned him the Chatti were planning to cross that night.

Marcus knew the Chatti. They were fierce, war-loving giants who weren't allowed to part their hair till they had killed their first foe, and who wouldn't stop fighting till they had tortured and killed every one of his men. They were savages who worshipped Mercury, to whom they sacrificed prisoners. Their women accompanied them to battle to cheer them on to victory, but also to jeer them to suicide if their gashes were too few.

Marcus' scouts estimated them at five thousand, while Saturninus was said to hold his fort with an equal force. Bitterly Marcus thought of the seven thousand praetorians Domitian held in check upstream. Though his own two thousand men would certainly be slaughtered that night when the Chatti surged across the river, he entertained no thought of ordering a retreat. If they could delay Saturninus by at least a day, there was a good chance Maximus Norbanus, advancing with his ten thousand men, could destroy the rebels before they gained momentum. Otherwise, Saturninus and his auxiliaries would swoop down upon Domitian and his demoralized men as a prelude to mobilizing the whole of the Rhine and Danube into the steamroller that Saturninus had bragged would crush Rome.

Anticipating a long and tragic night, Marcus retired to his tent to compose his mind before battle. He could see Saturninus' rebels preparing the great war machines with which they would hurl flaming darts and stones upon his all but defenceless men should they attempt to scale the hill. He could hear the Chatti battle chant – high-pitched and eerie – from across the Rhine, where they too mobilized. Apparently his own men were to be crushed between Roman science and primitive butchery.

As Marcus tossed on his cot, the Chatti battle chant seemed to reverberate through his tent. He remembered falling asleep twelve years ago to that same chilling sound, but then it was with a young man's confidence that he would survive, since the world was incapable of continuing without him. Now he no longer felt that invincibility: that had ended for him with the meaningless death of Helvidius Priscus. He no longer felt the invincibility of Rome. He had seen too much of her soft under-belly. With surprise, Marcus realized he didn't mind dying so long as his death counted for something. He still had enough vanity for that.

As he drifted off to sleep, it seemed to Marcus that the Chatti chant increased in shrillness and frequency till it was a single whine piercing like a hot wire through his skull. He remembered the tales the older legionnaires told about the ancient German gods, and especially the Valkyrie who howled and screeched as they hovered over the battlefield deciding which warriors to choose for death. From their pitch and resonance, the Chatti foretold the outcome of battle.

Passing into deep sleep, Marcus dreamt the nightmare he had had several times since Priscus' death. Once again the play-wright was at the Odeum mocking the emperor in word and gesture. Once again Geta rushed the stage, but this time when he grabbed Priscus by the offending tongue, it began to shriek and wail in the same strident tones as the Chatti, only sharper and shriller, so that it burned through Geta's hands. Dropping the tongue, Geta fell bellowing to his knees, his fingers stuck in his ears. The emperor too was writhing in agony in the royal box, his eardrums spouting blood. Now all the spectators collapsed before the howling tongue, pleading for mercy. Except they were no longer Romans. They were Chatti, in furs and leather breeches, their long blonde hair streaked with blood.

Marcus awoke with a jolt. So vivid was his dream that he had to focus on his armour, then his tent flap to assure himself he was awake. He could hear the Chatti across the river, but not half so discordantly as he had imagined. Had the wind changed or had his fears amplified the sound?

Getting up from bed, Marcus strode down to the riverbank where his men were diligently preparing fortifications. The wind *had* changed direction. He grinned. A far-fetched plan was forming in his mind that made him wonder if he were as mad as the emperor.

It was nearing sunset on this sombre winter's day. Assembling his tribunes outside his tent, he addressed them with more confidence than he felt. "Men, take heart. I know these Chatti. There are none braver once they have begun to fight, but none more fearful of joining battle in case they prove themselves cowards. Don't be discouraged by the numbers against us. Remember we are Romans with the backing of civilization. Let us use our brains against the superstition that savagery breeds. At nightfall let's move down to the river and, holding our shields before our mouths as amplifiers, we'll take advantage of the turn in the wind to set up such a counter-roar that our enemy will fear us to be ten times their number and supernatural to boot. Hear me, men, and use your throats with the same vigour you use your swords, for no man is more overwhelmed than when boldly topped by his own choice of lies."

Though Marcus' tribunes were skeptical, even this pantomime of defence seemed better than cringing in the dark waiting to have their throats slit. They cheered their commander and vowed to follow him wherever the fates should lead.

By now a light fog was floating in wispy fingers up the river.

As a cloudy, moonless night settled uneasily upon them, Marcus ordered his troops down to the shore. The Chatti chant was building to its climax when they would break off and swarm across the ice. At its shrillest pitch, Marcus lit a torch – the signal for his own men to step in front of their fortifications to begin an answering clamour. What started as a desultory chorus built to a hooting, howling crescendo as Marcus' troops discovered a release from their frustrations: Far better to be Valkyrie calling down death upon the Chatti than Romans marked for slaughter with friendly armies idle to the north and south of them.

Riding up and down the ranks, Marcus struck with boot and sword and shield all those who mocked his orders. He commanded his tribunes to do the same until the men – apparently overtaken by the same fanaticism Marcus had witnessed at the rites of Cybele – needed no more urging. Even when fog made a sneak attack probable, they continued to create such a hullabaloo without seeking cover, that Marcus didn't know whether to praise their courage or to rue the closeness of savagery to the civilized man.

When dawn revealed itself as a ruby claw through the thinning fog, the throats of Marcus' troops were raw but unslit. No Chatti had crossed the river. More importantly, none would. A gash, like black lightning, split the Rhine. The ice had broken. Spring – even in this god-forsaken country – had begun. Jubilant, the praetorians saluted themselves by clanking their swords on their shields. Incited by their bloodless victory, the boldest wished to rush the fort, but Marcus ordered them to withdraw to their camp in the pine forests, knowing their best tactic was delay.

When Saturninus learned of his opponent's successful ruse, he took to his ramparts, in his scarlet cape, exposing himself to every danger as he tried to provoke Marcus to attack. Without the Chatti's support, he knew he had to defeat the emperor before the arrival of Maximus Norbanus and his ten thousand men.

Saturninus' first stratagem was to send one thousand troops

down onto the plain, hoping to lure Marcus with easy game. When Marcus refused to budge from the forest – despite the eagerness of his men, grown cocky with a belief in their own immortality – Saturninus led a cavalry of two thousand down the far side of the hill, in a wide sweep to encircle the enemy. Though Marcus could have retreated to safety, his intention – as Saturninus had guessed – was to sacrifice his own force to stop the rebellion. After waiting till Saturninus' men were farthest from the fort, Marcus ordered a charge. With a savage cry, his cavalry dashed from their pine cover onto the plain, to begin the slaughter of the legionnaires used as bait.

For two hours they killed in the ratio of three to one, till they felt the tightening of Saturninus' noose. Now Marcus' men were falling in equal number. As Saturninus' cavalry forced them within range of his spearmen, the tide of battle turned against them. All that remained was for Saturninus' men to butcher them in a rush from the fort.

At this critical point, a trumpet blast was heard as standard-bearers crested a northern ridge: Commander Maximus Norbanus of Lower Germany was within an hour's march. Marcus' trumpeters blasted *Hail to the Golden Eagle* while his cavalry, cheered by this promise of victory, fought with renewed energy. It was now Saturninus' men who faced annihilation for a cause they had been forced to adopt. Many galloped off into the forest. To prevent mass desertion, Saturninus kept to the rear with a few chosen men. Then he ordered his soldiers to leave off fighting and dash for the fort.

Less than an hour later, Commander Maximus Marcus greeted Commander Maximus Norbanus – a stocky, scar-faced veteran – at the northern edge of the battlefield where his own wounded were being attended. The new troops pitched camp in a ring around Saturninus' hilltop fort, and criers called upon their fellow Romans to lay down their arms. Trumpeters even played *Victory* as if the battle were won.

Again Saturninus could be glimpsed on his ramparts urging on his troops. Such efforts were useless. His men could see how staggering the odds were against them. As the sun set, they lowered Saturninus' purple banner from its mast. A white flag was raised. The troops surrounding the fort gave a triumphant shout as they dotted the plain like tree stumps.

At last the door of the palisade creaked open. Commander Antonius Saturninus, impeccable in gilt helmet and scarlet cape, strolled to the lip of the hill, followed by a page carrying an axe on a purple cushion. Tossing his head like a stag with golden horns against the reddening sky, he started leisurely down the hill toward Commander Maximus Marcus, followed by the shivering page.

Dismounting, Marcus strode to meet Saturninus at the bottom of the hill. It was clear from the presence of the page with the axe what Saturninus wanted of him: Knowing death was inevitable, the rebel chief was staging it like a piece of theatre – his own time, his own place, his own audience, and even his own hand-picked executioner...if that executioner were willing.

The commanders saluted each other by smiting their chests. Saturninus removed his plumed helmet which he tucked under his arm. Both knew he could have fallen upon his sword and saved himself the long walk down the hill, but Saturninus did not like private or anonymous acts. Like most good actors he existed only while performing, and he yearned – in this final act – to experience his existence in thrilling totality.

Savouring his own melodrama, Saturninus ordered his page to offer Marcus the axe. If Marcus refused it, taking him prisoner instead, as were his orders, Saturninus would be condemned to torture at the hands of a madman. If Marcus himself executed Saturninus – the appropriate sentence for a fellow commander – he jeopardized his own life. Here was the sort of dilemma Saturninus liked to foist on the world.

Marcus eyed the silver axe, resentful of his role as pawn in yet another of Saturninus' theatricals. He thought of the October Horse, when Saturninus had awarded him the gold purse. He thought of Saturnalia, with Saturninus in a blonde wig. He thought of the secret meeting at Saturninus' villa, himself covered in sewer slime. Buried deep in his disgust, he found a grudging admiration for the courage and ingenuity of this man, and for his ability to fix and ferret out his own pretentions. He also remembered his promise to Domitilla.

Grimly, Marcus accepted the axe.

Gratitude overwhelmed Saturninus who realized, with a shock, that his joke had been no joke. He wanted to have Maximus Marcus execute him, for he admired the quality he had scotched in himself: his decency.

Handing his helmet to his page, Saturninus whispered: "Now general, a head for a head. Avenge your October Horse. Many would say it lived up to its pedigree more nobly than I."

Kneeling in the snow already flooded with the red light of sunset, he lay his head sideways on a stump. Marcus hefted the axe, a superbly balanced weapon, whetted to a fine edge. With the dispassion of someone who has killed often in the line of duty, he sized up Saturninus' neck.

As Saturninus gazed up at Marcus, he remembered the only person who had ever punished him – his mother's father, a man of towering rage and Republican rectitude. He smiled with a child's trust that the blow he so richly deserved would be strong and clean, then arranged his cloak for the greatest modesty.

Marcus brought down the axe. Two columns of blood spouted from Saturninus' neck to the height of a foot. The eyelids of the severed head flickered, the jaws opened then closed as the liquid rushed out.

Marcus examined the head lying by his toe, blue eyes staring. Something of Saturninus' last thoughts had transmitted themselves to him. He felt strangely moved.

Marcus sent a dispatch to Emperor Domitian, reporting the victory but saying nothing of the rebel leader. Domitian broke camp that same night and, with a vigour that astonished his men, marched north to claim his trophy. He arrived to find the midnight sky as bright as noon. The fort had been torched. It burned on its hill, a magnificent crown of fire, while the troops below drank and sang like pagans.

Domitian demanded that his two commanders be brought to him. Mounted on his horse, he watched them tramp across the plain with their escort of tribunes carrying torches – one tall and broad-shouldered, the other short and stocky, yet marching in unison, mouths set in the same stubborn line like two men who have their story well-rehearsed.

Flinging his arms toward the burning fort, Domitian demanded: "What is the meaning of this?"

"An accident," replied Norbanus. "The men in their drunken zeal fired it. The wind and dry timbers did the rest."

"What of the rebel's correspondence?"

"Gone," asserted Marcus with a long face. "If it existed, we saw none."

A tic twitched about Domitian's mouth. He knew the answer to his next question even before asking it. "What of Antonius Saturninus?"

"Slain in battle, my Lord and God," Marcus replied without hesitation.

Drawing a tighter grip on the reins of his horse as if upon himself, Domitian asked: "By whom?"

Marcus' face remained expressionless. "That is not known. It happened in one of the skirmishes while we were taking the fort." He even managed an authentic-looking shrug. "I myself found the body and chopped off the head."

Feeling the rise of fury, Domitian shifted his eyes from one to the other. He knew they were lying. Lies were the thing an emperor came to know early – the main means of communicating with him. Simple men became simpler when they lied, like these two blank-faced idiots. Inveterate liars became more elaborate.

Still managing to control himself, he focussed on Maximus Marcus. "Come here."

Marcus stepped forward. Taking a torch from one of the tribunes, Domitian leaned across his horse and peered into the commander's face, letting his eyes crawl, like spiders, across its flinty surface, searching for some small break in its line of fortification, a flicker of uncertainty, of fear. There was none. He scrutinized Norbanus behind him and then the phalanx of tribunes, their faces stony with loyalty. He knew what he would see if he looked into the eyes of his own officers: contempt, accusation, suspicion. Flinging the torch into a snowbank, Domitian gripped his horse so tightly the beast whinnied in pain. Not here in this alien place. Later, in Rome. That was the time to unleash his rage. To seek vengeance.

With an ingenuous smile, Domitian requested: "Bring me the head of Antonius Saturninus. I would like to see that it finds a good home."

The next day Domitian left Maximus Norbanus in charge of the newly captured fort and ordered his own army to strike camp for Rome. After a single morning's march, it was clear that a division had developed between Domitian's praetorians, restless from inactivity, and Marcus' veterans, full of braggadocio over their victory. To appease his own men, Domitian had them stop frequently en route to burn the Chatti's villages, to slaughter their cattle and to rape their women. Though Marcus would not himself have given such orders, he saw the wisdom in providing disgruntled soldiers with some of the sport they expected, especially when their victims were only savages. Well he remembered the thrill he had felt, as a youth, in burying his sword and fist in the entrails of an enemy of Rome; and when his officers presented him with one of the comelier Chatti virgins, he had no misgivings about enjoying her before passing her on to his men.

The emperor, for his part, seemed more interested in the devastation that fire could wreak upon this misbegotten country. He would torch hill after hill for no reason other than the pleasure it gave him to see the pine trees flare, groan, snap then tumble, and to melt the interminable snow. He especially enjoyed burning the forest in a ring around the camp so he could review his troops in his tunic without need of a cloak. His enemy seemed to be nature itself; and in his vanity, several times he risked fire-trapping his whole army.

CHAPTER FIFTEEN

News reached Rome that Antonius Saturninus had been defeated. The emperor and Commander Maximus Marcus would arrive in triumph within the month, and there would be three days' celebration including a mock sea battle. Already every citizen was out spending the bounty he counted on reaping from the arrogant good luck of being Roman. What were enemies for, if not to prove the might of Rome? What were emperors for, if not to provide bread and circuses?

Castor the page lurched drunkenly through the crowds. It was still a couple hours before dawn would bring an end to this night of celebration. Music, laughter and curses tumbled from every alleyway, along with the occasional body. Even the City Watch were casting dice with the rest.

As Castor stumbled toward the tavern on the next corner, he used one hand for his heaving stomach and the other to keep the buildings from crashing upon him. This arcade was beginning to look familiar: a bakery, then a blacksmith's shop. Like a pair of carrier pigeons, his feet had brought him home. Home, though she didn't live here anymore. Home, because he still paid the rent. Phoebe had fled like a magpie from her cage, stealing everything but the peeling fresco and her book of Ovid, which she had stuffed in a crack to keep out the wind.

After catching her with the baker, Castor remembered once having found a blacksmith's apron in her bedroom. Now when he dreamed about her, her body was plastered with black and white handprints, along with the red welts he put there himself.

Recalling for a shameful moment the filthy paddlings and pawings of the dwarf, Castor scrawled on the yellow stucco: *Fuck like mother, suck like son.* He pissed on the wall of the bakery and puked in the door of the blacksmith's shop before staggering on down the street.

The tavern was stuffy, smoky and smouldered with the threat of violence. Castor checked his pouch for a coin: nothing. Had he lost his money gambling with Parthenius or had he been robbed? He needed a drink. Something cool and refreshing to wash away the sour taste of vomit. An idea took shape...more of a vision, snow-white and shimmering...untainted, drawing him southward.

A girl so young she hadn't yet formed breasts, accosted him from the shadows of Porta Capena. Rubbing her scrawny ribcage against him she asked: "Are you game, lad? Three quadrans a go – eight for the night." He flung her from him so violently her skull cracked against the Servian Wall. Whimpering, she fell to the paving stones, holding her head.

Castor found the familiar path, heard the gurgle of water, then passed out cold in cypress bushes. Lying in mud softened with spring shoots, unable to get up, he watched the sky turn pink, then blue. He heard the rustle of branches, saw the flash of a white robe. Reaching out his hand, he expected it to slide right through as in his dreams. His fingers closed around a thick ankle. He looked up. A face rimmed in white stared down. "Hullo, boy. You going to lie there all day holding my foot?"

Castor crawled to his knees.

"You're the page, aren't you? From the palace."

Her face was round and fuzzed like a peach. Her brown eyes bulged from their sockets, and she had a double chin, but her smile was pleasant and her voice melodious. "What's your name?"

"Castor."

"I'm Diana."

That didn't sound right either.

"Well, you've had some party, haven't you?"

He moved aside to let her pass. Instead, she rubbed against him like the young bawd at the gate. Feeling the shocking collision of her warm plump body, he jerked backwards, losing his balance as she lost hers, so that they fell in a tangle of silver buckets. Her face was two inches from his.

"It looks like we're stuck on each other." She touched his lips with the tip of her tongue, then fumbled with a friendly hand at his crotch, giggling at the dismay on his face. "I'm not your first, am I?"

Castor felt a powerful explosion that spun him around so he was lying on top of her, ramming his body blindly into hers, possessed by the same fury that tormented his mother into giving freely what she resented selling.

"Hey, wait! That's not the way you do it." As she struggled to sit up, Diana picked leaves and dirt from her hair. "Now look what you've done!" She pointed to a large stain on her robes. "How am I going to get that out?"

He flushed. She grinned. "I *was* your first, wasn't I?" Taking his cloak and spreading it on the ground, she instructed Castor to lie on his back, then casually, amiably, took him into her mouth.

Diana was too busy scrubbing stains from her robe to notice Castor leave. Since catching Cornelia here with a man, she was no longer afraid of the chief vestal. She was still afraid that Agrippina would some day report her to the chief priest, and she would be stripped and beaten under the lotus tree. Unlike the other vestals, it wasn't the humiliation that Diana dreaded. She was terrified of the pain.

As Diana rubbed, fat shook in stormy waves down her arms, through her heavy body, making her feel airy and relaxed like when she made love. Puffing out her throat, she imitated the song of the thrush. There was still a blurry brown stain the size of a fist on her gown. Maybe no one would notice it in the folds?

Filling her buckets – conical so they couldn't be set down – Diana ambled off through the hawthorn trees, just bursting into bud. If a vestal spilled water, she was supposed to empty the rest and return for a refill. Diana had done that a couple of times and had been scolded for being late. Next time she had dipped the buckets at a crosswalk fountain. Then she was praised for punctuality. The lesson was obvious. From then on, Diana never returned for a refill though that was the excuse she would use today, unless something better turned up.

As she hurried through the awakening city, sweepers were already out with their myrtle brooms, carriers were filling apartment wells, bawds were yawning over their fires. The vestal waved to one person then another – a generous, good-natured girl who should, in all justice, have married and had children. As it was...Diana couldn't understand vestal life, and certainly not her vow of chastity. For as long as she could remember, she had known how wonderful it felt when a man petted her, then came inside her. She didn't understand why she shouldn't do something that gave everyone so much pleasure – only that she'd better not get caught. Nor did she understand why she was scolded for eating too much or sleeping during prayers. When gobbling food, Diana felt the same lusty fulfilment as when she managed sex, and when she slept those were the two things she dreamt about. Since she didn't understand the moral niceties that preoccupied the other vestals, she didn't know why everything she did was always wrong or why no one liked her when she liked everyone else.

As Diana entered the Temple, she rubbed once more at the back of her skirt, preparing her story. Pouring the water into the alabaster urn, she went behind the screen to replace Fausta at the hearth. When she opened her eyes after repeating the incantation, Agrippina was standing behind her.

"What's wrong with your robe?" Agrippina picked up the hem. "What's that?"

"What?" asked Diana, swivelling her head.

"That," said Agrippina, pointing to the brown mark.

"Oh that." Diana reached protectively for the stupidity she knew would exasperate Agrippina. "That's a stain."

"I know that. What is it?"

Diana's brown eyes bulged in their fatty circles. "Mud."

Agrippina was scandalized. "Mud!"

"I helped somebody – Castor the page from the palace. Some praetorians stole his money and dumped him near the spring."

Scowling, Agrippina rebuked her: "You know you're not supposed to talk to anyone unless commanded by a person who outranks you. Certainly not a page." She added sarcastically: "Even our chief vestal doesn't allow that."

Remembering, Diana grinned. "Oh yes she does."

"Don't contradict me!"

Excited at having something she could hold over someone else, Diana blurted: "I saw her. She met a man at the spring."

That was too much for Agrippina. "If you lie once more, I'll take you to the chief priest and have you whipped."

Mention of the whip started Diana quivering. "You'd have to take her too!"

Beginning to smell something not quite savoury in Diana's defiance, Agrippina demanded: "What do you mean?"

Diana backed down, knowing she had gone too far. "Nothing." Spreading a slack-lipped grin across her face, she closed her eyes, retreating further into giggles.

Agrippina knew she should pursue the girl, prod her, trap her, but who cared anymore about duty, piety, excellence? Since the death of Julia Sabina, she had been too ill to eat or sleep, yet in all that time the empress had not contacted her though she still sent Domitia regular reports. Feeling weary, unloved, unappreciated, Agrippina reached out a self-pitying hand and patted Diana on the shoulder. Pitched up for battle, Diana felt the other vestal's touch probe like a firebrand into her vulnerability. To the surprise of them both, she began to cry, large clotted sobs that rumbled and quaked through her flaccid body. Agrippina

213

stared at her in self-recognition: the unlovely ones, the leftovers, the outcasts. She put her arm around Diana, experimentally, the way she had seen Cornelia embrace the favourites, feeling tremors twang from her taut, tense body into Diana's lumbering one, yet unable to acknowledge the pain of her own needs, seeing this only as the triumph of honey over vinegar. Here was a creature more wretched than herself, someone it was her duty to save.

CHAPTER SIXTEEN

Triumphs were granted by the Senate to generals of the Imperial House who could prove a major victory. The most ludicrous was the one demanded by Nero to celebrate the 1,800 poetry and musical laurels he had won in "contests" throughout Greece. The most magnificent was the one celebrated by Titus and Vespasian for their crushing defeat of Judaea.

Emperor Domitian's return to Rome was a journey from winter to spring, from the fastness of Germany's pine forests to the cosy green hills of Italy. It was a trip made all the more salubrious by the message the emperor received en route. He had successfully intimidated the Senate into begging him to accept a double triumph for his defeat of the rebels and for his raids against the Chatti.

Wherever his troops billeted, Domitian ordered up entertainments that wreaked greater havoc on that province's economy than the damage his battles had done to his enemies. He also demanded slaves and criminals to be disguised as German prisoners to fight in a mock sea battle he was planning as a celebration.

The army's last night was spent in revelry at the Praetorian Camp outside the city walls – a fortress of brick and concrete built around the Temple of Mars, where Captain Geta lived.

At cockcrow the troops assembled outside the camp, then marched west around the city to enter through the Triumphal Gate.

First strutted the standard-bearers with their unit emblems on gilded poles; then litter-bearers, carrying a reclining statue of Jupiter; then decorated wagons heaped with booty and stage sets representing scenes from the war. These were followed by pipers, horn-players, and dancers, displaying three white bulls with gilded feet for sacrifice.

Next came captured German chieftains, unkempt and dirty, in two-wheeled carriages, followed by litters of their weapons, and a shambling line of chained prisoners in ragged cloaks fastened with thorns.

After them paraded the emperor's heralds and twenty-four lictors. Then the golden victor's chariot, drawn by four white horses, bearing the triumphant emperor in purple-embroidered gold robes, his face painted red, and crowned in laurels.

Behind the emperor marched his chief officers, including Maximus Marcus, then the praetorians wearing their gold helmets and rippling purple mantles, pinned with the decorations their valour had earned. Tramping behind them were the brass-helmeted legionnaires, singing the rude jibes no emperor dared forbid them:

"The old Bald Eagle went to bed,
As Maximus Marcus rode ahead.
Domitian fucked Vulcan, and fought the air
While Marcus and Norbanus took the enemy's lair.
They captured Saturninus, the rebel chief,
For Emperor Domitian, victory's thief.
He pillaged the provinces on the way home.
Better be an enemy than friend of Rome!"

The procession travelled down the Avenue of Triumph, through flower arches, to the Forum. People jammed doorways, balconies, rooftops, from which they pelted the prisoners with dung, and the emperor with flowers. As Domitian threw handfuls of coins, many toppled from their rooftops in eagerness for the booty, and some were trampled.

One person in the parade attracted as much attention as the emperor: a poor wretch chained to Domitian's chariot, with his head stuffed into the putrefying head of Antonius Saturninus, now buzzing with flies.

The procession flowed through the Arch of Titus into the Forum, where the milling crowds were thickest. Standing in his chariot, it seemed to Domitian that his head actually scraped the stone archway depicting his brother's sack of Jerusalem. Stretching out coin-filled hands, he heard adulation rise in crescendos: "Hail Caesar! Hail Caesar! Hail Caesar!" At last he felt the equal to his brother in both love and conquest.

The procession continued to the Capitoline, a two-crested hill that was both the military and religious heart of Rome. Dismounting, Domitian climbed its stone steps, followed by officials in ranking order, leading the sacrificial bulls. Towering over him was the Temple of Jupiter, the Greatest and Best, rebuilt by him in white marble, and mounted with three four-horse bronze chariots – one of Jupiter, one of Mars and one of Minerva. After escorting Domitian inside, chief priest Piso sacrificed the white bulls before an eighty-foot ivory-and-gold statue of a seated Jupiter. Then Domitian and his entourage descended the Capitoline to Tarpeian Rock, where criminals of rank were sometimes executed.

Here the official party mounted a dais to witness what was to be the most grisly act ever to debase a triumph. On Domitian's orders, the wretch already strangling inside the dismembered head of Antonius Saturninus was brought before him. While a crier delivered a chronicle of Saturninus' crimes, his scapegoat inside the wreath of buzzing flies was tortured with hot pokers.

Remembering the proud style in which Saturninus had died, Maximus Marcus felt particular disgust as he watched him being wrestled to the ground by four praetorians, who spread-eagled him over Tarpeian Rock as he bleated and bawled through his double mouth. Now Geta stepped forward with an axe. As if seeing himself in caricature, Marcus watched Geta bring down the axe once, then again, as the thrashing scapegoat eluded blow after blow.

217

At last the miserable deed was done. The head of Saturninus, hacked for the second time, bounced off the executioner's block and rolled over and over, down the dusty Forum paving stones, to nuzzle like a friendly dog at Marcus' boot. He peered down at the putrid mass, saw the eyes still blue (this time with the slithering backs of bottle flies), saw the lips twisted into a maggoty smile. Then he looked up at Emperor Domitian, his face gloating. Did that madman in triumphal robes actually think he had slain the rebel chief? If so, would this gruesome rite deflect vengeance from himself?

Marcus heard a long, low wail from the dais. Turning, he saw Domitilla fall back, her shawl wound around her face. He saw the vestal Cornelia rush to her aid.

The Field of Mars was a spectacular complex of parks, shops, art galleries and promenades on the right bank of the Tiber. Among its attractions were the Pantheon, the Mausoleum of Augustus, Domitian's Odeum, and also his new stadium – a 775-yard oval squared at one end, with two tiers of seats accommodating twenty thousand, and with an underground system of channels for converting it into a lake for mock sea battles.

It was at this stadium that Domitian's triumphal procession came to a halt. With much blowing of kisses, to the citizens of Rome, Domitian took his place in the royal box beside the Empress Domitia whom, it was noticed, he greeted perfunctorily after so long an absence. He was also attended by Maximus Marcus, Consul Clemens, prosecutor Messalinus, Captain Geta and the chief vestal Cornelia.

Now came the spectacle for which all Rome waited: A flotilla, manned by the prisoners outfitted as Dacians and Chatti, sailed into the stadium, followed by a Roman galley with an unarmed crew dressed in black. To ensure the prisoners would put up a good fight, Domitian had promised a pardon to the winning side – all but the black crew of the galley: those men, bearing the sins of Saturninus and his rebels, were doomed.

The trumpets sounded. The Dacians and Chatti rammed the black-draped galley. Boarding it, by means of the bridges and grapples with which Romans turned all sea battles into land battles, they soon reduced the unarmed men to a gruesome heap of heads and torsos. With whoops and slashing steel the prisoners now set about the grim task of slaughtering each other. When some attempted to save themselves by climbing the rigging or diving into the water, the spectators discovered a new amusement: the lake was stocked. Crocodiles tore their victims with such rapaciousness that, even when the reddened water was bobbing with enough meat for all, most combatants preferred to die by steel rather than to risk jumping.

As the spectators grew bored, the emperor signalled for his praetorians to fire flaming pitch into the boats so that soon the lake was afloat with charred and smouldering hulks. Only two boats now remained navigable, their decks clustered by men so gored and sooty it was impossible to tell under what colours they fought.

The sun had long since been driven into eclipse by a pall of clouds, smoke and floating ash. The May day was turning raw, windy and damp. Stomping and clapping in unison, the spectators shouted for the emperor to declare a draw. Annoyed, Domitian merely ordered robes and braziers to be brought into the royal box.

The prisoners fought on stubbornly but with little vigour. Many had lost limbs or were otherwise mangled. The livid skies grumbled and growled, and a chill wind whipped red waves foamed with pink the length of the stadium.

Now the spectators hooted and made catcalls. Some even stood up as if to leave. Domitian was enraged. How dare they spurn his beneficence? Climbing up on his chair for all to see, he ordered his praetorians to shoot fireballs into the stands so that Romans were treated to the sight of some of their own, clothes aflame, clawing each other for the privilege of plunging into crocodile-infested water.

Far from stopping the flight, this caused a stampede. With glowering face and shaking fist, Domitian urged on his praetorians, giving vent to the hysteria he hadn't dared unleash while off in an alien country.

Consul Clemens, Maximus Marcus and the vestal Cornelia converged upon the emperor. Though they knew they risked their lives, each tried individually, then as a group, to reason with Domitian.

"How can you kill Romans in a ceremony meant to give thanks for their safety?" pleaded Cornelia.

"Stop this bloodiness. Haven't we spilled enough Roman blood?" demanded Maximus Marcus in a voice too near command.

"This is madness," broke off Consul Clemens, speaking too closely the truth.

At last, in exhaustion, Domitian ordered the firing to cease. Breathing heavily, the sweat pouring down his face, he turned to his self-appointed advisors. "Since you three love the plebeians so well, what are you doing in the royal box?" Beckoning to Geta, he said: "See that my friends have an escort up to the top of the stadium so they can smell the garlic breath of those they champion."

He turned his attention back to the stadium. By now all the fires in the stands were extinguished, and the spectators had resumed their seats. Before Domitian could call an end to the day's celebration, the storm which had been so long threatening finally broke. The witchy skies opened. All those outside the royal box were deluged, and once more a few determined Romans headed for the exits. When they weren't impeded, others followed so that there was another exodus.

Enraged to see himself defied again, the emperor waited until all twenty entrances at the flattened end of the stadium were packed. Then he secretly ordered Captain Geta to raise the side of the tank. Water flushed through the exits in a tidal wave, drowning hundreds and causing another stampede. Millions of gallons poured into the streets of Rome, through shops and tenements, carrying corpses and crocodiles and the wreckage of ships.

It was as Antonius Saturninus predicted: Rome had another Caligula at its throat.

CHAPTER SEVENTEEN

The slave bazaars were also located in the Field of Mars. Here naked men and women were packed in pens reeking of human waste – Egyptians, Moors, Greeks, Arabs, Celts, Teutons, Jews. Those with white chalk on their feet were for immediate sale, and the red chalk notations on their pens stated their value. Whip or chain scars usually indicated recalcitrance. A brand on the forehead declared: *thief.*

Dealers answered all the standard questions: Did the slave take fits? Was he prone to running away? To attempt suicide? Did he have any skills? Did he speak Greek? Since each came with a six-month guarantee, sellers were inclined to stretch the truth rather than to lie. Except in the case of slaves with caps. That signalled: *Buyer beware.*

A standard price for a male slave was 2,000 sesterces, with the cost rising in accordance with the number of his skills. Since most slaves in wealthy households were for show, comeliness was the most expensive asset.

It was at the slave bazaar that Consul Clemens, ex-Consul Cocceius Nerva, freedman Clodianus and Maximus Marcus met to consider the assassination of Emperor Domitian. Clodianus, who owned a private booth for the display of skilled slaves such as physicians, school masters and chefs, suggested the location.

Enraged by the events in the stadium, Nerva seized upon it, for, as he asked rhetorically: "How do we senators differ from slaves, except that we have red on our hands instead of white on our feet? Let us sit down in the stench of fettered humanity till we draw enough courage to strike for our freedom."

Clodianus' booth was presided over by Mercury, god of thieves and merchants, and his motto – Profit is Joy – marked the door. Lounging on oversized couches and drinking from gem-studded cups, the conspirators pondered the first question: Was the emperor to be assassinated? All agreed such a thing must be considered, for as Nerva again summed up: "Our emperor has crossed the line from private perversity to public atrocity. No man in Rome could accuse us of acting out of self-interest."

On whom should the mantle of power fall? Both Marcus and Nerva urged it on Clemens, who refused. "I will not profit from my cousin's death."

The only other choice was Nerva. He agreed with reluctance. "At sixty-two I can be only the caretaker of power."

How could they secure military backing, especially of the praetorians still loyal to Domitian as the source of their high pay? "Captain Geta is a hard man both ways," asserted Clodianus. "By that I mean his price comes high both for including or excluding him. I'll sound out which we can best afford."

Remembering his friend the poet Priscus, Marcus stood firm. "Any side Geta is on, I am on the opposite."

"Can we say the same about prosecutor Messalinus?" asked Nerva. All agreed.

When was the assassination to take place? "As soon as possible, if it's to be done," Nerva urged. "Every minute lost adds an inch to Geta's blade and Messalinus' tongue."

How was it to be accomplished? Though historical precedents were many, here the argument became heated and divisive. At last Clemens was driven to exclaim: "I do not think I'm really quarrelling about the merits of belladonna versus steel. I know from the pain in my gut that I cannot stomach participating in my cousin's murder, though the reasons are many and compelling."

"The path of history is soaked with the blood of men of noble thoughts and no deeds," Nerva gently reminded him. "To spare the emperor's throat is to slit your own. To spare his head is, like the slave, to crop your own."

"My mind is made up, Nerva. Some men, like you, become revolutionary later in life. I have gone the other route."

"You mean your stomach has!" jeered Clodianus. "You seem to look to that like the augurers their chickens."

"I am not Brutus. I cannot move from a position of loyalty to disloyalty to one of my own blood, or swallow the end over the means, though I don't hold it against anyone who can."

It was here Clodianus surprised everyone with his eloquence. "I understand you, Clemens, for I am your opposite number. I know you all despise me as a man who would turn any trick for a coin, and sometimes I despise myself, but if I were a morally fussy man, I'd still be on the wharf at Carthage under a stinking pyramid of fish. I have forgiven myself, but it seems the gods have not. I am now a walking nemesis of the life I've led: bad bowels, worms in the belly, fire in the groin. I have nothing to fear from death, and though I can afford anything now – even scruples – it would be as much a lie for me suddenly to find mine as it would be for Clemens to lose his. The best way I know to give significance to my life is by an end that justifies its means. I see that in the assassination of this mad emperor. Gentlemen, I am your butcher."

A date was set for a second meeting, at Clodianus' Fullers' shop in the Subura, to make detailed plans. The conspirators left the slave bazaar at intervals, and one at a time.

As Clemens elbowed his way past the slave pens he felt clearer of eye and firmer of judgement than he had in a long time. He was a slave, as Nerva had said, but so was the emperor. A slave to his past, his image of himself, the expectations of others. Perhaps it was best to begin with that knowledge, clearly

223

focussed, and to make the best possible choices within the framework of one's own nature. Any justification of his life would have to be – as Clodianus had said – in the terms in which it had been lived.

Marcus too brooded long and hard about his own nature while leaving the bazaar. To kill an emperor. That was a deed on the level of patricide. A moral act outside of the recognized system of authority. To a man who had always accepted the given order as the natural order, that seemed like a contradiction in terms. He thought of the mock execution of Saturninus and the slaughter at the stadium. Where did loyalty end? When did silence become collusion?

Still disturbed, Marcus joined Clemens at the foot of the Capitoline. As they plodded toward home, Hermes the dwarf popped out from a pillar which bore the head of the god Hermes and a giant phallus – one of the many "Hermes" scattered throughout Rome. Tipping his scarlet cap, he handed each a scroll bearing the imperial seal. Each broke the seal and read: "You are commanded to attend Imperator Domitianus Caesar Augustus this evening for dinner before sunset." Both invitations were edged in black, and at the bottom the emperor had scrawled identical postscripts: "Given the long faces I see around me over that tiresome event in the stadium, perhaps mourning clothes would be in order?"

Flavius Clemens and Marcus hurried to the consul's Esquiline villa to don their mourning robes for the evening's "entertainment." Convinced this would be his last day on earth, Clemens asked his steward to fetch the chief vestal to transcribe his will for safekeeping in the Temple. "It must be the Lady Cornelia," he stressed. "No other."

Less than an hour later Stephanus escorted the vestal chief into the consul's office. She seemed breathless and flustered in a way that surprised Clemens. "I'm sorry, Lady Cornelia, to rush you over a job I've had sixty years to do. Delay is a luxury I can no longer afford." He smiled grimly. "Many men claim forebodings of death. Few receive formal invitations." He showed her the black-bordered scroll he had received from the palace. Before she could express sympathy, he directed her to a couch where she could write, and handed her a ledger along with some deeds.

Glad to busy herself with detail, Cornelia laid out parchment paper, pen and inkwell. She examined the consul's ledger, trying to recover her poise through concentration on her work. Though she had seen Maximus Marcus at the stadium, the public emergency had prevented compromising contact. If she could have sent Agrippina to this dangerous place, she would have.

"Your records are in excellent shape," Cornelia observed. "What is to be the disposition?"

"A simple one, Lady Cornelia, under the circumstances. All my properties outside Rome, except for my Como estate, have already been made over to my sons. My Como estate goes to Marcus. My Roman holdings to Domitilla until her death. Then those too go to Marcus."

As the consul dictated from his easy chair, Cornelia drew up the testament, which she handed to him to inspect. Barely glancing through it, he affixed his seal. Then he sat staring moodily into space, one hand over the document, the other fussing at his beard.

Sensing his worry, Cornelia asked: "Is there anything I can do, Consul Clemens? Any messages you would like me to deliver?"

"Messages?" He repeated the word vaguely. "Yes, there is one thing...something I have difficulty asking." Lowering his voice he said: "If anything happens to me, Lady Cornelia, will you help my Domitilla? It's hard to explain...this foolishness...this obsession."

Feeling guilty at such an apt description of her own condition, Cornelia protested: "I don't understand, Consul Clemens. Is Domitilla ill?"

He shook his head. "Nothing doctors can help. It's this other

225

thing. This Christianity – a disease of the mind she caught from her serving girl. Every day I see her fall further under its spell though she tries to hide that from me. It's a part of her I don't understand...this zealous part that denies reason. Once before... long ago..." He dismissed the end of his sentence with an airy wave. "Of course that was another matter. Something belonging to her youth that I thought she had overcome. An incident during the celebrations brought it back.... All these human problems worry me far more than the disposition of property." Leaning toward Cornelia, he seemed to beseech her: "Can I count on you? Will you promise to come to Domitilla if I'm stricken, give her wise counsel according to the examples of Vesta and Juno?"

"Certainly, Consul Clemens." Cornelia reached out her hand to comfort the older man. "I know your wife has been under great tension. Great fear for your safety. This cult offers eternal life. Her love for you naturally draws her to it." She repeated the words she had used to mislead Zeno and herself about her own confusions: "I'm sure it's just a phase – something that will pass."

Clemens bobbed his head, eager to be reassured. "Let's hope so. Her life has been lived in moderation." He handed Cornelia the document he had sealed. "Of course, if my troubles become... acute, I can't guarantee my legacies. Except for my strongbox." Pointing to an iron trunk in one corner, he explained: "If you are willing, Stephanus will deliver that to you after I leave for the palace. It's for you to use at your discretion, for the protection of my heirs, and however else you deem fit."

"I accept your trust, Consul Clemens."

Sighing, he arose from his chair. "Thank you, Lady Cornelia." As she stood up to accompany him to the door, he said: "Oh, didn't I mention? Maximus Marcus wishes to speak with you. He too received one of the emperor's invitations. He too wants to put his estate in order."

Her host was at the door before she could stop him. "Consul Clemens!"

226

Surprised at her note of hysteria, he turned. She could think of nothing to say that wouldn't seem mean or suspicious. Bowing her head to hide her confusion, she murmured: "I hope your fears prove groundless."

He nodded. "It's a good life sometimes, isn't it, Lady Cornelia?"

Returning in nervous haste to her couch, Cornelia rearranged her ink, pen and paper. Then, with her scroll propped on her knee, she wrote in a tidy hand that did not betray her: "MAXIMUS MARCUS, HIS LAST WILL AND TESTAMENT." The shock of those words tore a silent protest from her, especially when she also caught a glimpse of his ashy robes out of the corner of her eye. Though he was standing at the end of her couch, she did not look up. Not even when he spoke her name: "Cornelia." Not even when he sat on the couch, though it sagged under his weight.

In a crisp voice she asked: "You wish to prepare your estate?"

He made no reply though she could hear him catch his breath in the stillness at the other end of the couch. Again she dipped her pen and wrote more words, exaggerating the scratch of the reed on the parchment to fill up the space between them. Her page caught the shadow of his hand, before she actually saw it swoop, felt his touch. "Oh." She jerked back, blotting the ink. "How clumsy." Crumpling the parchment she reached for another. Again she dipped her pen and wrote the words that would expunge him: "MAXIMUS MARCUS, HIS LAST –"

This time he folded his fingers around hers, forcing her to drop the pen. "I can't speak of wills." His other hand crumpled the second parchment. "Look at me, Cornelia, please. There's so little time."

As always she felt his power, the loss of will, the betrayal of her senses. He said: "Tell me the truth. Do you ever think about what I asked you at the spring?"

Closing her eyes, she tried to blot him out, saw instead the red hawthorn berries and gold birches chiming in the wind – the magic place where she dwelt in fantasy. Slowly, with pain and yet with relief she replied: "I think of nothing else when I let myself...in the first stirrings of morning before my guard has come up. When my mind wanders in prayer. When I see a thing of beauty which opens my heart. When Helen or Poppaea do something thoughtful it would please me to share..."

Marcus moved toward her on the couch, then took her in his arms, despite the dangers even here. At first she resisted him. Then, with a moan, she collapsed against him, lay her cheek on his chest, felt the abrasion of his mourning robes and the beat of his heart underneath, clung to him, cried freely, felt his arms tighten around her, and allowed him to comfort her. He looked for and found her wet cheek, then her lips, in the tangle of hair and silk scarf. He whispered in her ear: "I'll survive tonight, I promise. Even if I have to cut my way out of the palace with a spoon."

Flavius Clemens said good-bye to Domitilla in their garden under the almond tree just pressing into blossom. "Words can no more express what is in my heart than a statue can speak."

Remembering the Temple of Juno Viriplaca, Domitilla replied: "A statue did speak, Clemens."

He kissed her with unbearable tenderness, wishing to urge: *Take care, my love, my life. Guard yourself.* Instead he said: "Remember to feed my fishes. I'm afraid I've spoiled them."

"You've spoiled us all, Clemens."

Just before sunset Clemens and Marcus travelled by litter to the Palatine. The sky over the western city was fumid with the smoke of hundreds of funeral pyres – bitter legacy of the massacre at the stadium. Domitian, it was said, had flooded where Nero had burned. He had laughed where Nero sang. Charon would need as many boats as the Imperial Navy to carry the dead this night.

Captain Geta met the two senators at the palace gate and marched them to a vestibule where other guards, dressed in black, were awaiting them. Without protest, they submitted to being stripped and searched for weapons, then to having their eyes bound with black scarves. As they were escorted through marble halls, Marcus could tell by the shuffling around them that others were being propelled in the same direction. When at last their blindfolds were removed, it made little difference to their understanding, for they were in an all-black room – walls, ceiling, furniture. As their eyes adjusted, they distinguished two companions – Nerva and Clodianus, the other conspirators!

Also wearing mourning clothes, the emperor was seated on a black throne, at a black table, with black dining couches on either side. He grinned and gestured. "Welcome. Your places are marked. Make yourselves comfortable." An ebony tombstone, inscribed with each man's name and birth date, headed each place on the reclining couches.

Clodianus' read: *Before I die, please pass the dessert.*

Nerva's was: *Some men grow wise. Others grow more foolish.*

For Clemens: *I compromised with life, but I cannot compromise with death.*

Marcus' seemed the most insulting: a blank with only the birth date and a dash.

As each guest reluctantly reclined, black slaves bathed their hands and feet with perfumed water from bowls made of human skulls. Then they were served wine in goblets shaped like funeral urns. Though Domitian's face was smeared with ashes as if in deepest mourning, he seemed in a jovial mood that jarred with the setting. Holding his goblet high, he announced: "To your health, my friends. A long life and a happy death." Then he drained the goblet.

Since all the guests had noticed their wine came from the same bowl as the emperor's, they drank with confidence though with little pleasure.

Now Domitian signalled for the entertainment to begin. Six flute-players filed through the black curtains, wearing shredded mourning robes. Shuffling slowly around the diners, they played a dirge that sent shivers up and down the spine. An actor in bloodied toga, and wearing the death mask of Julius Caesar, delivered a lamentation in which he cursed the villainy of men who joined their weakness to tear down the strong.

A platter of mushrooms was served. All noted that the emperor refused this dish, and they tried to do the same. "What, you turn down the food of the gods?" joked Domitian, using the name Nero had given the poisoned mushrooms served to emperor Claudius. Scooping up a handful, he tossed them one by one into his mouth, chewing each slowly, till there were only four left. These he passed out to each of his guests with the admonition: "I hope you love your emperor better than you love his food."

As the mournful evening dragged on, dish after dish was served – costly delicacies such as cockle pâté, roebuck kidneys, sea nettles and thrushes, marinated in piquant sauces. Sometimes Domitian ate from the common platter, sometimes he ordered his food served separately, sometimes he abstained. "An emperor has to keep his friends, as well as his enemies, guessing."

Four youths, their bodies naked except for black paint and cypress garlands, vaulted into the room. Each was wearing a "death mask" of one of the guests. With muscles rippling, they leapt and twirled to tambourines, then flung themselves at the feet of the man whose face they wore. They removed their masks. Smiling, they showered their patrons with kisses and caresses, making it clear they wished to share their couches. Marcus recognized the youth assigned to him: Castor, the page – having come down in life by moving up, as Priscus had predicted.

Fending off his intended companion, Clemens addressed Domitian wryly: "If you wish to kill me, cousin, do so with your dagger rather than with such kindness. I have not the desire, and my heart hasn't the stamina."

The youth at Clemens' knee burst into tears.

"He will be flogged for failing to please," warned the emperor. "Then his beauty will be ruined and he will have to work the quarries."

"Give him to Clodianus, who has flesh and appetite for all these youths and more, so your hospitality won't seem stingy."

Cocking his head like a sparrow hawk, the emperor agreed. "Very well, since it is you, cousin."

Marcus too was troubled by the emperor's "gift." Though male prostitutes were a commonplace in army camps, most were enjoyed bestially by the lowest classes, or in decadence by the patricians. True to his middle-class provincial origins, Marcus shunned such practices as an insult to his manhood.

As the emperor's eyes rested upon them, Castor began teasing Marcus' chest hairs and plucking at his loincloth. Remembering he would have had a boy just this age, Marcus was overcome with pity rather than desire. He put his arm gruffly around the lad, causing Castor to burst into tears. Marcus comforted him, yet held back, unwilling even during this, his last day on earth, to face such tender sentiments in himself. Captain Geta, a knife and a fist by Domitian's side, observed this behaviour with rare approval.

Growing bored, the emperor turned his scrutiny to Clodianus and to Nerva, who were performing more amusingly on their couches – Clodianus because he was a lustful pig, Nerva because he took a connoisseur's pleasure in his bisexuality. Indeed, Nerva's intimate tastes were well-known to Domitian, since they had had an affair before he became emperor. As the youths lent themselves to every pleasure that persons with the same sexual parts could devise, Domitian made imaginative suggestions, and especially to Clodianus, greedy to soak up with his spongy flesh all the sensations that a fast-fading life could still provide.

By firstlight all but Clemens were exhausted and sleeping. As each guest awoke, he exchanged sheepish looks with the rest: They were still alive then. Had it just been a macabre joke? Getting up from his throne, Domitian travelled from couch to couch, kissing his guests so effusively he left ashes all over their mouths. Then he presented each with a black scarf. "Any day in which I give nothing to my friends is a day wasted." Since this was an oft-quoted remark of his brother Titus, it was greeted with much discomfort. Was he still mocking them, or had he gone over the edge into madness?

Laughing into their fears, Domitian observed: "You have had a good night. Now I bid you good-day." He left his guests to his guards, who escorted each from the palace.

Marcus hiked down to the Circus to release his tensions in a long hard gallop on Priam. Clemens returned by litter to the Esquiline. Despite shortness of breath, the consul asked his bearers to let him out a distance from his villa so he could revel in the first glimpse of the almond trees overhanging his garden wall. Would he live then to smell their foamy blossoms? To savour their nutty harvest? Never did his little dew-spangled world look more inviting.

Pausing to enjoy the sunrise over the city, Clemens drank deep draughts of chill air, no longer tainted with the acrid taste of funeral smoke, feeling bands loosen from around his chest, beginning to relax. He entered his villa through the vestibule guarded by his mosaic dog, pleased to see no clients waiting, anxious to reassure Domitilla. He stopped in mid-stride. Putting his hand to his heart, he gaped. Something appearing to be a hive, buzzing with bees, was impaled on the head of his household god. He drew closer and gasped, incredulous. The black-tongued head of Antonius Saturninus, ripe with maggots and horseflies!

Now Clemens ran into his courtyard, shouting: "My wife, my wife!" Domitilla's maid Berenice was lying half-in, half-out of the fountain. She had been disembowelled, while her babe, still attached to her umbilical cord, floated beside her. Running from room to room, Clemens continued to shout: "My wife, my wife!"

Domitilla bolted toward him, her hair in an uncombed tangle. Even as she flung herself into his arms, two praetorians were yanking them apart. Standing between them, Captain Geta confronted Clemens. "I arrest you in the name of Imperator Domitianus Caesar Augustus."

232

Drawing himself up with patrician grace, Clemens demanded: "What is the charge, sir?"

Geta jerked his head toward Berenice in the fountain. "Harbouring an atheist and a Jew, an eater of flesh and a drinker of blood. That for now. There will be other charges later."

CHAPTER EIGHTEEN

Across the Aemilian Bridge,
the oldest stone span on the Tiber, were the wharves and warehouses and fish markets where Jews and Orientals traded second-
hand goods, told fortunes and lived in squalor.

In a round wattle hut of the sort built by Rome's first settlers,
Philip the Prophet – known to the Romans as Philip the Fishmonger – preached faith, charity and forgiveness, while existing
on fishheads and other refuse. It was to Philip's tiny hut, just
after sundown, that Stephanus and Domitilla brought the mutilated remains of Berenice, assisted by a woman in scholar's
cloak, whom everyone took to be Domitilla's freedwoman. Tall,
gaunt, with translucent skin and joints as gnarled as his oak
staff, Philip kissed Domitilla on both cheeks. "We have bene-
fitted much from your kindness." He clasped the hand of her
companion. "You too are welcome with us."

Berenice's relatives – shy in the presence of so fine a Roman
lady – provided Domitilla with coarse robes more suited to the
humble surroundings, then prepared Berenice's body with perfume and spices. Philip baptized her unborn child, and the two
were wrapped in the same winding sheet.

At dusk the body of Berenice was hidden in a mule cart under
bales of straw, and the mourners joined the horses and wagons
rattling northward out of Rome. Two hours later they reached

their destination: the catacombs of St. Peter, one of a dozen Jewish cemeteries that ringed the city.

Carrying a lamp, Philip stooped through the well-concealed entrance, followed by the others bearing the body of Berenice. Passages and crude stairs jutted off at odd angles from the tufa tunnel that was so low-ceilinged sometimes Philip had to bend double. Supported by her companion, Domitilla shuffled after his light to a roughly hewn chamber where a granite slab bore a silver chalice, a silver plate and a seven-pronged candelabra. Etched on the ceiling was a fish. Domitilla compared it to the carving on the bone handle of her fish knife, one of the few things she had brought with her. It was the same as the Christian symbol.

Lighting the candelabra, Philip knelt before the altar, and prayed: "Please accept, oh God, into your tender keeping the earthly remains of our beloved sister Berenice, who was one with us and is no more, and of her son David. Cleanse them of sin and embrace their spirits in the name of Jesus Christ, your son and our Saviour, so that they may enter the Kingdom of Heaven. Lift from our hearts, oh God, the pain of our grief and our anger. Fill us with joy everlasting. Thy will be done."

Philip poured wine into the chalice. "In the name of Jesus Christ, drink of this blood that we may be saved by his sacrifice." After offering it to all but Domitilla and her companion, he placed wafers on the silver plate. "Eat of His body that we may join Him in Paradise."

The bodies of Berenice and her unborn child were placed in a cleft gouged out of the rock. Philip sprinkled crumbled rock. "Earth our bodies become. Let our souls rise to heaven." As several mourners completed the burial, the others sang spirited songs, clapped their hands, and afterwards told stories of Berenice – joyful stories of her gentleness, her humility, her love of laughter.

Their songs and their faith seeped like sunlight through Domitilla's numbness. It was as if, in shedding her Roman garments, she had shed her Roman constraint and cynicism. The thrilling hope she had felt only in flashes about this religion of rebirth permeated her whole being. Here was the optimism she had sought in vain at the core of her Roman piety. Here was the love – an ecstasy that filled her without words. Domitilla began singing, clapping, swaying along with the rest, in the dusty rockbound room, expanding into the darkness of the cavern... becoming one with her new friends in the Mystery. She looked again at the symbol on her knife, then at the one sketched on the ceiling. Had she been travelling to this place – this cavern in the earth – all her life? She thought of the cave of Plato, with its shadows of shadows. Was it in this secret place that she would experience the blinding light of Truth? She laughed aloud, as she hadn't done in years. Sorrow had fled, and she felt like a child again.

In the midst of the celebration, Stephanus stood up and, grabbing one of the torches, bolted for the exit. When Philip tried to restrain him, he pushed the prophet aside. The companion of Domitilla joined Stephanus and together they stumbled up the tunnel gnawed through tufa, sometimes scraping a shinbone or knocking their heads, but never slackening their pace. At last they reached the dewy air. Smashing both fists against the rock, Stephanus sobbed: "I can't forgive! I won't forget! Don't taunt me with the joys of heaven."

Domitilla's companion lay a comforting hand on his shoulder. "I too am Roman." Withdrawing to a grove of plane trees, she folded back the hood of her scholar's cloak, revealing herself: Cornelia. Hugging one of the trees, she rested her feverish cheek against its peeling bark. Why had she come here? What mistaken sense of loyalty to a friend had led her to this pagan place? What could she as a vestal accomplish here, except the destruction of all she had tried to build?

The burial had been touching in its earthy simplicity – a contrast to the chasteness of the ceremonies of Vesta and the grandeur of those of Jupiter. It wasn't until Philip had eaten the bread and drunk the wine he believed to be human flesh and blood that she had felt the first intimations of panic. When

Domitilla – face flushed, hair unloosed from its matron's coil
and eyes glittering too much like Fausta's – had joined in the
singing, Cornelia's panic had exploded, collapsing the cavern
walls upon her so that the tunnels seemed to coil their dusty
tentacles around her, strangling her. Never before had she felt
such terror. Was it because her parents had been entombed at
Pompeii? Was it because of the dread that haunted every vestal – to be buried alive for breaking her vow of chastity?

The mourners emerged one by one from the catacombs.
Philip, Domitilla and Cornelia climbed into the mule cart, with
Stephanus lying face-down in back. They returned to Rome, to
the Jewish quarter under Janiculum Hill. Since Domitilla's life
was no longer safe on the right side of the Tiber, she was intending to remain with Philip. Clasping Cornelia's hand, her face
radiant, she said: "Thank you, my friend. I hope some day you
will come to us."

Cornelia hurried across Aemilian Bridge, her cloak husked
about her, not wishing to look down at the roiling water, too
much like the confusion of her thoughts. It had been foolhardy
to accompany Domitilla to the catacombs. Consul Clemens had
asked her to restrain his wife, not to help her reap the whirl-
wind. There were more important, more appropriate ways to
help. As chief vestal, it was her duty to request an audience with
the emperor when the safety of the state was at stake. Given the
temper of the present emperor, it was not a privilege much exercised, but one she could invoke. The very next day she would
seek an appointment with Domitian because of the bad auguries
which had marred the recent Festival of Foricidia. She would
connect these with the arrest of Clemens, then convince the
emperor that the consul was more useful to him alive than dead.

As Cornelia reached the Forum a grey mist that the superstitious called the shroud of Caesar was seeping up through the
paving stones of Sacred Way. Ahead, she could see the glow of
the Temple. Taking her key from Zeno's cloak, she slipped it
through the vestalry grating into the lock. The gate opened with
a metallic click that echoed through the moonlit gardens. Glanc-

ing both in gratitude and self-reproach at the vestal chiefs surrounding the courtyard pools, she slowly, silently climbed the stairs to her room.

Cornelia lay down on her cot without changing her clothes. Despite her exhaustion, her mind leapt nimbly from image to image snatched from the dark and ominous night...the wagon ride out of the city...the dusty tunnel down to the cave...the shining face of Domitilla with unbound hair...Stephanus banging his fists against the catacombs, energy pouring from his body in an envelope of light, a man in the extremes of love and grief....

As Cornelia's door closed behind her, the vestal Agrippina crawled up from her cramped position in the vestalry rose garden. Though she was chilled to the bone, nothing could have made her leave her spiky nest or take her eyes from the vestalry gate as she waited for Cornelia to return. In the steadfastness of her vigil, she considered herself as one with the line of vestals immortalized in marble: Aemilia, who proved her purity by re-lighting the cold hearth with wet linen; Tuccia, who answered false charges by carrying water in a bronze sieve; Agrippina, her namesake, who set herself aflame rather than let Vesta's fire go out after rain had drenched the faggots. How glorious seemed their sacrifices against the sloth of the vestalry today.

Agrippina had not intended to spy on Cornelia, but she had seen her sneak out in Zeno's cloak and – as a point of duty – had followed as far as she could through the crowds of the Forum. Where had Cornelia gone? If on Temple business, why hadn't she used a litter or taken her lictor? And why was she disguised in a man's cloak?

As Agrippina waited, hour by hour, her mind had grown rank with the images of orgies glimpsed, heard of, imagined – all fertilized by the tale Diana had told her about Cornelia's rendezvous at the sacred fountain...a tale she hadn't dared believe till now. She looked with satisfaction at the scroll of misdemeanours, grown soggy in her hand. Soon she would have enough to show the chief priest or her friend the empress. She smiled grimly. It was her duty.

The youngest vestal Poppaea was a light sleeper. She had heard Cornelia tiptoe past her room, then minutes later she heard Agrippina. As the fourth daughter of a stonemason, Poppaea had been used to lots of company in bed. Though her sisters had all complained about an elbow in the stomach and each other's snoring, she found she missed the cosiness, the turmoil. Her cot seemed too large, too white, too slippery for one person.

Poppaea climbed from bed. She padded out onto the gallery overlooking the courtyard, and peered down at the statues of the vestals reflected in three pools. Cornelia had said they were her ancestors – her family. Poppaea pretended the plumpest one was her real mother, who was also fat. She was afraid of being over-whelmed by the vestals.

Shivering in her shift, Poppaea crept to the door of Helen's room and put her ear against the shutters. She could hear Helen breathing – snoring like her sister Fannia, though both denied they did it. When Poppaea opened the door, Helen was lying in the centre of her bed, her hands folded neatly, her blonde hair fanned over the bolster, her mouth open – which was why she was snoring. Poppaea crept to the bed. Kneeling, she whispered: "Helen." Then louder: "Can I get in?"

Helen opened one eye. Without actually waking, she lifted the coverlet for Poppaea. Poppaea moved into the milky triangle, smelling warmly of flesh, then pressed her chilly body against Helen's fleshier one, the way she used to snuggle up with her sisters. It felt familiar. Wriggling closer, she lay her hand on Helen's breast. Helen stiffened. Propping herself on one elbow, the older vestal stared down at Poppaea with an odd unfathom-able expression. Turning over, Poppaea shifted away so Helen wouldn't make her leave.

Helen was now fully awake and trying to sort through her alarming feelings. At first she had liked it when Poppaea had touched her breast. Then it frightened her. Helen wished she knew more about her body. In a few months she would undergo a secret initiation in which her hymen would be cut and the blood offered to Vesta as proof of chastity. She yearned to know what that meant, but didn't dare ask Cornelia in case such questions were sinful. Cornelia's good opinion meant more to her than the bedevilling questions.

Once Helen had thought there were no answers – that such obscurities were all part of the Mysteries, like what Vesta looked like and what happened when you died. Later she began to suspect some people did know – people like Diana. Knowing the answers had more to do with how long you had lived "outside" than how old or how smart you were. Helen had been three when her father, the governor of Britain, had sent her as a ward to the vestalry so she wouldn't be killed by insurgents.

Helen tensed. Poppaea's hand had once more wandered onto her breast. Forcing herself to relax, she glanced down maternally at the sharp little face snuggled against her. Maybe it was all right because Poppaea was so young? As Helen continued to watch her friend, she had a more compelling thought: Poppaea had been ten before she became a vestal. Did Poppaea know the answers?

Poppaea opened her eyes. The girls stared crosseyed at each other, then both started to giggle. Poppaea tickled Helen under her arms, across her belly, between her legs. Helen drew back, shocked. She pushed Poppaea away, opened her mouth to scold, but instead blurted: "What does a man do to a woman?"

Confused by the change of mood, Poppaea regarded Helen with suspicion.

Helen whispered more urgently: "What is it vestals can't do?"

Frowning, Poppaea thought of the couplings between her mother and father, which she had routinely witnessed. She thought everyone knew that. Was she being tested? She answered cautiously: "He...puts his rod in her."

Helen's eyes widened. Here at last was the answer, if only – like the riddles of Delphi – she could unravel it. She thought of the chief priest's rod of authority. "How does a man use his rod?"

240

"He lies on top of you and puts it in, that's all."

Helen tried to imagine that. "What if he doesn't have a rod?"

Poppaea was incredulous. "Every man does, that's what makes him a man – oh, well, not the eunuchs. They have theirs cut off. That's what makes them eunuchs."

Seeing no light of understanding in Helen's eyes, she began to guess the depth of the older girl's ignorance. Kindly, matter-of-factly, Poppaea explained – as patiently as Helen had showed her how to make salt cakes – all she knew of men and sex. As she talked, she touched Helen's body with her fingertips. Feeling the response, she pressed her lips against Helen's, and caressed her breasts. Sliding lower, she sucked on them the way she had sucked on Fannia's breasts, until Fannia's baby had displaced her. Cautiously she nudged her hand between Helen's legs. This time Helen, cowed by gratitude and stimulated by curiosity, did not draw back. She moved forward.

Helen felt Poppaea's fingers touch the place she dared not touch – where she never dared look. She did not faint. She did not die. Instead, she became aware of a pleasing sensation arising in little spurts from Poppaea's fingers, like being tickled, only... She pressed her lips hard against Poppaea's. Poppaea pressed back, her ribcage pushing against Helen's belly. Helen felt a funny expectation begin to build in her body, and then something else started to happen – something that frightened her into thinking this was why you weren't supposed to do this thing, why it was bad. Her body was twitching like Fausta's body when she had a fit! Clinging to Poppaea, she imagined Fausta, grey hair sticking out in a thunderclap, and then *oh... oh...* Helen felt a spasm ripple through her, and then another, leaving her wet and trembling. Keeping her eyes closed, she felt fear discharge in prickles from her body, and well-being steal over her. She put her hands to her face. Her skin had not wrinkled. Her hair was smooth, not sticking out in spikes. She had not turned crazy like Fausta.

She opened her eyes. Poppaea was on her hands and knees grinning down at her. "Now do me..."

CHAPTER NINETEEN

Emperor Domitian's library was second only to the one in Alexandria. To this civil place, containing 200,000 scrolls and decorated with frescoes of Minerva, goddess of letters, the emperor's praetorians marched Consul Flavius Clemens to await an interview with the emperor.

Ten hours after his arrest, Clemens was still waiting.

He had passed through many moods. Shock. Grief. Fear. And – the safest if he weren't to break down – anger. In each he had composed a speech to be delivered in the appropriate tone of outrage, sarcasm, dignity. Then – still in his mourning clothes, and with the emperor's ash kisses still on his cheek – he stretched out on a reading couch to stare blankly at the ceiling. It seemed odd to Clemens that never once did he take down a book, either for comfort or to pass the time. His eyes travelled from pigeonhole to pigeonhole, each with its dangling red label – the wisdom of the philosophers, the precedents of law and history, the solace of the poets – and he brooded about his wife, about Berenice, about himself.

At last he heard the scud of praetorian boots on the slate tiles. After stripping and searching him for the third time, Geta marched him to the palace's residential wing.

The emperor's bedchamber was stuffy with the odour of unwashed flesh. Amidst overturned goblets, Domitian squatted on the floor with the dwarf, playing odds and evens. He rolled the dice, cursed his luck, then pushed a pile of markers to the jubilant dwarf. Glancing over his shoulder, he said: "Ahh, yes, my dear cousin. Greetings. I would have fetched you sooner, but as you can see I'm busy."

"Why have I been arrested?" demanded Clemens, determined to remain imperturbable now that he could see the game was to bait him. "Why was my wife's maid slaughtered?"

Domitian shook his dice. "Weren't you told?" He rolled two three's and a four. "The charge is the one I warned you about: harbouring a Jew."

"The girl was my wife's servant for three years. Her nationality was unimportant at the time of purchase."

"It became important, for it led to your second crime." Looking at him for the first time, Domitian smiled. "My consul's becoming a Jew."

"That's a lie."

"You deny it?"

"Most emphatically."

"You deny instructing the Jews to raise the floodgates of the stadium?"

"What? You dare to make that accusation?" Clemens laughed cynically. "The Jews burned Nero's Rome. Now they've flooded yours?"

Domitian picked up the dice box, returning to his game. "An emperor doesn't *dare*. An emperor *does*. That's the difference between us, cousin."

"I see," replied Clemens, still outwardly calm. "Now that the head of Antonius Saturninus is too rotten for use, I've been selected, with the help of Messalinus, to blame for the slaughter at the stadium."

Domitian snorted: "That's your story. Everyone in the stadium saw you in the royal box trying to distract your emperor while the Jews did their dirty work."

"Monster!" exclaimed Clemens, losing control. "I dared tell you the truth – that you have gone mad."

243

Rattling his dice loudly enough to end conversation, Domitian ordered: "Take him to prison, Geta. I'm sick of his face."

Tullianum Prison, at the foot of the Capitoline, was said to have acquired its name from a spring, or tullius, which the Jews claimed the apostle Peter struck out of a rock, then used to baptize his jailers. A less romantic legend ascribed it to an early Roman king named Tullius, responsible for its original construction. The prison had two chambers created from massive blocks of volcanic rock – ugly, durable, impervious to fire. The upper chamber was circular, with a cone roof, and divided into cells. The subterranean one was communal, reached only by a hole in its ceiling.

Tullianum was not just the oldest prison in Rome. It was the only one. Under Roman law, incarceration was not a punishment but an interim state. The top cells were for prisoners awaiting trial or public execution; the lower chamber was for the condemned awaiting torture or strangulation, with their bodies to be dumped through a trapdoor into the Great Drain.

Consul Flavius Clemens was thrown into an upper cell, with a high grated window through which filtered sickly tendrils of light. His only contact with humanity was a pair of boots, which each day kicked mildewed bread and cloudy water through a slit in the iron door.

To sustain himself, he tried to recall the values by which he had lived his life:

A belief in the natural order.

A belief in the authority necessary to maintain that order, including loyalty to the emperor's *imperium*, or power, despite the vagaries with which he wielded it.

The Stoic belief that a man should serve his state according to his talents.

A belief in the superiority of logic over feelings, of the civilized over the primitive.

A belief in human decency: that one must not degrade another human being.

244

A belief in happiness as the byproduct of a useful life, rather than the purpose of life, as the Epicureans believed.

A belief in this world as having precedence over all others, as the skeptics maintained.

Though Clemens admitted to having neglected the study of ethics for political philosophy, he had seen no evidence that the gods exist. No evidence that anything called a soul exists. No evidence of life after death, or of the Socratic world of Ideals beyond this material world.

As one day melted into the next, Clemens was chagrined to discover how much he, an ascetic, had counted on his little pleasures: freshly baked bread; honey from his own apiary; robes handwoven from the softest fibres; the tranquililty of his garden; the conviviality of checkers played with his cronies at the Julian Courthouse. Because he'd eschewed the ostentation of patrician Rome, he believed he had lived simply. Now he saw how privileged his life had been.

Clemens' second interview took place in the corridor outside his cell, at the pleasure of Catullus Messalinus. Wearing his prosecutor's sauve over his right eye, Messalinus tapped his way up and down the corridor, sniffing from a perfume bottle to cover the prison's stink, all the while spinning aphorisms and mixing metaphors, unable to pass up even this opportunity to show off his oratory. After haranguing for ten minutes, he at last broke off: "Clemens, this may come as a surprise to you, but I like you. I would like to help you to get out of here."

Clemens scoffed: "Your compliment would worry me more than my prison walls, if I didn't know you were the person who intrigued against me."

Messalinus chuckled. "The thing I admire about you, Clemens, is your gift of compromise. When tempted with great power, most men have to make a decision: either for or against. You never have. You always manage to wriggle onto middle ground when I would have sworn there wasn't any." He tapped Clemens' cell with his cane. "This time I've caught you. You have only one way to save yourself – a choice I myself have devised. Sign a statement confessing you killed your wife's maid when you discovered she was one of the Jewish mob who opened the floodgate at the emperor's stadium, and you will go free."

Stroking his beard, Clemens considered this generous offer. "Ah yes, Messalinus, now I understand. I understand why there is always so much applause when you speak in court. Given our profession's practice of paying claquers to applaud, it's always the worst speakers who raise the most noise. Your voice squeaks, your breath stinks, you jab the air like a fishwife trying to get a better price, and your metaphors – in fine shape when you stole them – all get mangled by a tongue that thinks each syllable worth its weight in spittle. When you began your public career, you received the acclaim your skill deserved: none. It was only when you started slitting throats, as an informer, that people began to notice you. This sinister second career of yours is the price all honest men must pay for your bad oratory."

With cheeks puffed like a galley in a squall, Messalinus sailed out of Tullianum.

Clemens' guards ordered the consul to strip. Wrapping him in a loincloth already infested with lice and soiled with body waste, they tied a rope around his waist and lowered him through a dank hole into the lower chamber of Tullianum.

A single lamp told Clemens more than he wanted to know. Some four dozen men, women and children squatted in straw and excrement. Judging by the stench, not all the bodies were alive. Such shocking ugliness befuddled Clemens, already humiliated by the filth of his loincloth. Always before he had had his senator's toga, his wealth and family to mirror back to him who he thought he was. Did Flavius Clemens exist in this foul pit, unheard and unseen?

To preserve his sanity, Clemens spent his first day inventing word games and mathematical puzzles. He marvelled at the Roman contribution to the world in law and in architecture, and dwelt with admiration on Latin as the supreme example of logic applied to human expression. Once he scratched his family tree on the wall, astonished at how many copulations from how many pairs of humans it had taken to bring him here to this spot on this day.

Each morning, food was tossed through the hole in the ceiling. Only the new prisoners rushed to eat it. When the water pail became empty, everyone licked the damp walls.

On Clemens' third day he discovered what happened when the chamber became overcrowded: A half-dozen guards descended by ladder through the ceiling to strangle prisoners at random and to heave the corpses through an iron door leading to the Great Drain. One of their choices was a young girl just into puberty, and here the procedure changed. All six guards raped her before strangling her since it was considered bad luck to execute a virgin.

As a lawyer, Clemens had done his decent best to keep clients out of Tullianum. Except in the case of friends, he had not bothered about what happened after the gates clanked behind them. Justice was the aim of Roman law, not mercy. That innocent men were sometimes ground up in the machinery did not invalidate the system.

On Clemens' fourth day he was summoned for another appointment with vested authority. When he was dragged by ropes through the ceiling, his eyes found it difficult to adjust to daylight and his limbs buckled. So thin were his hips they could barely hold up his loincloth. He no longer smelt his own stench.

Awaiting him this time was Captain Geta, who took Clemens to his shop where instruments were displayed: whips with lead burrs; mangles into which limbs could be fed. The stuffy, scummy room shook with the groans of the dying, for some of the instruments were in use. A man with ears, hands and feet lopped off begged for water from a heap of rags. Another hung in a harness over a tub of bubbling pitch. Several had wires tied round their limbs to cause gangrene.

Dispassionately, Geta explained the technical use and expected result of each instrument that might be applied to Clemens – unless he signed a confession.

"A confession of what?"

Geta shrugged. "That's up to Messalinus."

As Geta led Clemens from the torture room, he gave a drink to the man whose limbs he had chopped off; he wiped spittle from the face of another trussed in wires; he adjusted the harness – for comfort? – of the one suspended over pitch.

"You keep your victims happy?" mocked Clemens.

Fixing him with flat eyes rimmed in white, Geta said: "Pain is my job. It opens some men's mouths. It closes others. I don't enjoy it any more than you."

Clemens was lowered back into his cage, knowing he would never get the sounds and sights of the torture room out of his mind. For the rest of the day he pondered the word courage. He had often given speeches extolling it. What did it mean? Was courage charging into the hurricane for what you believed in, or resigning yourself to accept with dignity what you couldn't change? Was it taking your own life when there was nothing ahead but sorrow, or drinking life to its bitterest dregs? What took more courage: to stand firm for an unpopular opinion or to face down the enemy in battle? Who was the most courageous: the man who did what life required though his knees knocked, or the one who laughed in the teeth of adversity? Clemens knew nothing of his body except that it got him from one place to another and sometimes malfunctioned. Now he examined his arms and legs and chest as if seeing them for the first time. How much torture could he endure? Since he would have to sign the confession anyhow, could anyone blame him for bargaining for a quick slice of the throat?

As an experiment in suffering, Clemens scraped his hand against the volcanic wall, raising a small welt, drawing a little blood. Even that smarted. He thought of the earless, handless, footless man in Geta's torture shop and, groaning, bowed his head. Clemens had a cruel, clear vision of himself in triumphal robes at the Circus Maximus with the slave Nemesis whispering in his ear: "Remember you are mortal." As he wiped his eyes he knew he would give up all his honours for one last day at his villa with Domitilla and his sons, and his almond tree in full bloom, and yes...his fish tank.

When Clemens raised his head, some shift had taken place within him, as if his tears had cleared his vision. He began to see faces under their filth: a toothless old woman who made necklaces out of straw; an Arab who played tunes by clicking his tongue; a boy who nursed his father. Till now the ex-consul had kept himself apart from the other prisoners, unwilling to acknowledge any kinship with the pathetic scraps of rag and bone around him. He had been especially repelled by an enormously fat prostitute who willingly opened herself up to all comers, so that sometimes she seemed like a sow with a litter of piglets sucking at her. In the new "natural order" in which he found himself, he regarded her as one of the humanitarians.

Since Berenice's funeral, Domitilla had lived in a chapel gouged out of limestone under the hut of Philip the Fishmonger, sparsely furnished yet with every scrap of wall and ceiling painted in murals depicting the life of Jesus of Nazareth. Though these were ill-proportioned and without perspective, they had a power that held Domitilla spellbound. She was especially drawn to two portraits: one of Jesus in tranquillity with a dove in his hand; the other showing him with pierced side and crown of thorns. Both had been painted by a man called Josephus – one of two thousand Jews crucified on the road from Jericho to Jerusalem.

Though Domitilla knew her husband had been imprisoned in Tullianum, she had heard no further word. Never before had she been separated from him. She felt as if half her flesh had been slashed away. Though praying to the God of the Jews, she bargained in the Roman tradition with her wealth and even her life for his safety.

Philip, with whom she spoke daily, did not hold out false hope. As this room of martyrs eloquently testified, his experience was against such optimism. Instead he spoke of resignation to God's will...the peace that passeth understanding.

To fill the time that hung heavy on her hands, Domitilla fashioned an altar cloth out of the hand-woven purple cloak she had worn in her flight from her villa. She also accompanied Philip on his visits to the poor and the sick where her compassion and domestic skills were put to good use. Almost every night there were services in the chapel. Among these simple, zealous people, Domitilla felt again the joy she had found in the cave. Here at last was an altar on which to place her gift of passion – a gift which, during her whole life as a Roman matron, she alone had prized. A gift without receivers.

While living on the Esquiline, Domitilla had refused baptism out of respect for her husband. Now she felt no such inhibitions. She was baptized by Philip into the Christian religion – the first highborn Roman woman to be converted. In opening her heart to her new faith, she felt more at peace though the ache of her grief did not cease.

On learning from Jewish spies that Clemens was in the lower chamber of Tullianum threatened with torture, Domitilla vowed she would not eat till he was released. Her fasting heightened her gift of prophecy so that both sleeping and awake she caught visions of Clemens in a loincloth, his face dark with pain, like the face of the crucified Christ on her ceiling. After one such dream, she awoke to find herself staring at a detail of the mural that had escaped her: Christ's side was pierced with a knife bearing a fish symbol. Domitilla placed her own knife, with the same symbol, on her altar. Kneeling, she prayed the words she had embroidered on her altar cloth: *Thy Will Be Done.*

Flavius Clemens lay in Tullianum neither awake nor asleep, neither dead nor alive, neither mad nor yet quite sane. Already there had been one torture session. On behalf of Messalinus and the emperor, Captain Geta had demanded that he confess to converting to Judaism for the purpose of leading a Jewish conspiracy. When he refused, Geta had seared his sexual parts with a branding iron, the mark of the Jew. The pain was total, like a shaft of white fire consuming his body. He could never endure another test. One sight of that branding iron would reduce him to shrieking compliance.

The trapdoor opened over Clemens' head. Choosing to assume it was a guard throwing down slops, he paid no attention. "Hey, you!" shouted the guard. "You, old man."

Still Clemens made no response. Petras, a youth who had been arrested for scrawling Jewish symbols on the Flavian Temple, shook him by the arm. "You, father, they want you." With touching optimism, he added: "Maybe you are to go free."

Clemens looked toward the trapdoor. The guard's brass helmet lit by his torch filled the circular opening like a subterranean sun. The man was pointing at him and beckoning. As Clemens crawled to his knees, he felt his bowels release though there was nothing in them to soil him.

The guard was still waiting. Seeing the old man's frailty, Petras helped him to his feet. While Clemens composed himself for the ladder, the guard glanced fearfully over his shoulder then tossed a pile of rags into his arms. He slammed the trapdoor. As Clemens stared up at the ceiling, listening to the retreat of heavy boots, Petras eased him back to his patch of straw by the wall, where he then sat nursing the grubby bundle. Was it from the emperor? He remembered the head of Antonius Saturninus impaled on his household god. What macabre joke had been sent to mock him?

Clemens tried to push away the bundle, but his eyes kept returning to it.

"Aren't you going to open it?" asked Petras.

Clemens gingerly explored the outer wrappings. There was nothing in its weight to suggest it was anything but what it pretended to be: a bunch of rags. Layer by layer he unfastened it. Now he could feel something hard at the core. He poked and prodded. A knife! He clasped the handle. It was of bone. With hope too precious, too fragile to acknowledge, he held the handle toward the light. Yes. There it was. The carving of a fish with its tail worn smooth where her hand had held it to fillet the trout he caught near Como. *Domitilla's* hand. She was alive. She knew where he was, and was one with him in his suffering. Perhaps she had sought sanctuary in the Temple of Vesta? Cornelia could be counted on to contact Marcus who would spirit her out of Rome. Perhaps she was already on her way? Perhaps to their sons in Greece?

As Clemens turned the knife, trying to divine its story, Petras pointed in excitement to the carving of the fish. "Are you one of us, father?"

Clemens shook his head. "No, though that's the lie against me." Turning his back on Petras, sealing himself in his own private world, Clemens clasped the knife, crying openly now, allowing himself to remember the joy, the richness, the love, the peace of the life he was leaving.

When Clemens again looked at Petras, he was fast asleep. How much time had elapsed? Hastily wiping his eyes on the rags that had bound the knife – by far the cleanest thing in the cell – Clemens turned his attention, in resignation, from the handle to that other part: its blade. He dared not wait another moment! What if Geta should send for him with his deliverance in his hands? Holding the knife in grateful dedication to whatever gods might be passing through this corner of the universe, Clemens slashed his right wrist, then his left. As he observed the jagged gashes, already he felt detached from his body, so lightly worn by him. With a touch of impatience now that the decision had been taken, he watched the blood gurgle down his arms. He thought of all his friends who had chosen this path, and knew he need not confuse regret with shame.

Clemens shook the sleeping boy, whose head nudged his lap. The brown eyes looked up dully, then widened. Handing him the knife, the consul said: "For you, lad. Maybe you'll make fiercer use of it than I."

Consul Flavius Clemens lay his head against the family ancestry he had scratched on the wall, thought of his almond tree, and died.

Domitilla stared into the face of the man with the dove on his head and knew Clemens was dead. With her instincts as a Roman, she also knew where she would find the body. She took communion from Philip who, kissing her, said: "You are one with us, sister. God be with you."

Dressed once more in the robes of a Roman matron, Domitilla crossed Aemilian Bridge to the right side of the Tiber. She walked to the Steps of Mourning by Tullianum Prison, where corpses of political prisoners were tossed as an invitation to abuse before being dragged on hooks to the Tiber.

A silent crowd had assembled. A few recognized Domitilla and fell back respectfully. Others pulled their cloaks over their faces and scurried away.

Domitilla climbed down the stairs to the crumpled, naked body of her dear Clemens. He had not been a large man. Now the corpse seemed as small as a child's. After examining the encrusted blood on each wrist and the wounded genitals, Domitilla kissed the cold lips. By some kindly hand the eyes were closed. He seemed at peace. She cradled the body she had tended through pain and disease, urged to health, then provided with the instrument of death.

Domitilla felt a hand on her shoulder. Maximus Marcus was standing over her. Scooping up the frail body in his scarlet cloak, he carried it toward the speaker's platform in the Forum, trailing a small crowd of the curious.

Marcus did not mount the rostra, where Antony had stood with the body of Caesar; where Cicero, in payment for too much eloquence, had had his chopped head and hands displayed; where Priscus had mocked and mimed his own death. Without gesture or declamation, and speaking so quietly only those closest could hear, he said: "Flavius Clemens was a good man. He was your consul and friend. What is Rome when good men die – not by the will of the gods or through the enemies of Rome but by the hand of Caesar? What is Rome when to ask for justice for her citizens is to ask for your own death?

"You were at the stadium. You saw the madness of our emperor, who ordered his praetorians to shoot fireballs among you and then to release the floodgates to drown you. You heard the moans of the dying. You smelled the smoke from their pyres. Tell me, citizens, who was that man who poured his outrage into the emperor's ear? My friends, that voice which spoke for you has been silenced. Now, when you cry out, who will hear? Now, who will place his love between you and the tyrant's sword?"

Marcus spoke for one-half turn of the waterclock – less than a man's lawyer would speak for the loss of a jar of wine – before Captain Geta arrived with ten praetorians to arrest him.

CHAPTER TWENTY

Cornelia set out by litter for her meeting with the emperor – his first audience of the day. She could tell by the noisy rush of the crowd toward the northern end of the Forum that something was wrong. Some disturbance. Possibly at the rostra.

She thought of asking her bearers to sweep around that way, but decided against it. Having spent days preparing for this meeting, she couldn't afford any distractions.

Cornelia's litter mounted the Palatine, through the imperial gate to the public wing of the palace, with the usual challenges and security checks. Once inside, she was escorted by four praetorians to a reception room, where the emperor sometimes held private audiences. As she waited unattended for two hours, she felt confidence drain from her like liquid from a waterclock: in what condition would she find the emperor? Few had seen him since the debacle at the stadium. Some said he, like Caligula, had fallen from his tightrope into madness so that now he too swaggered the corridors of the palace in gold beard, casting thunderbolts. Others insisted he never left his bedchamber, where he conducted himself with a depravity unheard of since Tiberius. Rome had had much experience with imperial excess. Now her gossips made full use of it.

A praetorian informed Cornelia the emperor was on his way. She rose to greet him. Moments later he strode into the room in senator's toga, his hair unadorned. Settling himself in a mother-of-pearl chair the twin of hers, he indicated she too should sit down, and then, leaning toward her, fixed her with full and flattering attention.

Cornelia was relieved at his look of normalcy. She had never seen him so at ease. Always in the past she had experienced his arrogance as weakness. In his composure, she felt his strength. The articulate phrases she had rehearsed deserted her, throwing her back on lame salutation. "Lord and God, I trust you have been well though you have not been much around the capital?"

Without change of expression he replied: "The emperor has been well – for an emperor."

"That pleases me."

He smiled charmingly. "Why?"

Taken back, she replied: "The health of the emperor is of concern to the gods of Rome, and hence to Vesta's chief priestess."

"You have never before loved me enough to come and tell me. Perhaps you had better forget my health and explain why you have left your post."

"This is my post." Cornelia moved into her prepared text. "Last week at the Festival of Fordicidia the vestal Fausta pulled twin calves, joined at the heart, from the womb of a slaughtered cow. As she rolled about the floor of the Temple, clawing at her breast, she spewed words like Vesuvius its lava. 'How can such twins hold onto life, if one set of arms makes war on the other so that the blood shed by one is shed by the other? That is no less true when the two seem separate but are joined at the heart in love, as when two brothers or two cousins suckle at the same breast. If Romulus should strike Remus, what then will become of Rome?'

"Struck by the force of this vision, I heaped twigs on Vesta's altar and, in the eloquence of their flame, read Vesta's message: 'The two calves joined at the heart are Emperor Domitian and his cousin Flavius Clemens who, though not equal before the

256

gods, are joined in the protection of Rome, and suckled by the same mother, for did they not both adopt Minerva as patron? If one should smite the other, would not Minerva split herself in sorrow? Mark well my words, for the safety of Rome depends on it.'"

As Cornelia spoke, Domitian's face seemed to congeal around his frosty eyes. "Must I take this warning as coming from the gods, oh chief vestal, or merely from you?"

"My emperor, though I can't claim infallability, I was chosen above all others for this trust. Many omens foretold the Flavian family's rise to power – the dog that brought your deified father the severed hand; the ox that shook off its yoke and bowed to him; the statue of Caesar that turned and faced east, where he had just scored a victory; the blind man, and the lame, whom he cured with a touch. The omen I have just related is one of many recent portents in the Temple of Vesta, predicting grief for the Flavian House if these warnings go unheeded."

Though the emperor's mouth twitched, his voice was calm. "Why would the gods send me a warning they know will arrive too late? My dear cousin Clemens is dead – a suicide."

Cornelia jolted forward. "What? Consul Clemens dead?"

Domitian pulled a sober mask over a face that gloated. "For weeks I've been bombarded with information about the infatuation of my cousin with that Jewish sect. When I could no longer ignore the evidence, I put my duty before my love and had my cousin brought to me. I begged him to deny his attachment to these Jews so that I might punish those who blackened his name, which is also mine. He refused, and when I asked for an explanation, would give none. I had no choice but to send him to Tullianum, where I hoped in solitude he might redress himself.

"My cousin was questioned by Messalinus. This time he had the audacity to boast that the reports of his conversion were true, offering as evidence his naked organ with the Jew cross on the tip. Even when I still had it in my heart to think him more mad than treasonous, he took the dagger he had smuggled into his cell, and slit his wrists.... So, you see, if the gods you consult – *who consult you* – had foreseen my being hurt by my cousin, you might have been nearer the mark. Indeed, the more I think of it, the more I'm convinced that must be the meaning."

Cornelia no longer doubted Clemens' death, only its manner. "Where is the body of Flavius Clemens? How is it to be treated?"

Again the emperor assumed his mourning face. "The funeral has come and gone, though not as I would have chosen. That's what delayed me for our meeting. My praetorians, acting on their own judgement, threw the body down the Stairs of Mourning. It was claimed by Domitilla, who has been hiding out with her Jew sect. She was joined by Maximus Marcus, who drew about him a rabble at the rostra, till my guards put a stop to that by arresting both." His voice rose in self-pity. "So you see, chief vestal, the pain to an emperor who trusts that those close in blood will also be close in love!"

Cornelia's fingers tightened around her chair. *Marcus arrested. And Domitilla.* She tried to squeeze the panic from her voice. "What is to happen, my Lord and God, to Maximus Marcus and Domitilla? Where have they been taken?"

The emperor raised an amazed brow. "Where would you suggest after what I've told you? Would not a charge of high treason match the events?"

Cornelia shrugged. "In one way, but not in another. You didn't believe in the guilt of Flavius Clemens, despite the private parade of evidence which you heard. How could they believe with no evidence at all? They heard the body was crushed on the Stairs of Mourning, and rushed in grief to administer to it. That's all."

"In your mind, perhaps. Not in mine. Not in the mind of an emperor." He leaned forward, his mouth beginning to twitch. "How would you have me behave? With mercy?"

"With wisdom. Your people will be upset by the death of their respected consul, and think well of the man who forgives his widow and adopted son. To have their lives count *for* you, instead of their deaths *against* you, would seem no mean thing in the tinderbox that is Rome. It would also prove to the suspicious that Clemens did take his own life."

Domitian sighed. "There's something in what you say, but my mind's made up. At least as far as Maximus Marcus is concerned."

"What do you mean?"

"I propose to give him another chance to capture popular acclaim."

"You wish him to race again in the Circus?"

"No. I've got a better place for him to star. One where he won't have to share the glory."

"Where is that?"

"In the arena. Yes! I'll make him the star of my next gladiator show. Let him find his mercy – or his justice – there."

"Of mercy, there is none in the arena. Of justice – very little. I ask the emperor to reconsider."

Domitian leaned back in his chair, studying her. "This conversation was beginning to bore me. Now I find my interest grows with your intensity. Since you've been speaking of Maximus Marcus, your eyes have bulged from your face, your cheeks have flushed, and you find it hard to breathe. An emperor learns to watch others with the same curiosity as they watch him, for isn't a cat as interested in a mouse as the mouse is in him? Your love for my safety – which you insist brought you here – seems nothing compared to the love you bear the dashing Marcus. If you were not a vestal bound by chastity, I'd see something of the woman in that concern of yours."

"My emperor, this conversation has been a harrowing one for me. The concern I express now is the accumulation of my concern for everyone...for Rome. How can you compare my feelings for Maximus Marcus, a recent acquaintance, with my feelings for you as the spiritual head of Rome?"

Domitian laughed. "You lie so badly! Far from loving me, you barely manage to conceal your distaste." He held up his hand.

"Don't deny it, for it's written all over your face. Too bad, lady, for you have a mind and a character that interests me – no small compliment from an emperor, for whom the treats of the world are often a bore. It's too bad we couldn't have joined like the grafting of a tree, instead of playing our emnity off against each other."

"You misread me, my emperor. I love and admire you, as I have said. Maximus Marcus' popularity, along with the people's respect for Domitilla, may cause you more trouble if they are dead than if they're alive – that's all that concerns me."

"So, you persist, do you? You love him enough to add your lies to all the others that flatter and fawn around me, eh? I grant you this: the foolhardiness of Maximus Marcus today in the Forum proves he's no danger to me alive. He reeks of the amateur, who plays politics as if he expected the best man would win. That's why my mind seized on the arena. Let him test his theories there."

The emperor shrugged. "The truth is, lady, I don't care if he lives or dies. What interests me more is *your* concern. How far has it gone between you? What pretty words have been spoken? What vows exchanged? How much does a *virgin* like you dare, when the feelings you've bottled up begin to boil over? I have a taste for challenge of an unusual sort. What's the point in being emperor, with all the nuisance of that, if not to throw dice with the gods occasionally? I ask you this: What would you do, August Lady Cornelia, to save Maximus Marcus' life?"

She could not answer. Not even to herself.

"Aha! So that *is* it! Well – I'll tell you what my terms shall be, my vestal. Though I have no need to offer any at all, I'll make an exception for this rare opportunity to study human nature.

"Maximus Marcus *will* fight in the arena, against any odds I choose – that much is fixed. But if he wins, he can walk away from Rome a free man. For that, there is a forfeit." The emperor cocked his head. "Aren't you going to ask me what the forfeit is? Look at me. Raise your eyes when your emperor speaks!"

Cornelia did as commanded.

"That's better. The forfeit is this: you must bed with me." He held up his hand mockingly. "Don't thank me. There's time enough for that later. Don't berate me. Don't plead. Don't tell me how I jeopardize the safety of Rome. All that I know, and have dismissed." He teetered backward on his chair. "I'll admit it: this proposition has simmered at the back of my fantasies, interesting enough to fill a dull minute or two, but not to be put to the test till I knew you to be a woman like the others. A woman with human weaknesses. I am, after all, as well as your emperor, your high priest. The vestals of Rome are the emperor's women. You are – as chief of the vestals – the wife of the Imperial House. Ergo, you are the wife of the emperor of Rome." He laughed. "If your virginity doesn't belong to me, who does it belong to? Certainly not Maximus Marcus. Believe me, lady, I don't endanger Rome, I save it!" Folding his hands, he became crisp and formal. "So, there it is, lady, your challenge and your rationale. Say nothing now. Dream of your lover Maximus Marcus alive, then dream of him dead...and weigh the rest."

Cornelia left the palace by litter, as she had come. Clemens dead. Domitilla arrested. Marcus to fight in the arena. How stupidly prideful she had been to think she could re-direct the crooked imperial will. She thought of Marcus as she had last seen him, in ashy mourning robes. How cruelly prophetic that had been. She clasped her hands to keep them from trembling. She had to remember now that she was a vestal. Chief vestal. With responsibilities far greater than herself. Other good men, like Clemens, had lost their lives at the emperor's caprice. More would. There was nothing she could do about it – either out of love or pride of office. That had been proven. The emperor was mad – or close to it. It would take everyone's courage to confine the evil, to keep it from lapping like acid all over Rome. The challenge he had made to her – shameful as it was – she herself had allowed by her weakness. Against her vow, she had become emotionally entangled with a man. She had harboured illicit

261

fantasies, even watered and tended them like prize hothouse blooms. Now she must root them out, as she would advise – order – any other vestal to do. How did her situation differ from the foolish ensnarement of Julia Sabina, except in the greatness of the duty she was betraying?

Cornelia reviewed her conversation with the emperor as dispassionately as she could. If he had been able to read her guilty thoughts in her face, how many others had done the same? What gossip was there about her in Rome? What kind of an example had she been setting for the younger vestals? Was this the reason Agrippina and Diana had become so insubordinate?

The litter stopped at the vestalry gate. As Cornelia climbed out, she saw Agrippina forcefully propelling Helen and Poppaea toward her. Though she knew instantly that something was wrong, it wasn't until she observed Agrippina's face, with its blend of outrage and triumph, that she knew how terribly wrong.

Agrippina flung the two vestals like bags of soiled laundry at Cornelia's feet.

"That's enough, Agrippina," ordered Cornelia. "State your grievance."

Agrippina was only too willing. "They were supposed to be in the library, copying vestal history for the Vestalia. I found them in the archives room with their clothes off."

Agrippina's look of disgust spelled out the rest. As gently as possible, Cornelia asked the younger vestals: "Is that true?"

Sobbing, Helen replied: "Yes."

Poppaea, as stubborn as Agrippina, refused to answer.

Cornelia looked from one to the other, remembering in anguish that time when she and the vestal Junia had been caught by Fausta. They had been forced to strip before the chief priest, then whipped with his rod of office, under the sacred lotus tree.

"These vestals are unfit to tend the flame until they've been cleansed," exclaimed Agrippina, adding with malice: "They are unfit to be vestals."

Determined to seem unruffled, Cornelia instructed: "Take Poppaea and Helen back to the library. Don't speak to anyone about this matter until I come to you with my decision."

It was not the gloating victory Agrippina had expected. The doubt Cornelia always managed to sow at the centre of her righteousness had taken seed. As she marched the vestals toward the library, she flung over her shoulder: "We'll be waiting."

Cornelia watched them go with a feeling of nausea. As the dispirited little group disappeared into the library, she plodded toward the Temple where Fausta was tending hearth. The elder vestal had been lucid for several days now. Cornelia prayed she would be well enough for consultation.

Fausta was at the back of the Temple, draping fig-leaf garlands on the statue of Juno, her grey hair discreetly bound, her robe tied. "August Mother," greeted Cornelia, "may we talk?"

Fausta inclined her head. "That would please me." Putting aside her garlands, she sat on a marble bench, apparently completely restored to that vestal chief whom Cornelia had known for her dignity and justice.

"Agrippina has come to me with distressing news. She surprised Helen and Poppaea in the archives room, lying together with their robes unbound, and insists they be reported to the chief priest for discipline. Of course I know the rules, but wouldn't it be fairer if –"

Fausta held up her hand, her face stern. "Chastity is our one great gift to Vesta. That is what the state rewards us for sacrificing, with privileges and honour. Any carnal sin must be penalized so that every temptation in the future is overshadowed by the severity and certainty of punishment, and especially by its humiliation. There can be no compromise."

"But August Mother, once our girls were ignorant of what they sacrificed. That spared them curiosity. Now they go to an emperor's banquet and see what is denied to them enjoyed as heartily as the menu. Should we not bear such temptations in mind when confronted by experimentations?"

Fausta shook her head, and this time when she fixed her eyes upon Cornelia they pierced her heart. "It's often a loose society like ours that values all the more highly the chastity of its vestals, and punishes the more cruelly our infractions. I sense that kind of perversity in our emperor." She leaned toward Cornelia. "Be wise, my daughter. Restore seniority inside the vestalry. Use your lictors and order the others to do so. Veil yourself, as vestals of the past. You protect your sisters with strictness. You save their lives."

"Do you mean my mission is wrong? My hope that we might live in harmony, sharing equally the joys and burdens of the communal life?"

"Not wrong. But you have moved too quickly." Fausta smiled with kindness. "I too had such hopes when I became chief vestal. That's why I supported your candidacy so strongly against Agrippina's. That is why I have watched you – when Vesta has given me the clarity – with sadness in my heart and a lump in my throat. Bring your ideas back in line with tradition for the time being. Wait your chance. The only change acceptable in religion is the kind that isn't noticed." Lowering her voice to a whisper, she added: "Let me give you one more piece of advice. Leave politics to the politicians. No more visits to emperors. Your life as chief vestal is here. Higher walls keep the world out as well as the vestals in."

PART IV

CORNELIA

CHAPTER TWENTY-ONE

The Flavian Amphitheatre was begun in A.D. 72 by Vespasian on the site of Nero's Golden House, which he demolished to obliterate the memory of that emperor. Ironically, it became known as the Colosseum because of an immense statue of Nero placed near its entrance by Emperor Hadrian.

Built as a ponderous ring of stone supporting itself without buttress, the arena was a theatre for the ritual sacrifice of the enemies of Rome to Mars, the god of war. On its inauguration by Titus in A.D. 80, five thousand beasts were slaughtered in one day of the 100-day orgy, and two thousand gladiators during the total event. Such spectacles accustomed Romans early to their blood role as conquerors of the world.

The amphitheatre was constructed of travertine blocks, some weighing five tons, dragged by ox cart from nearby Tivoli, and secured with bronze pins using as little mortar as possible. Faced with marble, mosaics and gold, it had three floors adorned by columns of the Doric, Ionic and Corinthian orders, with archways for statues, and a top floor decorated with Corinthian pilasters and bronze shields. A ring of rods supported a voluminous yellow, red and purple canopy, with a centre hole for sunlight. To raise this canopy, one hundred sailors who maintained it were joined by one thousand others from the Imperial Fleet of Misenum.

The arrival of these troops was regarded by many as the true opening of the festival. With cheers and music, all who could flocked to the docks to escort them to the amphitheatre. As the sailors turned 160 winches in perfect unison to the ominous beat beat beat of drums, the ring of brilliantly coloured canvas unfurled in a spectacle so stirring that all who witnessed it felt the truth of the Roman proverb: "So long as the Amphitheatre stands, Rome will stand. When the Amphitheatre falls, Rome will fall. When Rome falls, the world falls."

Castor, page of the imperial court, lay on the Esquiline overlooking the amphitheatre, watching the banners of red, yellow and purple luff in the wind, feeling the thrill of what it was to be a man and a Roman, for wasn't the amphitheatre the foremost wonder of the world? From his vantage point, he could also peer into the barracks where the gladiators lived and exercised. Some were running around the sandy track in chains. Others grunted and cursed as they tried to maim their opponents even in practice. As an urchin bred on heroic dreams, Castor had often imagined proving himself in the arena – single-handedly holding off a half-dozen roaring, slashing gladiators, or wrestling a leopard with his bare hands. His victory proclaimed by the adulation of the crowd, he would then dump the carcass in front of the royal box and, with his true paternity proclaimed – here the story had many variations – he would gallop around the arena for all to acclaim him, and especially for the vindication of his mother.

Castor dreamed nightly of Phoebe, though he had not seen her since she fled their apartment. Dreams of beauty that tore out his eyes, dreams of depravity that scorched his loins. With a groan, he hugged his bony knees and rolled over and over, down the dusty slope to the boulders at the bottom. Tomorrow he would see Diana at the spring. Now when he touched her, she drove him off, frightened and angry so that he had to persuade her. Once he even forced her with his hand over her mouth. She told him she didn't want to see him anymore, that she was afraid of her friend Agrippina.

Castor couldn't help himself: a volcano simmered inside him which sometimes needed release.

Maximus Marcus had one week to prepare for the arena. As a member of the power elite, Marcus held his class' view of gladiators: They were criminals, enemies, deserters – doomed by the will of man and the gods. Wasn't it better for them to depart this world in a contest of valour, with their entrails dedicated to Mars, than in whatever gutter their inferiority would drag them?

Even now, Marcus had only to witness their brutality to harden him against them: the blasphemy with which they cursed the gods; their barbarous sexual stories, often ending with gloating descriptions of how they murdered or mutilated their partners; the irrationality with which one man would slit the throat of another over a crust of bread, or gouge out an eye because a companion had touched his armour or breeched some other superstitious ritual. These men were the scum of the earth!

On his first night in the barracks, Marcus received a measure of insult due his former rank, but his presence was soon reduced to the indifference with which the men treated everything that did not arouse their lust. Here there was no division between pro and amateur, as in the stadium. Here were only savages set upon survival.

There were sixteen modes by which a man might defend himself, each patterned on the armour and techniques of a conquered enemy:

The Samnites wore a plumed helmet, carried a large shield, a sword and a lance.

The murmillones, so-called for their fish helmets, wore metal leg and arm shields, and carried a short sword and oblong shield.

The Thracians, unarmoured, carried a small round shield and scimitar.

The retiarii, unarmoured, carried a trident, a dagger and a net with which they tripped their heavily armoured opponents.

It was fashionable to pit the heavily armoured against the lightly armed, with the odds lying only on the skill of the individual in exploiting strength or speed.

Given his large size, Marcus naturally chose to go heavily armoured as a Samnite. His first task was to familiarize himself with the equipment: the plumed helmet, large shield, lance and sword – blunted and twice as heavy for practise. Though he was in superb condition from battle, he felt no match for these case-hardened men. He concentrated on teaching his body the techniques of the heavily armoured, and his mind the tricks of the lightly armed, against whom he would certainly be pitted.

One man stood out in all the clash of arms: Xerxes, a heavily armoured murmillone, whom Marcus had seen demonstrate his awesome strength at the emperor's banquet. This hideously scarred veteran of eighty-seven bouts was a showman who liked to pick up a dis-armed opponent and, after crushing every bone with his steely arms, tear off the leg or even the head, and devour it.

Xerxes had another distinction: he fought for the pleasure of it. Some even said he was not born of woman, but had been shaped by Pluto out of the pitch and fires of Hades to deliver to him the most corpses in the shortest time. Since his nose had been slashed off, he wheezed like a whale through a blowhole. Resonating through the barracks at night, this sinister sound caused more than one terrified retiarius to choke himself by swallowing his blanket rather than face this monster in the arena.

One other person drew Marcus' attention: an emaciated old man some called Philip the Prophet and others Philip the Fishmonger, who had been rounded up with a raggle-taggle of Jews accused of being part of a rebellion instigated by Flavius Clemens. Since the Jews refused to fight in the arena, they were to serve as fodder for the wild-beast show which opened the games. Many of the gladiators fixed upon these unfortunates as the butt of their jokes, especially Xerxes, who turned his dull mind to inventing such diversions as having them scour his chamberpot or eat porridge with his spittle in it.

Though Marcus harboured a Roman's natural suspicion of the Jews, he was grudgingly won over by the equanimity with which this sect, under Philip's example, bore the vilest of insults. One evening when the bullying was especially galling, Marcus joined them for dinner, preferring them to his vulgar Roman companions. His authority, added to Philip's dignity, staved off all but the most incorrigible. When Xerxes tried to force upon Philip a cup of wine adulterated with urine, Marcus smashed it from his hand so that it flew into the giant's lap. Since Xerxes held the Roman belief that to stink of piss was to smell of the breath of Charon, he tore apart the dining room in a superstitious frenzy, breaking benches and uprooting tables, but he did not attack Marcus, and from then on went back to terrorizing the retiarii.

Marcus learned from Philip that Domitilla had been exiled to the island of Pandataria. From a Jewish lad called Petras, he also learned how Clemens had died. Showing Marcus the consul's fish knife, Petras confided that he himself had been intending to use it to jump a guard when he had been sentenced to death – or life! – in the arena.

Of all the Jews, only Petras had agreed to fight as a gladiator. The rest were to be fodder for the wild-beast show. While they prepared for martyrdom, Marcus practised his survival skills, such as running around the "cornmill" – an upright drum with two crossbars to duck and jump at risk of breaking a leg or splitting a skull.

At first Marcus enjoyed conversations with Philip, but he was repelled by the prophet's vision of another life, for which this was a preparation, when he learned that a man who earned honours in this world might be stripped of them in the next, while a man like Philip, who lived on prayer and fish heads, would be elevated for his belief. Marcus was also rankled by Philip's claim that he did not despise Xerxes, whom he regarded as an equal fallen into sinful ways. How did seeing only good in all men differ from Priscus' error in seeing only the bad? In honesty, Marcus did not blame the emperor for banning the Jews.

There were eighty entrances into the Flavian Amphitheatre, including the Triumphal Gate through which the gladiators paraded, and the Gate of Funerals, out of which the dead were dragged. On the first day of the celebrations, the populace of Rome streamed through these arches like sharks converging on blood prey. Magistrates and senators sat in the first tier of marble benches while the poorest jammed into the "chicken coop" under the awnings, making for a capacity crowd of sixty thousand.

The emperor and empress were borne through the Triumphal Gate to their cushioned stall, opposite that of the vestals. For the wild-beast show, the arena had been landscaped with trees, cliffs, streams and waterfalls. At a blast of trumpets, elevators brought animals up from subterranean cages for the comic warm-up events: monkeys in Faction colours racing chariots drawn by leopards; bears who balanced poles on their noses. Even here the preference was for acts that humbled these proud beasts to Roman domination: a tiger that licked the trainer who had just beaten it; an elephant that knelt before the imperial box and traced a D in the sand with its trunk.

As Poppaea clapped in glee, Cornelia cast a rueful glance sideways. She hadn't wanted the youngest vestal to attend today's wild-beast show, but Poppaea herself had begged and the chief priest had insisted.

The clown acts came to an end. Now the elevators released one hundred ostriches. Stunned by sunlight, they staggered about the arena, causing the crowd to laugh at their homely gait. The emperor stood up in the imperial box, a bow in his hands. As they loped by, he shot them with arrows handed to him by his page, and such was his precision that he decapitated or pierced the necks of twenty in successive shots. Many knights and senators also tried their skill, so that dozens of the birds were soon rushing around the arena, headlong and headless, like tattered scarlet flowers in a cyclone.

Giraffes were released. Again, their mottled necks made irresistible targets. Again, senators and knights took aim. The crowd was startled at the speed and grace of these seemingly timid, foolish-looking beasts, then at the ferocity with which they lashed at each other in their agony, their forelegs capable of breaking the back of an ox.

When this activity grew monotonous, the elevator delivered another load of unfortunates: thirty Jews, huddled and naked, followed by twice as many leopards. The leopards were surprised at their release into sunlight; the Jews were not. As the big cats adjusted dully, the Jews – led by a stately prophet known to the crowd as Philip the Fishmonger – climbed the highest peak in the arena, singing praises to their Jew-God.

Knowing the Jews would be as quick as fleas to claim this small respite as yet another miracle, Domitian aimed with bow and arrow. He picked off Philip with a barb through the brain, then signalled for his praetorians to shoot the rest, so that Jew after Jew was soon tumbling into the ponds, now bobbing with corpses.

The elevators disgorged the next amusement: elephants! As they milled in a tight herd, mothers and babes on the inside, wild dogs were released. Trained through torture and starvation to attack anything that breathed, these dogs charged the herd. At first, the bulls easily crushed them with ponderous feet, or tossed and skewered them with their tusks. Pack after pack of dogs were released: wave upon wave of snarling fury. At the same time, the praetorians hurled a volley of spears, aiming for the elephants' eyes. Blinded and confused, they lunged at each other, trampling the carcasses of birds and animals, churning the floor of the arena into gore.

The first beast lumbered and fell. It was beset by dozens of dogs, jaws slathering. Though their teeth could not penetrate the tough hide, they tore hunks of the softer mouth and ear flesh, driving the elephant so mad with pain its bellows shook the arena.

The big beasts toppled, one by one, their hides spewing blood from hundreds of wounds. Sensing at last who their true enemy was, they herded as best they could, and charged, first one side of the stadium, then the other, so that senators and even the emperor had to abandon their seats. The crowd stampeded and bellowed and trumpeted in imitation of the beasts' death throes. A stiff wind luffed the canvas roof, sending ripples of red and yellow and purple over the arena, and adding a sepulchral echo, so that some feared the amphitheatre would come tumbling down, thus fulfilling the prophecy about the fall of Rome, of the empire and the world.

More spears. More dogs. At last there was only one beast left. With its hide so pierced that no black showed, it reared on its hindlegs, thrashing its scarlet trunk. Receiving a dozen more spears on its exposed chest, it shuddered then fell. Now the elevators dispensed slaves with hooks, harnesses and teams of broken and tuskless elephants whose job it was to drag off their kin. Fresh sand was spread over the wood floor for the next entertainment.

Cornelia had not seen the elephants. Poppaea had become ill at the sight of the decapitated ostriches, and hysterical at the massacre of the singing Jews, so that Cornelia had rushed the child from the amphitheatre – as much for herself as for Poppaea. Though trained to view the sacrifice of beasts as dispassionately as a surgeon regards the amputation of a limb, Cornelia realized – through her response to Poppaea's nausea – how much this savagery repelled her. The Flavian Amphitheatre was a theatre of ritual murder for a people intoxicated with the smell of blood – the rough strong fruit of the Roman lust for conquest. There had been nobility in the climb of the Jews to higher ground. Would she have the same courage as Philip the Prophet to act with serenity and conviction for her beliefs? Conviction. That was the trouble. More and more often Cornelia found her conscience, and what others called her duty, on opposite sides of the weighscales. The doubts she had repressed about her role as a vestal were beginning to surface, and she felt terror.

The evening before they fought, all gladiators were provided with a banquet as lavish as any in the palace. It was food wasted. Many had no stomach for the exotic dishes, while the rest bolted plateful after plateful just to vomit it up again.

Marcus was astonished at the sentimentality these base men showed at this time. Some would burst into tears as they fondled a talisman, or dictate lamenting letters to wives about the care of children and the disposition of property.

The veteran of eighty-seven clashes, each notched on his belt, Xerxes was one who believed his power lay in defiance of the fates through excess. Since he loved the arena as his home, he was allowed free run of the city. After bolting down and puking up over a hundred dishes, he heaved himself up from the table with a loud belch and an even noisier breaking of wind. Then, relieving himself on the gaming table of a group of retiarii to prove his boast that his cock was longer than their tridents, he left the barracks. There was a brothel opposite the Circus Maximus that Xerxes sometimes terrorized with his custom. It was his habit to bellow his name at the bottom of the steps, then to stamp his way up through the rat warren, abusing the bawds as he desired. True to form, Xerxes preferred the broken-down whores on the top floors, whom he felt he favoured with his patronage. When he reached the fifth floor of this house, he was huffing and puffing in a way that might have alarmed him if he didn't believe all he had to do next day was swing his mighty sword while the retiarii died like flies from fear.

There was only one bawd in the heat of the eaves – a black-haired witch with two teeth missing. Announcing himself: "I am Xerxes, the man the gods sigh for!" he dragged her to an oil lamp to get a good look. "Who are you?"

Her lips barely moved: "Phoebe."

It was almost dawn when Xerxes left the whorehouse, carrying a birdwing fan and a tin box of powder in which he had found a gold coin. Being very drunk, he stopped at every earthenware urinal to relieve himself. As a youth, Xerxes had collected urine for the fullers' shop in the Subura, where it was used for cleaning. If anyone taunted him, he would heave a jar to his shoulder, then smash it down on the jester, thus proving the Roman proverb that piss was indeed the breath of Charon.

Xerxes lost his gold coin in the last urinal. Intending to smash it so as to collect his money, he heaved the jar, caught his foot on a paving stone, and tumbled in a crash of piss and pottery. When he got to his feet, he stank of urine.

Maximus Marcus did not sleep the night before he was to fight. Instead, his mind taunted him with the sweetness of life by casting up happy memory after happy memory, like dice that only roll high when the opponent is oneself. Consumed by impotent rage that made him want to curse the gods, to shatter their statues, to slit the throat of every person who had life to live, he understood at last that furious greed that goaded the "scum" around him to jam every lust into their last hours. Here there was not even the comfort of men before battle. Here there was no cause to serve, no camaraderie of shared purpose, and only a tenuous glory to win. Here was only the scramble for survival, in which any sentiment toward another human was a chink in one's own armour. How could you slaughter a man with whom you'd broken bread the night before, unless you had seen him only through a filter of hate...as a rival for that piece of bread?

As he tossed in the darkness of the barracks, Marcus heard a groan that was so poignant an expression of how he himself felt that he feared he must have made it. He roused himself on his elbows. The young Jew, Petras, was begging his god alternately to forgive him for deserting his friends and to deliver him from the arena. Marcus remembered seeing the boy on the exercise field, dressed as a retiarius, his trident awkward in his hands, his net dangling unfolded between his legs, too ashamed of the condemnation of his friends to commit himself to the practise sessions. Marcus wondered: *What if I look down my sword and see those miserable eyes staring back?* Turning from the boy in grinding resentment, he prayed: *Apollo, god of truth, don't saddle me with that one's pain.*

At cockcrow, Marcus roused himself for a cold plunge, followed by a massage, given to him by old Pollux who had loyally smuggled himself in for this ritual. He returned to the barracks to dress. As he reached for his tunic, he stepped into something warm and sticky on the cold stone. He looked toward Petras in the next cot. The coverlet was drawn over his face. Marcus pulled it back. The boy's throat was slit. His eyes bulged from a terrified face. His hand clenched Domitilla's fish knife. The mattress was drenched in blood.

Marcus pried the knife from the boy's fingers and stuck it in his own tunic. Closing the corpse's eyes, he drew the cover over the face, repressing compassion he dared not feel: *So be it.*

The gladiators streamed into the Flavian Amphitheatre through the Triumphal Gate, as gorgeous as peacocks in their plumed helmets and coloured cloaks, each in his own chariot with a slave bearing his armour. To the accompaniment of a hydraulic organ that could be heard sixty miles, they circled the arena, then greeted the emperor with raised hands: "I undertake to suffer death by fire, in chains, under the lash or by the sword as you shall decide. We who are about to die salute you." Xerxes inspired the loudest eruption of cheers and hisses, but Maximus Marcus aroused adoration. Women showered him with flowers, locks of hair, talismen and tear-drenched silken handkerchiefs.

The gladiators warmed up with practise weapons, while pygmies, cripples and freaks boxed with metal-weighted gloves or – one of Domitian's favourites – scantily dressed women wrestled in the mud.

The emperor signalled.

Thirty heavily armoured murmillones, with fish-trimmed helmets, metal leg and arm plates, oblong shields and short swords, confronted thirty lightly armed Thracians with small wooden shields and scimitars. Eager for a quick draw of blood, the emperor tested their weapons for sharpness. Since he detested the Thracians for no more reason than his brother Titus had favoured them, he urged on the murmillones with the wish: "May your weapons draw more blood than their share."

The chief priest tossed a scarlet napkin. The two lines rushed each other, swords and scimitars slashing – at first the air, then steel found flesh. As the spectators placed wagers, they shouted: "A hit! A hit!" "Over there!" "Watch out behind you!" Limbs were severed, chests and faces gashed. Sometimes a fighter put his foot on a dis-armed opponent's throat and raised his weapon to the crowd. Always the verdict was: "Kill him!" If any gladiator didn't attack brutally enough, a slave prodded him with a firebrand.

The Thracians gained the upper hand, so that soon twenty-four of them opposed twenty murmillones. The odds became longer: sixteen to ten; then fourteen to seven. At last four Thracians faced one desperate murmillone who managed, despite having only one arm, to kill another opponent before being brought to earth. The crowd hollered: "Save him!" The emperor's handkerchief went down: *Drop the swords.* His thumb went up: *Spare him.*

The victorious Thracians presented themselves to the emperor to receive their palms, and here Domitian showed his famous perversity. He ordered a pack of wild dogs to be unleashed so that two were torn limb from limb. When a Thracian supporter jeered, "To the dogs with our emperor!" Domitian had him yanked from his seat. Around his neck he hung a placard reading: "I spoke evil of my emperor," then threw him to the dogs.

This infuriated the mob, for they regarded the games as the one time they could express all sentiments free from punishment. The boldest continued to hiss, and when Domitian contemptuously used his dwarf to silence them instead of replying directly by voice or hand gestures or by writing on his slate, the boos and mutterings increased.

In the arena, slaves in masks of Mercury, the god of death, prodded fallen bodies with hot pokers to reveal fakery. Others, dressed as Charon, finished the job with mallets. Attaching hooks to the corpses' feet, they dragged them through the Gate of Funerals to be hurled into a mass grave. They also collected the losers' weapons, but not without challenge from the spectators, who considered a spear, wet with gladiators' blood, to be lucky for parting a bride's hair and for curing epilepsy.

Having insulted the mob, Domitian now sought to appease them by ordering the Great Xerxes to fight next. This giant in flashing silver armour, swinging his ruby-encrusted sword in an arc around his head, soon brought everyone to his feet, clamouring, "Retiarii! Retiarii!" Nothing pleased the crowd more than seeing retiarii with tridents and nets darting around Xerxes like monkeys while he leisurely bashed in their heads.

Requesting the chief priest to bring him the jar with the names of retiarii, Domitian drew a lot and showed it to the dwarf. Smirking, Hermes wrote the name on his slate, which he held up for the crowd: Maximus Marcus.

Catcalls greeted this announcement. Once more the crowd felt duped. It offended their sense of dignity to think of their hero forced to prance about this garish monster. Many called, "Foul! foul!" suspecting a substitution.

With arms folded across his chest, the emperor indicated that he could not be budged: Maximus Marcus would now fight as a retiarius.

Marcus received this humiliating command while in an underground cage, costumed as a Samnite. His armour was stripped from him, he was given a trident and net, then shoved onto the elevator. It was there he discovered the full danger of the insult: the trident was of wood; the net had holes in it. Contemptuously presenting his arms to the emperor, he warned: "Do not cut yourself on the point, my emperor."

Laughing, Domitian shouted to Xerxes: "Be alert, Xerxes! He'll pierce the fish on your helmet as easily as Neptune spears jellyfish."

Bareheaded and barechested, Marcus approached Xerxes standing, feet astride, tossing his scarlet plumes and braying like

279

a jackass. Taking the measure of the man, Marcus prayed, with some satisfaction: *Thank you, Apollo, for giving me a man I can despise.*

It had been Marcus' first impulse to toss away his useless weapons, but wiser instincts prevailed. Since only the emperor knew they were fake, why advertise his vulnerability? That was an act of bravado he could ill afford – like Priscus in the Odeum sticking out his tongue at the emperor, making it all the easier to lop off. This was a time for donning Clemens' leather trunks of compromise.

Continuing to advance on Xerxes, Marcus challenged then feinted. Though his net was damaged, it wasn't entirely useless. After arranging the lead weights for casting, he moved in as close as he dared and made an inexpert swipe at Xerxes' feet. Remembering how rankling Priscus' insults had been when they wrestled at the baths, he taunted Xerxes: "Hey, Big One! You stink of Charon's breath!"

The superstitious Xerxes slashed at Marcus with his jewelled sword. Nimble from workouts in the cornmill, Marcus evaded these wild blows. If his trident had been real, he could have caught Xerxes under the breastplate.

Marcus made another attempt to snare Xerxes. Beginning to enjoy the strategies of the underdog, he heckled again: "Hey, Pisspot! You foul the wind." Again Xerxes over-reacted with thrashings and snarlings that wore him down without hurting Marcus.

Though Marcus was no closer to winning without weapons, he could judge by these manoeuvres that Xerxes' timing was off and his balance uncertain. The jewelled armour was more suited for show than battle. What's more, he held his shield and sword in front of him like an amateur, rather than protecting a broader area.

As a soldier, Marcus had survived as many face-to-face encounters as Xerxes, for while the Romans had adopted all the long-range weapons of their enemies as easily as they adopted their gods, they still preferred to fight with short sword, granting a close look at the other man's eyes. Marcus wondered now how many of Xerxes' victories had been won by the fear his opponents brought into the arena after weeks of bullying in the barracks. He felt contempt for this flashy, soft-bellied giant who seemed to represent all that had gone wrong with the Roman dream.

As yet no blood had been drawn. Impatient, the crowd began to boo. Marcus could see slaves moving in on him with firebrands.

Pricked by the catcalls, Xerxes used his longer reach to slice Marcus' shoulder. Then he manoeuvred his shield so as to blind his opponent with the glare of sunlight. Driving Marcus backwards into a semi-circle of slaves with firebrands, he jabbed him again in the leg. Though Xerxes might have pressed his advantage while Marcus still reeled, he was too addicted to collecting plaudits from the crowd, so let the opportunity slip.

Marcus was not seriously wounded, but was now losing blood. To win, he would have to act quickly. Casting about for some way of surprising Xerxes, he caught the glint of sunlight from Xerxes' fish helmet and remembered Domitilla's fish knife stuck in his tunic. Despite the gash in his leg, he rushed Xerxes, faked a frontal thrust to attract his weapons, then flung his trident into his opponent's unprotected face.

While Xerxes dealt with what was little more than an insult to his dignity, Marcus spun so he was facing the slaves with firebrands. Raising his thumb, he advanced toward them as if seeking mercy. Then he wrenched a prod from one and wheeled to confront Xerxes. Smiting the giant across the forehead, he seared one eye. Bellowing in agony, Xerxes brought up his shield to his injured face. Here was the mistake Marcus had been awaiting. Experiencing the odd sensation that overtook him on the battlefield when every sinew seemed so perfectly pitched for survival that time slowed down, he ploughed into Xerxes' belly with his prod, catching him under the breastplate while snaring his feet in the net. Heavily weighted in decorative armour, Xerxes crashed backwards. Leaping over him, Marcus yanked back his head by the fish helmet as he drew Domitilla's knife from his tunic. Now was the time to sue for mercy on Xerxes' behalf. As Marcus' fingers gripped the hilt, he saw the terror in Xerxes' one good eye, so like the terror he had seen on the face of Petras. Feeling a surge of hate so primitive nothing could stop him, he plunged his knife into Xerxes' throat, savouring the warm spurt of blood around his fist and the last pitiful struggles of the giant as he vomited up his entrails. Closing Xerxes' one remaining eye, he felt in some small measure to have avenged Petras' death, though the real culprit there was Philip.

The crowd cheered, threw scarves and flowers. Still revelling in the orgiastic thrill of having conquered a despised foe, Marcus acknowledged the adulation from these screaming mouths that seemed to meld into one giant mouth the size of the amphitheatre. He remembered the last time he had heard that roar: at the Circus before the slaughter of his horse Helen. He remembered also Priscus' question: Would he prefer the laurels or the horse? Now he knew he would take the horse, and he would know what to do with it.

By the time Marcus reached the imperial box, he felt only contempt for himself, for these people and the man who ruled them. That man lounged amidst purple cushions, sniffing the perfumed handkerchief which – if dropped – would spare Marcus' life. As Marcus presented himself in mock humility, the emperor leaned over the edge of the box, his face enigmatic. Toying with his handkerchief, he looked across the arena at the chief vestal.

She was standing in the stall opposite. She too held a white handkerchief. Though Cornelia had not intended to respond to the emperor's insulting challenge, she had risen to cheer with the rest and, paralyzed, had remained standing when they sat down. Now the wind tugged one corner of her handkerchief as she pinched the other. Glaring across at the emperor, intending to defy him, she saw instead the proud back of Maximus Marcus, the wind riffling his hair. The wind also caught her handkerchief, spun it upward, then floated it down like a fallen leaf to the blood-soaked sand. Now committed, Cornelia raised her thumb: *Spare him.* The emperor dropped his handkerchief.

With a joyful bray, Castor leapt from the imperial box, carrying the victor's cape and laurels that the emperor refused to present. As he flung them into Marcus' arms, the gladiator gripped his hand, muttering: "Priscus was right."

While slaves wearing the mask of Mercury dragged the once-mighty Xerxes through the Gate of Funerals, Marcus strode through the Triumphal Gate a free man.

CHAPTER TWENTY-TWO

After Maximus Marcus left the Flavian Amphitheatre, Cornelia numbly pretended to watch an event in which six retiarii were slaughtered by six Samnites. Then, pleading illness, she fled to the vestalry, went directly to her room, closed her door and lit the fire at her vestal altar. Laying her bulla of office and her sacrificial knife before it, she recited her vows, then asked Vesta: "Shall I take my life?" When she received no answer, no omen of any kind, she repeated the ritual, this time including a confession of her feelings for Maximus Marcus. Again she received no response from Vesta – neither in the way the twigs burned, nor in the curling of the smoke, nor in any supernatural phenomenon such as the sudden rising of the wind.

Remaining in her room for the rest of that day and night, and then the next day and that night, Cornelia repeated her question, refusing either to eat or to sleep, stressing her guilt and her unworthiness, dreading moment by moment a summons from the palace.

Eyes stinging from the smoke, throat hoarse from her incantations, she began to wonder if her fears had been groundless. Had the emperor meant only to humiliate her? Had she, through guilt and the pride of self-importance, exaggerated his threat? Was that why Vesta had remained silent – to punish her for her arrogance? Surely even this emperor could not take so lightly the defilement of a priestess of Vesta.

Cornelia cracked open the door of her bedchamber. With the first rush of warm, moist wind, she flung it wide and, sucking in a deep breath, held it in her lungs, savouring it: She had forgotten there was such a thing as fresh air.

It was stilltime, the magic hour not quite day or night when the stars cling to the brightening sky. Down in the courtyard Helen and Diana were weaving garlands of orange blossoms and verbena. Of course! How could she have forgotten? It was June 9 – Vesta's own day and Cornelia's favourite in all the year. The Vestalia: a time of hope and new beginnings. She felt a surge of joy so powerful it brought tears to her eyes. Was this Vesta's message to her? Was this her omen?

After washing then dressing in a clean gown, Cornelia ran down into the courtyard, growing more hopeful at each step. Diana was sitting with her back toward her, singing like a meadowlark with the fragrant blooms heaped around her feet. Hugging the radiant girl, Cornelia noticed her slenderness. Agrippina's purgings and fastings seemed to have released her spirit like the bird whose songs she sang.

Piling their arms with garlands, the vestals carried them to the Temple. Here Agrippina and Poppaea, working under Fausta's exacting eye, had scoured every nook. Together, the vestals decked the columns and statues with yard upon yard of blossoms till the Temple was as sweet as a garden.

The first rays of sunlight were just beginning to shoot in a fiery crown over the Sabine Hills. Draped in jasmine, Cornelia stationed herself at the Temple door. Carrying his rod of office and an unlit torch, Pontifex Piso led a priestly procession from the Regia, across Sacred Square and up the steps of the Temple. Accepting the torch, Cornelia plunged it into the hearth. "I consign to your care the fire of Vesta."

Now with the burning torch, the procession returned to the Regia. After Cornelia doused the hearth with wine, Fausta collected the ashes to be spread under the Regia lotus tree, magnificently in bloom. Agrippina and Poppaea scrubbed the hearth, while Diana relaid the fire and Helen sprinkled the Temple with sacred water.

All six vestals returned to the vestalry – freed for one day of their hearth duties. Shedding their robes and sandals so they were clad only in white tunics, they unbound their hair and crowned each other with flowers. Now each vestal recited a page of Temple history: how King Numa, Rome's second king after Romulus, and his wife Oppia gave birth to five daughters of unsurpassed beauty and modesty; how Numa's arch-enemy Tiro tried to burn Rome and to rape Oppia on Numa's own household altar; how Oppia, preferring death to violation, had prayed to Vesta to rekindle the hearth; how Vesta had answered this prayer by sending fire from Oppia's own thighs to consume Tiro while saving Oppia by drenching her robes with tears. In gratitude for Rome's safety, Numa vowed never to let the flame die in his hearth. In gratitude for her own deliverance, Oppia bound herself and her daughters to the hearth in chastity.

A banquet of sweetmeats was served, along with the finest wines from the emperor's cellar. For the rest of the afternoon the vestals danced to the flute and the lyre, till – giddy on wine and freedom – they leapt into the pools and pelted each other with white blossoms so that the air was a blizzard of them. Soaked to the skin and covered in petals like a great swan, Diana imitated every bird in the aviary, while Hello the magpie flapped round and round her head, shrieking in confusion. When even Agrippina joined in, Cornelia saw the first delicate budding of her hope for a vestalry united in love, faith and loyalty.

As the sun began to sink behind the Palatine, the vestals prepared once more to take up their duties. After donning clean robes bound with sashes tied by the intricate Hercules knot that only a bride's husband has the right to unfasten, they twisted each other's hair into six braids held by white ribbons and wound into cones of chastity, over which they fastened their head scarves.

In silence and solemnity the vestals filed into Sacred Square, where a crowd of matrons with unlit torches had assembled. Kneeling before an altar prepared with tinder and two twigs from the lotus tree, Cornelia began a friction of twig to twig, praying that Vesta would favour her and the Temple with a good omen.

The crowd waited in a hush.

Cornelia felt the twigs grow warm in her anxious fingers. A spark flew to the tinder. Then another. The corner of the tinder smouldered. Flames spurted. Helen caught the lighted tinder in a bronze sieve and, shielding it from the wind, ran up the steps of the Temple. As she threw it onto the freshly laid altar, Fausta and Agrippina worked the bellows. The flame caught, then flared. A cheer went up from the matrons in Sacred Square as a plume of smoke rose through the cone of the Temple: the hearth of Rome burned brightly once more.

Carrying a lighted torch from the Temple of Vesta to the chief priest at the gate of the Regia, Cornelia proclaimed: "Vesta gives you new fire and renewed good fortune." The matrons rushed to light their torches at the Temple, thus to share in the luck of Vesta.

Feeling radiantly at peace, Cornelia crossed Sacred Square, with Poppaea and Diana, an arm around each. As she reached the gate of the vestalry, a dumpy figure in scarlet detached himself from the crowd still milling around. Taken unawares, Cornelia stared at him like a bird that has been struck by a stone but has not yet begun the dizzying plunge. Doffing his scarlet cap, Hermes smiled his yellow-fang smile. "You are summoned to attend the emperor." Stunned, Cornelia shook her head. This could not be. She had just received Vesta's blessing. The sweet fragrance of jasmine still clung to her hair, her fingers were warm from the twigs of the fire.

Bowing, Hermes gestured toward a purple litter guarded by four praetorians. "You are to come with me."

Veiling her face, Cornelia hurried after the dwarf, propelled more by guilt than by obedience. She stumbled into the litter. Hermes drew the curtains. The bearers lifted their burden.

Lying numbed among the cushions, eyes closed, Cornelia heard the familiar sounds of the Forum ebb and flow, as if coming to her over a great distance: the slap of the bearers' feet on the travertine paving then up the steps of the Palatine; the demanding and receiving of the first password; the creaking then the clanging of the imperial gate. Now they were sprinting through gardens, gushing with fountains and redolent with spring flowers. Another password, another door. Now the bearers were padding down silky marble corridors, where she could see torches burning at intervals through the litter's purple curtains. Another password. Another door. This one closed behind them with a muted sound, as if they were in a chamber with many cushions and wall hangings. Halting, the bearers deposited the litter. A black hand parted the black curtains. A black face peered through the gap. Chamberlain Parthenius beckoned to Cornelia. She stepped from the litter into the emperor's bedroom.

The emperor lounged on an ivory couch, set in an apse of golden mirrors. He was wearing a white silk robe elegantly knotted with a purple cord, and drinking from an amethyst goblet which he extended. "To the vestal Cornelia. Join me."

Though he smiled, his voice held the ring of command. Cornelia took two shaky steps forward, then stopped, her hand on her bulla.

The emperor laughed. "Well, all right...for now." He dismissed Hermes with an airy wave. Scowling, the dwarf glared at Cornelia, then at Parthenius, as if holding them responsible. Delaying as long as he dared, he snatched up his stool and hopped from the room.

The emperor turned his full attention to his guest. "I trust you have come to me to make good our bargain?"

"I did not come to you," protested Cornelia, still clasping her bulla. "I was sent for. I made no bargains."

The emperor arched a silky brow. "No? All of Rome saw you drop your handkerchief. Only I knew its meaning."

"I exercised my prerogative as chief vestal to urge justice."

"You said yourself there is no justice in the arena. I exercised clemency, for which there are now favours due." He held out his goblet to Parthenius, his eyes fixed on her face. "I thought we had a bargain, but never mind. For an emperor, all the world is an arena into which the dogs can be unleashed at any time."

Breaking his gaze with laughter, he leaned back into the purple cushions, his casualness fed by her anxiety. "You see, I have only to clap my hands to take up the story of Maximus Marcus exactly where it was left off – to turn this room into an arena." Slipping his hand under his cushion, he withdrew an ivory-handled dagger and flashed it so she could admire its sharpness. "Should I order Captain Geta to bring Marcus here to us now, this evening? Shall we ask Geta to cut out his tongue, the way he detongued the rebel Priscus? Better yet, shall we urge Geta to castrate him for tempting a vestal?" Grinning, he offered her the knife. "Maybe you'd prefer to do the job yourself, to avenge your tarnished honour? Frankly, I find spectator sports boring. I'd hoped for a more interesting use for our evening. What, after all, is Maximus Marcus to me but a bargaining point between us? The truth is...I find, to my surprise, that I've never desired a woman more." He dropped his voice to a husky whisper. "I could take you now, as Zeus took Leda, and I will, if I must, but sometimes I'm a man like any other. I'd prefer your enjoyment.... Well?"

Cornelia was spinning at the centre of many uncertainties. Had Maximus Marcus been arrested before he could quit Rome, or was the emperor bluffing? She tried to collect her thoughts, to reason, to protest, but two days of fasting and the jubilation of Vestalia had disoriented her. She felt out of synchronization with the world, like Fausta, who heard a question one day then answered it the next.

As he drank from his goblet, the emperor studied her over the rim. "Am I to take your silence for compliance?" He waited a few moments more for her response. When there was none, he snapped: "All right. I grow weary. Those who can speak, will. Those who can act, will." Dismissing Parthenius with a toss of his head, he rose from his bed and, eyes caressing the vestal, climbed down the dais. Forcing the amethyst goblet into her hands he wrapped her fingers around it. "Drink."

Lifting the goblet, Cornelia sipped. As the liquid burned her throat, she clasped the goblet in both hands and drained it. The emperor chuckled. "You have a strong thirst for a vestal. I hope you bring the same thirst to the rest of our evening."

This wine, combining with all Cornelia had had at Vestalia, blurred then melted the room into rippling rings around her. All that now seemed clear was the fire in her throat and the sternly sculptured face of the emperor just two feet away – the long thin nose with flaring nostrils, the moist lips from which the faint scent of wine drifted, and especially the blue eyes in their gouged sockets boring into her.

The emperor lay his hand on Cornelia's cheek – feverish to his cool touch – then slid his fingers up into her hair. He unpinned her head scarf and, holding it by the corner, he let it fall the way they had both dropped handkerchiefs in the arena. Grinning, pleased with the symbolism, he fumbled with both hands in her hair till he found, one by one, the six bronze pins that held it in its cone of chastity. Patiently he removed them, letting each fall to the floor on top of the head scarf. He unwound the six braids from their cone, each bound in a white ribbon. After untying the ribbons one by one, he unwove each braid.

The emperor took hold of the Hercules knot that bound the sash of her vestal robes. Tugging her to him, he unfastened each loop with lingering fingers, in the tradition of the bridegrooms of old. Letting the sash fall to the floor, he again placed his palms on the vestal's cheeks – more feverish than before. Again he slid his hands into her red-gold hair, running his fingers in a fan through it, loosening it, smoothing the crimpings of the braids. Still without touching her body, he drew her to him. "I am King Numa," he said. "You are my bride. I claim you openly as my lawful right, in the name of Rome." Kissing her, he thrust his tongue deep inside. Then, releasing her with the shock of his taste still in her mouth, he held her in submission with his eyes – through his authority as emperor, high priest and, he chose to believe, as a man. "I command you. Remove your vestal robes."

For a long while the vestal stared at him; at last her hands went to her gown. Her fingers plucked then fumbled at the fabric, finding it too slippery to hold. She made an awkward attempt to lift it, abandoned that. Hesitated, then *at last, at last,* started to move inside it, drawing one arm slowly through its hole and then the other, with the robe still enveloping her like a tent.

Once again, she hesitated. He intensified his stare, now fuelled by the first impatience. Again she moved inside the gown, raising it slowly up from her neck, getting lost in the voluminous folds till her head disappeared down the hole. The emperor watched in a hush and rage of desire, itching to get his hands on the damnable fabric, to yank it off, but controlling himself. At last, in a marvellously deft movement – surprising after so much delay – she not only removed the robe but collected it in a bundle in front of her. The emperor reached for the bundle. She clung to it. Gripping her wrist, he squeezed till her hand whitened and grew numb...the threat of force. She released the bundle. He tossed it from them.

Standing before the emperor in thin cotton shift, the vestal tried to defy him, as she always had – to oppose – but was unable to overcome her years of terror for this one thing: the threat to chastity. She trembled to the toes of her white sandals, with her bulla heaving on her chest. The outline of her body was clear through the sheer fabric, the tip of each nipple, the stain of her sex. Cupping his hands under her breasts, feeling the curve and pulpiness of each in his palms, the emperor swept her up – still in the tradition of the bridegroom – to the ivory bed.

The emperor lay the vestal on his bed. He inspected her – this virgin – not yet stripped to his fantasies. Though she did not resist, she was still too frightened to arouse. Indeed, she seemed dazed to the point of unconsciousness. Again her dread fed his patience. Kneeling at her feet, the emperor unlaced one white sandal then the other. Fondling one foot then the other, he sucked each toe, enjoying the delay better than any aphrodisiac, recalling all his old craft as a seducer which, in the privileges and pressures of dictatorship, he'd chosen to forget. Though her legs were naked to mid-thigh, they were glued at the knees. Covetously, he picked up her shift by the hem, gripped it in his fists, and tore it to her neck.

The chief virgin of Vesta now lay naked on the emperor's bed, as lovely as he had imagined – her red-gold hair unbound, her slender body marked with dark nipples, and here and there a shimmer, a brush of gold. Propping her head so she was forced to look at herself in a burnished mirror, he wooed her: "The wine you drank was an aphrodisiac. You won't be able to resist my will or the desire I will unlock in the deepest part of you." As she stared at the naked girl shimmering in the mirror, fascinated and bewildered, pushed further into unreality, he discarded his silk robe, then posed like the god Priapus so he too was reflected in gold, displaying himself to her, fondling himself, enjoying the surety of himself and the promise of power, the more intrigued when she turned away in fear. Kneeling by her on the bed, he lay his hands on her breasts, and bent low to kiss her lips, sucking on them, coaxing them, trying to insinuate the tip of his tongue, feeling her nipples stiffen in his palms. Shifting his weight, he straddled the virgin, his knees brushing her hips, and lay his sex across her belly. He slid it upwards, nudging between her breasts, displacing her bulla from its moist nest.

He took the virgin's hand in his and forced her fingers to the shaft of his cock, ran them down the smooth-to-bursting skin. She touched him as if touching fire, then snatched her hand away.

Shifting once again, the emperor propped himself on his elbows, stretching his body over hers, with his sex nudging persistently along her silky threshold. She remained stiff, unyielding, her jaw clenched, her legs glued. Sliding down beside her, he took a nipple in the fingers of one hand, then the other, teasing them into erection – the only vulnerability in her line of fortifications. He pinched them till tremors passed through her. Pressing his lips hard on hers, he let her feel the sharpness of his teeth, pinching even harder. When she opened her mouth to cry out, he penetrated it with his tongue, subdued her tongue with his, wrestled it to a standstill, filling at least this cavity to bursting...the enemy now within. Gripping her nipples with all his strength, he pinned her body as she thrashed beneath him, unable because of his tongue to scream, feeling deeper spasms flush up from her pelvis. She hugged her knees all the tighter, held for a few seconds more, then convulsed and went slack. The virgin surrendered.

Generous in victory, the emperor became solicitous once again, tenderly licking the nipples he had abused – affording now to give better terms. He stroked her belly and thighs – his touch featherlight. He blew in her ear, tangled his lips in her hair.

Rising from the bed, the emperor lifted the virgin by the hips, drawing her so her legs and thighs overlapped the end. He caressed the hair sliding down between her thighs – not much of it, like a child's – and spread her legs. With delicate fingers he stroked the inner thighs, faintly dusted in red-gold, where even the sun had never dared touch.

With curiosity, the emperor knelt between the virgin's thighs and examined her sex – a small cleft discreetly folded in upon itself, the most inaccessible place (so all history decreed) in the Roman Empire. Extending the tip of his finger, he touched it. Tickled it. Stroked it. Tried to insert his finger. *Patience, patience, still too tightly closed.* Drawing back he turned to a row of pots which he kept by his bed for just such occasions, and selected one of porcelain containing honey. He dipped three fingers, then smeared the honey liberally between the virgin's thighs – around the cleft and dipping a little inside. Once more kneeling between the thighs of the virgin, he extended his tongue like a bee's to a flower. He licked her sex – around and around, then easing down inside.

The emperor kissed the lower lips of the unawakened vestal,

and felt the quiver of her thighs. He rolled his tongue, and pierced her. A spasm passed through the vestal. Burying her face in the pillows, she began to cry. Sucking and probing with his tongue, he lost himself in the sweet convolutions of flesh, sorting it out layer by layer, outer lips and inner, velvety tabs and the gash between, with the taste of the honey giving way to the musk flavour of the vestal's own juices. He could feel her breathing more deeply now, and the pitch of her flesh losing control under his lips. The emperor slid his tongue, like a sticky caterpillar, up her sex, nudging through the slippery hair, slithering up the belly, plundering through the valley of her breasts, with her bulla like a rock now pushed aside. He lay his lips, thick with honey and musk, on the lips of the crying vestal. He stretched his body over hers. His sex found the tunnel inviting him inside – open now, her stubbornness dissolved, pushed aside like the bulla, engorged with blood, letting him insert the tip of himself.

The vestal widened to receive him. Fully engrossed, the emperor tongued her lips, not forcing her, making her accept him through enticement, centimetre by centimetre, not hiding his triumph nor letting her cover her face, binding her hands so he could witness the crumbling of her pride, enjoy the interplay of fear and shame with surprise and desire, her total bewilderment at the vulnerability she had nursed unknowing between her legs, watching the transformation he alone was able to command, the mottlings, the sweatings, the ripplings, the heavings, remembering a snake he had seen swallow a rabbit, just like this, with the anatomy of course reversed – the same terror, with victory as inevitable and as complete.

He yielded some of the ground he had gained so he could thrust more powerfully, withdraw, thrust again, wallowing in his own responses now, his own needs and desires, thrashing in a bubble of heightened awareness, glorying in the heat pulsing up to engulf him, she an extension of him now, soft to his hard, his odours mingled with hers, her cries entangled in his, a shudder in him producing a shiver in her, joined by the same draw of breath, the same throb of blood. The emperor had never before felt so potent. Here was something neither the charm of his brother nor the gall of Tiberius had dared to do. Feeling his climax start, he clasped the vestal to him, and poured his sperm in a hard hot stream into her womb. He *was* King Numa fucking his virgin bride on a burning hearth. He was Rome!

Emperor Domitian lay spread-eagled upon his bed, luxuriating in the afterflow of victory. Beside him, hidden in the covers, was the vestal. Lifting her gently by the hair, he lay her face against his genitals. Again he felt himself begin to rise.

Hermes the dwarf paces back and forth outside the emperor's bedchamber – a jackal who can smell the flesh but can't get at it. He snarls. He growls. He rolls his eyes. It is an outrage, a thing unheard of! Here he is – the emperor's official taster of wine and women – outside the imperial chamber while Parthenius – traitor! sneak! betrayer of dwarfs and emperors! – is inside. *He* will pay. *She* will pay. *They* will pay.

Back and forth. Head up. Head down. Fists pummelling the air. Fists knotted in back. At last he sees Parthenius – a slender shadow in the hall, *banished too!* In relief, he hops after the black man. With a flying tackle, he snares him by a leg. "Wait! Stay!"

As Parthenius peers down his long torso to the knot around his ankle, Hermes catches his breath, wipes his brow, smirks up at him, pretending aplomb but without releasing the other's leg. "A drink, Parthenius? How about that? Some of the emperor's finest? A game of odds and evens? How about that?" He giggles as he ticks off Parthenius' short list of vices. "I feel lucky tonight."

That last is a joke, for Hermes has been losing steadily to Parthenius for over a month – an act of politics more than ill-fortune since he usually steals the money back within the week. As for the emperor's wine, that too costs him nothing beyond enterprise. Only three people have access to the emperor's cellar: his wine steward, through a complex set of keys; the emperor, through the wine steward; and Hermes, through a drainage tunnel into which only he can squeeze.

Still gripping the chamberlain's leg, Hermes witnesses a silent struggle up on the other's face. Will Parthenius report to the Empress Domitia about the vestal Cornelia, or will he go with Hermes to drink and gamble? Seeing men torn between their vices is almost as amusing to Hermes as the more classic struggle between good and evil, especially since he is confidently pitting Parthenius' first two vices against his third choice. Inevitably, Parthenius leans toward Hermes which, given the simplicity of the black man's nature, means Hermes has won. Releasing the leg, the dwarf playfully grasps Parthenius' rump. "Let's go where we won't be found. How about the basement?" He jerks a thumb toward the emperor's bedchamber. "We've got lots of time. Our Lord and God is in for a long night."

Parthenius and Hermes trot down the hall – the one in a lazy lope, the other bunched at his side like a noon-time shadow. After stealing a torch, they sneak into one of the palace storage rooms, smelling of spices. As Parthenius sticks the torch in a wall bracket, Hermes produces the promised goatskin of wine. Anticipating, Parthenius bounces his amber dice from his elbow, from each knuckle, from his thumbs. Grinning, Hermes urges the goatskin upon him, intending to be as prodigal tonight as he is usually stingy.

As bad luck would have it, Hermes does have a winning streak. Twice Parthenius tries to quit, so the dwarf has to refill his goatskin and double the stakes. Fortunately, obliterating Parthenius proves easier than he dared hope. Could it be that the chamberlain's double life is catching up on him? Hermes watches the spidery fingers take longer and longer to collect the dice. At last – with the wine guttering his chin – Parthenius leans way over to count the spots, and never gets up again. Pulling open his eyelids, Hermes examines the yellow and black orbs: out for the night.

Coming briskly to life, Hermes borrows one of the storage attendant's wax slates. He writes: "To the Empress: When is a virgin not a virgin? When she stokes her firebox in the palace instead of the Temple. This is the very night when all of Rome burns – especially our two chiefs. I trust you will know how to douse the flame?" Sealing the slate with a ball of wax, he impresses it with his forged imperial signet just to demonstrate what he can do.

With his slate under his arm, Hermes skips up the tunnel from the storage room, proud of the crab-like speed with which he rides his deformity despite the pain throbbing through his joints. Once Hermes toured the world as ringmaster to a caravan of freaks. He was absolute emperor of his pathetic court. He still views the world as a collection of freaks for whom he is ring-master. It is an illusion, absolutely necessary for his survival in a life of misery and pain – an illusion he will give that life to main-tain.

The chief vestal Cornelia hid inside an unmarked litter that stole down the steps of the Palatine – still in dead of night. The Hercules knot binding her robes was improperly tied; her hair, underneath its head scarf, was loosely twisted rather than bound into its cone of chastity. Once again she was seeing the emperor hovering over her – the wetness of his mouth, the sheen of his eyes. She was feeling again his fingers part the soft, unbearable, untouchable flesh, clinging to those moist images and yeasty smells, keeping at bay the world outside her litter. If only she could get to her room in the vestalry, then maybe she could sort through her chaotic thoughts, consult Zeno, confess to Pontifex Piso, scourge herself, kill herself...whatever she must do.

Voices were battering like fists against the curtains of her litter. She heard the clanking of armour, the scuffing of boots. Men were quarrelling. Her litter had been halted at the bottom of Victory Stairs; her bearers were being challenged. As the angry voices rose, Cornelia tugged her borrowed cloak about her, shrinking into the pitchy darkness, too traumatized to understand the encounter.

The curtains of her litter were swaying. A hand – large-knuckled, hairy – tore them aside, bringing a rush of cool air. A face in praetorian helmet poked through: brutish, bulbous, pock-marked; black irises rimmed in white, cold and unblinking. She gripped her bulla: Captain Geta.

His lips scarcely moving, he announced: "I arrest you in the name of Imperator Domitianus Caesar Augustus."

She heard her voice inquire: "What is the charge?"

Scowling, he demanded: "Do you dare to ask?" Reaching inside the litter, Geta yanked open her cloak, exposing her throat. With cold fingers, he fumbled between her breasts and, seizing her bulla, tore it from her neck, leaving a rawhide gash. Pushing a torch into her face, he asked his companion: "Do you recognize this woman?"

Without raising his eyes, the other praetorian replied: "Yes."

"Identify her."

He mumbled: "Lady Cornelia, Chief of the Temple of Vesta."

Releasing her, Geta jerked the curtains back in place, and ordered: "To the Regia."

In shock, Cornelia buried herself in her cushions, her hand to her throat, hearing the splash of feet through puddles, the rattle of wagon wheels, tavern laughter, dogs barking, a man singing.

Next time the curtains were opened, Pontifex Piso's liver-spotted hand poked in. As she stumbled out of the litter, Cornelia was assisted by the other praetorian.

His red apex at a perilous angle, the chief priest led Cornelia, flanked by her guards, into the Regia, down a shadowy hallway ending in a stuffy room with a metal cot. Cornelia fell face-down upon it. Other persons pushed into the room. Lamps were lit. Everyone seemed to be shouting at once. As Cornelia felt herself lose consciousness, a hand clasped her shoulder. "August Lady, please..." said Piso, shaking her gently. "We must speak with you."

Cornelia gazed up into a ring of faces: Pontifex Piso, Captain Geta, prosecutor Messalinus and the emperor's physician, Rufus Felix. Their noses seemed as large as potatoes, while their eyes hung like broken eggs from the sockets. "There's been a misunderstanding – some terrible mistake," apologized Piso, clutching his heart.

Pushing the priest aside, Messalinus took charge of the interrogation. Offering neither title nor greeting, he demanded: "Where were you coming from at the time of your arrest?"

Cornelia stared up in silent fascination as the prosecutor's mouth pursed, pouted and parted in the centre of his face, sending out words in bubbles of saliva, marvelling at how much he resembled the scavengers in Consul Clemens' fish tank as they sucked up refuse from the bottom. Half an hour later, Messalinus' questions came to an abrupt and frustrated end. The swarthy fingers of Rufus Felix took over with a harsh eloquence of their own, slithering and insinuating while the sibilant voice of Messalinus hissed instructions, again violating her vestal robes. As Cornelia hid her face against the wall, her repelled flesh congealed around the shimmering girl she had glimpsed in the emperor's mirror, entombing her once more.

Emperor Domitian awoke mid-afternoon, feeling youthful, bursting with energy. Too often lately sex had left him glutted, drained. Today he felt revitalized. Yawning, he ordered Parthenius to draw the bed-curtains, to throw open the shutters, to invite in the sunlight.

A scroll had been conspicuously placed on a table by his bed. Examining it, he saw Pontifex Piso's seal, which he broke with his thumb. His mind still unfocussed, he read: "Your instructions have been carried out in full." He frowned. What instructions? Was Piso senile? He tossed the scroll aside. He would look into the matter later.

Domitian sent for Zeno. Today he was anticipating his secretary's buoyant enthusiasm, which on less promising mornings struck him like a draught of cold water. As irony would have it, Zeno slumped in wearing a tattered mood, his perpetual smile looped downward. While he was glumly arranging the imperial correspondence from routine to more complex, the emperor seized upon an item that had been bedevilling him for weeks – a thorny matter involving fraud. In sudden inspiration, he began dictating a long yet concise letter to his imperial agent in Byzantium. Not only did Zeno fail to keep up, but twice he had to ask the emperor to repeat the name of the man charged.

"Damn you, Zeno! If your fat fingers can't pace my tongue, fill in your name on the next execution order and get out."

"Please, my Lord," begged Zeno, mopping sweat. "I've been up since before cockcrow dealing with the Lady Cornelia's arrest. I've never seen such an ugly mob around the *Gazette*. I was pelted with protests the moment I set foot in the Forum – some with sizeable rocks in them."

"What? What is this nonsense?" Domitian's eye shot to Pontifex Piso's note. What was going on here? Ever cautious of plots, of traps, of conspiracies, he backtracked: "The mob is easily aroused without knowing the facts. But you are right. Let's put aside this irksome correspondence and attend to closer matters...Parthenius, fetch the chief priest. You may go, Zeno." He clapped his hands: "Quickly, quickly..."

As soon as the door closed, Domitian pounced on the scroll from Piso. He reread: "Your instructions have been carried out in full." No more. Trust the old windbag to choose this moment to be terse. He was still staring at the cryptic message when he deduced from the wheeze of asthmatic breathing that Piso had entered his bedchamber, apparently having been in the vestibule. The emperor raised his eyes from the scroll to the author's pale and dithering face. Attempting to kneel in strictest protocol, Piso locked his leg and would have sprawled on his face if his body slave had not caught him. "Get up, get up!" exclaimed Domitian.

"I beg pardon, Lord and God. It's been a week in a single night."

Controlling his impatience, the emperor tapped Piso's scroll. "Tell me. What exactly have you done?"

"As you instructed," replied Piso promptly.

Waving his hand in irritation, Domitian growled: "Yes, yes, but how did you proceed, and when?"

"Your order arrived before cockcrow. I was in bed when –"

"Did you bring the order?"

"Yes...Cato has it."

Producing another scroll from his tunic, Piso's slave handed it to Piso, who passed it to the emperor, who read: "To Quintus Piso, Chief Priest of the Colleges of Jupiter, Mars and the Flavian Cult, from Imperator Domitianus Caesar Augustus: I have ordered Petronius Geta, Captain of my Imperial Guard, to arrest the August Lady Cornelia, Chief of the Temple of Vesta, this night, on charges of breaking her vow of chastity. She will be delivered to you this morning under armed guard, to be detained at the Regia in suitably secure quarters. Immediately on receipt of this order, I instruct you to send for Catullus Messalinus, prosecutor of the Imperial Courts, member of the Flavian College; and Rufus Felix, imperial doctor, also a member of the Flavian College, so a suitable physical examination can be conducted as evidence to support the charge."

Domitian flicked the note, his face twitching. "You carried out these instructions?"

"In full," repeated Piso, daring to add: "With much regret."

"All in power must do things we regret," snarled Domitian. He waved the scroll. "Leave this." Dismissing the chief priest, he ordered Parthenius: "Fetch Geta. Tell him to bring every imperial order he received during the past twenty-four hours."

The door closed. Pouncing on Piso's order, Domitian examined the broken imperial seal. Not perfect but very like. Hearing the thump of praetorian boots, he raised his eyes. Captain Geta bore four wax tablets, his face inscrutable.

"You had no difficulty with last night's orders?"

"None."

"I would like a doubling of my bedchamber guard."

301

"Yes, my Lord."

Domitian reached for the waxed tablets. "Zeno made a botch of things. No records were kept for the archives." He lifted his signet finger. "Enough, but stay close."

As Geta marched from the room, Domitian swooped on the tablets. Picking the latest, dated June 9, he read under his own name: "Proceed to the foot of Victory Stairs. Stop every litter travelling down the Palatine. Arrest the Lady Cornelia, Chief of the Temple of Vesta, on the charge of breaking her vow of chastity. Escort her to Quintus Piso, Chief Priest of the Colleges of Jupiter, Mars and the Flavian Cult, at the Regia. Post a guard."

Domitian threw aside the tablet. Who was behind this impudent and treasonous act? Was the arrest intended to discredit him? Who had anything to gain? His mind took a more practical turn. Who, besides himself, knew of the presence of the chief vestal in the palace? Summoning Parthenius, Hermes and his bedchamber guards, he questioned each about their activities of the evening before, and what they had observed in this wing of the palace. Badly hung over, Parthenius seemed only remotely aware of how he had spent the evening, while Hermes cheerfully provided an alibi for both. Who would have the audacity to hatch such a scheme? Who would dare forge his signature? Who was capable of it? Whom was he neglecting?

The word *neglect* launched a small arrow of suspicion that did find a target – one that gave him a measure of relief, for it indicated he had a domestic rather than a political problem. With the twitchings of a smile, he pointed to Hermes: "Bring the Empress Domitia."

It had been a long while since Domitian had invited his wife into his bedchamber. He ordered Parthenius to get out his purple silk robe, to plump his cushions, to freshen the room with rosewater.

Minutes after her summons, the empress arrived, elaborately coiffed, fully made up, wearing an orange gown – his favourite colour. She smiled, despite the peremptory manner in which she had been fetched – a cause for suspicion in itself. Approaching the dais, she inclined her head. "My Lord and God." Ha! Almost a confession.

Domitian handed her Geta's forged order. She read it, then returned it without comment.

"Well?"

She shrugged. "What do you wish of me?"

"Your opinion."

"I suppose my opinion is the same as any other Roman's – your order is long overdue."

Startled, Domitian inquired: "What do you mean?"

Play-acting for the amusement of both Hermes and Parthenius, her royal spies, she declared: "All of Rome is wagging its tongue. Some even swear she has been seen at Cybele."

"*Who* has been seen at Cybele?"

"The chief vestal, of course. That's who we're talking about, isn't it?" Repressing a smile at how easily she could entangle him in her web of innuendo, she sighed as if drowning in boredom. "But why involve me? You must have evidence or you wouldn't have arrested her."

The emperor felt a sharp rise in temper. "For a wife who spends all her time in her bedchamber, you know a lot about Cybele."

Pretending to feel his rebuke, she demurred. "Of course, the report may be false. What is Rome but a breeding ground of gossip."

"Gossip spread by you, and no other!"

She toyed with the white amulet around her neck – the vestal Cornelia's amulet, taken from Maximus Marcus. "What else do you leave for me to do except chatter with my slaves? I can tell you, there is little comfort for me in knowing how slyly the *virtuous* of Rome lead their lives. Though it's hard to sort fantasy from fact, I do know that the chief virgin of Vesta prowls the night dressed as a man."

"What? You dare to make such an accusation unsupported?"

"Who says I am unsupported?" She thrust out her jaw. "I can prove it. I have another vestal's word. But why have you sent for me? You know politics bore me."

Tapping the forged imperial order with his signet finger, Domitian insisted: "You sent this."

She met his cynical gaze. "If you are accusing me, what's the point in protesting? Who else accuses me? On what evidence?" As if in despair, she flung her red-tipped nails in the air and began to pace the chamber. "I spent last evening confined to my room, as I did the night before and the night before that – as you have imprisoned me. What is the vestal Cornelia to me beyond my admiration for her clever double life?"

His wife was lying. He knew it. She knew it. What gall! What a magnificent performance. He should have her executed right now. Instead, he found himself overwhelmed by prideful nostalgia, remembering how the two of them had once play-acted together – scenes of jealousy, of intrigue, of deceit. What perfect partners! He'd never seen his wife more alive, more beautiful.

Relieved, the emperor dismissed the empress, giving her credit for easing his anxieties rather than discredit for causing them. No conspiracy. He smiled smugly. Just a jealous wife.

Settling back, Domitian tried to salvage the day. The fake imperial orders were still on his bed-table. He couldn't rescind them now the arrest was public. He couldn't admit he hadn't sent them. How weak and foolish he would seem – as ridiculous as the idiot emperor Claudius wrapped around his concubine's sticky fingers. He thought of the vestal Cornelia – of what she must be thinking, how she must be feeling. He thought of their remarkable evening, already receding in the press of events. Frowning he thought of the empress' outlandish accusations: that the vestal had been seen at Cybele; that she prowled the night as a man. Could there be any truth to such charges?

That kind of suspicion sent a destructive riptide over the previous night as Domitian thought he had experienced it. If the vestal was no virgin, he was not King Numa. If she had deceived him, he had not seduced her. If he had not seduced her, she had seduced him. Suddenly feeling unsure of himself, weak, drained, Domitian called for Parthenius and Zeno with the last of his will power. Ordering the chamberlain to bring him the turquoise box he kept in a secret compartment under his statue of Minerva, Domitian removed a signet ring bearing the head of Alexander – the signet Augustus had used till he replaced it with his own profile. Putting this on his right hand, Domitian tapped the coverlet with both rings, imagining himself twice as powerful. Then he dictated to Zeno: "Henceforth, all imperial orders must bear both the seal of Augustus and the seal of Alexander."

Ordering the room to be shuttered and the curtains drawn, Domitian pulled the covers over his head. History would have to run its course without him...till tomorrow.

From the benches of the Senate to Rome's baths and brothels, no one could talk of anything but the arrest of the chief vestal. The mood was one of outrage. The emperor had gone too far. Many of Domitian's statues were defaced or broken, and an imperial guard was posted at the Flavian Temple to prevent reprisals. Speeches were made from the rostra proclaiming Cornelia's innocence and denouncing "those in high places" responsible for her arrest. Crowds gathered around the Regia, chanting: "Free her! Free her!"

CHAPTER TWENTY-THREE

From the moment Maximus Marcus left the Flavian Amphitheatre, he had but one desire: to quit Rome by the shortest route. That meant travelling southward through Porta Capena. Once outside the gate, he considered hiking north to Como, but the optimism with which his family had launched his Roman career contrasted too bitterly with its collapse. Better to join the beggars, peasants and tradesmen in their jostling wagon train streaming south.

The Ostian Way took Marcus over the Pontine marshes, through woods and meadows, supporting sheep, horses and cattle. Though limping from his leg wound, he walked rapidly, not stopping to rest, expecting to be overtaken by praetorians but not caring much, not allowing himself to think or feel till he was far enough away to gain perspective.

In four hours he reached Ostia – Rome's first colony at the mouth of the Tiber, a fortified camp that had grown into a seaport, granary and resort of fifty thousand, subservient to the needs of Rome. Still wearing his gladiator's cape, he strolled through the commercial city with its efficient grid of streets and red-brick public buildings, contrasting to the marble and serpentine grandeur of Rome, starting now to explore beyond the tunnel carved by his eyes and feet, to orient himself.

It was late afternoon. Hundreds of Ostians crowded the

beaches, playing ball among the overturned rowboats, splashing in the palmy green water that served their needs as well as the splendid baths served the senators and tenement-dwellers of Rome. Joining them on the sand, Marcus sluffed off his cares in the lap of water and the cheerful tug of salt wind. He discovered he was still wearing his laurel crown and pitched it to three small boys who were building a Roman fort. They spun it from one to the other, initiating a boisterous new game among themselves.

Now trekking northward, Marcus passed mile upon mile of warehouses on his way to the harbour, which completed the subjugation of the world to the desires of Rome; for if all roads led to Rome, it was now equally true that all navigational lines did as well. Dominated by a 200-foot lighthouse, it berthed a tangle of ships from every province – three weeks by sea from Alexandria, six months from India. Elbowing his way down the teeming, clangorous wharves, he watched dusky workmen transfer cargoes to riverboats powered by sail, oars or oxen for the trip to Rome. Here were silks from the Orient, incense from Arabia, tin from the Scilly Islands, glass from Syria, gold from Dalmatia, lead and silver and copper from Iberia, venison and timber and wool from Gaul. And most important – since Rome had long ago stopped feeding herself – the grain of Africa, Numidia and Egypt.

Almost at random Marcus chose a bireme from Crete which had disgorged a cargo of marbles and was loading Italian oils and wines. The captain – an amiable enough fellow – told him the *Neptune* was sailing next morning for Sicily, Piraeus and several Greek isles, before returning home. Exchanging his cloth-of-gold cape for passage, Marcus shipped aboard.

The bireme – a short crescent with two banks of oars and an oblong sail – pulled anchor at firstlight, plying southward under stiff winds and misty blue skies, from the polluted waters of the Tiber into the blue Tyrrhenian Sea. After a few hours the mist clotted into thick grey clouds, so that the *Neptune* was overtaken by a short, sharp squall that damaged her masts and threatened to run her aground on the rocky spur known as Capri. The captain, who might have prevented this had he not been celebrating a successful launching with retsina, ordered his crew to shelter in the island's harbour. As the keel struck sand, cockleshell boats, manned by the fishermen who harvested these waters for mullet and prawns, challenged the heavy surf to take ashore the captain, his officers and Maximus Marcus.

High seas kept the bireme landbound for three days. On the fourth, repairs to the mast and hull were begun. Taking advantage of this idyllic June day, Marcus set out to explore the majestic arrowhead which he had visited seventeen years before, with Cornelia's brother Nestor. Dressed in sandals and breechcloth, he climbed the precipitous spine that split the island, through wildflowers and silvery olive trees, watching the village drop away along with the crumbling tufa walls from the old praetorian camp built by Emperor Tiberius when he lived here. Rejoining the imperial road, Marcus hiked upward toward Tiberius' fabulous Villa Io, on the highest promontory. Along the route were broken statues and erotic mosaics, more easily reclaimed by nature's greening hand than the memory of that randy tyrant who gave the island its name: *Caprineum*, the old goat.

Tiberius had not left Rome because it was evil, but because it was not evil enough. Here, free of the censure of friend and foe, he had given full rein to the unnatural lusts he had repressed during earlier years. Boys and girls called *spintriae* were trained to perform upon the vile old man; babies as yet unweaned were forced to suck at his diseased organ; virgins, with arms and legs bound, were thrown over the cliff so their death struggles might arouse his waning passions. Never had such revolting practices defiled a spot so beautiful. Yet Tiberius was the emperor Domitian admired most. His were the memoirs he read and reread, by way of envy and example. Should such a man be allowed to live, let alone to rule the world?

Flavius Clemens had said yes. He had remained faithful to the *imperium* of the emperor – to order and to form, to working within the system. Priscus, the rebel, had thumbed his nose at it. His father, the Stoic, had publicly opposed it. Philip the Prophet had set up an alternative system. All had died for their views. What was Marcus to make of such examples?

He remembered, as he had not done in years, a fussy old Greek tutor he had once had by the name of Artemon. Impatient at having to learn Greek before he could learn Latin, Marcus had taunted Artemon with the fact that all the engineering texts and war manuals were in Latin, which he claimed was why the Greeks had lost their empire. Artemon had countered by making him stand on one foot and decline by the hour, "Marcus Porcius Cato has said that the roots of science are bitter.... Bitter are the roots of science, Marcus Porcius Cato has said..." twisting the words like wet towels to wring out their meaning.

Unchastened, Marcus had resisted all Artemon's attempts to teach him of a world beyond the building of bridges, the fighting of wars, the racing of chariots, dismissing that world and its tutor as impractical, decadent and dangerous. Now he tried, with a certain wistfulness, to open the box of memory. To recall the Stoics, with their faith in reason and law. The Epicureans, with their belief in pleasure as the pursuit of life, but especially the pleasures of the mind. The Ideals of Socrates, existing above and apart from the material world. Marcus shook his head. Greek abstraction gave him a headache. Perhaps when he got to Crete?

At last he saw the blinding-white ruins of Tiberius' villa, shimmering in the rocks and shrubs above him. Three olive-skinned boys shouted at him from a grotto where they were splashing. For two quadrans each, they offered to escort Marcus through Io, and to reveal the filthy exploits of the emperor who built it. For another three – less than the cost of a prostitute in Rome – they would demonstrate, for his pleasure, the tricks of the *spintriae.* Dancing naked in front of Marcus, they blocked his path, snatching at his breechcloth so he was forced to beat them off with a birch wand, outraged that Rome's depravity had pursued him here.

Marcus veered away from the villa to the opposite side of the island, with its needle spires that dropped brutally to water of uncanny blue. After watching the sea dash itself into foam, he gazed up into the sky where two seagulls arced and swooped, catching sunlight on their broad white wings, remembering the acrobats in the Baths of Titus as they dove, arms outstretched.

Marcus was overtaken by a more powerful image: a childhood memory frozen in pain. His mother and father standing hand in hand on a cliff at Como. His father had jumped first – in dignified acquiescence to the disease that gnawed his vitals. His mother, in devotion, had leapt after him, with their togas spread like wings, then wrapping them round and round as winding sheets while they hurtled down into the streaked blue water. Marcus had been nine years old. He had not understood. He had felt afraid and angry, as if he had done something wrong or were being falsely punished. Marcus discovered – to his dismay – that he still did not understand, that he still felt afraid and angry and falsely punished.

Now climbing partway down the cliff to a ledge, he dove, arms outstretched, cutting the surface cleanly, glorying in the bite of cold water as it slid over his sweaty skin. He stroked his way around the promontory back to the village, spotting a skiff headed from the mainland into Capri harbour, thinking of little beyond the next breath.

Pleasantly exhausted, Marcus hauled himself up onto the silvery rocks and stretched on his back, staring up into the sky. As he dozed, he remembered a cave he and Nestor had visited here seventeen years ago. A blue cave – a wonderful sight. An old fisherman had taken them. Instructing them to lie on their backs in his boat, he had pitched through a gap in the cliff on the crest of a wave. A dome had opened overhead – mysterious, silver-blue, phosphorescent. As infinite, or so it first appeared, as the sky. The fisherman had swirled his oars in the water, stirring up luminous whirls of quicksilver...so quiet, so still, *remarkable, remarkable.* Marcus imagined himself back in that magic cave with Nestor's head against his chest, stroking the

310

flame-coloured hair...not Nestor's head, of course. Nestor's sister's head.

Marcus sat bolt upright on the rocks. He scrambled back to the beach and headed for the village, his pleasure in the afternoon spoiled by hopeless thoughts of Cornelia. Never before in his life had there been anyone so unique, someone for whom he would subjugate head to heart, subvert his goals, risk death. How to account for the longings that thrilled his nights and tormented his days, the fantasies that compelled his thoughts like a powerful lodestone? Even the Greeks had no answer, no matter how long he stood on one foot or how many sentences he declined.

He remembered the vestal as he had last seen her, proud and silent and white amidst a chaos of screaming mouths and shaking fists, her handkerchief in her hand. Never had she seemed more desirable or more remote. Had she risked her life to save his? He groaned. Every time he had tempted her from her duty or taken her in his arms, he had endangered her. Their love was impossible, even if he were still welcome in Rome. Consul Clemens had been right, as always. What he needed was a wife. Some ordinary but loving woman to bear him children...a son.

Marcus thought of the wife he had once had. Calpurnia, dark-haired and pleasant – pretty, he guessed, though no beauty. Plain in dress – nothing like the style of the women he'd known in Rome. He realized, with belated regret, that he knew almost nothing about her. She had been a cousin. Shortly after they married, he had left on campaign while she stayed in Como. When she had died of malaria, he hadn't known about it for two weeks. Nor his son. Now, when he pictured young Marcus, he saw only Castor the page.

Marcus turned from such disturbing thoughts. He had been eighteen when he married – no different from all the other ambitious, young knights he had known. To the extent that he had love to spare, he had given it to his concubine Damaris, whom he had left behind in Egypt. Damaris had been a spontaneous, fun-loving companion, and a skilled mimic. What a mar-

311

vellous time she would have had undercutting the pomposity of imperial Rome – and his own.

Now as Marcus plodded through the sand, he spied the mast of the *Neptune* in the harbour, flying the Crete flag, along with the skiff he had noticed ploughing in from the mainland.

A tanned and grisled man shambled toward him. By his unsteady gait, Marcus assumed it was the captain already celebrating this new launching. Lifting his head, the man grinned. Marcus quickened his pace. "Pollux!"

Stretching his arms across the sand, the old man loped toward Marcus. "Yas! Yas!" He pointed to the skiff from which he had debarked, and waved a letter.

Clapping Pollux on the back with an outpouring that surprised him, Marcus asked: "How did you find me?"

The old man mouthed: "Cape." Then "ta-vern."

Apparently the *Neptune*'s captain had lost Marcus' gladiator's cape, sold for passage, in a dice game – the same cape Marcus had worn, along with his laurel crown, from the amphitheatre to Ostia. Marcus laughed. If he had wished praetorians to hunt him down, he could scarcely have made it easier.

Frowning, he accepted the letter from Pollux: news from Rome. Had he any reason to expect good news? Breaking the seal, he discovered it was from Zeno. Scowling with what was now foreboding, he read: "Cornelia arrested. Trial to be held in Alba." He looked at Pollux with astonishment. What had happened? As Pollux painfully expressed what he knew, Marcus watched the *Neptune* preparing to set sail at firstlight tomorrow. Return to Rome? It was the last thing he would have chosen.

312

CHAPTER TWENTY-FOUR

It was customary for the wealthy to flee Rome during the stifling summer months. At first this was to avoid the malaria that bred in the bogs around the Tiber; later it was for the salubrious enjoyment of the countryside.

White villas dominated the hills for hundreds of miles around the city, offering a panoramic view of vineyards, grazing lands, seacoast and forest. Domitian's summer estate was located fifteen miles southeast of Rome, above Lake Alba in the Alban Hills. It included baths, a race course, a library, gymnasium and amphitheatre, lavished with every kind of marble, stucco, precious metal and mosaic. There were as many dining rooms as hours of daylight; graceful porticos caught balmy breezes and exploited every vista.

Greatest attention had been focussed on the gardens, for Romans liked to force, control and dominate nature as much as they liked to mould in marble and concrete. Myrtle, bay, fig and plane trees had been sculpted into animals, urns and pyramids. Box trees spelled DOMITIAN. Streams had been rerouted to create fountains that danced, waterfalls that cascaded, grottos where guests, partly submerged, could eat from miniature flower boats. Flocks of flamingos, doves and peacocks roamed shady parks and even these challenged nature, for all were albinos in celebration of the region's historic name.

At firstlight on July 1 the emperor, his guards, sixteen members of the priestly college and one hundred senators set forth in a train of fifteen hundred carriages along the Appian Way, the world's finest road. Their purpose was twofold: to move the emperor's household to the mountains for the summer, and to conduct a trial to determine the fate of the vestal Cornelia.

The emperor's habit was to journey by litter so he could read, write letters and sleep in comfort. Because of his desire to quit the hostility of Rome as quickly as possible, this time he travelled by two-horse carriage, with the sepulchres lining the route setting an appropriately baleful tone.

The trial of the chief vestal was to be held in the villa's amphitheatre, more often used for poetry competitions, cockfighting, bear-wrestling, and death duels between snakes and mongooses. At dawn of the first day the jury, which consisted of the sixteen priests of the three sacred colleges, ranged itself in the lower marble seats, with the senators behind. Catullus Messalinus, the prosecutor, occupied a canopied stall to the right of the stage. Ex-consul Cocceius Nerva, the defence counsel, accompanied the vestal Cornelia in a stall to the left. Pontifex Piso, judge of the proceedings, sat at centrestage by the witness box. A higher stall, amidst the stage's Dionysian frieze, was intended for the emperor. This day it remained empty: Domitian had declined to attend the opening session.

Judge Piso called the court to order. Though many had dismissed him in latter years as a silly and ineffectual old man, the gravity of this trial and his affection for Cornelia brought forth physical and moral strength. His voice was sonorous and his manner authoritative as he intoned: "Be it resolved before this court and the people of Rome that Cornelia, chief vestal of the Temple of Vesta in Rome, did – against her solemn oath of chastity to Vesta – engage in sexual intercourse with a person, or persons, as yet unnamed." He requested Cornelia to rise. Recognizing a vestal's right to give testimony without taking oath, he questioned her as she stood: "How do you plead?"

Staring straight ahead as if carved in marble, she made no reply. Rising by her side, Counsel Nerva confronted the court. "Not guilty!" he boomed.

The judge struck his gavel. "Let us proceed."

Prosecutor Messalinus called his first witness: Cinna Celer, one of the two praetorians who had arrested Cornelia and escorted her to the Regia. As the centurion took the stand, his chest covered with medals, it was clear Messalinus had made a wise choice, for the mere presence of the detested Captain Geta would have prejudiced the assembly against his case.

Pacing the stage to the *tap tap tap* of his ivory cane Messalinus elicited information from Celer about his long and honourable military record. "Is it not true that you are the first centurion of the first cohort, in charge of your legion's eagle? Is it not true that you were awarded the oak crown for saving a comrade? Is it not true that you have won a siege crown for rescuing a garrison?"

To each question, Celer nodded his ropy grey head, creating a modest and manly impression. In the same respectful tone, Messalinus asked Celer about the arrest of the chief vestal, slicing each question into as many segments as possible, and preceding each with "Is it not true...?" to imply every positive response from this military hero was yet another piece of damning evidence against the vestal. "Is it not true that on the night of June 9, Captain Geta of the Imperial Guard showed you an order from the emperor? Is it not true that this imperial order required you to halt a black litter fleeing down the Palatine?"

Pausing before the witness box, Messalinus asked: "Would you point out the person you found hiding in that unmarked litter."

As unhappy as his droopy moustache, Centurion Celer nodded in Cornelia's direction.

"What was the condition of her hair and clothing?"

Celer mumbled: "Can't say."

Messalinus swung his ivory stick. "Can't or won't?"

Eyes downcast, Celer refused to answer.

"What conclusion would you have drawn about the character of such a woman, seen at such a time and place, if she hadn't been a vestal?"

Counsel Nerva rose majestically. "I object to this line of speculation. I would have objected earlier to the prosecution's use of the words *hiding* and *fleeing* but I wished the court to observe how far my colleague would go in concocting his flimsy case."

Judge Piso nodded. "Objection sustained."

Messalinus shrugged, as if it scarcely mattered. "No more questions." Then he sat down.

Nerva strode toward the witness stand, exaggerating his bulk, his age and authority, in contrast to Messalinus' slick and darting manner – an imposing barrel-chested man with glowing white hair and dark bushy brows. Gesturing to the clerk not to bother reversing the waterclock, he addressed the witness. "Since my opponent has established your distinguished career, I'll spare the court repetition. I wish to ask you only one question. Knowing the sanctity of a vow to Vesta, and knowing August Lady Cornelia's unblemished record, would it be more reasonable to assume she was engaged in secret Temple business when arrested or –" here a disdainful toss of the white mane toward Messalinus "– as this gentleman insinuates?"

"On Vesta's business," exclaimed Celer. "As Jupiter is my witness, she is innocent!"

The court all but cheered.

"I object!" shouted Messalinus, who had been waving his cane to attract the judge's attention. "I demand that question and answer be stricken from the record."

Judge Piso nodded. "I so move."

As Nerva strode back to the defence box, Messalinus called his second witness: Rufus Felix, the emperor's physician and a priest of the Flavian cult. The doctor from Alexandria – very much the dandy in scarlet-and-green silk mantle – took the stand and was sworn in. Again Messalinus elicited detailed information relating to his witness' prestige – much of it based on his fashionable reputation for treating diseases of the sexual organs, known familiarly as Dionysius' Curse. Delighted at being able to expound his questionable theories, the doctor answered fulsomely – a digression not unwelcome to elderly members of the court, happy to receive free advice on such a worrisome subject.

Tackling more serious matters, Messalinus again bombarded his witness with rapid-fire questions designed to bring the weight of the doctor's prestige against the accused. "Is it not true you were summoned by imperial decree to the Regia before cockcrow on June 10? Is it not true you were asked to examine a woman who had been arrested by Captain Petronius Geta of the Imperial Guard and Centurion Celer? Is it not true you discovered the person to be –" here he swung around, poking his cane toward Cornelia "– chief priestess of the Temple of Vesta? Is it not true you were asked to examine this person for evidence of sexual intercourse, in contravention of her solemn oath of chastity?"

Ceasing to pace, Messalinus spun around to the court as if consulting them in the delicate wording of his next question. "Allowing for your caution as a man of science, and forgetting the person we are discussing is *technically* a virgin of the Temple of Vesta, would you conclude from your examination that the accused had ever had sexual intercourse?"

Having caught some of Messalinus' flair for suspense, the doctor rolled his eyes upward as if considering. Judge Piso leaned forward in his seat. Some of the members of the court cupped their hands around their ears. At last the witness replied: "Yes, I would."

Triumphant, Messalinus pressed on. "What would lead you – as a scientist specializing in the sexual organs – to that conclusion?"

The doctor launched a self-important lecture, which Messalinus allowed to go on long enough to sound impressive, before interrupting. "In layman's terms, please."

317

The doctor folded his hands on the witness box. "In layman's terms, the skin sealing the vaginal opening was ruptured."

"You mean, what is commonly called the virgin's veil?"

"Yes."

"It had been torn."

"Yes."

Daring one more question based on character assessment, Messalinus asked: "Would you care to hazard an educated opinion, doctor, as to whether sexual intercourse had taken place within...let us say...the last six hours?"

The doctor hesitated – not because of any lack of arrogance as to his medical knowledge, which was limitless as Messalinus had judged, but from fear as to how far he dare go politically. He glanced nervously at the empty imperial box before replying: "I cannot answer that question."

Straining forward in what had become almost self-parody, Messalinus asked: "Can't or won't?"

"Can't *and* won't!" snapped the doctor, furious at having to admit there was anything he did not know.

"You mean it is beyond your skill to tell?"

"I mean," replied the doctor with hauteur, "it is beyond the skill of Hippocrates himself!" He pointed to a broken urn that was part of the stage decorations. "You might as well ask me how long since that dry pot was filled."

The court burst into laughter – partly in relief and partly out of satisfaction at seeing Messalinus bested.

Smiling through his teeth, the prosecutor bowed, in deference: "Very well then, let us clarify." Stroking the doctor with oily solicitations so as to lure him back into the embrace of the prosecution, he asked him to describe how the medical examination of the vestal had been conducted: who was present in the cramped room, and where they stood; how the vestal was arranged on the metal cot; what clothes she was wearing, and their condition; what instruments he had used, and how her sexual parts differed, exactly, from the sexual parts of a virgin – thus feeding, for the better part of the afternoon, the prurient fantasies of the court, so there was scarcely a man who did not believe he himself had intimate knowledge of the vestal.

Many times Counsel Nerva objected, but Judge Piso, though distressed, seemed to think Messalinus' questions relevant. At last the prosecutor turned to Nerva. "Your witness."

Though it was late enough for the priests and senators to be yearning for their baths, Nerva dared not leave the court to mull this vicious testimony. Ambling toward centrestage, he said: "I'm sorry, my distinguished friends, to hold you to your hard seats when the emperor's gardens are so inviting, but since my opponent has sweated so windily to prove flowers are thorns, I wish to take a little of your time – and common sense – to change them back."

He approached the Alexandrian doctor preening himself in the witness box. "I have no intention of disputing your credentials, but I do have one question pertaining to your credibility." His voice hardened. "In your practice – dealing largely with cases of impotence, infertility and sexual excess – does your clientele include many virgins from the Temple of Vesta?"

The doctor's head jerked back in surprise.

The counsel sarcastically rephrased his question. "Do vestal virgins flock to your office seeking your special sort of services?" His black brows converged in his famous oratorical scowl. "In short, have you ever examined one before?"

Fine feathers ruffled, the doctor replied: "I have not. They *are* women like all the rest, are they not?" He smirked at the assembly, seeking more applause.

"When born, of course!" snapped Nerva, cutting him short. "But are you not aware of the ceremonies by which a young girl becomes a priestess of Vesta?"

"I am, indeed. Are *you* not aware that I am a priest of the Flavian cult?"

"Then I suppose you are familiar with the bridal symbolism of those vestal ceremonies – the flame veil, the cutting of the virgin's tresses, and the white robes bound with the knot of Hercules?"

319

"I am."

"Are you also aware of the significance of the vestals as daughters of the imperial house, and of the chief vestal as the bride of the state of Rome?"

"Of course."

"Are you aware of a later ceremony, after puberty, in which novices present their chastity to Vesta?"

The doctor shifted uneasily. "I know there is such a ceremony."

"Do you know how that ceremony is conducted?"

"I do not." He growled: "Nor do you."

"I agree. The rite is a secret one which no vestal can reveal. However...can you imagine, given the significance of the ceremony, the form it is likely to take?"

The doctor scowled. "I cannot. No one can. As you admitted, that rite is secret."

"Could you imagine that such a ceremony – offering chastity to Vesta – might leave physical evidence consistent with a woman's having had sexual intercourse even though she had not?"

"I know when a woman is a virgin and when she is not!"

"Do you, doctor? Even when she has become the bride of the state of Rome? I wonder." Nerva strolled to the row of urns that had provided the doctor with his "dry-pot" metaphor. He picked a lily and held it high. "If I were to find this lily by the side of a path, I would not know, by its broken stem, whether it was plucked by the wind or by human hand, and I doubt you would either." Striding to the prosecution's stall he laid the lily before Messalinus. "Take care. The gods will not forgive those who sling mud on their anointed one."

Judge Piso adjourned the court.

Nerva escorted Cornelia from the amphitheatre, collecting discreet congratulations en route. As they withdrew to a quiet nook far from the lavish banquet the others were enjoying, he held the vestal's arm with fatherly reassurance. "Please, my dear

320

Cornelia, don't be depressed. Messalinus is a dishonest show-man, far better at whitewashing the guilty than at blackening the innocent. When confronted with goodness, his slickness coils against him so he strangles on his own tongue. All Rome is on your side – at least, the honest part."

The vestal stared listlessly into space.

"You know, of course," Nerva continued, "that I cannot question the genesis of your arrest since it was by imperial decree. That means only that the emperor signed the document, not that he initiated it. Do you know anyone who would try to destroy you?"

Cornelia was non-committal. "No enemies I can state."

Cocking a brow in imitation of his opponent, Nerva asked: "Can't or won't?"

The question hung unanswered.

He tried once more. "The doubt weighing heaviest against you is where you had been when arrested. If you could confide in me, I could use that information to root out any suspicions Messalinus sows."

The vestal inclined her head. "I'm sorry, Nerva. Though I trust you more than any man, I cannot tell you."

"Very well. I'll ask no more. I need only stage a show for my colleagues since they expect it. The star of the defence is you. Your words and your esteem will shine through any murkiness Messalinus stirs up."

Cornelia's level gaze met Nerva's. "I will not speak in my own defence."

"What? Are you sure? I know how insulting it is to reply, but your accusers bray with strident voices. A simple statement of innocence from your own lips is all decent men will need. Surely Vesta wants you to speak on her behalf?"

"I don't know what Vesta wants," returned Cornelia flatly. "I will not testify."

Tapping his stylus against his teeth, Nerva studied her with thoughtfulness. "Very well. I'll have to work a little harder then."

The trial of the chief vestal continued for five days, sometimes with Nerva winning the session, and sometimes Messalinus. Not once did the emperor put in an appearance, preferring to stalk stags through his forests (on good days) or to float aimlessly about Lake Alba (on bad ones) with the oars of his dinghy muffled against frazzling noise.

On many of these occasions his companion was a youth of eleven named Varus, from the village of Alba Longa, whose grandmother was summer midwife to the royal household.

On the third morning of the trial, Domitian ordered Varus to row him about the ponds stocked with ornamental fish, so he could shoot them with gold-tipped arrows. After each shot, the boy would retrieve the fish pierced by the arrow. Holding it high for the emperor to approve, he would toss it onto a pile of spotted, striped, rippled, mucus bodies that lay in a broken rainbow, some still gasping for air.

Domitian aimed at a goldfish with a red eye on its side – the most exacting marksmanship. Though he never missed a shot, he took longer each time to line it up. This was partly because the fish were becoming less numerous and partly because of the tic in his left cheek. Though he was balanced on the peak of a high mood, he knew by the clammy sweat seeping through his tunic he was about to plunge. The zing of the arrows – by relieving internal pressure – kept depression at bay.

Though Domitian avoided the amphitheatre, the trial had much effect on his state. With a tremor of excitement, he wondered what the vestal Cornelia might be thinking at this moment, feeling joined to her by his power over her the same as he was joined by his arrow to the fish hiding in the reeds. Did she blame him for the arrest? What would she guess his motive to be? Did she imagine the seduction to be a political act to ensnare her? Would she suspect he was exercising personal domination over her? Did she hope the trial was just a warning, that he would reverse a verdict of guilty? Would he?

Domitian had intended to halt proceedings against the vestal but he had never managed to do it. Then it had become easier –

more interesting – to let events unfold, like a good play, with their own momentum.

He heaved a self-pitying sigh. That was the trouble with power. The more he had of it, the more there was to do and the less time to do it. The more he reacted to events instead of initiating them, the more passive he became. Life unfolded its spectacle like a peacock its tail, while he watched from his throne, adding a little business here, subtracting a little there, till in boredom and frustration he strode down the dais and, taking the peacock in both hands, wrung its neck.

Domitian released the arrow. It pierced the red eye of the fish. With a cheer, Varus waded waist-deep through the reeds, then held up fish and arrow for him to see: bull's-eye. Domitian admired the boy as he scrambled back into the boat, his lean brown legs shedding water under the leather tunic, his smile winsome. Perhaps he would amuse himself with Varus this afternoon? If depression didn't overtake him.

In the meantime... Domitian tightened his bow and cast about for more fish. Were there none left? He felt the twitch in his cheek. *Ahh, yes,* he spotted one near the bow of the boat – a silver fish the size of a child's hand. It darted into the reeds. He waited. It reappeared but too far away.

He thought again of the vestal. The mastery he had felt that night he had taken her, the joy, the release. And yet, when she had left – hastily robed, her hair unbound, trailing her clouds of broken glory – he wasn't sure he wanted to see her again. Romance was a young man's game. What he needed at this stage in life was greater detachment. The detachment of a Tiberius, who could make love, then kill. Or kill, then make love. Without remorse. His problem was in being somewhere between.

Besides...what of the vestal's true guilt? That suspicion had begun to rankle. Had she been a virgin, as she pretended? Had she already betrayed her vow with Maximus Marcus, or at Cybele? Domitian's thoughts turned rancid. What did he know of the innocence of women? All he had experienced was their perfidy!

323

The fish. He let fly his arrow. It pierced the silver-white body, drawing blood from a large red hole. Clapping his hands, Varus stepped flirtatiously into the water, aware of the emperor's eye.

Domitian fitted another arrow and searched for another fish. In the reeds? Behind a rock? Grinning, Varus waved the impaled silver one. The bow taut against his twitching cheek, Domitian turned toward him. He released the arrow. It pierced Varus' forehead. The boy's laughter turned to disbelief, as his head snapped and his torso arched like the bow Domitian gripped. He tumbled backward, the foam rustling around him like a silky skirt, as he struggled feebly.

Domitian steered the boat to the boy, with one of the muffled oars. Gazing down at the pretty face with its matting of dark curls, and the arrow stuck so absurdly in the middle of his forehead, oozing blood from its efficient little death hole, he patted the soft cheek that would never wrinkle, remembering his sister the day she had drowned. She had called to him, but he had been sulking about something she had done, and he hadn't rowed quickly enough. She had been swept away...her body bloated and unburied, chewed by millions of little fishes like the slimy heap in his boat.

Domitian retrieved the arrow from the boy's forehead and drifted slowly away, feeling the darkness close in around him. Even his lovely Alban villa was losing its charm.

Day by day news of the trial at Alba leaked back to Rome – presumably through prosecutor Messalinus, since the evidence, unsifted through the prestige of Nerva, all pointed to the vestal's guilt.

Speculation centred on what was known as "God's business or bawd's?" Why would the vestal be travelling through Rome before cockcrow in an unmarked litter? There seemed only two explanations: sex or politics, and for a woman, suspicion leaned overwhelmingly toward sex. There was also much titillation about the vestal's physical examination, with the more conservative maintaining that even to have submitted was a breach of her vow of chastity. It was the vestal's duty – even more than Caesar's wife – to be above suspicion.

The most damning gossip swirled around two secret witnesses called by Messalinus on the last day of the trial. Under elaborate security precautions – as much to intrigue as to disguise – he spirited them out of Rome by fast gig then billeted them backstage in the amphitheatre. Such tactics, of course, assured a full house. Only the emperor could not be enticed from other pursuits.

The witnesses were not present when Judge Piso called the court to order. He turned to Messalinus: "The prosecution will proceed."

With a sly smile, Messalinus stalked backstage, his cane flicking before him. When he returned, the identity of his witness remained a mystery. He, or she, was draped in a mourning veil. Standing at centrestage, his hand fingering the veil, his blind eyes ricocheting in excitement, Messalinus said to Judge Piso: "I request permission to dispense with the oath." Flicking aside the witness' veil, he revealed the vestal Agrippina – a thin, vertical line of defiance confronting the court.

While Judge Piso re-established order, Messalinus deferentially guided her to the box. "Would you please identify yourself."

Clutching a scroll in both hands, the vestal replied: "I am Agrippina, second eldest vestal of the Temple of Vesta." She added with a flick of tongue over dry lips: "Acting chief priestess of the Temple."

"How long have you served as a vestal?"

"Twenty-eight years, six months, two weeks and four days."

"How long has the accused served as chief priestess?"

Agrippina was equally precise. "Seventeen months, two weeks and two days."

Having learned something of the power of brevity, Messalinus plunged into testimony. "During the accused's tenure as chief, did you notice anything unusual in the operation of the Temple?"

Agrippina tightened her grip around her scroll. "Laxity! I noticed laxity in the Temple! Improper forms of address are used. Seniority isn't respected. The younger vestals speak without being spoken to. They laugh in the Temple. They wander about Rome without litters or lictors." Holding her scroll inches from her eyes, Agrippina began to read: "On the seventeenth day of November the vestal Cornelia did sprinkle four drops of the blood of the October Horse on the altar of Vesta before speaking the incantation. On the thirteenth day of December –"

As spectators shifted impatiently, Agrippina ticked through her meticulously inscribed misdemeanours. Several times Messalinus tried to interrupt, but Agrippina overrode him. At last he cracked his cane on the witness box, causing Judge Piso to bang his gavel. "Order! Will the prosecution please confine itself to questioning the witness." He turned to Agrippina. "And would you please stay with evidence pertaining to this trial."

Putting her scroll resolutely behind her, Agrippina began to recite: "On the evening of the seventh of May, just after sunset, I was in the vestalry garden when I saw a person in a dark cloak come down the stairs. It was a brown cloak – a man's cloak – though no man is permitted in the vestalry after sunset. I saw this person look left, then look right. I saw this person sneak out of the vestal compound."

"Did you see the face of this person?"

Agrippina shook her head. "I saw this person's hair. It was red hair – the vestal Cornelia's hair."

Tapping his cane, Messalinus inquired: "Did you attempt to address 'this person' by her name?"

"No. I followed her out into Sacred Square."

"Why did you do that?" The answer had been carefully rehearsed: *Because the vestal Cornelia had not seemed well lately and I was worried about her health.*

Licking her dry lips, Agrippina replied: "Because of laxity, laxity in the Temple!"

Messalinus heard the rattle of parchment and was gripping his cane as Judge Piso snapped: "Please, Lady Agrippina, confine yourself to *this* trial."

Agrippina picked up her recitation. "I followed the vestal Cornelia – *this person* – from the vestalry. I followed her past the Regia and down Sacred Way. I followed her down the Street of the Yoke-Makers out of the Forum. The way was dark. The street was full of ruffians and whores and soldiers. Of drunks and thieves and bawds of Cybele." Agrippina's eyes grew round with the vividness of her recollections. "I was frightened. I returned to the vestalry."

"Then what did you do?"

"I went to Cornelia's room."

"Was she there?"

"She was not."

"Are you sure?"

"I called to her. I searched the room."

"Was she anywhere else in the vestalry or at the Temple of Vesta?"

"She was not."

"Are you sure?"

"Yes."

"How do you know?"

"Because...I waited for her in the garden. I saw her sneak back in through the gate."

"What time was that?"

"Many hours later...almost dawn."

"What was her condition?"

The cords of Agrippina's neck grew taut, her eyed bulged. "I think she was drunk. She seemed...unsteady."

Messalinus spun around in triumph to Nerva. "Your witness."

Grim-faced, the counsel shook his head. "I waive, till after the second witness."

Eyes fierce, back ramrod straight, Agrippina stepped down from the box.

"Next," said Judge Piso.

Again Messalinus prowled his way backstage, and again he returned with a witness draped in a mourning veil. When he flicked aside the covering this time, he revealed: the vestal Diana, thirty pounds lighter than last seen publicly, her eyes darkly ringed.

Messalinus turned to the judge. "I request the oath be waived."

Judge Piso nodded. "I so grant."

Unwilling to risk exposure of his terrified witness, Messalinus again came swiftly to the point. "Will you please tell the court what you witnessed on or about the date of February 2, which pertains to the guilt of the vestal Cornelia."

With downcast eyes, voice faltering, Diana testified: "I was at the spring of Egeria. I was fetching water. It was morning – just after dawn. I was running. I thought I was late. I would have been late except Cornelia – Lady Cornelia – was already at the spring. I had forgotten she told me she would fetch the water."

Diana peeked nervously at Messalinus.

Whipping his cane behind his back, he said: "Let me clarify... The vestal Cornelia told you *she* would draw the Temple water on the morning in question?"

"Yes."

"Did she tell you why?"

"No, sir."

"What did you do when you saw her?"

"I hid behind Apollo."

"Why?"

"I heard voices."

"Ahhhh." Messalinus chuckled. "You heard voices. Whose voices?"

Diana took a gulp of air. "The vestal Cornelia's voice."

"Yes, yes. Who else?"

"A man's voice."

"A man's voice?" Messalinus ran his cane through his fingers. "Did you see this man?"

"Yes. He was wearing a uniform. A commander's uniform."

"A commander, eh? Can you identify this man?"

Diana's voice was almost inaudible. "Yes."

Messalinus ordered: "Will you tell the court whom the vestal Cornelia met at the fountain of Egeria on or about the morning of February 2."

Diana mumbled into her chin.

"Beg pardon?" Messalinus cupped his hand around his ear. "Speak up, please. I may be the only blind man in court, but there are many deaf ones."

Diana's face reddened. She glanced toward Agrippina, who nodded slightly. "It was Maximus Marcus."

The court erupted with noisy exclamations as this name buzzed from seat to seat. *Marcus Marcus Marcus.*

"Order!" demanded Judge Piso. "Order in the court!"

After waiting dramatically for silence, Messalinus leaned toward the box, his white prosecutor's eyebrow cocked. "Did you hear any conversation between the vestal Cornelia and Commander Maximus Marcus?"

Diana shook her head. "I was too far away."

"Did you see anything that might be of interest?"

Breaking into a slack-lipped grin, Diana became animated for the first time. "I saw them hug! I saw them kiss! I saw them go off together in the bushes! I saw them come out again. She had mud on her robes – a big stain as big as your fist. He was picking leaves out of her hair. They were laughing together. She washed her gown in the spring."

Cornelia jumped to her feet. "Diana, that's not true! Tell them it isn't true!"

"It *is* true!" exclaimed Diana. She looked in terror at Agrippina. "It's true! It's true!"

Judge Piso declared a recess.

It was a muggy day, with fog blotting out the Alban Hills. When the court reconvened several hours later, a sticky pall hung over the amphitheatre, so that the emperor's villa seemed isolated from the rest of the world.

Throughout the trial the senators had ranged themselves on the side they supported. Before the testimony of the two vestals, the defence side of the amphitheatre had always been conspicuously full of well-wishers. The rumour had even gone around that the emperor's absence meant the trial was merely a warning to those who opposed him and that the vestal was to be acquitted. Now the senators were not so sure. Most bunched in the centre or sat as spectators toward the back.

Though Nerva seemed fatigued, his voice was strong and his mind sharp as he went back and forth over Agrippina's testimony, poking holes in all her certainties. How could she identify the person who left the vestalry when her eyesight was so poor she had to hold her scroll to her nose to read? How was her own offence, in leaving the vestalry after nightfall, less than the chief vestal's – if, in fact, it was she? And so on.

Under Nerva's steely assault, Agrippina gave up some of her damaging testimony – especially that pertaining to the condition of Cornelia on her return to the vestalry – but in her conviction that it *was* Cornelia, she was granite.

The vestal Diana at first seemed like butter to Nerva's hot knife. Wadding her robes, she shifted back and forth as to time and circumstances, and even as to the identity of the officer. However, she clung to the portion that was most damaging: she *had* seen the chief vestal go into the bushes with a man; she had seen her emerge "a while later" with mud and leaves on her robes and hair; she had seen the vestal wash her robe in the spring.

Turning from Diana with contempt, Counsel Nerva declared his cross-examination at an end. Judge Piso adjourned the trial.

There remained only the summations to the jury.

As the court reassembled for the last day, the principals took their places: the accused Cornelia, composed after yesterday's outburst; defence counsel Nerva, grimly full of purpose; prosecutor Messalinus, ebullient with self-confidence; Agrippina, stiff-spined and flame-eyed, as if she carried the hearth of Vesta stoked inside her; Diana, wan, with drooping head like a broken flower.

Even Emperor Domitian was present. Cupping his chin in his hand and propping his elbow on his knee, he sat in the royal box as motionless as if he were part of the marble frieze.

The prosecution spoke first.

Already savouring victory, Messalinus was verbose, flamboyant, even obnoxious as he strutted about the stage, swinging, stroking and tapping his cane. He spoke solemnly of the historic importance of the vestals to the safety of Rome, of their awesome rights and responsibilities, and of the significance of the oath of chastity as a beacon of morality in an evil world. He cited those times in history when important battles were believed lost because of corruption in the Temple of Vesta. He reminded the jury of six other times when it had been necessary to demand the death penalty for an errant virgin. He reviewed the evidence against the chief vestal, and praised the courage of her sisters Agrippina and Diana in giving testimony.

Nerva, in turn, was cogent, gentle and dignified. After apologizing to Cornelia for the trial's cruel and inhuman torture, he eulogized her years as a vestal, with no hint of scandal. He reminded them of the wonderful auguries that had attended her elevation as chief vestal, and cited the omen she had recently received at Vestalia when she struck flame instantly for the hearth as another sign of her favour with the gods. He agreed with Messalinus – "a rare enough thing" – in the importance of the cult of Vesta to the safety of Rome, and warned them that they dared not condemn a vestal in error. He referred to Agrippina and Diana as "poor wretches caught in the prosecution's web" and, staring from one to the other, urged the gods' forgiveness. He stressed again the gentle yet courageous character of the chief vestal celebrated throughout the empire, and he exhorted the jurors to join that which was most honest in themselves to fight for her acquittal.

As Nerva drew to an eloquent close, several members of the court brushed tears from their eyes and some dared to cheer: "Bravo! Bravo!"

And yet when it came to sifting the evidence, crucial questions remained: Cornelia had been arrested before cockcrow travelling in an unmarked litter. This was not – according to her own sisters – the first time she had left the vestalry for appointments which could only be described as clandestine. Her physical condition did not – to put it kindly – preclude her having had sexual intercourse. There was the suspicion of a liaison with Maximus Marcus – depending on how much credence was given the testimony of Diana. Under normal circumstances, few jurors would take the word of Diana or Agrippina over that of the chief vestal; but Diana's stupidity and Agrippina's piety seemed to legislate against outright lying. More compellingly: why had they not heard of the chief vestal's innocence from her own lips? Why only through her lawyer Nerva?

Also weighing heavily was the significance of the vestal's arrest *by imperial order*. What was the political intent of her trial? While Nerva had the respect of the Senate, Messalinus often functioned as an extension of the emperor's *imperium*. Did he speak for the emperor now?

In such ruminations, the jurors were in line with Roman concepts of justice, for influence and deference to authority were an acceptable part of it. Nor was there any need to consider "reasonable doubt" – a nicety of a later age. It was each juror's right to vote according to his own prejudices and best class interests. In this case, conscience and politics were not necessarily opposed. The prosecution had produced enough evidence to favour the direction they now believed the imperial wind to be blowing.

The vote was taken by show of hands. The court clerk confirmed what everybody had seen: four priests for acquittal, with twelve opposed. All eyes swung to the emperor. Would he quash the verdict? Judge Piso asked: "Does the vote please my Lord and God?"

The emperor remained expressionless, as he had throughout both jury addresses, for the day's proceedings had taken him entirely by surprise. During the depression which had followed the death of young Varus, he had lost contact with everything except his own despair. From his last assessments, he had thought the jurors would neither wish nor dare to find Cornelia guilty. If by some misguided sense of politics they had done so, he had intended to pardon her as an act of popular justice launching him toward the love that was his brother's birthright, denied to him. The damning testimony of Cornelia's sister-vestals, along with private reports from Geta that Rome was violently against the vestal, had changed all that.

Seeking answers, Domitian stared at Cornelia as she sat in the defence box, her profile proud and beautiful, the only person in the court who would not look at him. Though he had toyed with the idea of her guilt, he realized now that he had never seriously doubted her. His experience of her innocence, and his mastery of it, had been too powerful a memory. All the torturing questions he had put to himself had been merely the characteristic suspicion with which he tore, like a mongrel, at all the good things that happened to him. Now, surrounded by confirmation of his ugliest fantasies, he was forced to put the question to himself rationally. Had the vestal been a virgin, as she pretended? Had she visited Cybele, as Domitia had accused? Had Maximus Marcus seduced her? Had the lovers planned his seduction to gain influence? Had he, the emperor, been their dupe?

As his belief swayed from one side to the other, prosecutor Messalinus – bypassing Judge Piso – asked permission to speak.

"Does this pertain to the case before us?" asked the emperor.

"Oh yes, my Lord and God." He smirked. "I have just received startling revelations from Rome."

The emperor nodded: "Speak."

Savouring this new turn in the limelight, Messalinus approached the imperial box. "A bawd from the Temple of Cybele, whose identity must remain secret to protect her from

333

prosecution, has sent me a trinket which she claims to have received as payment from Maximus Marcus, and which Maximus Marcus received as a love pledge from the vestal Cornelia." He held up a white amulet on a white silk cord so it caught the fire of the sun. "The vestals Agrippina and Diana have identified this trinket as belonging to their chief, Cornelia."

The court burst into such noisy speculation that Judge Piso was unable to restore order. All eyes swung to Cornelia. The look of shock, guilt and dismay that stained her face was enough to persuade two of those who supported her acquittal to change their votes.

Murderous jealousy consumed Domitian. Drawing his bow against his twitching cheek, he let the arrow fly. "I accept the verdict as rendered: guilty."

Judge Piso bowed his head. "We, the members of the Colleges of Jupiter, Mars and the Flavian Cult, do find the August Lady Cornelia, chief of the Temple of Vesta in Rome, guilty of breaking her solemn vow of chastity. We sentence her to that fate prescribed by the laws of man and of the gods: that she be buried alive in the Field of Ill-Luck, there to await death at the pleasure of the gods, whom she has so grievously offended."

Judge Piso adjourned the court.

The priests and senators filed from the amphitheatre to return to Rome.

CHAPTER TWENTY-FIVE

The verdict of the Sacred Colleges was announced in the Forum by a bronze plaque posted beside the *Daily Gazette*. Because of rumours as virulent as swamp gas, few Romans were surprised, though most were still shocked. A second plaque announced the elevation of Agrippina as chief priestess of the Temple of Vesta. Her inauguration was to take place the next morning in the garden of the Regia.

Cornelia – again imprisoned in the Regia – could see the ceremony by climbing on her bed and pressing her face to the window grating. Agrippina stood under the lotus tree, from which Cornelia's banner of hair had been stripped. After placing the bulla around Agrippina's neck, Pontifex Piso led a procession from the Regia. Cheers greeted Agrippina in Sacred Square. As she mounted the steps of the Temple, she took out her miserable scroll, and chanted it from beginning to end. Cornelia saw her raise her arms to denounce corruption in the Temple of Vesta and in the city of Rome, then heard the jubilation as Agrippina promised piety and purity in the future.

The unruly mob would not disperse. Many shook their fists toward Cornelia's window and cursed. As Cornelia slumped upon her metal cot, she touched her neck, which had been gashed when Captain Geta stripped her of her bulla. She thought of Philip the Prophet and the certainty with which he had climbed to his martyr's death. She thought of Domitilla – of the radiance she had found in the cave where Cornelia felt only fear. Rubbing her turquoise ring she tried to conjure up in love the man who had given it to her, as compensation for her suffering; but his features melded with those of the emperor, whose hands had become confused with the humiliating thumbs and fingers of Doctor Rufus Felix. Sometimes she remembered it pure. Sometimes at night her body would relive what her mind had repressed, so that she would awaken in a stew of erotic images – sometimes with Marcus, sometimes with the emperor – but then Doctor Felix would touch her with one oily finger and she would numb up, freeze over, wind herself around in her icy vestal robes.

As Cornelia gazed up at her grated window, still hearing the threats and jeers of the mob, she was overcome by panic – the same panic, prophetic now, that had smothered her in the catacombs. She kicked against her bed in frustrated fury. Was she to die by the testimony of two sisters who had lied for their own advancement? Was the man who had betrayed her to continue to rule the world? Where was the lover for whom she had sacrificed her life? When prosecutor Messalinus had held up her amulet in court, she had feared Marcus had been arrested and the amulet stripped from him. Then she had remembered, with a lover's fondness for detail, that he had not worn it for their meeting at the spring, nor at Consul Clemens' house before the emperor's dinner. *Had* he given it to a bawd of the Temple of Cybele? And what of Vesta, to whom she had devoted her life? Where was she when Cornelia had sought guidance? Where were the parents who bound her to this hell? Why wasn't she allowed to lead a normal life, with love and affection freely exchanged, with husband and children?

What was expected of her now?

Who wanted it?

Why?

Agrippina's first act as chief was to visit Vesta's hearth to denounce again the sloth of the previous administration and to reconfirm her promise of better things to come. She begged Vesta's forgiveness for having participated in incorrect hence sacreligious rituals under the vestal Cornelia. She regretted the need to corrupt Vesta's Oath of Silence for the purpose of saving the Temple. She promised absolute precision of ritual in the future with severest penalties for infraction. She thanked Vesta both for revealing to the priests of the Sacred Colleges their fallacy in valuing beauty over piety and also for giving her a plain face as an invitation to modesty and a guard of chastity. She apologized for having been resentful of the ridicule heaped upon her from birth because of her ugliness – an assault which made her strong.

She assured Vesta of her humility. She explained that she wanted to be chief only because she could do the job better than Cornelia, and she reminded Vesta she had tried to help Cornelia by pointing out her errors and by informing against the other vestals. Once Cornelia's jealousy had forced her into silence, it had been her duty to keep a private record of all infractions, then to testify against Cornelia, and to give Diana the courage to repeat the story she had confessed to her.

The longer Agrippina prayed, the more agitated she became – the colder her hands, the drier her mouth. Seizing the bulla that burned like an ember between her breasts, she cast herself before the altar, confessing to herself the brutal truth: the auguries marking her elevation had been no better this time than last, though she had hidden the evidence. Of twelve doves sacrificed, all had diseased or discoloured entrails. Why did the gods again reject her? Why had Vesta disdained her gift of service?

The empress had not come to Agrippina's inauguration. Both Helen and Poppaea hated her. Fausta pretended she was mad when she wasn't. Her best friend Diana – her only friend now that the empress shunned her – cried in her room and would not talk to Agrippina, would not even look at her after all Agrippina had done to save that girl from her wretchedness.

The new chief vestal unloosed a wail that rattled through her chest then gagged in her throat. Why was she, alone, without friends in all the universe? Why had she been born with the mark of the claw on her chest? Why could no one understand her torment? Why did no one see the yearning for love, for beauty, for companionship, locked inside her?

Agrippina drew her scroll from her tunic – the scroll that anchored her to her duty, to her one reality. Kneeling before the altar, she dipped her pen into the blood of a dove she had offered in sacrifice and, holding it over the parchment, suddenly discovered the trap. Now that she was chief vestal, there was only one person to make book against...herself. Groaning, Agrippina wrote in large red letters: "IF I BREAK THIS VOW OF SILENCE, O VESTA, LET THY FIRES CONSUME ME AND THY RAGE DISEMBOWEL ME." She collapsed against the altar, knowing from the stench and stickiness of her vestal robes that she had soiled them.

The rabble Agrippina had inflamed refused to leave Sacred Square. Joined by toughs from the taverns, they loitered about the Regia singing the newest drinking song: "Hail to our head maid, who lost her maidenhead!" Geta's praetorians waded into the mob with whips and clubs, but though they cleared the square, the gangs rampaged through the city. They raided brothels and smashed naked statues. A man and a woman caught kissing in public were paraded through the Forum with the sign: "We are depraved." A man was flogged for using a coin with the Temple of Vesta engraved on it to pay for a urinal.

Thugs fired the whorehouses across from the Circus owned by Clodianus. As the tenements went up like torches, bawds darted shrieking from the lower floors, and some who escaped were forced to fornicate with pokers. Others appeared at upper windows, some with their hair already aflame. One in a top gable fanned herself as if for business, apparently undisturbed by the fire.

"Jump!" shouted a youth, spreading his cloak as if offering a safety net. The rest took up the cry: "Jump, jump, jump." Smiling in trust, the bawd ventured out onto the roof, then leapt for the cloak. The punk yanked it away while his friend caught her on a pitchfork.

The stucco face of one then another of the houses crumbled, sending pans of plaster crashing into the street. The drunken pack scattered like rats up every alley, many convinced this was the vengeance for evil predicted by Agrippina.

The next time the new chief vestal appeared in public, she was cheered.

CHAPTER TWENTY-SIX

Emperor Domitian slouched in his bedchamber, his feet soaking in sulphur water, sipping a bitter brew of herbs and vinegar prescribed by his physician, Rufus Felix. The shutters were closed. Rags had been stuffed into the cracks of doors and windows, despite July's heat.

While fishing at Alba, Domitian had caught a cold he couldn't cure. His father Vespasian had died, age sixty-nine, from a chill contracted at the baths. His brother Titus had died, age forty-two, from the same affliction. He felt his mortality weighing heavily upon him.

To counter his fears, Domitian had called for his most reliable soothsayers – Asceletarion, the famous augurer, and Larginus Proculus, the astrologer – neither of whom had ever presented him with an unfavourable prediction. He peered at his bedchamber door: Where were they?

Domitian gulped from his goblet, forgetting it was medicine. He spat the brackish mixture on the head of the dwarf, curled by his bed. "Wake up, freak! Where is my cup-taster? Someone is trying to poison me." Holding the dwarf's nose, he forced the liquid down his throat, then kicked the sulphur footbath down the step. His peckish energy spent, he slumped back into his cushions.

Parthenius escorted in a swarthy little man as wizened as a raisin.

"Asceletarion!" exclaimed Domitian. "Your face fills me with delight, especially when compared with the drab ones around me." He extended his palm for the soothsayer to kiss, an unusual mark of favour. "Other prophets I consult by whim. You I seek out when in need of good prophecy. You have never failed me."

Asceletarion replied with a dignified bow: "It is not I who give the omens but the gods. Every step you take I read by the creatures of sea, land and air. If you had not called me soon, I would have come to you."

Domitian rubbed his hands in glee. "See, Parthenius? See, Hermes? Was there ever a subject more loyal? One more sweet prediction, Asceletarion, and I will promote you to chief priest!"

Asceletarion nodded gravely. "First, emperor, hear the augury."

Domitian chuckled. "Ahh, what a bargainer you are! What will you settle for? My two signet rings?"

In a voice startlingly deep for so tiny a man, Asceletarion pronounced: "Hear and judge, O emperor! In every imperial augury since the arrest of the vestal Cornelia, there has been a diseased or discoloured organ."

Domitian leaned forward, eyes glittering, for this matter of the vestal was much on his mind. "Are you saying the vestal is being falsely punished?"

Asceletarion shook his head. "No, my Lord. I know nothing of that. The augury is for you alone."

"What do you mean?"

"Prepare yourself, my Lord," intoned the soothsayer. "Make peace with this world and the next, for your death is near."

"What? You dare to tell me that, old man?"

"When the gods speak so unequivocally, there is nothing to do but accept. You will not live out the year. You will probably not live beyond October Horse."

Flinging his goblet at the soothsayer, Domitian bellowed: "Recant, old man! I *give* death, I don't receive it. I command you: make a better augury!"

"My Lord, I cannot."

Glowering at the soothsayer with head thrust out from bunched shoulders like a vulture, Domitian asked: "Tell me, old one, do you read your own oracles?"

"Yes."

"Do they tell you how and when you will die?"

"Yes. I will die very soon. By wild dogs."

"Then, Foulmouth, hear how false you speak." Clapping for his praetorians, Domitian ordered: "Take this filthy scrap of flesh down to the Forum. Bind him hand and foot and burn him." He beckoned to Castor. "Go with him, and report to me when the deed is done: how long it takes, and what parts burn first; how many times he screams, and his exact words when he recants."

Arms folded, he turned to Parthenius. "Now fetch me that other soothsayer who awaits outside my door."

Parthenius ushered in Larginus Proculus, as large, white and roly-poly as the other was small, brown and wizened – a ball of bread dough to the other's raisin.

Since flattery had failed with the first, Domitian tried intimidation on the second. "Well, Proculus, I've already rid the world of one soothsayer who displeased me. I hope you won't give me cause to kill off another. Let mine be a good fortune and a quick one, for I've never felt more like rewarding cheerful news and punishing bad."

Without speaking, Proculus hopped from one foot to the other, a parchment in his hand.

"Well, does the brilliance of my future stop your tongue?" heckled Domitian.

Proculus unrolled his scroll – an astrological chart plastered with black-and-red notations. He smoothed the creases, then tried to rub out the sweat marks. Pointing a pudgy finger to various symbols in the astrological houses, he came at last to a conjunction of planets around Saturn. Taking a deep breath, he blurted: "There will be blood on the moon as it enters Aquarius."

Domitian rubbed his two signets against the coverlet. "So?"

"You will die!"

Domitian smiled. "We all die, Proculus. How does that affect me more than most?"

Proculus gulped more air. "You will die by steel."

"That is a prediction I have heard before," scoffed Domitian. "What better way for a triumphant commander than to die in battle?"

"You will die from one close to your bed."

"That, alas, is the fate of many emperors."

"You will die at the hour of three."

"Then I will have had the pleasure of seeing the sunrise."

Proculus paused before blurting once more: "You will die on September 18 of this year."

Now Domitian's face exploded in a dozen tics. "The last soothsayer gave me life till October Horse, and I gave him death by fire. You have taken away a month. For that I must devise a more painful leave-taking."

Falling to his knees, Proculus quivered in every fat cell. "You will die at three on September 18."

Domitian shook his fist. "No, Proculus, *you* will die on September 18, after your prediction of my death has proven false. Your death will be agonizing and well-attended, for it will be the entertainment for my birthday banquet."

He jerked his thumb toward the dwarf. "You! Take this forktongued white elephant out of my sight."

He pointed to Parthenius. "You! Fetch me Zeno, Messalinus and Captain Geta who, if they value their lives, will be outside my chamber now." Reaching for the dagger under his pillow, Domitian caressed the ivory hilt, tested the blade and waited. Not for long.

Zeno bustled through the door, followed by Messalinus and Captain Geta. Without a greeting, Domitian started in to

343

impress his will upon them and the world. "I wish to rid myself of faces that displease me." He scowled around the trio, as if trying to choose among them. "Does anyone in the Senate plot my death more vigorously than usual?"

Finding the emperor's eyes on him, Zeno deflected with familiar sycophantism. "When men shine as brightly as gods, my Lord, there is always jealousy, but none more pointed than usual."

Messalinus' response was, as usual, self-serving. "Nerva is preparing a pamphlet giving his version of the vestal's trial. He is also circulating Stoic tracts by Helvidius Priscus the Elder."

"Aha!" pounced Domitian. "The old thunderer strikes again." He poked a long finger at Zeno's slate. "Write down Nerva. That man is a boil on the backside of my patience. Make the letters small for there will be others."

"If Nerva goes, I will need twice the praetorians to keep order," said Geta. "Two hundred for the Forum. A double guard on the Regia. Double on the palace. Rome is restless."

It was the longest speech Geta had ever made. Reluctantly Domitian reversed himself. "Scratch Nerva. Let him wait till after the vestal." He twirled the dagger on his palm. "What we need are rich ones to fatten the treasury."

"Clodianus," suggested Geta.

"Capital! Who's to mourn there?" Pointing to Zeno, Domitian ordered: "Put down Clodianus."

Messalinus tapped his cane. "Beg pardon, my Lord, but that's a fat goose the better left for plucking. Remember that fellow Stephanus – Consul Clemens' Jew-steward? He's been after Clodianus to plan a conspiracy. It's worth waiting to catch those two vipers in the same nest."

Domitian's eyes narrowed in excitement, for he now believed in the Jewish uprising he had invented. "Good work, Messalinus. Keep your nose into that one. Every day I receive a dozen petitions demanding the recall of my pious cousin Domitilla. I'd like more dirt to bury her. Besides, the longer I wait for Clodianus, the wealthier he grows. Never did a man turn a strong stomach to greater profit." He laughed. "I have it! Let's promote him instead – make him my Dispenser of Patronage, knowing he'll make generous dispersals to himself. Then when we get around to butchering him, it will be for a feast worth celebrating."

Zeno rubbed Clodianus from the slate. The list was getting shorter instead of longer. The only person proscribed this morning had been...*Domitian himself!* The emperor swigged from his goblet, then spat. "Write down this name, and prick it hard so it stays: Rufus Felix. Say he makes bad medicines – no, better claim he tried to poison me. Word the charge prettily, full of coy innuendos and fancy curlicues, the way he flashes his rings and perfumed handkerchief. You know the ridiculous style, for you use it in your own poetry. But when the vestal's funeral is past, and we accuse Nerva, see you use high dudgeon, indignation, as if he were condemning himself – which is the idea."

Domitian looked from Geta to Messalinus. "Don't I hear protests? No bleeding hearts for the good doctor?" He chortled. "That's a relief. I thought you were growing soft." Now questioning Geta, he demanded: "How does that other matter sit? I mean Maximus Marcus, our virgin's lover?"

"Orders have gone out over every road of the empire. He is to be arrested on sight."

"How long will it be?"

"A week. Two at most."

Domitian continued to play with his knife, spinning it around and around in his palm. "In the meantime, look for another dupe. Someone to assure the populace. Perhaps a praetorian you want to get rid of? I leave it to you."

A clang and a clatter in the corridor – Castor is catapulted into the emperor's bedchamber.

"What is this?" demanded Domitian. "You look as if you've seen a ghost." He remembered the boy's errand and grinned. "You *have* seen a ghost. Our soothsayer is dead, I trust? Fried to a grease spot."

345

Castor nodded, throwing himself at the emperor's feet.

"What is this snivelling? Stand up and speak like a Roman."

Castor scrambled to his feet.

"You *did* throw the old coot into the fire, did you not?"

Castor nodded.

"You bound him hand and foot?"

"Oh yes."

"And he *is* dead?"

"Yes."

"Then what is the problem?"

"Oh, please, my Lord, the fire blew out."

"So?"

"The wind was high and the wood too green."

"But the man *is* dead?"

"Yes."

"My guards ran him through with their swords?"

"Yes, my Lord and God – that is, they tried, but we were attacked."

"Attacked? Who would dare attack my guard in the Forum?"

The boy burst into tears. "Wild dogs, sir. They tore the body to bits and dragged it away."

Insane with fury, Domitian climbed down from his couch and began kicking the boy again and again, so that if the dwarf hadn't thrown himself in the way and abjectly absorbed half the blows that followed, he would have finished the page off. "Get out!" screamed the emperor, shaking his fist at Castor and the dwarf and then at everyone else. He pitched his bedside table at Parthenius, a wax slate at Zeno, his chamberpot at the dwarf. "Get out, do you hear? Get out!"

Though blind, Messalinus was first through the door. He ducked into a niche around the corner from Domitian's bed-chamber, then waited for the others to fan off in various directions. Flicking his hand through his slick black hair, and adjusting his toga till he was sure his appearance in no way reflected the indignities he had just experienced, he stepped back into the corridor. With his cane sliding along the wall to guide him, he hurried down the hall, passing four sets of guards, and delivering four passwords: *Avenge. Saturn. Homer. Senate.*

Shortly, he broke from the palace into the gardens, keeping close to the buildings to avoid the sunlight that blotched his white skin, flicking his ivory staff like a serpent's tongue across his path, confident...*anticipating*.

He could tell by the rise in humidity and the drop in temperature that he was approaching the first grotto leading to Domitian's famous Portico of the Fountains. Knowing she would be waiting, he slowed his pace. Already he could smell her scent – musk with a touch of jasmine.

He halted. Tapped his cane. "I know you are there. What do you want?" No answer. He giggled. "Don't pretend. This makes the third time you've waited for me. Yesterday I was with Geta, the day before it was that chattery fool Zeno. When are you going to show yourself...my empress?"

She caught her breath. "All the time we were passing I could hear you breathe like a defective bellows. I could smell your perfume – quite distinctive. I found myself becoming more animated so the others wouldn't notice, forgetting in my anxiety how little those with eyes can see. I came myself today, so you could reveal yourself."

Messalinus heard the rustle of fabric – silk with a cross-stitch of cotton. With a sulky sigh, Domitia stepped from the grotto. Putting his palm on her chest, he pushed her back. "Are you entirely stupid? I wanted you to reveal yourself *to me*, not to the Roman Empire. Not everyone is blind all the time."

Messalinus pressed into the grotto, imprisoning Domitia against the rough wall, behind the noisy curtain of water. He rubbed his thighs against hers. He fondled her breasts. "Don't deny me, Domitia. Be kind, be kind. Let me enjoy the warmth of your flesh. Ahh, yes...you radiate heat, you pulsate with it. All women are hotter than all men – that's why the poor burn female corpses with the male ones, to save wood. But you're special, Domitia – a furnace of heat. I can smell your blood as it burns through your veins." Sucking her lips, rolling her nipples, he felt her body quicken despite her resentful struggles. "Aha, do you forget yourself, *my darling*, in the skill of my hands? What else – besides this – do you want from me?"

"One small thing," she managed to gasp.

"No no no. You want three things – one small, one medium, one large. The small thing – that's the thing you came to ask. The medium thing – that's what I have been giving you. The large thing – that's my promise not to report you to the emperor."

Again he rubbed against her, now in full erection.

She held him off. "Not yet, not yet."

He smirked. "Of course. *Small* things first. What do you want?"

"Where is Maximus Marcus?"

Messalinus exhaled in a long low hiss. "Our new senator is in vogue today. Why are *you* after him?"

She shrugged. "I want to see him."

He laughed. "Since your husband wants Marcus' death and you seem to want him alive, could it be that some day soon you will want your husband's death?" He felt the startled expression on her face and sighed. "Oh, Domitia, Domitia.... How foolishly high you aspire in politics, and how low in love. Take a lesson from my life, for I've enjoyed several regimes and intend to live out this one before dying of natural causes. Aspire only to be useful to emperors, never to replace them. The secret of your success is that you are both shallow and lazy. Either ambition or love would destroy you."

"I want information, not advice!" snapped Domitia.

"Beg pardon, beg pardon, my empress. I'll find out what you want to know – that one small thing. I'll keep my counsel – that one large thing. If you will now lean back against this wall – for that one medium thing. Don't be coy, my darling, for I know you're the best bawd in Rome – and one not often satisfied. I can smell it on you – both your desire and your frustration. Here, let me help you. Let me lift your gown with the tip of my little finger. Let me place my little hand on the curl between your legs. Ahh, yesss, that's right, so soft..." He swayed in the warm, wet, wondrous grotto. *As soft as his rabbits with quivery noses and wet pink mouths waiting for him to feed the carrots in.*

Messalinus closed his blind eyes, hearing silvery jets of water, gushing and rushing...smelling dripping limestone and squishy moss...feeling the scrape of stone and the flutter of feathery fern. He chuckled. Though few people wanted to believe it, Messalinus was a happy man.

CHAPTER TWENTY-SEVEN

Putrid yellow fumes from Clodianus' Fullers' Shop could be smelled from the Subura to the Forum. Within the shop's tufa walls, slaves scrubbed fullers' earth into stained tunics or stretched togas on wicker frames to be bleached by sulphur smudge pots. Other slaves chained at the feet tramped clothes in vats of urine and chemicals, to the beat of fullers' songs. Occasionally one would collapse, choking, against the vat or onto the pavement, as hot as the smudge pots.

Since his return to Rome with Pollux two days ago, Maximus Marcus had been heaving jars of urine from donkey carts into the fumid vats – the same job gladiator Xerxes had once had, though for Xerxes it marked a step up from the stone quarries. At last he saw what Pollux had told him to wait for: a white laundry cart from the Temple of Vesta, driven by a plump man in scholar's cloak. There was no mistaking the pouchy face that peered from the brown hood like a gopher from its burrow. "Zeno!"

The tutor tossed a sack of soiled robes into Marcus' arms. "Hurry."

Marcus vaulted into the cart. They drove through the Subura where merchants were setting up their stalls, and clients in greying togas that could have done with the fullers' services rushed to appointments.

"I'm not a brave man," sighed Zeno, wiping globules of sweat from his face with his sleeve. "If these alleys were wider, I would have bolted back to the vestalry."

Marcus lay his hand on the tutor's arm. "Steady, my friend. The cause is a good one."

Their donkey cart turned up Silversmiths' Rise.

"Pollux said you would have a message for me from Nerva."

Zeno nodded. "There's a meeting this morning in the baths of Titus. Nerva. Clodianus. Stephanus too has joined us. Since his pretty wife Berenice was slaughtered there's no man more anxious for the emperor's throat. The trouble is...Domitian seldom leaves his bedchamber. Since the soothsayers made their predictions, it's rule by pillowcase."

By now Marcus could see the smoke from the Temple of Vesta. He asked the question preying on his mind: "How is she? Have you seen her?"

"No one has seen her since the trial, though Fausta and Helen send petitions each day."

"What are the arrangements for her rescue?"

"We storm the Regia at midnight tomorrow. All's set except to warn and arm the lady inside so she can protect herself if a guard tries to kill her."

"How will that be done?"

"By you. Tonight. Pay attention now as we enter Sacred Square. See the guards, at six-yard intervals. There's only one place where it is possible to scale the wall – the corner, with trees both inside and out. The guard who stands there tonight has been handsomely bribed, as have two others on either side – we have Clemens' cashbox to thank for that. You and I will come through the square at night, pretending to be drunk. While I engage the guard, you can gain a foothold in the trees. She has her freedom inside the Regia and spends most of her time in the garden, even after nightfall – that's Pontifex Piso's contribution to our plan though he doesn't know it."

"But why this double breach of the walls – tonight and then tomorrow? Why don't we double the bribe instead so I can bring her out tonight?"

"Because if the vestal escapes, the whole guard is to be

executed – Geta's orders. You can't bribe a man enough to pay for his life. What we've purchased tonight are visiting rights. You're supposed to be a brother who yearns to see her one more time."

They were even with the Regia. Marcus studied the corner of the wall with its twist of plane trees, then shifted his eyes upward to the grated window where he imagined her to be imprisoned.

"This cart has to be off the street before sunrise," Zeno reminded him. "I'll take you to the baths now – your next job is as a bath attendant."

Marcus held up his reeking tunic. "A good choice."

Sometimes Cornelia spent the balmy summer evenings under the sacred lotus, talking with Centurion Celer, the guard with whom she had developed a gentle friendship. Sometimes she read poetry. More often, as the day of her funeral approached, she sat in solitude, watching the sun turn the massings of white roses and dewy-sweet gardenias into a golden glow that pinkened then darkened till moonlight licked them silvery grey.

Her anger had passed and with it her guilt. She had simply come to accept herself as two persons – the vestal in white robes who strove to do her duty; and the other person – the shimmering stranger with unbound hair she had first glimpsed in the emperor's mirror but whom she now realized had always been with her. She was that confidant, curious and eager for life, who had fed vicariously on Julia Sabina's passions while her vestal self doled out sensible advice. She was the heartstrong girl who had shared forbidden embraces with Junia, who had pursued her infatuation with Maximus Marcus, had dropped her handkerchief in the arena, and had given in to the emperor's lust. Because Cornelia's vestal self had been punished so often for this other person, she had become ashamed of her. Now Cornelia realized it wasn't so simple. It was this spontaneous self who had loved rather than served Vesta; who comforted instead of scolded the younger vestals when they failed their tasks; who laughed when her vestal self suffered from the sin of pride.

The two sides of Cornelia were almost reconciled to their mutual fate. In her soul, the vestal still believed she was dying for a crime she didn't commit. In her heart, the girl in the mirror still believed what she had done was not a crime.

What was chastity after all...that tongue-clicking little word that filled the mouth with bristles? With much pomp and ceremony the burr of chastity had been implanted between Cornelia's legs...to block her emotions, to isolate her, to subjugate her to duty and to the state, at the same time as it gained a market value in privilege and status. The emperor had removed the golden burr, releasing and reducing her at the same time, robbing her of her specialness yet restoring her humanity. He had acquired the accidental power of destroyer and liberator, the way strangers coupling on a battlefield acquire, in those few mythic moments of life-before-death, the icon of each other's eyes.

Cornelia heard a rustle in the shrubbery. Looking toward the lotus tree blowing with swatches of vestal hair, she saw a shadow move. A man was hiding behind the tree. Celer? He was a head taller yet there was something familiar about his profile. He stepped from the shadows. Cornelia leapt from her bench. Maximus Marcus. They embraced. She wanted to scream: *Why are you here? Get out of Rome, run while you can....* But she could not speak.

He wanted to say: *Listen, listen, we have no time...tomorrow night....* But he could not speak.

They clung together under the lotus tree, then sank to their knees on the moss. She was feeling the shagginess of his tunic, marvelling at the largeness of him, the pull of hard sinew across his back, the crisscross of scars through the wiry hair of his chest – the imperfections, the rough details, the maleness of him eliminated from her fantasy of the ideal. He was relishing again the uniqueness she had for him, the wonder, the glow – all the luminosity he had tried to expunge from his portrait of her so as to make her ordinary, therefore controllable, therefore forgettable.

They lay down together, hearing the thud of each other's hearts. She smelled boot leather and briny flesh mixed with loam and mouldy leaves, heard the heave of his breath through the rustling of petals, felt the tickle of grass against her bare legs and the twist of roots and sharp pebbles through her thin green tunic. He touched her shiny hair – it came unbound. He felt the ripeness of her breasts through her tunic, lifted the fabric gently – an easy thing to dispose of. Kissing her nipples, he found them substantial: they did not melt away, she did not slip from his grasp as she did in his dreams. He put his hand here and then here, spanning her creamy flesh, hugging her close to him, enveloping her, one white bird scooping up the other white bird in flight.

His square hands were upon her – calloused and warm, caressing her cool, wind-stirred flesh. His large, pulpy tongue was inside her – no invasion this, no subjugation, no ruination, no working of wills. Shivers passed through her, then spasms as her body rose like yeast to embrace, receive, envelop his.

Now his hands slid down the thin gold line of hair ending in the silky arrowhead that marked her sex. A cave of the deepest, darkest longing opened between her legs. At her lover's touch, she spread her thighs.

He slipped gentle fingers between her legs, imagining that marvellous blue cave of Capri, with his oar stirring the luminous water, spinning off shivery spirals of quicksilver; sliding his fingers deeper into the pithy darkness of her, where he would fit; feeling his body grow taut with a thrilling expectation, the skin tighten across his midriff, his sex stiffen. Reaching out for it, she stroked it with cool moonlit hands, traced the branching of veins, cupping the stalk with its strange fruit, so unfamiliar, in her palms, laying it between her breasts, feeling the pulse and kissing, with a flutter, the tip.

He shifted his position in the fragrant white petals, the squishy moss, the filtered moonlight, raising himself between

354

her thighs, nudging her, a small persuasion, feeling her roll open to welcome him. He slid inside, gasping for breath now, sucking in long silvery draughts of it, feeling himself fill up with air, expand, grow lighter, rise, sail off.... She embraced him with her thighs like great white wings, and again he envisioned the coupling of his two birds in flight...the rush of freedom denied him in life by the dizzy plunge of those other two – like stones, not birds – from the cliffs of Como, making him cling to the monuments of the earth, to stand foursquare on rock and build with stone, to climb but never to dare to fly for fear of falling, yet in flight now, feeling with joy the stretch of his wings, not falling, staying up there, his body melded with hers...holding.

She felt him penetrate then pierce her, not at first an easy size nor a convenient rhythm, rock-hard, foreign, too much of him, she too full of him, and now the familiar beginnings of panic, of smothering, of strangling, unable to catch her breath...the desire to throw up, beat him off her with her fists, too much...feeling his sweat dribble upon her, and the crush of grass and rotting brown petals, too sweet, against her bare back, then – when she might have pulled away – giving in instead, her body catching his rhythm, his fire, his need, his desire, adding a pulse and a frenzy of her own, feeling his sex as a root grounding her, clinging to it with tendrils sprouted from her own flesh, his arms no longer clamps but vines leafily wrapping her around, protecting her, no longer afraid of the cave inside of her, no longer in terror of the catacombs, no longer trembling on the peak of Delphi in her vestal robes, unwilling to gaze down into that black hole in the earth that moaned with prophecy, no longer even aware – with his arms enclosing her and his sex inside her – of the loneliness of the cave.

They were moving together effortlessly now, flesh of one flesh and yet some part of each still standing aside, the better to marvel. She gazed up into his eyes, seeing a swirl of white petals like laurels around his head, and beyond that – ever so much farther and higher yet somehow still a piece of his eyes – the spinning galaxies of stars. Yet still she felt the earth. He gazed down into her eyes, green like the moss, saw the fire of her red hair, heard the snap of twigs, smelled the loam, yet he felt the rush of wings, saw the stars. He was the arrow in flight, she the moss where the tip imbedded. He was the bird. Having been the bird, she wanted to be the egg.

Turning her face into the moss, she cried – not out of shame now, not out of submission. He had touched a place inside herself, a place no one else had touched...the cave where she would die.

Afterwards they lay with limbs entangled, feeling the fragile world they had spun from strands of love and hope cross-stitched with desire begin to fray, exposing them to fears, anxieties. She thought: *This is selfish. I am risking his life.* He thought: *This is foolish. I am risking our future.* Moving away, he snatched up discarded clothes, hurriedly put them on. "I must leave, but listen, listen. Tomorrow Zeno, Stephanus and others will storm the Regia. You and I will escape from Rome through the sewer system. Saturninus taught me that – no information, it seems, is wasted in Rome. The horses will be waiting outside the walls – Priam and the fastest mare money can buy. We'll be half an empire away before your funeral time." Drawing a fish knife from his belt, he wrapped her fingers around it. "Take this. It has an honourable history. You may need it before you leave this garden. To kill your guard."

Cornelia stared at the knife, its bone handle carved with a fish, seized by hope, with the thrill of a desperate fate averted. Running her thumb along the blade, feeling it nip the flesh, she shivered in power and then in fear, remembering her lover's casual instruction: to kill your guard. Staring at the single red tear on the tapered blade, she imagined plunging it into the chest of her friend Celer. *Impossible, impossible.* She returned the weapon. "Marcus, I cannot. My life isn't worth so much."

"But you must!" He refused to take it. "Think of your guard as a sacrifice to Vesta – you have the right." Curling her fingers around the handle, he tried to make it stick to her flesh. "The arrest was unjust. The trial false. These men are praetorians

356

trained to kill. If they die doing their duty – that's part of it too. Scooping her up in his cloak, he kissed her long and tenderly. "What is my life without you to share it?"

She groaned. "What is my death unless you go free?" Pulling back from the safety of his arms and this temptation to life, she urged: "Go, Marcus, please. Before my guard returns and the two of you are forced to fight. Go. Let this be our good-bye. Don't try to rescue me tomorrow. I forbid it."

"Is life such a poor thing in your eyes? This makes no sense."

"It's all the sense we have. Marcus, Marcus, what's the choice? If the rescue fails, you will be killed, with Stephanus, Zeno and the rest. If you succeed, my guards will be killed, and Geta will be after us with a price on our heads. If by some miracle his praetorians don't catch us, there will be reprisals against the pontifex and the vestalry."

Again she tried to return his knife. Again he refused it. "I'll take the knife on one condition – that you'll come with me now. Tonight. Over the wall. It may be that's the best plan yet – I know the guard can be taken."

She shook her head. "No, I can't. That's no different."

Arms folded, he leaned against the lotus tree. "Two can be as stubborn as one. Come with me now, or I swear they'll find me rooted here when the sun rises."

Again he tried to sweep her up into his cloak, but she held him off. "Marcus, no...I must tell you this, though I'd sooner tell you anything else." Looking him in the eye she took a deep breath. "I'm guilty, as charged."

He laughed, turning her glance aside. "I don't believe you. You lie to protect me – to get rid of me."

"No, Marcus. You must believe me. I did break my vow of chastity."

"I know that. With me. Tonight." He frowned. "If I've undermined you, my darling, if I've done anything that –"

"No, Marcus, no." She shook her head as she plucked at her green tunic. "It's all right now, I'm defrocked. Not with you. With someone else. Before tonight. That's the truth." She

357

grabbed his arm. "Look into my eyes, if you don't believe me. Read my testimony."

Compelled, he studied her face. As their eyes met, she saw disbelief turn to uncertainty, then to pain that seeped like acid down lines in his cheek not there a few months ago. "By god, I think you *are* telling me the truth." He shook his head as if trying to clear his vision. "How can that be? Has everything between us been a lie?"

"No, Marcus. I love you. Never more than now." Feeling her resolve dissolve in the pain from his eyes, she pushed him from her, as if in impatience. "Go to whatever happiness you can find. These things are hard and not always what they seem. You haven't been in Rome long enough."

He ran his hands over his face. "Lady, I have been here too long. I don't know how to take this thing. Nothing in my life has surprised me more."

They continued to stare at each other, neither able to break away. *In a few moments I will tell him what I have done, and why.* Impulsively tearing her turquoise ring from her finger, she lay it in his palm. "Who knows? Another time, another place. I'll love you then as I love you now." She turned away.

Folding his fingers around the ring, Marcus walked stiffly, pridefully, toward the garden wall. She spun back toward him, yearning to call to him, to cling to him, to steal a few seconds more of love and life...to burden him with her sacrifice. As he put his hand on the plane tree, his face stony with rejection, she felt her sadness turn to resentment.

"Take better care of the ring than you did the amulet!" she called after him. His head swivelled around, his bitterness shattered by guilt. Then he slid over the wall and was gone.

Cornelia slumped against the lotus tree, tears running down her cheeks, already regretting her rebuke, any small satisfaction swallowed up in her grief and his suffering, trying to comfort herself, to console herself with her own hands, hugging herself, pretending her hands were his hands, sliding them under her tunic, touching her shivering body as he had done, seeking out again the forbidden opening to herself, still mysterious but no longer frightening, no longer the enemy, a wondrous part of herself – her birthright – now reclaimed. She dipped her fingers inside, into his sperm, all of him that was left and, like a child with fingerpaints, traced it over her thighs and belly, becoming calmer, rededicating herself, remembering step by step everything that had happened to her since she dropped her handkerchief in the arena, knowing she would make that decision again, despite certain knowledge of her fate, resigned to seeing this sour adventure through with grace, for she knew now why she must die. The thing was so simple. Each path in the labyrinth coiled back like a cobra to this place. She had no choice.

CHAPTER TWENTY-EIGHT

Cornelia spent the last day of her life in the Regia garden, pruning dead leaves and blossoms from the white gardenias and roses. By special invitation she dined that evening with Pontifex Piso who lay propped on his couch, looking shockingly fragile, his pulpy skin rotted by brown liver spots like the wasted blossoms she had just plucked.

Greeting her with affection, he spoke cheerfully of everything that had happened that day in Rome – one whole issue of the *Daily Gazette* committed to memory except, of course, for the item announcing her funeral.

When conversation waned, Cornelia took his thin hand in hers. "Now may I tell you my story?" In a calm, deliberate voice, she told him of her first meeting with Maximus Marcus, leading to her decision in the amphitheatre, and the betrayal of her vow of chastity with the emperor. As she finished, the elderly priest tearfully bowed his head. She watched him for a few painful moments, then asked: "Do I disappoint you so much?"

He raised his rheumy eyes. "Disappoint me? You thrill me! Having witnessed day by day the depth of your devotion, I now know the power of your humanity. I understand the fierceness of your conflict, and what must have been the agony of your decision." His frail hand clasped hers, his face glowing. "For a statue to sacrifice its life, what does that matter? For a beautiful woman full of yearning for life – that is another story." His voice grew stern. "There can, of course, be no reward for what you have done – you were right not to accept rescue. But neither should there be punishment...beyond the inevitable unfolding of the event. Be compassionate with yourself, Cornelia. Take no remorse, no regrets, no recriminations with you to the grave. The gods of Rome value courage over perfection. As for the people of Rome –" he shrugged "– when the world is corrupt, every man is his own judge and jury."

They embraced in sorrow. "Your confession has honoured me," declared Piso, wiping his eyes. "With your permission, I will tell Fausta and Zeno, both of whom love you, and will understand your pain." His voice choked. "In failing your duty, I believe you have been more moral than I have been in serving mine."

As the stars poked one by one through the darkening sky, Cornelia wrote letters to the people she loved: to Helen and Poppaea, asking them to take good care of each other; to Zeno, thanking him for his wise and loyal friendship; to Fausta, in appreciation for her example of dignity, decency and justice; to Diana, urging her to be true to herself; to Agrippina, calling for Vesta's blessing in the difficult task of running the Temple. Several times she began a letter to Marcus, then crumpled it. Either he would come to understand or he would not. The truth would hurt him more.

A knock on the door. *So soon!* Helen and Poppaea flew into Cornelia's arms. "Fausta sent us to dress you," exclaimed Helen.

Cornelia's burial garment lay on her cot: a grey tunic with matching sash. As Helen drew the tunic over her head, Poppaea waited to bind it. Looking from one to the other, Cornelia felt reassured. Poppaea was a tough little fighter, while Helen was maturing into a woman of strength and character. Now the vestals combed Cornelia's hair. As Helen started to plait it, Cornelia shook her head free. "No, let it be."

361

With their sombre tasks completed, the vestals buried their faces in Cornelia's lap and cried freely. "If you were my children, I couldn't love you more." She lay her hands on the two stiff cones of hair. "You *are* my own."

Another rap on the door. *This time.* Easing off the two vestals, Cornelia rose to answer it. "My guard is a good man. He'll be punished if I'm late."

His homely face stretched tight under his droopy moustache, Celer offered Cornelia his arm and together they walked from the Regia into the morning's first spill of sunlight.

A silent crowd already filled the square, some with faces shielded. Waiting by the Temple was a black cart drawn by two black horses with muffled feet and a black-robed driver wearing a mask of Mercury. Celer helped Cornelia mount the bier. For a poignant moment she looked toward the Temple of Vesta with smoke curling from its fiery core, like Vesuvius last time she had seen it, then she lay down, offering her wrists to be bound and her mouth to be gagged. With a contemptuous oath, Celer threw away the thongs and gag.

Led by torch-bearers, the funeral cart proceeded north along Sacred Way in unbroken silence. The sky was as blue as Cornelia had ever seen it. Seven white doves swooped low, circled once, then spiralled upward, turning silver before disappearing into the sun. From the Forum the cortege progressed eastward toward Quirinal Hill and the Field of Ill-Luck, with the crowds in their togas parting before it like the foam before a black ship. A gang of drunks on a tavern roof pelted Cornelia with dung. Otherwise, only silence.

Now the black cart crept up the Quirinal where the burial party waited. It halted at the foot of a grassy hillock with a gaping hole near its summit: a grave, freshly opened.

Cornelia saw the emperor, face waxy, robed as high priest; the empress, looking bored; chief priest Piso, so feeble he could not rise from his litter; Messalinus, nonchalantly leaning on his ivory cane; Nerva, shoulders hunched, eyes buried; Zeno, his sleeve over his face; Agrippina, piously clutching her scroll; Diana, eyes downcast, hands to her bosom; Fausta, very pale, very sad, very dignified.

Centurion Celer helped Cornelia down from the bier. As she climbed the hill, she was profoundly conscious of the stir of wind through her grey robes, the squish of dewy grass under her sandals, the throb of the sun on her red hair exposed in public for the first time.

Cornelia stared down into her grave – the mouth of Pluto, ready to devour her. Captain Geta was striding toward her with a birch rod to scourge her as a mark of her shame. She turned with dignity toward Emperor Domitian, her face as expressionless as his. Though no sign passed between them, he raised his finger and Geta laid down his birch rod.

A ladder protruded from the opening of the tomb. Geta offered Cornelia his arm, but she brushed him aside. Gripping it in both hands, she fumbled with her foot for the first rung, then the second. The gloomy pit swallowed her to her knees, then her waist. Pausing, she looked up at the sun, then at the driver of her black funeral cart. He had removed his mask of Mercury. Tears ran down his cheeks. He lay his fist over his heart in a last farewell: Maximus Marcus.

Still a patch of sky. That too was stolen by a wooden plug. Darkness. Total. She heard the thud of earth, shovelful by shovelful, against the plug, and felt the rise of panic...*to be buried alive.*

Dropping to her knees, Cornelia explored the loam floor, the plaster walls and ceiling. She found a rough wood bed with a musty blanket and fell upon it, listening to the continuing thud of the earth, trying to control the dizzy spiralling of her panic, feeling the walls begin to collapse around her, to grind slowly in upon her, smelling the dust rise to choke her, to smother her, knowing again the terror of the catacombs. Cornelia flung out her arms to push back the walls, hold them at bay, and remembered Maximus Marcus as she had just seen him. There had been suffering in his face, but acceptance too. She remembered his arms around her, remembered him filling the lonely cave inside her.

Calmer now, Cornelia again explored her prison, found a loaf of bread and a crock of water – not provided out of compassion but to spare those who buried her the guilt of having killed a vestal. Well, she would eat the bread and drink the water, eking out her existence for a little while. She touched the knife inside her tunic, the last gift of her lover. The gift of choice: not if but when.

To cease to exist ...what a strange idea. Her name would be stricken from all vestal rolls and chiselled from plaques and statues. Once that had seemed an unbearable humiliation – now it scarcely mattered. Better a record of flesh than one of stone.

Cornelia became aware of a difference in the darkness around her. An absence of sound. They had stopped shovelling earth on her grave. Her last connection with the outside world had been severed. With spasms passing through her body, she opened her mouth, expecting to hear a wail. Instead, she started to sing, at first in a quavering voice, then gaining in timbre. She went through all the songs she had ever heard Diana or Helen or Poppaea sing, unaware till now that she knew the words; songs caught in snatches through open tavern doors, at emperor's banquets, even songs from the catacombs. She thought of her parents buried in the ashes of Vesuvius. This too was how they had died; how she would certainly have died if she had stayed in Pompeii. She thought of a hunting expression her father had used: *gone to earth.* It meant that a rabbit had slipped the dogs and dived to safety in its burrow. *Gone to earth.*

As Emperor Domitian watched the grave-diggers pile earth on the condemned vestal, he barely noticed it start to rain – a thin drizzle, giving everyone who wished it an excuse to leave, soon turning into a downpour which drove off the rest. Only two persons remained: the emperor and Maximus Marcus, slumped in the funeral cart, his mask of Mercury in his hands. With curiosity and even some envy, the emperor studied this person whose grief outdid the pelting of the gods. After waiting till the grave-diggers replaced then tamped down the sod, he signalled Captain Geta: "Arrest that man."

Rain deluged Rome for seven days. Watery claws tore away banks, tumbling houses into the Tiber. Whole areas of Rome were evacuated, and many feared an outbreak of pestilence.

Toward evening of the eighth day, the rain slackened, the sky began to clear, and all gave thanks that the worst was over. A hot wind gusted in from the west. It began gently as the rain had done, then built to gale force, uprooting trees like turnips, ripping off roof tiles like leaves, hurling statues from their bases. The superstitious were quick to connect these omens with the burial of the chief vestal, and some claimed to have seen her ghost on the Quirinal, red hair crackling like fire in the wind. A party of zealots even climbed the Capitoline, scourging themselves, to sue the gods of Olympus for mercy.

Bolts of lightning fell in fiery shards from the dry yellow sky. One hit the Temple of Vesta while Agrippina and Diana were tending fire, illuminating the hearth with a wild blue light, flinging the vestals to the floor, scattering embers and ashes. When they came to, there was no fire of Vesta. The hearth of Rome had blown out.

PART V

EMPEROR DOMITIAN

A.D. 51 TO 96

CHAPTER TWENTY-NINE

Emperor Domitian was unable to shake his chill, which worsened at Cornelia's funeral. Doctors prescribed sweatings, purgings and fastings, as well as all manner of vile medicines.

During the depression that clung to him like sticky cobwebs, the only visitors he allowed into his bedchamber were prosecutor Messalinus, who fed him lies to fatten the proscription lists, and Captain Geta, who carried out the executions, all on evidence so flimsy many thought the two informers were trying to topple the emperor. To complaints of his harshness, Domitian replied in a lugubrious wail: "Miserable is the lot of emperors who only by their deaths can prove their throne has been assailed."

A complex system of riddles and passwords gave grudging access to the emperor's quarters. The mirrored corridors were polished hourly, and moonstones imbedded at the corners as reflectors. Since servants were required to fix bells to their ankles so the emperor could hear them, they acquired the nickname of "bell-footers." Domitian forbid his praetorians to bear arms in his presence, so that the only weapon in his bedchamber would be the dagger he used to stab flies. Since few flies ventured here, Parthenius was obliged to catch them for release. This led to the mock dialogue whispered throughout Rome:

"Where is Caesar today?"

"He's busy killing flies."

"Or senators."

"What's the difference? He kills senators like flies."

"And flies like senators."

Since soothsayer Proculus predicted Domitian would die by steel, he had his food ground by his nurse Phyllis, and poured into a goatskin with two teats – one for him and the other for the dwarf as official taster. This led to another jest:

"Did the emperor dine well this evening?"

"That depends – did the dwarf? Like Romulus and Remus, they have the same chef."

"You mean, the same she-wolf."

Surprisingly, Domitian received foreign delegations and presided over morning court, where he dealt with the affairs of ordinary citizens and the provinces with scrupulous fairness. This brought another quip: "Justice begins in the Subura and ends at the door of the Senate. Justice begins in Parthi but quits at the gates of Rome."

As September 18 approached, Domitian dwelt morbidly on the deaths of his father and his brother, rerunning through the tragic theatre of his mind everything he knew of their last moments. A dozen times daily he would repeat how Vespasian, feeling life ebb from him, joked about the deification of emperors: "Dear me, I think I'm turning into a god." And then, as violent dysentery ended his life: "Help me rise. An emperor must die on his feet."

His brother's last words gave Domitian more distress. Gazing at the sky from his litter, Titus complained: "Life is being taken from me unfairly since I have only one sin I regret."

There had been much speculation about this enigmatic remark. Many who hated Domitian claimed Titus regretted not having murdered him and thus spared Rome. Others, including Domitian, suspected Titus felt remorse at cuckolding him through an affair with Domitia. Over the years he had begged

370

the empress with tears, with anger, with love, with bribes, with threats, to confess her guilt, but she adamantly refused. Was that because she knew this crime of incest was one he could never forgive? Or did she just want to torment him?

Now Domitian raked through the ashes of this antique crime, putting his accusation to Domitia at least once a day, while grinding his teeth so fiercely the gums bled. She rebuffed him with increasing coldness – a rejection which whetted his appetite so that he would order her into his couch, demanding to be both serviced and comforted.

Every time his clammy fingers touched Domitia, she felt as if she had crawled into a nest of worms. How could she have loved such a pathetic bundle of fears and raw nerve-endings?

As she cringed by her husband's side, the empress dreamed of the one man she could love with an all-consuming passion: a soldier like her father, as strong, as hot-blooded, as fearless. She had not been able to take her eyes off him at the chief vestal's funeral. Even before he had removed his mask, she had recognized the sinewy arms that had embraced her; the contours of the head she had pressed to her breasts; the swell of his cock through his buskins.

A plan formed inside Domitia, fertilized by revulsion and midwifed by lust. She would rescue Maximus Marcus from Tullianum Prison and together they would assassinate the emperor.

Such a contingency sent Domitia back to prosecutor Messalinus, who ordered her to his favourite trysting place, the Flavian Crypt. Amidst the deified remains of the Flavian family, they made love on the pedestal engraved with the date of Domitian's birth, plotting Maximus Marcus' deliverance and the emperor's death.

After a week of rendezvous, Domitia decided that Messalinus was the strong, passionate, courageous lover she had been seeking. Though her conspiracy continued, with hopes of conscripting Clodianus, Stephanus, Nerva and perhaps Geta, Maximus

Marcus dropped from her thoughts now that she no longer had use for him.

While maintaining the fiction that Domitia was the patron and Messalinus the client, both knew that the prosecutor had seized control of the conspiracy and their love affair. Pretending boredom with her, he would tease her almost to climax, then refuse to continue until she described in meticulous detail the sex organ he could not see, comparing him most wonderfully to all previous lovers – in size, shapeliness, colour, endurance and force.

After one such exasperating session, Domitia swivelled her hips to imbed him more deeply, and demanded: "What of us, Messalinus? What of our life when Domitian is dead?"

Messalinus laughed his wispy laugh. "*Our* life? Do we only have one between us? *My* life will be safe due to my habit of serving all masters with equal disloyalty. As for you – why should you worry since I've already given you more ecstasy than most women dream of in a lifetime?"

Groaning, her mind blotted up with pleasure, Domitia sucked greedily on Messalinus' lips, as he obliged her by moving into a faster rhythm, even bothering to sweat a little. "Instead of the future, let's consider our responsibility to history. What of Parthenius? Is he delivered?"

"He will be this evening. By the same channel you treat so cavalierly."

"Good, then everything is ready. Only one other weapon will be in the room – the dagger under the emperor's pillow, for which I have plans."

"And the day?"

"September 18, of course. The doomsday the soothsayer chose. Just after the predicted time when he thinks he is safe, and is again celebrating his immortality."

Matching his final instructions to his thrustings, Messalinus drove the business meeting and Domitia tortuously, skilfully, deviously, to simultaneous climax.

They climbed down from Domitian's final resting place,

sticky from their pleasures. With sensitive fingers, Messalinus traced the inscription on the pedestal: IMPERATOR DOMITIA-NUS CAESAR AUGUSTUS, Born: October 24, A.D. 51. Scratching with Domitia's jewelled fibula, he added: "Died: September 18, A.D. 96."

"He'll give us no trouble," predicted Messalinus. "For him, death is the only adventure left."

Though Domitia had forgotten Maximus Marcus, Domitian had not. Every morning he would travel by unmarked litter down the tunnel Nero had carved from the Palatine to the Forum. Passing through doors and trapdoors, through groans and excrement, he would greet his former commander with the cheerful humility of a client visiting his patron.

Marcus was located down one of the corridors spiking out from Geta's torture shop, where prisoners undergoing long-term programs of humiliation and dismemberment were incarcerated. In a high, narrow cell of volcanic rock, he hung naked from a harness that bound him around the wrists and chest. Though his body was scored and scarred from floggings, and his wrists ulcerated from his chains, he had not yet undergone the systematic disfigurement that would inevitably lead to death; most of the time his feet were propped on a wood stile so he could slump against the wall.

Sometimes when Domitian came to visit, he would casually remove the stile to perch upon while he sipped calda and gossiped, seemingly unaware that Marcus dangled in agony with his shoulders yanked from their sockets. Usually the emperor would turn the conversation to his seduction of the vestal Cornelia – except in his version she had lewdly and ambitiously seduced him. While he played with her opal amulet, which he kept with him at all times, paddling and smudging it in twitching fingers, he would describe in picturesque detail each embrace, swear he'd never before had such a skilful bawd, then whip himself into a jealous frenzy till his head seemed to split like rotten

373

fungus, spewing curses, threats and obscenities. She had made a mock of Vesta and a brothel of Rome. He should have let the dwarf pump her till her belly hatched midgets like maggots. He should have tied her naked to her own altar so every guildsman with a finger to spare from his greasy sausages could stick it inside. He should have dipped her in honey and thrown her into the royal apiary.

At this point in his ravings, Domitian was likely to burst into sobs over the perfidy of all women and, confusing the burial of Cornelia with the banishment of Domitia, and Marcus with the pantomimist Paris, he would clasp him around his legs and fondle and suck his sexual parts, drawing from Marcus' humiliation, his grief, his outrage, his despair, the emotions he could remember, even act out, but no longer feel.

Finding the emperor's visits as tormenting as his chains, Marcus would glare down at this grotesque and numbing display, asking himself why he was here. Why hadn't he fled Rome when Cornelia had rejected his rescue? Who was that sentimental fool who had followed her to graveside, refusing to leave her funeral cart, knowing he would die for his tears?

In respite from these disgusting parodies, Marcus painted his cell with scenes from his childhood: peaks of blazing white and lakes of blinding blue. *He had climbed those mountains with the frosty air stinging his lungs, his head scraping the clouds. He had dived into the creamy foam, pulling out trout with his bare hands.* His years as soldier and would-be statesman gave him less pleasure. Now he saw that he had led a shallow life, full of restless activity, seeking nothing beyond what he knew how to achieve, never stretching himself toward the unknowable or trying to touch the impossible. A practical man. A man of honour, he hoped. But yet like one of his well-constructed roads: leading from nowhere to nowhere.

As one week blended into the next and the emperor's visits continued, Marcus developed, through his own suffering, a measure of pity for this other agonized man who walked barefoot through a landscape of thorns as torturing as his own, and

374

in the emperor's pathetic babblings began to piece together a story quite different from the one Domitian thought he was confiding.

It was a tragic story confirmed by a strange visit Marcus received on his fifteenth day of incarceration when Pontifex Piso suddenly appeared at his cell door. To the astonishment of everyone in Rome, the pontifex had, minutes before, sat upright on his funeral bier as he lay in state in the Regia. Adjusting his red apex, he climbed down and tottered off along Sacred Way, gaining strength and resolution at each step. Appearing at Tullianum in his burial robes, his lips a mouldy blue, his skin and spiky hair the colour of hoarfrost, he had so terrified the guards that they let him pass without protest. Waving his ivory rod at Captain Geta, he demanded an escort to the cell of Maximus Marcus, where he confided to its dangling occupant all the details of the vestal Cornelia's confession. Then, complaining of the heat, the pontifex turned around and stumbled out of the prison, not quite making it to the sunlight before he choked on Charon's gold coin, which had lodged in his throat, and died (for the second time that day, as some insisted).

Under ordinary circumstances, the knowledge of Cornelia's sacrifice would have tortured Marcus with unspeakable guilt. So startlingly and miraculously received, it sustained and strengthened him, making it possible for him to endure, through her love, the torments of each bitter day. Even to hope.

Now when the emperor ranted, Marcus dwelt upon their last embrace, high above the rooftops of Rome in a swirl of stars and white petals. He recalled with joy the last time he had seen her – trailing her radiance down into her grave, taking with her into the womb of the earth all the mysteries he had yearned for, felt missing from his life, yet could not name. Now he knew he would do it all again, just for the privilege of being there, of bearing witness, and that thought drenched him with sunlight.

On September 17 the emperor visited Marcus, as usual. However, instead of becoming crisp and formal, as he replaced the stile under Marcus' feet he lingered inside his bubble of sentiment, patting Marcus on the rump and brushing tears from his own eyes. Then, hooking Cornelia's amulet around Marcus' foot, he told him he didn't think he would be seeing him again, and asked him to give his love to Julia Sabina if he should see her first.

Signalling to Captain Geta, who had been watching this mawkish spectacle, stone-faced and disaffected, he proceeded to the cell next to Marcus, where the centurion Cinna Celer hung from a meat hook. Here the meeting was brisk and efficient.

"Has our virgin-lover broken yet?" demanded Domitian.

Geta shrugged. "Tomorrow."

"Good. Take him to the Forum when the crowds are thickest, and flog him to death by the Temple of Vesta where he can scream his guilt to those inside. There's been too much fear in this city since the hearth blew out and Agrippina could not relight it without the younger vestals' help. Let all of Rome be convinced, once again, of Cornelia's guilt. That whole vestalry is a cesspool!"

Jerking his thumb toward Marcus' cell, Geta asked: "What of him?"

Domitian nodded. "Yes, it's time to bring him along." He recalled Maximus Marcus at the vestal's funeral with tears rolling down his cheeks. "Start with the eyes. I'd like to have them as hors d'oeuvres for tomorrow's banquet."

CHAPTER THIRTY

To the astonishment of everyone including himself, Emperor Domitian awoke early on the morning of September 18 in high spirits. Commanding Parthenius to draw the curtains so he could admire his garden, he noticed the maple leaves near his window were stained scarlet. "Blood!" he exclaimed in bravado. "Some say the moon will be splashed with it tonight as it enters Aquarius."

Phyllis brought him his goatskin of premasticated food. "What's this? Gruel for pigs?" He dumped it on the floor. "Bring me food fit for an emperor!"

Parthenius offered him a selection of fruits. Choosing a Matian apple, he cored and sliced it with his ivory knife, raving over its tartness, its crispness, its juiciness. The knife slipped, nicking his finger. Laughing, he held up the wound for all to see. "Everywhere I look the prophecies of Larginus Proculus are being filled. An emperor's blood has been shed today!"

Domitian demanded the menu for the evening's banquet jointly celebrating his birthday and Jupiter's, then made a number of changes so that sweet courses alternated with savoury ones, and adding two dishes he especially liked, lark's eggs and lobster in tuna sauce.

With the same efficiency, he requested the plans for Larginus Proculus' execution, which he was adamant in making the evening's showpiece. The fat astrologer was to be skewered and rotated over hot coals till his skin baked. After peeling it off in inch strips, he would be flogged, then dismembered for fish food.

On impulse, Domitian decided he would attend today's scheduled court sittings. Dressing vaingloriously in triumphal robes he greeted his few remaining friends with effusiveness, even kissing Nerva on the lips.

That day the emperor was especially magnanimous in all his decisions:

He refused to accept an inheritance from a wealthy senator because "his four children have more right to it, by blood and need, than your emperor."

He excused, with a small fine instead of flogging, a freedman from Syria who had illegally purchased a Roman citizenship, for "such is the radiance of Rome, and myself as her protector, that who can blame the wretch for aspiring?"

More surprisingly, he forgave a legionnaire who had beheaded one of his statues on a drunken dare. "Who am I, the gods' anointed, to take heed of quarrels in plaster so long as this man serves Rome with his blood?"

Tired though still ebullient, Domitian returned to his bed-chamber. As he lay naked on his bed, his eyes chanced on Castor, whom he had treated with contempt since debauching him. Imagining the page resembled the boy Varus left floating in the fish ponds of Alba, and perhaps wishing to make amends, he patted his couch: "You are a pretty fellow. Come lie with me, unless you find me too repulsive."

With an obliging smile, Castor did as requested, applying his lips so dexterously to the emperor, then presenting his cheeks to be mounted with such affectionate compliance that afterwards Domitian exclaimed: "I commend you, Hermes, for the skill with which you have trained this boy. Never have I had a piece of flesh open beneath me with such grace. Look at those cheeks, smooth as a babe's yet ribbed with muscles that know their business." He stroked the boy's sweaty forelock. "You must have been blessed by Venus, for this requires natal talent."

As the emperor prepared to retire till time to dress for the banquet, Parthenius entered with a petition from Crispinus Clodianus.

Glancing through it, Domitian demanded: "Why was this not presented to me in court?" He laughed. "My subjects seem to be of two types: those who think every assassin's knife a shadow from my imagination, and those who imagine my doom in every shadow. This is one of my doom-seers." He read aloud in mocking tones that grew more serious: "Lord and God, as your servant it pains me greatly to have to inform you, on the day of your birthday celebration, of a conspiracy against you. It would pain me far more to withhold this information a fatal moment too long. I have been invited by the Jew Stephanus, steward to that traitor Flavius Clemens, to join a conspiracy of Jews and senators who plot your death. Under torture, that steward has produced the names of those conspirators, though not without a scuffle in which I had the pleasure of slicing the scoundrel's arm. I request permission to present him to you today, to make full confession of the ignominy that hourly threatens you. Be advised by one who is your humblest servant, except in the aspirations of his love."

Frowning, Domitian tapped the scroll against his palm. "My petitioner knows my tastes very well. A Jew conspiracy. A plot of senators. More evidence of my cousin's villainy."

"Too well," muttered the dwarf in unusual solemnity. "There's time to take up this matter tomorrow, after the appointed hour of death, when fear is put to bed."

"Fear? Who fears?" quavered Domitian. "Didn't you see the way I exposed myself in court today? Do you think the prophecies of idiots scare this emperor? It would be amusing to have that list of conspirators for the night's entertainment – perhaps Proculus would feel less lonely with more bodies on the spit." He turned to Parthenius. "What time is it?"

Knowing it was three o'clock, the time Proculus had pinpointed as the hour of death, Parthenius held up four fingers, lying by one.

"What, so late?" Domitian rose from his couch in jubilation. "Then the thing is already beaten!" He spun around to Hermes. "Hear that, you hairy toad! Were you afraid there would be no pension plan for dwarfs who outlive their emperors?"

He ordered Parthenius: "Have our petitioners thoroughly searched, then bring them in." Arranging himself on his couch, Domitian caressed the hilt of the knife under his pillow, then nudged Hermes with his foot. "Get me wine."

As the dwarf handed Domitian his tortoiseshell goblet, the emperor exclaimed: "What? Aren't you going to taste it? Since the hour of danger has passed, I thought you'd welcome a chance to gulp your emperor's vineyard." Pouring half the wine on Hermes' head, he downed the rest. "To Larginus Proculus – may his last hours be eventful."

Parthenius re-entered the bedchamber, escorting Clodianus who dragged Stephanus on a leather leash. As reported in the petition, the steward's left arm was bandaged. Terror-stricken, he fell to his knees, grovelling for mercy.

"Was it mercy you and your friends intended to show me?" jeered Domitian. "Get up, traitor, and let me hear the names of the lice I harbour in my hair."

Holding up a parchment scroll, Clodianus passed it to Stephanus, saying: "Tears would blind my eyes to read such an infamous list to my emperor. Let the viper sting them with his own forked tongue."

Stephanus reached as if for the list. Instead, he drew a dagger from the bandages around his left arm. Ever alert, Domitian caught the flash of metal and jerked his body away, deflecting the weapon into his groin. Gripping Stephanus' wrist with one hand, he snatched his knife from under the pillow and raised it to plunge. *There was no blade!*

With a whoop of laughter, Castor held up the blade for the emperor to see.

"Throw it to me!" shouted Domitian, not yet understanding the extent of the plot.

Parthenius ran to bar the door. Dodging behind the emperor,

Clodianus pinned him so Stephanus could strike a vital organ. Stephanus stabbed again, this time in the chest. As the dwarf sprang to the emperor's aid, Castor grabbed him by the throat and flung him to the floor. He jabbed the emperor's blade into Hermes' throat, his belly, his chest, his genitals, over and over, screaming: "Die, filth!"

Parthenius rejoined the assassins. Though it took seven wounds – one in the groin, two in the face, one in the throat and three in the chest – they at last overcame Domitian's sudden zeal for life.

The praetorians smashed through the door, seizing Clodianus just as he pierced himself through the heart. Stephanus strangled one guard and made it out to the hall before he too was slain. Castor was sobbing so uncontrollably over the bloody mass that had been the dwarf that all assumed his innocence.

Parthenius alone heard the emperor's last words: "What? All of you? Then I have nothing but regrets."

CHAPTER THIRTY-ONE

The body of Imperator Domitianus Caesar Augustus was carted off, by common litter, to the public undertakers where it lay unclaimed for several days until his nurse Phyllis bore it away. After cremating it in her own garden on the Latin Way, she spirited the ashes into the Temple of the Flavians where she mixed them with those of Julia Sabina.

Elated at the death of the emperor, the Senate quickly assembled and, to assure a united front against the military, its members took turns denouncing Domitian, now competing in vehemence as they had once competed in flattery. Amidst cheers and rude jests, they donned slave caps of freedom and, calling for ladders, pulled down his votive shields and smashed his images. Then they unanimously decreed that all inscriptions referring to Domitian be effaced, all record of his reign be obliterated, all his gold and silver statues be melted down for coinage. Though they had been at the emperor's mercy while he lived, they now found his immortality at their mercy, and the measure to which they shamed themselves by compliance was the measure to which they sought revenge.

Cocceius Nerva was chosen by his peers to succeed Domitian. Though the praetorians were furious at power passing to the

Senate in this way, they had no candidate of stature to oppose him. For compensation, they demanded that Parthenius – the only surviving assassin – be handed over to them. Though Nerva himself defended the chamberlain as having acted for the good of all against a mad despot, the praetorians were unappeased. For the sake of a tenuous alliance, Nerva was forced to acquiesce.

After a mock trial, a tribunal of praetorians cut off Parthenius' testicles and stuffed them in his mouth to replace his tongue. Then they crucified him – a death reserved for the vilest of crimes. So Parthenius, a dignified, gentle freedman and the least of the conspirators, was forced to bear the stigma of fifteen years' tyranny and its aftermath.

By freeing all political prisoners including the soothsayer Proculus, to whom he awarded 400,000 sesterces, Nerva more clearly made his liberal feelings known. One of those prisoners owed his life to a spark of humanity in Captain Geta. Having pieced together the story of the emperor's debauch of the Lady Cornelia, and having formed a favourable opinion of Maximus Marcus because of his compassionate treatment of Castor at the emperor's black party, Geta made his first decision of conscience over authority. He falsified a report confirming the gouging of the senator's eyes, and delayed his execution scheduled for the morning of the emperor's birthday banquet.

One by one, Marcus' chains were struck from him. One by one, locks were unbolted and doors flung wide. Maximus Marcus stepped from Tullianum Prison into the sun-bleached Forum, leaning on a spear given to him by a sympathetic guard and feeling a rise in jubilation as his limbs, though weak, continued to hold.

COCCEIUS NERVA ruled Rome for less than two years – time enough to overturn the habits of the previous regime and to set an example for the future. Modest and charitable, he punished informers and helped to restore the patrician families, only half of which survived the Flavian dynasty.

DOMITIA LONGINA, Empress of Rome, passed from history on the death of her husband, though it is believed she outlived him by some forty years.

FLAVIA DOMITILLA died in exile on the island of Pandataria. Some reports say she was burned alive for her Christian beliefs, but this has never been authenticated. The Roman Catholic Church declared her a saint, and named a catacomb outside of Rome for her. Her feast day is May 12.

CATULLUS MESSALINUS outlived Domitian by only a few weeks, dying, as he always predicted, of natural causes.

AGRIPPINA committed suicide shortly after the death of Cornelia by disembowelling herself as if seeking a good augury, then climbing upon the hearth of Vesta and setting herself aflame.

DIANA fled from the vestalry that same night – the first vestal to escape in over two hundred years.

HELEN succeeded Agrippina as vestal chief and ruled in harmony for sixty years.

FAUSTA lived in dignity to a ripe old age.

ZENO astonished himself by actually writing the stern political treatise upon which he had pretended to be labouring.

PETRONIUS GETA, captain of the Imperial Guard, found it no more difficult to serve a good emperor than an evil one.